Harriet's Escape:
Harriet Tubman Reimagined

N. D. Jones

KUUMBA PUBLISHING

Copyright © 2024 by N. D. Jones

All rights reserved.

All rights reserved. This book is a work of fiction. Names, characters, places, and incidents are the products of the author's imagination or are used fictitiously. Any resemblance to actual persons, living or dead, events, or locales is entirely coincidental.

No part of this publication may be reproduced, distributed, or transmitted in any form or by any means, including photocopying, recording, or other electronic or mechanical methods, without the prior written permission of the publisher, except in the case of brief quotations embodied in critical reviews and certain other noncommercial uses permitted by copyright law. For permission requests, write to the publisher, addressed "Attention: Permissions Coordinator," at the address below.

Kuumba Publishing – 1325 Bedford Avenue, #32374, Pikesville, MD 21208

Book Cover by Atlantis Book Design

Edited by Chris at Hidden Gems

Illustrations by Midjourney

Paperback ISBN: 979-8-9871464-8-4

Digital ISBN: 979-8-9871464-9-1

Content Warnings: implied adult sexual assault, talk of/threatening child physical assault, talk of suicide, on-page attempted suicide, on-page bullying, on-page physical assault, off-page physical assault, on-page death, off-page death

Dedication

Harriet Tubman (Araminta Ross)
1822–March 10, 1913
Daughter, Sister, Aunt, Friend, Wife, Mother
Abolitionist
Social Activist

"I was the conductor of the Underground Railroad for eight years, and I can say what most conductors can't say; I never ran my train off the track, and I never lost a passenger."

Acknowledgment

Bound for the Promised Land:
Harriet Tubman:
Portrait of an American Hero (2004)
Special thanks to Bound for the Promised Land by **Kate Clifford Larson** for serving as a pivotal resource in the creation of Harriet's Escape. The comprehensive research and insightful narrative of Larson's biography has been indispensable, ensuring that Harriet's tale is told with the honor and detail it rightfully commands.

DRALOX COUNTY

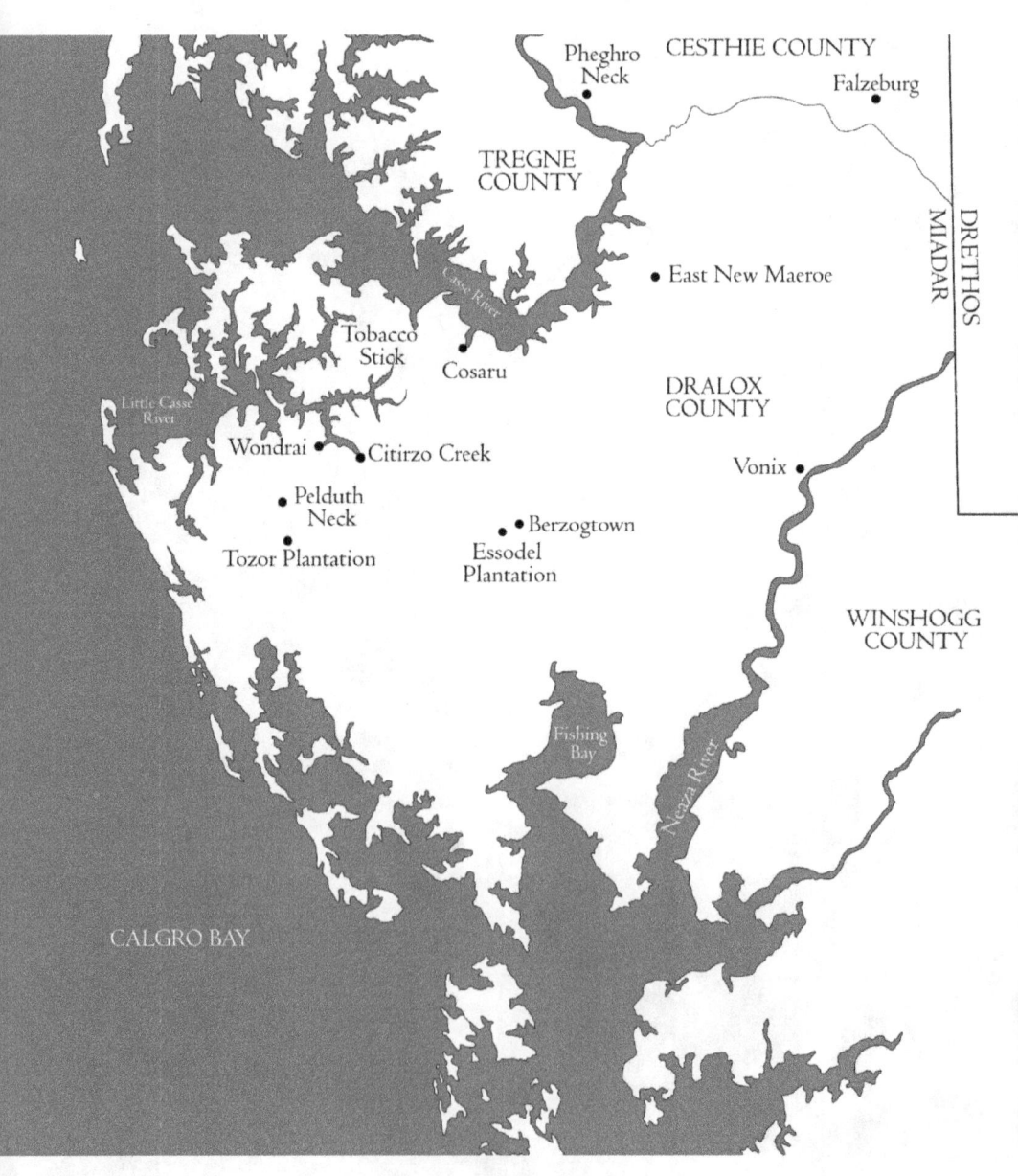

THE MUTOATH-DUPA LINE

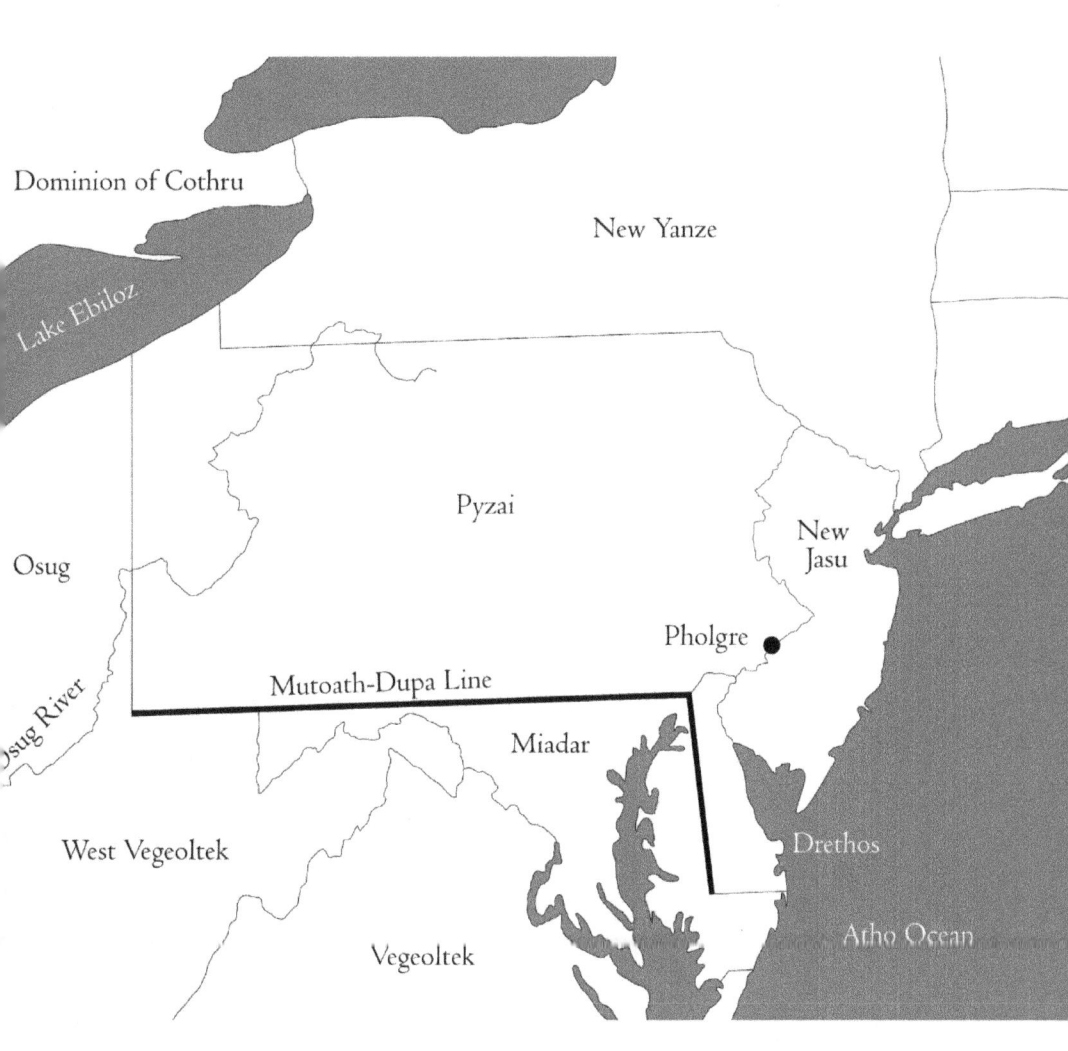

HARRIET'S TRAILS TO FREEDOM

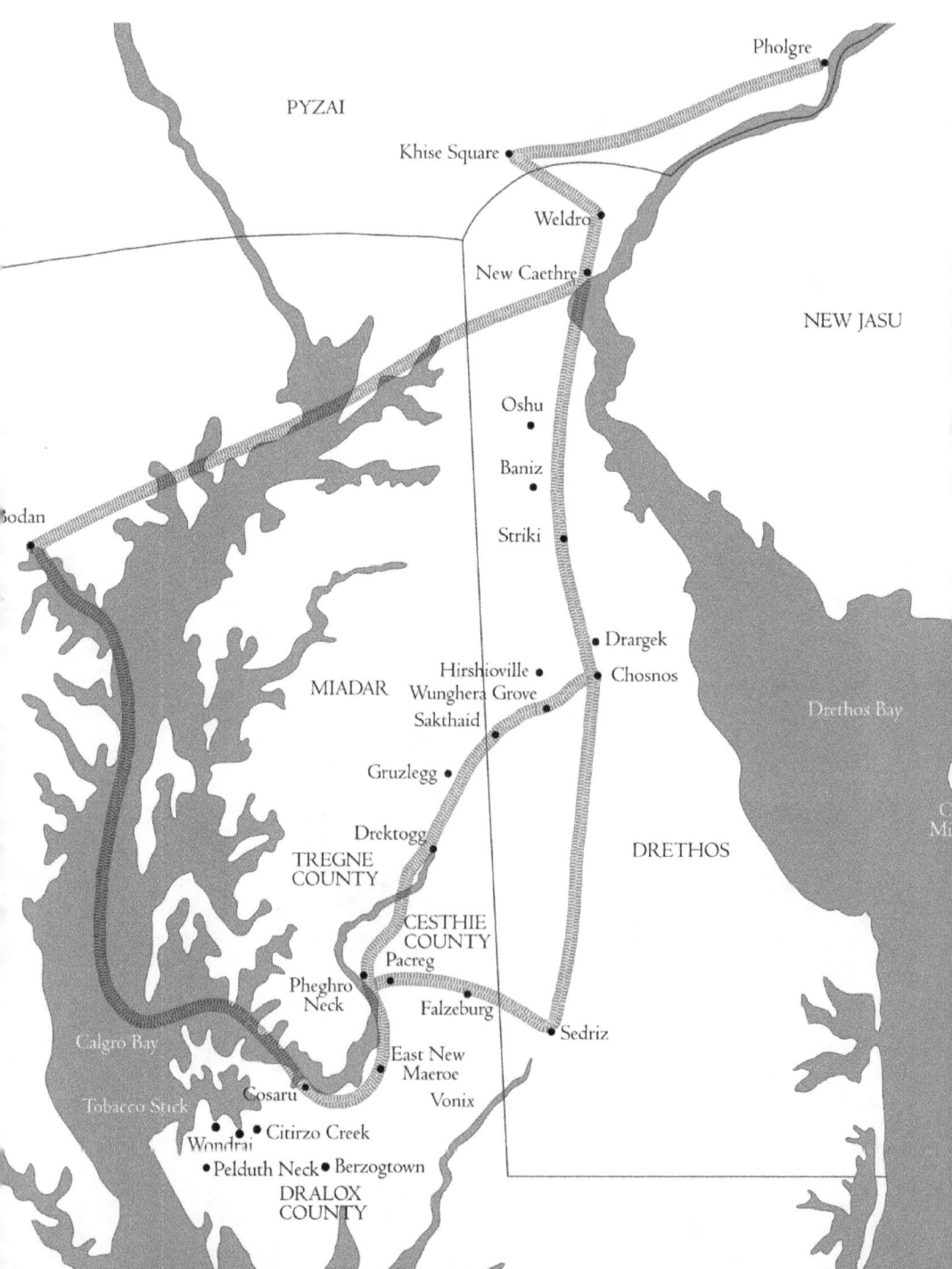

Prologue

1492

The Harpyfolk Land of Ciloth
Krieww Territory

Essodel opened her wide mouth, parting pointy white teeth sharp enough to cleave a seven-ton elephant in two. Heat raged in her belly, a boiling inferno that warmed her core, breaking down flesh, feathers, and bones from her last meal. They dissolved satisfyingly; a delicious treat too meager to satiate her greater hunger. A vortex of fire churned in her throat, spiraling up a neck corded with thick muscles overladen with rows of deadly spikes that grew in length and strength the closer they got to her arched back. When air from her open mouth met the internal heat that defined her place in the vast world of predators and their prey, the vortex surged forward, escaping its confines in a raging stream of molten hot fire.

As always, Essodel's aim was true; the circle of burning grass and screaming harpies were a sensory feast to her eyes and ears. Flapping wings the span of the gray clouds above that threatened to douse her ring of fire with an early morning shower, Essodel lowered her clawed feet to the ground. The dry spring grass crunched underneath her massive weight. A rain shower would do the ground good, but she was fond of her fire and not yet ready to lose her flames or the terror they invoked in the harpies cowering behind its sizzling walls.

"W-we d-d-don't have any g-gold." The female harpy who'd deigned to speak . . . to lie to Essodel, she was sure, pushed two children behind her. Barely fledglings, the two boys clung to the female's waist, their humanoid bird faces buried against the harpy's back. Their nude forms glistened with sweat, and their skin smelled of fear. The harpy female's clawed fingers plucked at the bits of gold attached to a crudely made necklace and bracelet. "T-this is all we have. No more."

One by one, the other harpies gestured to the same type of jewelry they wore.

"No more than this," the harpy repeated. "I . . . I . . . we will give you whatever gold we have."

Essodel watched as each harpy imprisoned in her ring of fire, be they adult, subadult, juvenile, or fledgling, removed the specks of gold jewelry and placed the meager collection in a pile.

"An offering," the harpy said, nodding to the insignificant pile with a tight expression Essodel interpreted as cautious hope.

If she were in her human form, Essodel would've laughed. She'd never been so insulted in her long life. Did these uncivilized half-bird, half-human creatures think Essodel, Eater of Bravehearts, Champion of the Deathlord, The Dark Dygen, Eternal Fire, would swallow their lies, accept their pathetic offering, and then fly away from this bountiful land, her scaly warrior's tail between her legs?

No. Essodel had traveled to this uncharted land, flying across a vast ocean at the behest of the King and Queen of the Dragonkin Kingdom of Targainth. She would claim this land and these heathen harpies for the leaders of her great nation.

"I'll have my hoard of gold," she said, projecting her words into their minds in a language they understood. A gift, for her kind, the ability to use telepathy in the recipient's native language. *"You'll show me. Every rock formation. Every small waterway. Streams, rivers, creeks. Every inch of this rolling land. From ocean to ocean. It will all belong to the Dragonkin of Targainth."* With a wave of a wing, Essodel extinguished her ring of fire, leaving scorched earth and coughing harpies with wide, round eyes that stared up at her as if she was death incarnate instead of their savior, their civilizer.

This newfound land will be my reward for the long journey across the ocean. If I must, I will claim it with claws and fire. Let the other Dragonkin kingdoms come. I'm the discoverer of this land, and my name, Essodel of Targainth, will be remembered as the greatest explorer. I will stake my claim here. Grow my hoard, beginning with these pathetic harpies. They will serve me well. And when I am done with them, the flightless Sankofa birds of Sika await.

Before that, this village of harpies would be made to understand the new status quo. Meaning . . . Essodel whipped her spiked tail around her body, a gliding arc of swift might.

Off came the head of the harpy who had spoken for her tribe. It tumbled to the ground, like an acorn from a tree, but with an open-mouthed *thud*.

The fledglings' screams followed, but they soon went silent, as did the other harpies, when she wrapped her tail around the young ones' shivering bodies.

"Let us try again. Take me to your gold mines. Every. Single. One."

PART I

"SLAVERY IS THE NEXT THING TO HELL."

Chapter 1
Beautiful Fledglings

1823

United States of Ungathu, formerly Harpyfolk Land of Ciloth
The State of Miadar, formerly Krieww Territory
Dralox County
Berzogtown
Essodel Plantation

Ben despised much of his life, but marrying Rit and producing five wonderful children with her was not among his life's trials. Yet, the injustice, the abject cruel horror of being the literal property of another, conflicted with everything it meant to be a person, parent, and spouse. So, Ben leaned against one of the many sweet gum trees native to Miadar's Eastern Shore region. Long before him, enslaved Birdfolk would hollow out the trunks of the trees and use them as a cradle for their children. Ben and Rit had benefitted from their ancestors' ingenuity. The seventy-foot trees with bright green, star-shaped leaves were made even lovelier in the fall when they turned a magnificent scarlet. But the medicinal benefits of the yellowish resin revealed when the bark was stripped away told the sad tale of enslaved life on the Essodel Plantation.

Thankful for the hand-me-down boots he wore, Ben's feet were protected from the sweet gum's prickly burrs but not from the inhumane creature who stood before Ben, telling him the unthinkable.

The unconscionable.

From a height of twelve feet, Master Gyzad spoke to Ben in a tone he knew well. His mind was made up, and he would not be moved no matter how Ben or anyone else felt. But sometimes, though rarely, a sliver of something akin to pity would enter the Dragonkin's golden reptilian eyes.

Brief. Shallow. But, in the end, inconsequential.

"I purchased a mine in Pelduth Neck, so I need a servant of your caliber to grow my hoard. You'll be the head ground-scraper among the other servants. That will please Rit. Make her proud of her husband."

As always, Ben remained silent, revealing none of his internal thoughts. Dragonkin did not have conversations with the so-called ground-scrapers. No equal exchanges of ideas and opinions existed between dragon masters and the flightless bird shifters they referred to as "servants."

Master Gyzad is only gifted at talkin' his mother into payin' for another one of his hoard-makin' schemes. They've all failed, so he can't afford but one slave. I ain't no servant. Servants have a voice and a choice. They define their future and control their present, includin' where they live. He thinks that because he permitted me to marry my Rit, I should be forever grateful for his "kindness." Damn him, I am grateful. But Master Gyzad don't do nothin' from his heart. Me and Rit gave Mistress Essodel five more slaves to add to her hoard. A slave, that's what I am. I don't care what Master Gyzad calls me. What his kind has created on this continent is a system of slavery. Plain and simple. What they choose to call it matters not a squat. No more than my righteous anger changes where I'll go in a week.

Golden eyes watched Ben, but he gave the Dragonkin nothing other than cool silence, satisfying Master Gyzad's craving for absolute obedience. "Good, then it's settled. You'll travel with me to Pelduth Neck. Be my overseer." Master Gyzad threw his bald head back and laughed as if the sweet gum behind Ben had morphed into a traveling menagerie. Even if the tree could and had, Ben found no humor in being forced to leave his wife and children and made to oversee fellow enslaved Birdfolk. Since silence was all he had to latch on to, he pulled it to him with both hands. "A ground-scraper in a province of gryphon slave catchers. With me as your dragon master, not one of those impure hybrid bastards will dare lay a talon on you or question your authority over my servants. Yes, yes," he said, his boastful arrogance punctuated by another loud bark of laughter. "So, don't look so forlorn, Overseer Benjamin Wren."

A hand wider than the span of his face slammed onto Ben's right shoulder.

He winced, unable to conceal the pain of having even a Dragonkin in human form lay a meaty hand on his person.

"Did that little touch hurt, Ben?"

The answer was obvious, but that wasn't the point of the question. Long, rough fingers dug into Ben's shoulder, pushing against delicate bones he'd rather not have broken again.

"So skinny and frail, you ground-scrapers. It has never taken much to snap one of you in two. Yet, despite God not blessing you with strength, size, flight—hell, much of anything physically useful at all, you make excellent servants." Tightening his grip and ripping a whine of protest from Ben, Master Gyzad grinned and nodded as if literally pressing his point into Ben elevated him to godlike status. "Don't think I don't know what your quiet acquiescence means. Birdfolk may be weaker than Dragonkin, but you are more intelligent and resourceful than most. Don't get any ideas into that bird brain of yours of escaping when traveling between towns."

Master Gyzad's thumb pressed hard against Ben's clavicle. He had no doubt the dragon shifter's instinct was to break the bone as an indisputable example of his predatory might over a weaker creature. But self-restraint or common sense stopped him from injuring his new overseer. Ben might indeed be a flightless bird, a damn ground-scraper, as the Dragonkin had taken to calling bird shifters like him. Still, even a physically weaker shifter traveled faster in their animal form.

"Mother wouldn't like it if I made it difficult for you to travel. She wants us both in Pelduth Neck in a week, and I'll be damned if I carry you on my back." With a hard squeeze and then a shove that would surely leave a bruise, Master Gyzad released Ben.

He wanted to breathe a sigh of relief. No, he wanted to gather his family and fly them far away from there. But Birdfolk did not fly. His wings were useless for anything as lifesaving as carrying his children away to freedom. But Ben had known no other life save this one, which did not stop him from dreaming about one day having his freedom.

I'll be a free man. A bird shifter owned by no one but myself. My family, too. We'll all be free. But first I must keep them safe. I ain't skinny or frail. How could I be when I've labored my entire life?

Still, there was no greater foe or hunter than the Dragonkin. Physically, Birdfolk did not compare.

Legs as weak as a nestling taking its first steps, Ben slid down the tree like the skinny, frail ground-scraper Master Gyzad had called him his entire life.

Master Gyzad's mocking laughter hurt his pride in a way his rough fingers had not. "I told Mother you would react this way. But not me. Distance from our mate and hatchlings means nothing to the Dragonkin. But to Birdfolk and Harpyfolk, you live for nothing but your flock. It's how the Harpyfolk of this beautiful nation were defeated so easily. You should've seen it back then. It was nothing but indefensible villages and acres upon acres of untamed and unclaimed land. They were doing nothing with all of this bounty."

Ben closed his eyes, uninterested in another one of Master Gyzad's distorted history lessons. In his mind's eye, he saw his lovely wife, Rit, surrounded by their five children. They turned and smiled at him, as always when he was the last to enter their cabin at the end of a grueling day. Their smiles propelled him from one day to the next, giving him hope in a way the Dragonkin's God never had.

There's nothin' to be done. I gotta sit with Rit and figure out how to prevent my move to Pelduth Neck from tearin' our family apart. Dragonkin has never cared about Birdfolk families. Master Gyzad reminded me of somethin' I shouldn't have forgotten. I won't forget again. Never.

Opening his eyes, Ben pushed to his feet, wiped the dirt from his pants, and stood to his full five-ten height. Nothing compared to the twelve-foot Master Gyzad, but size and physical strength did not make a person of consequence; their character did.

"Well, look at Overseer Ben. All grown up at the tender age of thirty-six. You'll need that spine when you come face-to-face with Pelduth Neck's gryphons."

Ben did not fear gryphons any more than he was afraid to die. But Master Gyzad and his mother, Mistress Essodel, knew Birdfolk well. As long as Rit and their children were owned by Mistress Essodel and resided in her aviary, Master Gyzad would be assured Ben would always return to his family. Because what did freedom matter when no one was around to share it with?

"I'll explain everything to my wife."

"Good, good. Don't forget to tell Rit you'll be my head man in Pelduth Neck."

"She'll be proud, as you said. So proud." Ben smiled, granting Master Gyzad what he craved—obedience, even when given with an invisible spoonful of sarcasm. Without waiting for his dragon master's permission, Ben strolled away from the old sweet gum tree and the even older Master Gyzad, and toward his family and home.

Little Araminta, or Minty, as the family called her, was only eighteen months old. Would she remember him after being away from home for weeks? Shaking off the dread, Ben picked up his pace and ran the rest of the way home.

"Bring them all the way inside, Rit. I want to see how much they have grown."

Rit never liked the intrusive sound of a Dragonkin in her mind despite never knowing any other existence. What she despised even more, however, were times like these. Refusal had never been an option, not if she valued her life and those of her children. So, holding Minty close to her chest, Rit tightened her grip on seven-year-old Robert's hand, who, in turn, looped his free arm around Soph's waist, Rit's ten-year-old daughter.

"Come along," she told the children, nodding to her two oldest daughters, Linah and Mariah, to follow. As they did each time they were summoned to Mistress Essodel's mountain, Linah's and Mariah's customary joviality shriveled like rotten fruit on a vine.

Few Dragonkin still resided in the mountains, but Mistress Essodel was from a bygone era, preferring her scales and fire to anything human and weak. Despite the voice in Rit's head, Mistress Essodel did not dwell at the mouth of the mountain, which would've made her command an easier task to complete. Instead, Rit and her children had to walk the long distance to reach a dragon who, if there was indeed a merciful god, would've died years ago. But no, Mistress Essodel coveted her life as much as she did her hoard.

"Momma," Minty whispered against her neck. "Scared."

So am I, baby, but I have no choice. I'm sorry.

"Don't want to."

Minty did not cry or scream about being called before the ancient dragon, as her older siblings had. Rit hadn't scolded her children for acting instinctively. No more than she would admonish Minty for voicing her genuine fears.

Rit nuzzled the side of Minty's head, a natural response to the tightening of the arms around her neck and the legs that struggled to stay wrapped around a protruding stomach that, not too long ago, had kept Minty safe and warm.

"I know you're scared. But we talked about this before we left home. Do you remember what I said?"

Minty's head nod was answer enough.

Fire-smoothed limestone surrounded them on all sides. It was an unnatural look. Rit couldn't begin to fathom how long it had taken Mistress Essodel to transform the mountain into a home suitable to her exacting tastes.

"Good." Rit shifted to her left, checking on Robert, who reminded her so much of Ben in his steadfast bearing and intense silence that her only son was Ben Junior in all but name.

"I'm fine, Momma," Robert said, sensing her eyes on him. "I won't cry this time. I promise."

"Me either," Minty said, letting Rit know she remembered their conversation, too.

"Do your best. But, if you can't keep it in, try to cry quietly."

"Yes, Momma," Minty and Robert said in soft, sweet voices captured by the limestone and tossed back at them in a gentle reverberation.

They plodded along, Rit acutely aware of Linah's and Mariah's barefooted steps behind her, just as she was of their heavy exhalations.

"Momma?"

"I know, Mariah," she said to her twelve-year-old, "I see them."

"B-but . . ."

"Don't look," Linah told Mariah.

"I'm tryin' not to, but . . ."

Linah blew out a deep breath, a sign of her own unsettlement. "Give me your hand and close your eyes. You, too, Soph. I'll lead and make sure you don't step on anything. Or anyone. We'll walk around the bits and—"

"Linah," Rit said, but not fast enough to prevent the first part of her sentence from slipping free and reminding the younger children that the path to Mistress Essodel was paved with, as Linah was about to say, bits and pieces of spat-out cow and Birdfolk remains.

"Yes, ma'am. Enough said about that. I got them."

"Thank you."

Linah is only fifteen, but she's had to grow up fast, just as I did. Just as we all must, but maybe my Minty will have a little more time to be a child. Carefree and unbothered by the ugliness that is our lot in life.

"Except for me and Linah, everyone should keep their eyes closed. Nothin' is important to see until we get to Mistress Essodel."

That wasn't true because this mountain portion revealed an ugly, enduring truth about Dragonkin like Mistress Essodel and her offspring. Not only did much of the mountain floor contain evidence of Mistress Essodel's disregard for the lives of Birdfolk to the point of permitting baby dragons to feast on any unfortunate slave, but the walls served as a morbid reminder of what happened to slaves who deigned to escape.

Whereas the earlier parts of the mountain were a mix of browns, blues, greens, and yellows, the walls in this section were scorched black with human- and bird-shaped indentations.

Now that Linah is fifteen and capable of runnin' away and survivin' on her own until she reaches a slave-free state, Mistress Essodel wants to remind her, remind all of us, what will happen if we try to escape. No one has ever escaped Mistress Essodel and her sons.

The sights above and below sickened Rit, but she trudged along because no good options existed.

"Ah, there you are. I expected you sooner, Rit. Did you encounter one of my grand-hatchlings on the way?"

That sentence was meant to frighten my children because we both know her son's latest brood of dragon babies only visits when Minister Breembat does on Sundays. And they've already come and gone, thank God.

Rit halted at the entrance to Mistress Essodel's lair. It opened into a cavern that extended four hundred feet east to west and double that length south to north. Even in the mountain's depths, light beamed inside but not from the yellow glow of the morning sun.

Piles of glistening treasure filled the cavernous space. Perhaps greed and power drove Dragonkin to obsess over collecting anything they deemed beautiful, unique, and valuable. Rit couldn't understand such a drive, especially since it led to the near extinction of the indigenous Harpy-folk tribes of this country.

No matter how many times she saw Mistress Essodel, Eater of Bravehearts, Champion of the Deathlord, The Dark Dygen, Eternal Fire, as she liked to remind Rit, not that she knew what a dygen was, the sight of the tremendous scaly beast never ceased to take her breath away.

At 164 feet, with a wingspan equally long, few modern-day Dragonkin could rival Mistress Essodel's size. Like her oldest offspring, Master Gyzad, most dragon shifters stopped growing at seventy-five feet, which was still a lot of dragon to contend with.

Mistress Essodel did not perch atop her hoard of treasure, shined to demanding perfection, but was curled around the piles of gold goblets, coins, and priceless jewels.

The obscene majesty of so much consolidated wealth against the backdrop of such a menacing creature was a disturbing visual display.

But Rit had stood before Mistress Essodel many times, and this day would not mark her final occurrence because the dragon collected more than jewels.

She stepped forward with her children, wanting this face-to-face meeting over as quickly as possible but knowing Mistress Essodel would not be rushed.

"Good day, Mistress Essodel. I've come as commanded."

"As you shall always. Why do your young ones not look upon me? Tell them to do so now."

"No, Momm—"

"Hush and do as our mistress says," Rit whispered to Minty. Then, "All of you," Rit added in a louder tone, infusing her directive with as much comfort as she could offer them.

One by one, the children complied, including Linah, who had slammed her eyes shut the second Mistress Essodel had come into view. Now, every member of the Wren family, except for Ben, stood wide-eyed before Mistress Essodel, their owner.

"*Well done, Rit. You and Ben make beautiful fledglings. Tell me their names and ages.*"

Rit bobbed her head in acknowledgment, then proceeded to reintroduce her children to Mistress Essodel, knowing the dragon had forgotten nothing, least of all the slaves that had added to her hoard.

"This is Linah, my eldest. She turned fifteen last month." Rit handed Minty to Linah, who met her gaze with banked tears before going to her sister. She continued the introductions, standing behind each child as she said their name and age. "After Linah is Mariah at twelve, followed by Soph at ten and Robert at seven." Returning to Linah's side, she placed a soothing hand atop Minty's woolly hair. "And this little one is Minty. She is—"

"*One year and six months in March. They are lovely, indeed. But I want to know how much lovelier they can become.*"

She means their value. Today was unavoidable. I'd hoped for more time before Soph would be expected to work like me and her older sisters.

"*Show me,*" Mistress Essodel demanded, her voice a low hiss of power in Rit's mind. Lifting her head from the cave's floor, her slight movement caused an avalanche effect. Shiny gold coins slid downward until they joined others already at the base of her body.

Rit stripped off her dress, turned her back to Mistress Essodel, and smiled at her children. "I know we haven't done this much, but you know what to do."

Barely. Only children ten and younger were permitted to transform without permission of a Dragonkin. Birdfolk who were Minty's age couldn't shift at all, making them "useless" to a dragon with Mistress Essodel's taste until they turned five and could perform the act. Until then, her youngest was safe from the Dragonkin's obsession with Birdfolk like the Wrens. Unfortunately, with an uninspired color palette, boys like Robert were destined for harsh mines or plantation work.

"Like Mistress Essodel's gold coins, you have two sides. Unlike her coins, neither side is visible at the same time. To show our other side, we must transform or shift our shape from one version of ourselves to the other. It ain't difficult. You just need to hold the image of your other self in your mind. Hold it and see yourself becomin' it on the outside."

To demonstrate, Rit closed her eyes, not because her transformation required the act, but because, for young shifters, limiting external stimuli aided the process. Still, she conjured an image of her avian form, a lithe body with multicolored wings.

She didn't break apart. No painful cracking of bones, realigning of organs, stretching of the skin, or any number of physical changes enslaved children assumed occurred with the shift before being taught the truth by a parent or community elder. Rit simply relaxed, relishing the pleasure of being permitted to take bird form. The sensation of air she'd never felt under her wings washed over her, caresses so strong she trembled from the breeze of euphoria that was her avian form. But her jubilation was as short-lived as the feeling of flying through the sky was nonexistent.

When Rit returned to herself, she stood as a five-three Sankofa bird native to the Birdfolk continent of Sika, which, ironically, in the language of her ancestors, meant gold. A bright green plumage led to wings the color of a ripe dragon fruit tipped in the peach-pink of a juicy papaya.

"*Gorgeous,*" Rit heard Mistress Essodel say, a tendril of speech across her mind as if the dragon hadn't meant to project her thought.

Rit agreed with Mistress Essodel on little, but she did her assessment of the majesty of Sankofa Birdfolk. Yet, her life, and the lives of the millions of Sankofa stolen from their homeland, would've played out differently had Mistress Essodel and her ilk not thought them "gorgeous."

But the cruel hands of fate could not be turned back in Sankofa's favor, so Rit pushed away thoughts of what could have been. Instead, she continued instructing her children in a way the Dragonkin could not. For all their might, the Dragonkin could not speak aloud in their animal form, and their telepathy, while unique to them, was limited by proximity and the number of recipients of their message.

Yet, Birdfolk physiology permitted verbal communication in both forms, so Rit told her children to "Envision your Sankofa form — vibrant feathers, a long, thin beak, eyes capable of seein' far and near, toes forward facin', and talons sharp. See your bird. Become the bird."

While Mistress Essodel may have found Rit's form attractive, the mother in her couldn't have been prouder as first Linah, then Mariah, and finally Soph transformed. Their chest feathers ranged from the same emerald green as Rit's to Ben's sapphire blue. Whereas her wings were a mix of peach and pink, her children's wings combined blue and green in a vivid gradient effect. Striking, but without the kaleidoscope of colors the most enchanting Sankofa birds were known to have.

"Well done," Rit praised her children, her voice chirpier than her human one.

"Yes, well done, indeed. Quite the investment. You have added nicely to my hoard. This is the future. Beauty and entertainment." With a flick of a wing, Mistress Essodel shoved mounds of her expensive jewelry aside, creating a ripple effect that shook the mountain floor. *"Show me why I am the smartest Dragonkin in this state and beyond. Show me why those*

abolitionists will always live on the fringes of society, their ideals naïve and their pockets wastelands where influence goes to die."

I've never met an abolitionist. One wouldn't dare show their face on Mistress Essodel's plantation. But Birdfolk have been enslaved by the Dragonkin for hundreds of years. I don't think we will ever be free if we haven't gotten our freedom in all that time. But I can still hope, right?

Mistress Essodel shoved even more of her finest gemstones out of her way, and Rit knew what would come next.

She turned to Robert while gently using her wing to push a silently sobbing Minty to her older brother. "Go home and take your sister with you."

"B-but, Momma. That's a far walk back through the mountain. It's dark, Minty is crying, and . . ."

Rit did not have time for her son to be a typical seven-year-old. Mistress Essodel only saw her slaves' children as another piece of her collection, not people with feelings, except for the emotion of fear, which she took much pleasure in evoking.

"Do as I say. Go home. Follow the same path we took, and you and Minty will be fine. There's nothin' else in these mountains but us and Mistress Essodel."

She hated sending her children home alone, but the trek was safer and shorter than staying for what was to come. Rit didn't want her youngest to see what would happen next, although the aftermath wouldn't be much prettier. Still, once they saw her and their sisters again, they would be in human form, the transformation hiding some of the brutality done to them.

Robert cried neither silently nor briefly, but with racking sobs that had Rit wanting to wrap him in her wings and fly him away to safety. But the power to do either was beyond her, no more than she could shield her daughters from Mistress Essodel's intentions. Rit wasn't a violent woman. She'd never struck anyone, least of all her children. Yet, each time she was summoned before Mistress Essodel, by herself or, worse, with her growing children, she wished she had the might to bring the mountain down on the dragon's head, crushing her under its unforgiving weight.

But, like Robert, she possessed nothing that could alter her circumstances. So, just as he took Minty's little hand and walked away, Rit returned her attention to Mistress Essodel.

"From this day forward, Rit, I expect you to bring your fledglings to me as soon as they can transform. The ones here resemble you and Ben too much for me to keep claiming originality. The colors, while lovely, do not represent the spectrum of the Sankofa. Perhaps the other two will diversify my offerings. Only time or more nestlings will tell." Mistress Essodel rose to her full height while seated on her hind legs. The spikes on her back grazed the mountain wall behind her. *"Now, dance until I tell you to stop. Dance until I've been entertained. Then, and only then, will I permit you to stop. When that is done, when you have served your lady well, I will take my feathers, for everything you have belongs to me. Now dance!"*

Rit danced. So, too, did her daughters. They danced and danced and danced.

When they finished, when numb toes and trembling legs had them crashing to the ground, they had no energy left to protest when a shifted Mistress Essodel plucked every colorful feather from their body.

Every.

Single.

One.

Chapter 2
I Was Scared

Ben rushed ahead of Rit. "Is there somethin' I can do for you? I can get you some resin." Without waiting for his wife's response, he yanked back an old used bedsheet they'd rescued from the trash. From Master Gyzad's tossed-away items, Ben no longer recalled. But he'd once heard an elderly slave say something about one person's trash being another person's treasure. He thought the sentiment was too much of a leap because sometimes trash was just trash, no matter the perspective. But he understood the saying well enough since his family had received many of Mistress Essodel's family's castoffs.

From clothing well past their prime, to broken and discarded furniture, to faded and stained linen, to weekly food rations no dragon hatchling could subsist on, much less a family of seven, Ben and Rit took what they were given because survival was preferable to death. Although, from the ghostly look on Rit's, Linah's, and Mariah's faces when they dragged themselves into their cabin home, halfway undressed and pulling off the rest, they appeared like death warmed over.

Holding back the bedsheet, a makeshift bedroom door in a one-room cabin, Ben waved his wife inside. As soon as she was, he quickly added the softest pieces of linen to their bed, a board box nailed against the wall with straw as a mattress. It wasn't much, neither the straw nor the recycled bedcoverings, but they were clean and theirs.

He wished she would wait for him to retrieve the resin from a sweet gum tree before crawling onto the bed, but she didn't, wincing when her tender flesh met the thin, linen-covered straw.

Ben winced, too, because Mistress Essodel treated her slaves equally. She had no favorites, granting certain slaves privileges while denying others the same. If anything, the slaves Mistress Essodel considered most valuable, most likely to add to her hoard and standing in Dragonkin society, were more likely to receive her attention and defeathering. Because Mistress Essodel had an eye for beauty, and there was no lovelier Sankofa bird in her aviary than Rit, he'd tended to his wife's injuries more often than she had cause to tend to his.

Who will care for Rit and the girls the next time they come home like this? I won't be here to help them to bed or cook for them. Robert, I suppose, and our friends. But it should be me here with them.

As if proposing again, Ben lowered to a knee, careful when he took ahold of Rit's hand. "What do you need me to do? Get some resin?"

Dark brown eyes blinked at him, and because he'd chosen the mother of his children and the keeper of his heart well, Rit conjured a smile for his benefit. "The children need you more than I do. Knowin' you're here to care for them will ease my mind and help me sleep. Rub the girls down before you do me. But bring Minty here first. I can't stand to hear her cryin' for me."

Neither could Ben, but the last thing Rit needed was a clingy one-year-old beside her in bed. Still, he did as she asked, disagreeing but trusting her to manage their toddler in a way that would soothe Minty while keeping Rit safe. But he needn't have worried about Minty because the child seemed to understand her mother's delicate physical condition. So, instead of tugging and climbing on her the way she often did, Minty's way of competing with her siblings for her mother's attention, she simply curled close to her mother's chest and, with a kiss to her forehead from Rit and a soft assurance of "I'm fine," she fell asleep.

Soon after, so did Rit, leaving Ben awake and angry. He used the latter as fuel to get himself going. Not that he needed a boost to take care of his children, especially Linah and Mariah, who, by the time he'd finished rubbing them down with the yellow resin perfect for soothing skin irritations and healing wounds, they were fast asleep in a board box they'd shared ever since Robert came along. Like everything else his eldest daughters possessed, the bed was too small for one teenage girl, much less two. But they made do, just as they would after Ben moved to Pelduth Neck, he knew. Yet, resilience came at a high, unfair price for the enslaved of this nation. Even for the many free bird shifters Pelduth Neck was known to have.

There's a thrivin' free bird shifter population there. Abolitionists, too, not that I can be caught talkin' to one of them. So, maybe not all bad. There are things I don't know and can't learn livin' here under Mistress Essodel's clawed feet. But in Pelduth Neck and as an overseer, I'll have more flexibility to move about on Dragonkin business.

With his upcoming separation from his family, Ben needed any glimmer of hope, an advantage to him being elsewhere instead of at home with his Rit. So, he latched on to the potential hope that a free bird shifter population in Pelduth Neck could offer an enslaved Sankofa bird with limited knowledge of life beyond Mistress Essodel's aviary.

Ben settled beside the bed that contained Soph and Robert. Like her sisters and mother, his Soph was asleep, skin glistening from a healthy coat of resin and her thumb in her mouth. At ten, she should've passed this developmental stage, and if Rit saw her, she would give her a gentle scold. But Ben couldn't bring himself to disturb her sleep, especially not after her ordeal in the mountain.

Instead, Ben kissed Robert's soft cheek and hugged him close, holding his son tighter and longer than usual. But Robert didn't seem to mind. The child's arms gripped Ben just as fiercely.

"I'm proud of you. You did good gettin' Minty back here all by yourself."

"I was scared I wouldn't remember the way. I was scared that . . ."

Ben accepted Robert's light weight as he scooted from the bed and onto his lap, a sweet ball of understated courage.

"You did good." Ben repeated the three words, needing his son to understand and accept his bravery in facing their harsh reality. "You did good, son, and I love you."

"Love you, too, Poppa. But I hate Mistress Essodel." Robert had spoken the second sentence without any tears in his voice but with a hardness beyond his seven years.

Hate was a strong word that Ben and Rit disapproved of within their family and community. But the Dragonkin was neither, so Ben found no fault in his son's emotion, deeming it justified.

His and Robert's.

Yes, hate was a strong word, but so was slave.

Dralox County
Pelduth Neck

Mudspike loved an excellent hunt; few were better than chasing down a slave who thought themselves entitled to freedom. He'd spotted the fool, Barbury, the moment he'd slipped away from the mining camp. A cotton sack on his back and neck on a swivel, the slave rushed away from the camp and into the moonlit night, squinty eyes searching the darkness.

Seeing no one, the slave sprinted until the dusty ground had met plush green. Breathing deeply, he'd plunged into the woods. Mudspike could've sworn he heard the male's deep exhalation at having made it that far without capture.

These ground-scrapers are so much fun. I love it when they flee, thinking they can cross into Pyzai before they're caught. Even when they manage to, I always catch them on the other side and drag their scrawny asses back here. Too stupid to be free. They never even look up when running away. They only look forward and backward, as if the creatures they're trying to evade would lower themselves to their flightless level.

Tracking the runaway with his keen bird's eyes while using his strong wings to keep his robust lion's body above the tree line, Mudspike followed his quarry. He could've captured him the moment it became apparent he was fleeing his bondage—stealing himself away to freedom, as the slaves had taken to calling the mad dash to Pyzai, the slave-free northern state that bordered Miadar.

Flapping wings took Mudspike farther away from Pelduth Neck, and he enjoyed the leisurely flight. There was nothing like the feel of crisp air between his feathers, the fresh, watery scent of clouds before a rainfall, and the sound of the stuttering footfalls of a barefooted slave running over spiny, prickly burrs that pierced calloused, unprotected feet.

Was this his plan? To run until his legs gave way, his lungs burned, and his feet bled from the sharp burrs? Does he even know the direction he should be running in? Did he bring food or water? That could be what's in his cotton sack. I could end it here. I could fly down there, knock him around a few times, and then march him back to his master. But what would the fun be in that? He got me all the way out here. I should at least let myself be entertained more. See how far he can run. Maybe I'll learn the secret of their escapes. Some have made it to Pyzai, not on my watch but on others. Perhaps I'll discover something interesting I can take to the Dragonkin. For a big payday, of course. I don't do this work for free, no matter how much fun I have playing with my prey. Then again, I didn't eat before leaving home.

Decision made, Mudspike swooped downward and toward his quarry. He traded in stealth for the delectable taste of terror.

"W-where did you come from?" The slave ran faster than Mudspike would've thought possible after the long trek from the mining camp and on feet that left a bloody trail in his wake. "I-I'm not going back. I'd rather die than go back."

That could be arranged, but Mudspike had his own little hoard he intended on adding to with this slave's capture. So, he flew faster, careful not to clip his wings on the trees. But it was challenging the deeper into the woods the bird shifter ran, darting around sweet gum trees with surprising agility.

Dammit. I don't remember these trees being so close together. I can barely—

Slam. Thud.

Mudspike glared up at the tree he'd smashed into but shook off the collision, the broken branches, fallen leaves, and . . . *Shit, those burrs hurt.* Pushing up on his thick lion's legs, Mudspike calculated the odds of him not crashing into another tree if he took to the air again. The odds were not in his favor, so he bolted after his prey on four legs.

This is better. I'm faster this way. He won't get away from me now. Come here, little birdie. I got something for you.

With each long stride, Mudspike drew closer. The scent of fear and piss perfumed the air like a freshly cooked game pie.

"I'm not goin' back." The slave stopped. His back was to Mudspike, and his cotton sack was lost somewhere behind them. A cotton shirt clung to his back, tight across trembling shoulders, with sleeves rolled up to defined forearms used to physical labor.

Unused to land pursuits, Mudspike opened his beak, letting in cool air and exhaling deeply. *I'm going to make him pay for this. I'll take a hand, maybe an entire arm. I'll tell his master he lost it during his failed escape. If I leave him with one good hand and arm to work, the Dragonkin won't mind me returning damaged goods.*

Mudspike crept closer to the slave, his bird head held high and his lion's feet a soft approach.

"I said I'm not goin' back to that life." The young Birdfolk's snort felt like a gust of mockery in the night air. "Life. Slavery ain't a life but a cruel, unendin' death sentence." Without warning, the bird shifter, a teen no older than sixteen, swung around, bringing the hand Mudspike intended on claiming up to a throat that, at once, appeared both fragile and robust. Or, perhaps, the hand that held the blade that radiated an aura of might.

"Don't you dare," Mudspike warned, determined not to lose his finder's fee.

"Let me go."

"Not happening, kid. Come on. You don't want to do that. You want your ma to cry when I drag your dead body back to Mistress Shandoth?"

"You don't know shit, gryphon."

Slash.

Chapter 3
Say Goodbye to Your Poppa

With fingers tightly interlocked with Ben's, Rit and her family trailed behind the throng of Birdfolk making their way from the ramshackle cabin homes and toward a familiar clearing at the base of Mistress Essodel's mountain.

"Are you okay?" Ben whispered.

Sensing his gaze on her, Rit refused to meet his eyes, knowing what she would see in their depths would match the sad pounding of her heart. So, she marched along, denying a truth her husband already knew. His leaving the family to move to Pelduth Neck wasn't Ben's guilt to harbor, yet he shouldered it all the same.

"I'm fine," Rit said. Her answer was a response to both her physical and mental state. It was a lie, of course, on both counts, but she didn't want to spend their last day together adding to Ben's burden. As with most things in their lives, they had little choice but to follow the decisions made by others, no matter how unjust and thoughtless.

As it was, the children, on learning of their father's impending separation from the family, had clung to him, especially Robert. Even now, as the family followed the tide of bodies to Mistress Essodel's cave, Minty rode on Ben's back while Robert had taken hold of his father's hand. Their three oldest girls walked behind their father so closely they would crash into him if he suddenly stopped.

Rit understood because she felt the same, but she vowed not to wallow or weep, although she'd cried plenty when Ben had relayed Master Gyzad's dictate. Now, she only desired to get through this obligatory service so she could return home with her family. Master Gyzad wanted to be on the road to Pelduth Neck before nightfall, which left them with a few meager hours.

One would think a weekly event that brought together over a hundred Birdfolk would be a cause for celebration and good cheer.

The crowd stopped two feet in front of Mistress Essodel's mountain home. Knowing the expectation, they dropped to the ground without being told to do so, heedless of the dirt and their discomfort. Children Minty's age and younger sat cradled in an adult's arms while the oldest among them leaned against a sturdy friend or family member.

Mistress Essodel may not have stood before them, but her presence was keenly felt because the Dragonkin who did wielded nearly as much power over them.

Just shy of ten feet, Minister Breembat, Mistress Essodel's youngest offspring, did not need to command the Birdfolk to be seated for him to tower over them in his human form. But their lower positions, physically and in society, did not prevent the male from strutting through the crowd, forcing them to move out of his way, lest they be stepped on.

"Good morning," Minister Breembat said in a booming voice from the group's center. Rocking on his heels and hands gripping suspenders, gleaming white teeth sparkled almost as brightly as his golden-brown eyes. "It's good to see everybody on this fine morning. Yes, such a fine morning our God has given us."

"God is good," Rit said, her voice one among many.

"Yes, yes, he is. And you know who else is good?"

"Obedient servants," Rit answered in unison with the others. Even children as young as Minty knew what to say when prompted by Minister Breembat. Rit and Ben ensured all their children did because they'd witnessed what happened to those who did not.

"This is a joke," Ben said so softly against her ear she felt his words more than heard them. "He can kiss my—"

As quick as a slave stealing away to freedom, Rit silenced her husband with a peck to the lips and a gentle "Hush. We can't afford trouble." Rit disliked Ben's return frown, but she'd take it and his silence over Minister Breembat's ire.

"God knows what is best for each and every one of us. In his wisdom and everlasting kindness, he led the Dragonkin to your native land. Before the Dragonkin took ground-scrapers under their wings, your people ran wild, worshipping trees, rivers, and the sun. But we rescued you, saved your souls, and set you on a righteous path to heaven."

Minister Breembat weaved through the crowd, barely waiting for people to move before slamming his big foot down to take the next step. Around he went, spouting one of many versions of the same sermon Rit had endured since she was a child.

"In exchange for our mercy and guiding hand, God asks only two things from you in return. And that is to serve Dragonkin without question and with loving devotion." Minister Breembat halted, plucked a suspender, and then patted the head of the person nearest him—the fifty-four-year-old Aveline.

To her credit, the older woman did not flinch or withdraw from the minister's touch despite the liberties he'd taken with her body when she was younger. The aftermath of Minister Breembat's unwanted attentions sat on either side of Aveline, twin sons with their father's golden-brown eyes. Both sets glared up at the Dragonkin, and if a look could sever the hand rubbing Aveline's head with a possessive touch, Minister Breembat would've lost his twice over.

But, like Aveline, Rit, Ben, and every other enslaved Birdfolk, the thirty-year-old fraternal twins, Efron and Abbott, knew better than to openly challenge a Dragonkin, even their own father, not that Minister Breembat had claimed any of the offspring he'd forced upon enslaved women. Still, the desire to protect ran deep within Birdfolk.

Lanky and lean but taller than the average bird shifter at seven feet, Abbott jumped to his feet. His outstretched hand flew to his mother's, who took the offering so fast that she was upright and dancing before Rit grasped the twins' ploy. Simultaneously, Efron had also pushed to his feet. Shorter and stockier than his twin, Efron used his entire body to make music. Hands clapped and feet stomped. His body swayed in a rhythmic pattern while his hands returned to his mouth repeatedly, tapping his parted lips in a fast, musical cadence.

Minty bolted to her feet, followed by her siblings, who danced in a circle with little Minty in the center. Rit's children laughed and laughed, and, for a priceless moment, she forgot both the twins' ploy and Ben's impending departure.

Soon enough, Rit and Ben joined their children in dance, as did everyone else. Overworked and underfed bodies moved to a hopeful tune of their own making, each gyration a silent prayer, each clap and stomp a plea to the ancestors to see them through.

Swallowed by the pulsating crowd, Rit could no longer see Aveline and her twins. But she could hear each time Efron called out, "Rock my soul," to which the crowd responded, "In the bosom of Abraham."

Rit had never enjoyed the Dragonkin church services, and today's gathering had proven no different. But she could not deny the joy that overcame her when in the presence of her family and community. Yet, the feeling doubled when they met in secret and beyond the watchful eyes of the Dragonkin. During those times, Rit could express herself fully and freely.

But she would not squander a second of her time with Ben, so she flung her head back and laughed as he strutted around her like the handsome Sankofa bird he was, even without his glorious blue feathers on display.

"Have I told you how much I love you?" Ben asked, having pulled Rit close.

She smiled against the shoulder to which her face was pressed, knowing he neither expected a reply nor required one. Then he sang. The warmth of his breath and baritone voice formed an invisible bubble around them, a cocoon of love, friendship, and trust.

"I got shoes, you got shoes. All God's children got shoes." Ben sang the song none of them would dare in front of Minister Breembat. "Everybody talkin' 'bout Heav'n ain't goin' there." It was a song about hypocrisy; one Rit knew the twins really meant when they rescued their mother in the only way they knew how, by giving Minister Breembat what he desired — obedient slaves who loved his God to the point of song and dance.

Rit smiled through the singing of the rest of the song, her husband careful not to step on her bare feet with the boots Master Gyzad had given him from a runaway slave who'd returned to the aviary after getting turned around for days in the woods. Rit didn't doubt the unfortunate man's burnt body was one of the dark marks on the wall she'd passed on her way to Mistress Essodel's lair.

"Abner won't be needing these anymore," Master Gyzad had said to Ben, tossing the turned-up, scuffed boots at his bare feet. "You should be able to work better in those. Faster. Harder. But don't get any thoughts of stealing away because those old boots won't serve you any better than they did that fool, Abner." Ben had relayed the story to Rit.

The song's last words returned Rit to the present and the boots that would take Ben away from her. "I'll be fine. I have Linah and Mariah to help me with the young ones."

"I know, but . . ." Ben hugged her tighter, and Rit understood his concern extended to himself as much as it did to their family.

"Have I told you how much I love you?" Rit asked, repeating Ben's question instead of letting on she knew that he worried about his loneliness without his family.

But then he laid his hand on a stomach that, over the months, had swelled to the size of a large watermelon. "I've never missed a birth, and I won't start now."

"He'll wait for his poppa."

The hand that slid from one portion of her stomach to another settled near her right ribs and where, if Rit wasn't mistaken, her child poked her with a foot or elbow. "A son, huh?"

"Yes. There's somethin' about your singin' that stirred Robert as much as it does this little one."

"Is that your way of sayin' our girls don't know good music when they hear it?"

Rising on tiptoe, Rit kissed Ben's smiling lips. "Our family continues to grow and survive, as families should."

Rit wouldn't mention Linah and the young, enslaved man who wanted her to be his wife. Not that Ben was unaware Linah was courting or that she would be old enough to start her own family when she turned sixteen next year. Their children wouldn't need their permission to marry. But they would need Mistress Essodel's, which Rit assumed she would grant since all children born from an enslaved woman belonged to the mother's owner.

The moment this child took root in me, he belonged to Mistress Essodel. None of my children are truly mine, no matter that I birthed and cared for them as best I could. It ain't right. Ben's mind must be goin' through the same thoughts, but he's never spoken them aloud. Each pregnancy brings him joy, while each of our children's unknown fate adds worry lines to a face kissed by the sun.

Rit kissed Ben's lips again, having faith they were strong enough to endure whatever existed on the other side of hope.

Dralox County
Pelduth Neck

Despite Pelduth Neck being only ten miles north of Berzogtown, the difference could not have been starker to Ben. He'd heard of mining towns. But the aviary near Mistress Essodel's mountain would not constitute one by any stretch of the imagination.

No wonder Master Gyzad was so anxious to move here. Look at this place. I've never seen a hotel before. I've counted two of them.

Trailing behind a flying Master Gyzad, Ben allowed the sights and sounds to wash over him. He chronicled everything he saw, from a general store with a constant flow of customers to open bars but closed brothels with a promise to open at sundown, to meat markets, boarding houses, and restaurants with delectable scents that had his mouth watering and stomach growling.

There are people everywhere. Dragonkin, Harpyfolk, and Birdfolk, but I haven't seen no gryphons. Maybe they don't live in the central part of town. It's hard to tell the enslaved folk like me from the free bird shifters. But I've never seen so many of us out and about and by ourselves. No mistress or master in sight. Except for me, because Master Gyzad likes to command attention wherever he goes. He might as well have hung a sign around my neck announcin' me as the newest slave in town. He's paradin' me around town as much as he is lettin' the town people know that Mistress Essodel's power and wealth extend beyond Berzogtown. I'm sure no one here needed remindin', especially when a seventy-five-foot, steel-gray dragon with spikes down his tail flies overhead. He acts like he didn't see the no-flying sign at the town's entrance. I can't read, but I know what crossed-out images of a flying dragon and gryphon means.

"Stop gawking. You look like a country bumpkin. No class, Ben. I can't have my overseer coming off like a know-nothing hick who has never seen the clean side of a barn, much less the inside of a house of ill-repute, as Breembat calls it."

Master Gyzad's laughter rippled through Ben's mind, a disturbing sound for all that went unsaid about Minister Breembat's forked tongue and lascivious ways. *"I won't tell Rit what you do on your days off. You have five hatchlings, so I know you like the feel of a woman. Understandable. Your wife is as pretty as your kind come."*

Ben stumbled as if Master Gyzad's words had manifested a pile of dragon manure in front of him. Righting himself, Ben held his head high, stared forward, and bit the inside of his jaw, tasting blood but swallowing pride.

This is what he does. He goes beyond limits. He thinks he's better than Minister Breembat because he doesn't force himself on women, but abuse can look different. I can't let him get to me. I promised Rit I wouldn't allow Master Gyzad or anyone else to take me from her and our children. I want to be here to meet our newest child. I won't leave my Rit to raise our children on her own.

Ben clamped down on the inside of his other cheek, Master Gyzad continuing to invade his mind with chatter he'd rather the Dragonkin kept to himself.

"I spoke with Mother about Breembat before we left, which was better than speaking to him directly about his actions with some of the female servants. It's unnatural. Dragonkin and Birdfolk reproducing."

Despite the one-sided conversation, Master Gyzad had flown ahead, leaving Ben to continue to jog after him. Rit had packed him what she could — his work boots, a couple of shirts and pairs of pants, a hollowed-out dried gourd for retrieving and drinking water, and a fat piece of toasted pork. It wasn't much, neither the clothing nor the food, but he'd refused to take more supplies from his family, who, he reasoned, needed them more than he did.

Once packed, Ben hugged and kissed his family one last time before transforming into a bird the same five-ten height as his human form. Rit had tied the torn sheet she'd used to store his meager possessions around his neck. She'd done an excellent job, too, because it hadn't come loose despite his hardy pace and eventual shift back into his human form when he'd reached Pelduth Neck.

"Everyone knows Mother has the purest Sankofa in all Miadar. The purest and loveliest. Except for the half-breeds. If not for their superior work in the fields, Mother would sell them to a buyer from one of the southern states. She still might."

If Master Gyzad had a point, Ben wished he would get to it so he could get out of his head. To his surprise, Master Gyzad had set a grueling pace, proving a blessing in disguise. Fatigue and focus left little room for thinking. But whenever Master Gyzad mentioned home, his words conjured memories of Ben's children's teary goodbyes.

"I don't want you to leave," Robert had said, arms crossed over a chest that, in time, would expand into manhood. But that was years into a future not guaranteed to any of them.

Linah had kissed his cheek, hers wet from tears she was unashamed to shed in front of her younger siblings. "I'll visit," she'd told him as if her fifteen-year-old self had the power to transform her statement into an unbreakable promise.

Mariah and Soph each had taken an arm, pressed their faces to the appendage, and wept so silently he feared his heart would tear apart.

"Say goodbye to your poppa." Rit had given Minty an encouraging pat on her back, but his little girl had sniffled into her shirt sleeve and then had given Ben a look so full of betrayal it made him gasp out a shaky, "Poppa loves his Minty. I'm sorry I can't live here with you anymore."

Minty had hidden behind her mother's legs, refusing to look at Ben, much less give him a goodbye hug he desperately needed to shore up his resolve for the separation.

My Minty is as mulish as they come. She hardly talks, but I can tell she has lots to say. Her eyes are so expressive. And her words are smooth yet sharp. She'll need to be careful when she gets older. Very careful.

"Breembat knows he better not touch your wife and girls, or he'll have not just me to answer to but Mother. Your family belongs to Mother and you to me, which means you're all off-limits to my brother."

Again, Ben's knees threatened to buckle and pitch him face-first onto the dusty ground. But he remained upright, if not woozy, from the prospect of Minister Breembat ignoring whatever threat Mistress Essodel may have leveled. Then his logical mind kicked in, reminding him of Mistress Essodel's unwavering demand for absolute obedience, even from her kinfolk.

Master Gyzad must think I'm an idiot. Aveline is also owned by Mistress Essodel. That fact held no sway over Minister Breembat. It's the first part of what he said. I wonder how much of a hit her reputation has taken in the Dragonkin community. It isn't as if Minister Breembat is the first or only Dragonkin to rape a Sankofa slave. The small but growin' population of Birdkin is evidence that Minister Breembat is not alone in his brutal but not illegal act. Because we slaves have no rights. We're nothin' but property to the Dragonkin. Used, abused, and discarded when no longer of use. For now, Mistress Essodel and Master Gyzad still have use for my family and me.

"You owe me, Ben."

Of course the bastard would want me to think that. He also knows I'm smart enough to interpret his unstated threat to Rit and my girls. If I don't do my job well, if I don't manage the silver mine and the enslaved miners to his standard, my punishment will fall on my family of females.

"Now, pick up the pace. We have gryphons waiting for us at the camp. I can't wait until they get a look at you."

Ben's eyes fell to the ground, convinced he waded in a lake of dragon droppings, his movements hindered and the stench dehumanizing.

He quickened his pace.

Chapter 4

Promise Me You'll Be a Good Big Sister

Okay, so maybe Ben was slightly fearful of gryphons. Or perhaps it was just these gryphons that set his flesh tingling and his heart racing.

He gulped, hoping the group of four male gryphons couldn't smell his fear or hear the rapid beating of his heart.

Ben and Master Gyzad had arrived at the mining camp, a crude collection of cabins and tents that made his former aviary home appear like a palace in comparison.

No wonder the former owner sold this place. It don't look like he tried to make a real go of it before throwin' up his hands and givin' up. Did these gryphons come with the sale, or were they hired as needed? And where are the other slaves I'm supposed to supervise?

Ben refused to look over his shoulder and to Master Gyzad, who had shifted into his human form minutes earlier. He did not want to give the gryphons any reason to think he needed his dragon master to stand between him and five-hundred-pound creatures whose only form was that of an animal.

They didn't so much surround Ben but stood in a menacing arch in front of him, sizing him up from heights of seven to nine feet and with eyes that ranged in color from black to brown. But there was one among them, the smallest at about seven feet and the only gryphon with evidence of a recent encounter with prickly burrs from a sweet gum tree, who glared at Ben with hostility beyond anything reasonable for a first meeting.

His eagle face and neck were marred with dots from where the spikes had pierced his skin, including near his eye, which was red but not swollen. Ben didn't know whether the gryphon knew how fortunate he was that a burr hadn't become embedded in his eye. His encounter with the burrs did not end with his face, for his lower body, a dirty yellow-gold coat, contained random specks of burr that hadn't been completely removed.

Either this gryphon doesn't have family or friends who can help him out and clean him up, or he thinks runnin' around with burrs attached to him, painful to anyone who has had the misfortune of fallin' or walkin' in them, is a sign of strength instead of stupidity. Seeing him like this tells me all I need to know about this gryphon. I need to stay far away from him because he's comfortable being friends with pain. No, thank you. I'll give him no reason to chase after me, especially not anywhere near a sweet gum's burrs.

"This is Benjamin Wren. Ben will be my eyes and ears at the camp. It will be like I'm here when he speaks, so you better listen to him." As naked as any shifter after a transformation, Master Gyzad sidled up beside an equally nude Ben. As he'd done the other day under the sweet gum tree, Master Gyzad placed a hand upon his shoulder. Unlike the last time he'd done the same, it wasn't to hurt and intimidate Ben but as a physical reinforcement of his words to the gryphons. "Tomorrow, the servants I hired will arrive. Twenty, to begin, all from different parts of Dralox County. Some you'll recognize from the previous owner's hires, but others are new."

All the gryphons, except for the one who'd waged war with burrs and lost, watched Master Gyzad as he explained the new power dynamics at the mining camp. However, the fourth gryphon stared at Ben with an expression that was neither unreadable nor unfamiliar. So, his words, "I'm not taking orders from a ground-scraper," did not surprise him.

Neither did the movement of the hand that rested on his shoulder. One minute Ben felt the weight of Master Gyzad's heavy appendage; the next, his partially shifted hands were wrapped around the mouthy gryphon's neck, reminding them all that dragons were deadly creatures in various states of transformation.

Ben used the unfortunate gryphon's predicament to slip into a pair of pants and boots needing resoling. They flapped as loudly as the mouth that had gotten the gryphon under the dragon's skin.

"If you had a mate or mother to give two rabbit foots about you, Mudspike, I'd rip off your neck, eat the worthless cat bits of you, and then hand deliver your"—Master Gyzad shook Mudspike, lifting him several inches off the ground—"scrawny head and neck to your next of kin. But killing you wouldn't be much fun without anyone to mourn your passing." Master Gyzad dropped Mudspike to the ground, and Ben had to give it to Mudspike. He hadn't gasped for air or pleaded for mercy.

Maybe this gryphon does enjoy pain. Either that or he has a death wish because Master Gyzad would murder him without a second thought or a morsel of regret.

Ben shoved the last piece of Rit's perfectly toasted pork into his mouth. It wasn't enough to sate him, but it tasted like home, a better kind of full.

"As I was saying," Master Gyzad said, his hands still a strange mix of extended human fingers covered in a layer of thick grayish scales with sharp curved claws, "Ben is in charge when I'm not here. You're carryovers from the previous owner, so I don't know or trust any of you. But gryphons are as good as any guard dog comes, so I'm keeping you on as long as you're useful to me and remember your place."

Master Gyzad just made life more complicated for me with the gryphons when he ain't around, implyin' he trusts a slave more than he does beings with rights and freedom. Master Gyzad is a liar who thinks I'm a fool. The only person he trusts is Mistress Essodel. He's deliberately turnin' them against me so they'll work harder to gain somethin' they cannot earn.

Like the obedient guard dogs Master Gyzad referred to them as, the gryphons sat, awaiting his orders, including Mudspike. But Ben knew fake compliance when he saw it, and so should Master Gyzad. Yet, the Dragonkin only smiled, finally shifting his hands into that of a normal human appendage.

"This might be a silver mine, but I'll pay you in sparkling gold."

Ben's gaze flew to the gryphons' long lion's tails, curious whether they would wag in response to Master Gyzad's surprisingly generous offer.

Master Gyzad laughed, perhaps because one of the gryphons wagged his tail after all.

An involuntary reaction or a ploy, Ben couldn't decide Mudspike's angle. People did not shift from defiant to obedient in minutes, and he did not think gryphons were any different. But they had settled down at the prospect of making a fortune and under the threat of a dragon devouring.

It wouldn't last, not that Ben thought he would find allies among the gryphon slave catchers. He would not. But, tomorrow, the camp would be filled with Birdfolk. Surely, despite him being Master Gyzad's overseer, he could convince them to trust him. Make friends.

He hoped.

If not, well, Ben did not want to think about that. No more than he liked to think about what Master Gyzad would demand of him as payment for permitting him to return to Rit's side for the birth of their sixth child.

Ben walked away, uninterested in listening to Master Gyzad discuss the gryphons' compensation for capturing slaves in search of the freedom owed to them.

He claimed the only cabin without a hole in the roof. He decided the mice already in residence were preferable to being alone. So, he found a corner not as dirty as the others and used his boots to clear away mice droppings before plopping onto the floor, his back against a wall.

Closing his eyes, he conjured images of his family, not imagining what they were doing in Mistress Essodel's aviary but of them living free on the Birdfolk continent of Sika. Though a small solace, the thought kept the tears at bay, even if not his bone-deep loneliness.

Berzogtown
Essodel Plantation
"Come on, let's play."

Seated on the steps of her cabin home, bare feet cold against the rough wood, Minty glanced from Mariah's outstretched hand to the closed door behind her.

"Momma is gonna be awhile."

"How long?"

Huffing as if she'd done something wrong by asking a simple question, Mariah marched to stand in front of Minty. "You took forever to get here. But we all waited. Me, Soph, and Robert played while Aveline, Poppa, and Linah helped Momma push you out."

Minty did not understand most of Mariah's words. Still, she grasped the more significant point because Rit had told her, "I'm growin' a baby inside of me. You will be a big sister, Minty. Will you like that?"

She'd nodded, feeling both happiness and sadness at the prospect of no longer being the baby of the family.

Pulling the oversized shirt over scraped knees still healing from the last time Minty tried to keep up with her older sister, Mariah, she poked her tongue at her.

Instead of getting mad, Mariah laughed and poked her tongue at Minty in return. "Momma would scold us if she saw. But she's in there, and we're out here." Mariah reached for Minty again, and this time, she permitted her sister to pull her to her feet. "I know it's kind of chilly, but we can warm up if we run around."

Minty was cold, and she liked it when her sisters were at home to play with her, which, since her father went away, occurred less frequently because they, too, were often sent to work elsewhere. So, Minty decided she wouldn't waste this alone time with Mariah.

She held on to her hand, smiling when Mariah grabbed hers tightly and skipped away from the cabin. As always, Mariah chatted, telling Minty things she was too young to fully understand.

"On my way home from the Ailron Plantation, I stopped to see Soph and Robert. But their temporary owner, Mistress Bargu, wouldn't let me see them. She said they were workin', and I needed to be on my way. I tried to tell her that Momma would have her baby soon and that it would be nice if Soph and Robert could be there. But she threatened to . . ." Mariah halted and grinned down at Minty with one of her many adult-looking expressions despite her being only twelve. "It don't matter. I just wanted to see my brother and sister. It's been weeks. And that mean dragon won't give me even a minute. Just a minute. That's not much. Is it?"

"Not much," Minty said, unsure how long a minute was but thinking it probably couldn't be long if Mariah was so upset. "Mean dragon," she repeated, trying to sound older than her not quite two years.

The effort may not have had the effect she desired. But Mariah's laughter brightened her wilted features, which was an infinitely better response.

Bending to Minty's level, Mariah kissed her cheek before pulling her in for a tight hug. "I hate it at the Ailron Plantation. But I can't tell Momma or Poppa because it'll make them worry more than they already do. Mistress Essodel is rich. I don't know why Minister Breembat hires us out. There's plenty to do around here and in the mine."

Again, Minty was too young to respond with anything other than an innocent child's "It's okay," followed by a kiss on Mariah's cheek.

"When we aren't around, you'll have to help Momma with the new baby."

"Play."

"You'll have to feed the baby, too, sometimes. And clean the baby's poop and pee."

"Poop and pee," Minty repeated, knowing she sometimes soiled herself. When that happened, Rit would remind her, "Big girls don't go to the bathroom on themselves."

"Promise me you'll be a good big sister."

That wasn't a hard promise for Minty to make because Linah, Mariah, and Soph had always been good to her. Some days, she would confuse Linah with Rit because her eldest sister was the next best thing to a mother that a girl could have.

"Promise." Because she wouldn't be the baby of the family after today, and her second-oldest sister had spoken a more profound truth into existence, a sense of responsibility and kinship that would drive her future adult self for eight long years, Minty maneuvered out of her sister's arms and around to her back, where Mariah still knelt. "Back ride?"

"I can do that. Hop on."

She did, and Mariah took off, whooping and hollering as she ran around the aviary. Darting between cabins, jumping over real rocks but imaginary lakes, Mariah ran and ran, a prelude to a future neither sister could imagine for themselves on the day of another Wren child's birth.

"The baby's finally here."

Recognizing Linah's voice, Minty jumped from Mariah's back and darted toward home. As her sister had, Minty ran and ran—slow, winded, but determined to reach her destination. But she stumbled and fell.

Tears threatened.

But before a single tear escaped, Linah and Mariah were there. Scooping her up, Linah checked her for injuries and, seeing none, wiped dirt from her legs, hands, and face. "Our clumsy Minty. Try not to fall on Momma. Now get inside and introduce yourself to our little brother."

Beside her, Mariah whooped. "Momma said she was havin' a boy. Named after Poppa?"

"Benjamin Wren Junior. You're as dirty as Minty. Both of you get in here."

"Yes, ma'am," Minty and Mariah said, then poked their tongues at each other. But Linah returned their silliness with a playful wink, a reminder that she was only sixteen despite her grown-up ways and fiancée status.

Knowing better than to run to her mother, Minty bolted for her father, who she knew would . . . Ben lifted her into his arms and showered her with kisses when Mariah had gifted her with only one.

"How's my sweet girl?"

"Good."

"You see the baby down there?"

"Hear him. He's loud."

"That's a good sign. Strong lungs. Strong body. Momma is tired, so we gotta let her feed little Ben and then nap."

Minty understood that meant for her not to disturb either of them, which was fine because she'd never heard a baby cry so much as her new brother. It wasn't a pleasant sound for Minty, she realized, but one she would have no choice but to get used to.

But those were future responsibilities and hardships. On this day, her family was mostly together; Minty was in her father's arms and held against a solid and true chest, like the male himself.

Linah and Mariah apparently felt the same because they turned Minty's moment with Ben into a father-daughter group hug with Minty squeezed between them.

The little girl giggled, unaware how, in two short years, Ben's move to Pelduth Neck would turn out to be the first of many separations forced on their loving but enslaved family.

PART II

"I GREW UP LIKE A NEGLECTED WEED, - IGNORANT OF LIBERTY, HAVING NO EXPERIENCE OF IT. THEN I WAS NOT HAPPY OR CONTENTED."

Chapter 5

Where's Mariah?

1825

The State of Miadar
Dralox County
Essodel Plantation

Minty sat on the cabin floor, her back against the wall and her arms full. "Chubby, chubby Rachel," she cooed, proud of herself for holding her little sister the way Rit had shown her. "Little piggy toes. Little piggy legs."

Minty laughed low, mindful of a sleeping Ben Jr. in the board box across the room.

"Piggy, piggy toes. You a piggy, piggy, Rachel." Minty squeezed her sister's baby-soft stomach and tiny feet. "Piggy, piggy," Minty continued to sing over and again. "I'm hungry," she whispered to the four-month-old.

Spying a basket with beets and turnips across the room, Minty frowned, knowing she didn't know how to prepare the food in the basket. Besides, she only liked vegetables when her mother cooked them.

"A little bite," she told Rachel, eyes the same shade of pecan brown as Minty's and Ben Jr.'s. Placing Rachel onto the floor, Minty crossed the room to the basket. Soon enough, she had a mouthful of a raw turnip.

"Want some."

Minty turned to see Ben Jr. awake and seated upright on the board box. One hand rubbed an eye while the other reached for the half-eaten turnip in Minty's hand. She wasn't done with the turnip and was still hungry, but she'd been taught to share. So, she bit off a piece for her younger brother, chewed it some, and then spat the smaller pieces into her hand.

"Here." She ensured all of it got into Ben Jr.'s mouth before repeating the process twice, and the turnip was gone.

"Hungry." Ben Jr. glanced at the vegetable basket.

Minty knew better than to permit either of them to have another turnip, and Rachel's cries reminded her she had more than one younger sibling to look after.

"Come on, Bennie." Taking hold of his hand the way Mariah always held hers, gentle yet firm, Minty helped Ben Jr. to his feet and to the other side of the cabin.

Rachel's whimpers did not change with their nearness, but Minty caught her sister looking from her to Ben Jr. She knew the signs when the baby wanted to play, so Minty grabbed her by her sleep dress, seized hold of her ankles, and swung her back and forth.

Rachel's bushy head of hair and greenish-blue feathers skimmed the floor, her weight pulling her down. But Minty forced her arms up as high as she could hold Rachel, swinging her around and around.

The baby's cries intensified, and Minty did not understand why. They were playing. She was doing what big sisters did: care for the young ones. Minty couldn't feed Rachel the way Rit did. She'd seen her mother feed Rachel and Ben Jr. from her chest. But Minty understood her little girl's body was different from women's bodies like Rit and Linah, who she'd also seen feed her own baby—Kessiah.

But play sometimes helped Minty forget her hunger, so she reasoned the same was true for Rachel and Ben Jr. Yet, Ben Jr. was too big for her to play with the way she could Rachel, so he must wait his turn.

Gripping Rachel's ankles with all her might, Minty swung the baby around and around, her arms dipping closer to the cabin floor with each rotation.

Rachel's bellows turned into whimpers and finally into silence. Still, Minty swung the baby around, her forehead skimming the floor. This was much better, Minty thought when her sister stopped crying and moving.

"Piggy, piggy toes. Piggy, piggy legs. Piggy, pigg—"

Thud.

"Wah, wah, wah!"

"S-sorry. S-sorry." Minty dropped to her hands and knees beside a wailing Rachel. "So s-sorry." She didn't know what to do, so she glanced over her shoulder at her brother. Their gazes met, his as wide as his open mouth, and in the time it took Ben Jr. to lift an accusatory finger at Minty, she'd burst into tears.

Big girls weren't supposed to cry, but she couldn't help herself. She hadn't meant to hurt Rachel, but she had. Minty only wanted to be a good big sister like Linah, Soph, and Mariah, but she was clumsy and afraid and did not know how to stop Rachel from screaming.

Cradling the baby to her, Minty held Rachel close. She kept her eyes closed, not wanting to see the horrified look of judgment on Ben Jr.'s face. Within minutes, though, she felt a small, soft hand on her shoulder, then the weight of a head and the sound of sniffles.

Minty still did not know how to make her sister feel better, but having her brother beside her, touching her, made her feel warm and less alone in the still cabin.

"Noooo!"

"Momma?" Ben Jr. jumped to his feet.

"No! No! No! He wouldn't do that. He wouldn't."

Minty placed the crying Rachel on the closest board box as carefully as possible.

"No, Minister Breembat wouldn't do that. He wouldn't do somethin' so awful."

"Rit, you gotta calm down."

"Momma," Ben Jr. repeated, and Minty agreed because she too recognized her mother's voice, but not the man with Rit. It wasn't her poppa's voice, or even Linah's husband, Harkless.

"Calm down? Calm down? I can't. I need to know. I gotta go find my baby, M-Mariah. Oh, God, M-Mariah. Please let the rumor be false. Please, God, please."

"Rit."

"I gotta go. I gotta know the truth."

"Fine, then I'll go with you. I can't let you go there by yourself. Not at night and not in your state."

The voices grew lower and fainter until Minty stopped hearing anyone in front of the cabin.

"Where, Momma?" Ben Jr. asked Minty.

Minty had no idea where Rit had gone. All she knew was that her mother's voice had halted her movement toward the door, her desperate, cracked voice worse than Rachel's shrill cries after hitting her head on the floor.

"I'm scared, Bennie." Minty did not possess the words to explain the emotions she'd heard in Rit's voice, no more than she was old enough to comprehend the context of the conversation she'd overheard. Still, Rit's raw emotions hit Minty in a way her parents never had, even when she'd done something deserving of a scold.

Wiping away tears that had fallen the moment she'd heard the way Rit had spoken Mariah's name, broken sobs between the syllables, Minty took Ben Jr.'s hand and returned to the board box.

And there they stayed, with Ben Jr. curled against Minty's side. She held Rachel, her thumb shoved into the baby's mouth. She'd seen Soph suck her thumb, and while Minty did not see the appeal, Rachel seemed to like it well enough. So, she permitted the baby to gnaw on her thumb and drool everywhere, but Rachel was finally quiet.

Tired and hungry, Minty lay down with Rachel in front of her so she could continue to suck her thumb. Ben Jr. scooted closer, and she was grateful for such a sweet baby brother. He rarely left her side except to play with their father when he visited. She wished Ben were there because Rit hadn't returned.

Knock. Knock. "Minty, it's me, Aveline. Abbott, too. We're comin' in."

Minty liked Aveline and Abbott, but they weren't her momma or poppa, so she didn't rush to them when they entered the cabin. She did, however, sit up, careful not to pull her finger from Rachel's mouth.

"Oh, you poor things. Abbott, gather them up and bring them to my cabin. I don't know how long Rit will be. We can't leave them here alone. This poor baby been tendin' to her brother and sister all day and part of a night."

Instead of doing as his mother advised, Abbott approached Minty and lowered himself to his knees. "I'll stay with them and wait for Efron to bring Rit home. You saw her. Heard her." A big, gentle hand ruffled first Minty's feathered head and then Ben Jr.'s. "How do you think Rit will react if she comes home to find these three gone, too?"

As if deflated by Abbott's words, Aveline sank in on herself. "Even if we had somethin' to write with or on, we don't know our letters to leave Rit a note. You're right; she would have a fit worse than the news of Mariah's—"

"Mom, don't."

Pulling out a chair from the small table beside where Minty had taken the turnip from the basket, the older woman sat. Her smile reached her eyes, but Minty sensed she kept a secret behind them.

"Again, you're right. It's not my place to say. But it's a terrible thing, Abbott. A terrible thing."

Minty wanted to ask Aveline and Abbott a question, but she didn't know what to pose other than when her mother would return home. But neither seemed to know, so she lay back on the board box, a wave of relief weakening her.

For the first time since Rit left to entertain Mistress Essodel, leaving Minty to care for Ben Jr. and Rachel, she did not have to make adult decisions. The lifting of the overwhelming weight of responsibility would not last, though. It never did, not even when it was Rit or one of her older sisters who did the relieving.

Minty disliked crying because it made her head hurt and her eyes swell, but she found herself doing it all the same. She didn't know why the emotion of sadness had come over her or why the thought of her older sisters never returning to their cabin home had forced its way into her head, causing a different kind of pain.

"It's okay."

Minty did not protest when Abbott lifted her from the board box, but she did shake her head when he opened the cabin door.

"They'll be fine with Mom. Don't worry." Abbott closed the door behind them, shutting off her view of Ben Jr., who'd claimed her place beside Rachel, his thumb going to her seeking mouth. "You're a good big sister, Minty. Kind, patient, and smart. Stay a good girl, especially for your momma."

Some days, Minty wished she were older than three. If she were, she would understand adults and their words better.

"Let's go for a walk. While we're out, Mom will clean Rachel and cook up whatever Rit has in the house."

Giving herself permission to relax, Minty slumped against Abbott's broad chest, her head on his sturdy shoulder and her tear-itchy eyes closed.

Minty did not recall falling asleep, no more than she could remember the last time every member of the Wren family had gathered in her cabin home. Not even Linah's marriage to Harkless or the birth of their daughter, Kessiah, were noteworthy family events permissible for a family gathering. But there they all were—Minty's parents and siblings. Harkless and Kessiah, too, as were Aveline, Efron, and Abbott.

Rising from the board box Minty shared with Ben Jr. and Mariah whenever Mariah, Soph, and Robert were home simultaneously, she did not dare make a sound. Not that she thought anyone would hear or notice her presence over both loud, angry curses and deep, ragged sobs.

"I will slit his throat where he sleeps." Rit.

"Mariah. God, our Mariah. H-how could a l-lovin' God let this h-happen?" Ben.

"I saw her just two weeks ago. This must be a dream. A dream. No, it's a nightmare." Linah.

"Poppa, we gonna go get Mariah, right? We can go get her and bring her home." Robert.

"I knew when I saw Momma beggin' Mistress Bargu to let her bring us home that it wasn't good. But this." Soph shifted next to Ben, wrapped her arms around him from the side, and buried her face against his arm. "No beatin' has hurt more than this. It hurts to think of never seein' my sister again, but not as much as it does knowin' she's alone. No family. No flock. No one to love and care for her."

"That selfish, inhumane dragon. I'll see Minister Breembat dead. I swear it, Ben. If it's the last thing I do in this life, I'll take his."

Despite her threat, or perhaps because the probability of a bird shifter killing a dragon shifter was so slight, Rit burst into tears and crumpled to the floor, clutching at her chest where Minty had seen her feed Ben Jr. and Rachel.

However, she did not comprehend everyone's extreme behavior or why they were there. Well, everyone except for . . . "Where's Mariah?"

As if the sheet Rit used for privacy had been flung aside, revealing the small space where she and Rachel slept, and Ben, when he was home, the entire room of people turned to face Minty. She realized not only had Ben and Rit cried but also everyone else because she was struck by the range of red and rage in their eyes.

The open door exposed the cabin to the sharp coolness of late autumn and the bright reassurance of the sun, letting Minty know she'd slept much longer than she'd thought.

Part of Minty saw Linah and Harkless take the babies and Ben Jr. into Rit's room, patting the babies' backs and rocking them into quiet calmness in a way Minty had not mastered. From the corner of her eye, she saw Aveline and her sons exit the cabin, pulling the door closed and plunging the cabin into morbid darkness. At the same time, Robert and Soph worked together to open the shuttered windows, bringing renewed life to the cabin but not to Rit's and Ben's faces.

Her parents knelt before her, faces contorted into something scarier than any nightmare she'd had because this was real, and she'd never seen her parents at a loss for words.

They opened their mouths as if gobbling up air to breathe. Their hands shook like a leaf forced from its tree home by the wind. Eyes filled and overflowed with tears—a relentless, body-racking, heart-piercing act that had Rit tugging Minty to her and crushing her to the point she feared she wouldn't be able to take her next breath.

Minty did not know why she cried other than it hurt something deep within her to see her parents and siblings in so much pain. So, when Ben told her, "Mariah won't be comin' home again," she cried harder.

Minty's endless stream of tears did not come from a knowledgeable place of comprehension but from the deep, empty well of a child's ignorance and fear. Much of her young life was spent caring for her younger siblings while waiting for her older siblings to return home. Being there for a short time and then gone for longer was a vicious cycle Minty neither liked nor could change.

So, she did not see how this occurrence with Mariah differed from the other times Minister Breembat hired her out to neighboring slave owners. Yet, from her family's reactions, Minty knew it must be.

"I'm sorry," Ben said with a voice that sounded like wood that crackled and popped in the fireplace they used for heating and cooking. "I'm so sorry I wasn't here when you all needed me. I'm sorry. I'm so damn sorry."

Ben apologized repeatedly, his long, strong arms around Minty and Rit. Above her, Robert and Soph cried, too, and it didn't take much to detect Linah's stuttering sobs.

Her family cried for Mariah, while Minty cried for her family's pain. It would be years before Minty heard anyone in her family speak Mariah's name again, much less discuss what Minister Breembat had done to her and a fifteen-year-old enslaved boy on the same day. But it would take considerably less time for the three-year-old Minty to forget she had an older sister, Mariah.

Mariah Ritty, she would recall much later in life, not because she harbored personal memories of the short time she'd had with Mariah, but because her parents had, after many years of deliberate repressiveness, forgiven themselves for choosing survival over death and revenge.

Mariah Ritty Wren.

Born in 1811.

Sold in 1825.

Fate unknown.

Chapter 6
We Own Them

Pyzai

Breembat did not do this enough, and he despised little more than being denied his delicious pleasures. So, he flapped his bluish-white wings, from which the most brutal bone and icicles framed the appendages. Softer icicles formed a beard-like structure under his chin. At the same time, a sturdier row of them began at the top of his head and continued down the center of his back, where they stopped at the tip of a tail that fanned out like a smaller wing.

"Why are you flying so fast?"

Breembat ignored his older brother. Gyzad was also larger because he'd taken more after their mother than Breembat, who favored his ice dragon father. Not that he'd seen the male more than a handful of times in his two hundred years of life. If the rumors surrounding the fate of Gyzad's father were true, at least Breembat's egg donor had survived his union with Essodel, Eater of Bravehearts, Champion of the Deathlord, The Dark Dygen, Eternal Fire.

Essodel had adopted the ancient practice of claiming the Dragonkin title of each dragon she slayed, be it rival or lover. In Gyzad's father's case, Choldred, The Dark Dygen, Essodel ripped his chest open and devoured his still-beating heart when he challenged her for the hoard they'd built together.

"We don't have a Dragonkin title," Breembat replied instead of answering his brother's question.

Gyzad, a majestic steel-gray dragon capable of breathing potent streams of fire like their mother, closed the distance between them. Gyzad did not fly beside him but above, both as an act of protection against any dragon foolish enough to challenge them and as a reminder of their difference in status.

"Once my silver mine yields enough profit, Mother will grant me my title. I already have a respectable collection of fine jewels, paintings, and rugs but not enough to tilt the scales in my favor with Mother."

"This is the New World, Gyzad, not the old one. Gold and fine jewels do not carry the same weight and favor here. The currency is cash, which we are both wholly lacking."

"You're wrong, little brother." To emphasize a double truth Gyzad never let Breembat forget, a heavy wing swept down toward him, shoving him off course.

"Ash licker."

His brother's mocking laughter rippled in his mind as he righted himself and continued on his way. Breembat didn't have a destination in mind. These flights were never about the where but served as a reminder of the what. He was a dragon. His kind ate what they wanted, had sex with whomever they liked, and killed anyone standing between them and adding to their hoard. Well, dragons of old, like Essodel, used to be that way. However, this new breed of dragon left much to be desired as far as Breembat was concerned.

"Gold, silver, and diamonds still matter to the Dragonkin who practice the old ways. They can be converted into the currency of the day."

"Not easily. And not every creature who now claims this continent as their home is Dragonkin. They see no purpose in hoarding treasures the way we do. They don't view our collection as a sign of power and strength, but of wasted effort because we live in poverty despite our great wealth."

The steel-gray wing came again, hard and fast. The attack knocked the breath from Breembat and sent him spiraling downward.

"What in the hell, Gyzad?" Breembat didn't dare return to his position, flying below his brother's scaly body because Gyzad had turned a simple disagreement between brothers into a fight they both knew Breembat had no chance of winning. He did not understand the mood shift. *"I've been sober for weeks and have stayed away from Mother's pretty Sankofa birds. I swear I haven't touched any of them."*

With speed Breembat could never match, Gyzad flew at him, smacking his left wing and sending him into a nosedive.

"You sold Mariah."

Breembat might have been smaller and weaker than Gyzad, but he was still a force of ice nature, so he snapped his wings out and halted his descent. Hovering miles above the slave-free state of Pyzai, he glared at his brother, contemplating an ice counterattack. But he decided on a different tact when he saw Gyzad's golden-brown eyes shift to volcanic eruption red.

"*I didn't. I sold a male teen ground-scraper, James, I think, and a female ground-scraper named Rhodes or Rhody.*"

"*Not Rhodes or Rhody, you idiot. Mariah Ritty. Mariah Ritty Wren.*"

"*Okay. So, I got the name wrong. What do you care about a ground-scraper? We've sold off Mother's servants before. We'll tell her they ran away, and she believes us and then gives us gold coins to replace the servant. We buy a young, cheap one with high resale value and pocket the difference. That's what we do. It's how you really afforded that silver mine you're always going on about.*"

To Breembat's discomfort, Gyzad flew closer, but he refused to play the coward. So, he forced himself to stay put and not to look away from a predator who, if Gyzad had half the courage as his father, would've challenged the elderly Essodel to her mountain hoard. And if Breembat was less of a lover and dragon of the faith, he would fight alongside his brother to bring old Essodel down.

But they knew each other's limitations and weaknesses, so they hovered in the sky. Dragons still ruled, but they were no more prosperous for their schemes to separate Essodel from her gold because power no longer resided in the sky but on the ground.

"*You sold one of Ben's daughters. Before you ask who Ben is, he's my overseer at the silver mine camp. Every so often, I knock him around a bit. Break a bone or two. But nothing serious. Nothing his Birdfolk body can't heal from sooner rather than later. I remind him I'm always in charge, even when not beside him. But you, the forgettable, drunk fool that you are, sold one of his kin.*"

"We own them. They have no rights to their family, not even their hatchlings. If he wanted his offspring to be born free, he should've had them with a free ground-scraper, not one in service to a Dragonkin."

Gyzad's wing flinched, and Breembat thought he would smack him again. Thankfully, the movement only displaced a bold bird who'd decided a dragon's wing would make for an ideal perch.

"None of that matters. What does is that Ben and I have an unspoken agreement. He does my bidding without complaint or resistance, and I leave his family in peace. The servants I've hired at the mine not only like Ben, but they respect him to the point of following his orders and working hard. None of them have tried to flee, which is nearly unheard of in an area with so many free ground-scrapers running around as examples of what life could be like not under a Dragonkin master's yoke."

Turning in the opposite direction Breembat had been flying in, Gyzad flew away from him, which did not signal the conclusion of their conversation but a nonverbal command for him to follow.

Breembat did, as obedient as that overseer Gyzad seemed to favor more than a Dragonkin should a piece of property.

"As soon as he learned of Mariah's sale, he returned to Essodel's aviary and Rit. He's been gone for two weeks. Do you know what that means?"

Breembat slowed his pace, putting him beyond the easy wing reach of his brother. He also knew a rhetorical question when he heard one, so he refrained from replying.

"It means he defied my orders to stay at the mine camp except on Sundays when I've permitted him to return to Berzogtown for your service and a visit with his family. No matter his fatigue or the weather, Ben never misses a Sunday. Loyal. Dedicated. But he defied me. The hired-on servants know it, and so do the gryphons."

Breembat did not see the issue Gyzad had with the sale of the girl. He'd made good money. If she'd been a little older or her Sankofa feathers as lovely as her mother's, Breembat could've sold her for more.

"He'll return; when he does, I'll have no choice but to make an example of him. I can't have the ground-scrapers and gryphons thinking my word means nothing, that they can, when the mood strikes them, defy my orders and do as they please." Gyzad's long neck swung to Breembat, a gurgled snarl in his throat. "You might enjoy the game of physical dominance, but I do not. It's uncivilized and beneath me. But, because you chose unwisely with Mariah Ritty's sale, I must punish Ben despite knowing he'll return soon enough and that he only left the camp to comfort his wife and see after the well-being of his offspring."

"I sold her for more than a month's worth of your silver mining. So, don't beat that Ben overseer of yours too badly, brother, because he and his wife make beautiful birds. A breeder of his caliber is more profitable than any silver ore."

"And that's the difference between us. This master-servant system we've established here will not last forever. It cannot last forever. When it eventually dies, as all things do, what will you have? Will you live like the land walkers? No hoard to buttress your long dragon life. A mother who will scorn your short-sightedness, tossing you a few pitying gold coins to get you out of her mountain and off her land. Emancipated ground-scrapers who'd rather set fire to your home when you're in a drunken stupor than permit you to sell them back into servitude. No, little brother, the time of us living off the labor of ground-scrapers is slowly but firmly ending, even if you and most of them do not yet grasp the inevitable."

Breembat wasn't a fool or an idiot, as Gyzad had taken to calling him when he engaged in an act he disagreed with. With Gyzad's ire piqued, however, Breembat knew to retreat. As Gyzad needlessly reminded him, dragons were long-lived. So, while he could not afford much, he could be patient because Breembat had plans for the priceless Wren family, just as he did for Gyzad and Essodel. Emancipation of the Birdfolk might come, but it would be Breembat on the winning side of history.

Chapter 7

I'm Gettin' a New Master?

1828

Berzogtown

Essodel Plantation

"Dance for me," Rit told Minty.

Slapping a hand over her mouth, Minty giggled.

"What's so funny?"

Minty laughed again, not from how her mother had mocked mean Mistress Essodel's booming dragon voice but at her three-year-old sister

Rachel's failed attempt to catch a baby bunny. A family of rabbits had wandered into the aviary three months ago, and despite never having enough food rations to go around, the rabbits hadn't made it into anybody's stew.

"You and Rachel are funny, Momma." Minty twirled, enamored by how her new dress felt against her skin and how wonderful it flared out when she moved with far less grace than her mother. It didn't matter, though, so Minty twirled and twirled, catching Rit's smiling face as she watched Minty from the steps of their cabin home.

"As soon as you visit Mistress Essodel, I want you out of that dress. I can't have you gettin' it dirty before . . ."

Minty ceased twirling, curious as to why Rit had stopped speaking mid-sentence.

She looks sad again. I don't like that look on Momma's face. Since Minister Breembat bought me my new dress, Momma has looked at me differently. She won't tell me what's wrong. Only that I must dance for Mistress Essodel. Show her that I can dance and what I look like as a bird. I'd rather not go back to that scary mountain or see that old dragon, but Momma said I have no choice.

"I won't get my pretty new dress dirty, Momma. I promise."

Rit snorted a laugh, and Minty knew her mother recalled similar promises she'd made. Each one ended with Minty dusty and dirty, and with a new cut or scrape from jumping out of a tree. Minty was convinced God wouldn't have given Birdfolk wings if he hadn't meant for them to fly. So, every chance she got, Minty would climb one of the black walnut trees on the property, going up as far as she dared, then she would shift into her bird form and leap from the tree, convinced, one of these days, her wings would carry her away. To date, every experiment had failed, but Minty hadn't given up faith that, one day, her wings would take her far away from there. Not that she had any desire to leave her siblings, parents, and friends. But the six-year-old reasoned, if she did manage to get her wings to work and fly away to freedom, she'd use the same wings to return for those closest to her heart.

"You stayin' clean. From your mouth to God's ears." Rit made a twirling gesture with her index finger, a signal Minty understood for her to dance.

Lifting her arms high, the way she still sometimes did when her father visited, begging him to pick her up the way he would Rachel and Ben Jr., Ben would twirl her about the cabin, not so different from how she twirled her thin frame, careful to hold her head high and back straight.

"Good. Don't forget to dip at the end of that move. Yes. Good. Do it again."

"Good, good," Rachel said, sounding like a mini version of Rit. "I wanna dance, Momma." Apparently, Rachel had given up her pointless pursuit of the bunny because she sidled up beside Minty, her hand outstretched.

Excited to have a dance partner, Minty accepted the offer. In fact, she grasped both of Rachel's hands and began a jaunty dance that had the sisters going around and around. With each fast heel-toe move, they kicked up dirt, and Minty didn't care that Minister Breembat hadn't also brought her a pair of shoes to go with her new dress.

She'd never had a pair of shoes, and while she thought they would be nice to keep her feet warm and protect her from rocks, she imagined they would constrict the movement of her toes. Minty liked to wiggle her toes. But what she enjoyed most was the affirming feel of the ground under her bare feet when she played and danced.

Minty didn't think herself a good dancer, especially compared to her older siblings. But she could keep a tune well enough, and Rit often praised her ability to remember the dance moves she'd taught her.

What Minty most enjoyed was how much better she could manipulate her body in bird form. During those times, when Minty would dance like a "wild child," as Soph had once called her, she felt as if she could do anything, no biting chain or vile dragon capable of keeping her where she did not wish to be.

Rit clapped, adding a musical cadence to the one Minty had in her mind. She clapped and Minty danced, careful not to drag her sister along in her enthusiasm while still flinging her whole self into the moment.

Minty knew better than to dance this way when she went before Mistress Essodel, revealing her heart and soul with each foot tap, tongue click, and body heave. But she danced there, elevated by Rachel's trust to safely lead her and buoyed by Rit's acceptance of everything that made her Minty.

And when she yanked off her new dress and handed it to Rit, her mother kissed her forehead and simply said, "Show me your bold abandonment."

Her mother's soft, confident words were all Minty required to see herself not as a slave in an invisible cage but as a bird whose cage door had been left open. She bolted from its confines, her body a flutter of multicolored feathers.

"Go, Rit. Breembat doesn't like it when the servants are late for Sunday service."

Minty latched on to her mother's side, looking up at her with big brown eyes that begged Rit not to leave her alone with the dragon.

Extracting herself from Minty's grip, Rit knelt to her level. "Mistress Essodel will call for me when she is ready for you to leave. Or, if you want to show me how much of a big girl you've grown into since the last time we visited, you can meet me and the others at the exit. Even if the service ends before you're finished, we'll wait for you to join us."

They always had a family dinner before Ben returned to Pelduth Neck and her siblings to whatever Dragonkin Minister Breembat had hired them out to serve. But their weekly family dinner came after they spent the day together, laughing and catching up. Minty did not wish to miss even a minute because it was rare for them to all be together.

This Sunday, they'd all returned to Mistress Essodel's aviary, but she couldn't join them.

Minty fell into one of Rit's supportive hugs. It was the kind of embrace that did not allow for lingering but was a physical reminder she was never alone, even when Minty was without family and friends by her side.

"Mistress Essodel wants to see how well you dance and how pretty you are in your bird form. When she's satisfied, when you have done yourself proud, join the family."

Minty wished she hadn't detected the hitch in her mother's voice. It always preceded something terrible, even when, at the time, Minty did not know what life's event had troubled Rit's mind.

"Go, Rit. I won't tell you again."

To her regret, Mistress Essodel's growled warning had Rit pulling away from Minty and leaving her alone with the dragon.

"Turn and face me, child."

Minty knew better than to disobey, no matter how painfully her stomach twisted in knots each time she came face-to-face with her owner. Hands fisted in her new dress, Minty shifted toward the dragon.

Even with her head resting on a small pile of gold and jewels, Minty had to look way up to meet Mistress Essodel's piercing golden eyes. They blinked slowly, and Minty wondered how such a massive creature preferred dwelling in a musty old mountain to soaring through the vast open blue sky.

"*Even for a fledgling, you are a tiny thing.*"

To Minty's surprise, the voice in her head softened, sounding less brutal and demanding but no less old for its gentleness. The change, however, did not put her at ease because this visit was only beginning.

"*Breembat wants to hire you out. He tells me you are prettier than Rit.*"

Minty did not think it possible for a dragon's gaze to heat her skin, but Mistress Essodel looked at her with such scary intensity she felt she would burst into flames.

"*Breembat boasts about much and lies about even more. Considering Rit presented you to me in that dress instead of your normal servant rags, Breembat has already spoken to her about your new residence and temporary master.*"

My what? I'm gettin' a new master? What does residence mean? Oh, I get it. Linah, Soph, and Robert no longer live with us in the cabin. They live and work someplace else. Momma says I can't visit them. I must wait for them to return home. I don't like that. But I've never been anywhere but Mistress Essodel's aviary.

"I'm goin' on a trip? An adventure?"

"*You are young, indeed, but hopefully not stupid. Do take that dress off, little Araminta Wren, and let me determine if Breembat's eyes are as keen as his taste in liquor.*"

Removing her dress far slower than when it was only Rachel and Rit as her loving audience, Minty took her time folding the blue dress with yellow dandelions. Usually, she wouldn't place something as special as her new dress on the ground, but considering this was a dragon's lair, the mountain floor was surprisingly dirt-free.

The low hum of a growl behind Minty let her know she'd taken the dragon's patience as far as she would allow. So, Minty made haste. Closing her eyes to block out the sight of Mistress Essodel's penetrating gaze and warning growl, Minty envisioned her Sankofa form. With how much she delighted in strutting about as a bird, Minty had taken to the transformation with an ease that had pleased her parents.

The tingling sensation that heralded her shift from human girl to young bird washed over Minty like a warm breeze tickling her sweaty skin after a hearty climb up her favorite black walnut tree. The change never ceased to amaze Minty. Where smooth skin once shaped the landscape of her body, now soft feathers did. The toes she loved to wiggle were gone, replaced with talons that, if a tree were near, she would ask permission to climb it because Minty was an even better climber in bird form.

Mistress Essodel's large head rose from its resting spot, halting Minty's musings and dulling the joy of her transformation.

Her stomach clenched like a hard fist, and she stumbled backward.

"Breembat did not lie. In my thousand years, I've never seen my hoard so extravagantly represented in a single Birdfolk. The green feathers are that of a brilliant jade, a pure green hue. No blue or yellow secondary hues to bring down the price. Perfect."

Mistress Essodel's head lifted even more, and Minty thought the distance between them would've made her more difficult to see. But it appeared to have the opposite effect.

"Yet, your purple feathers are as dark and precious as my collection's finest, highest quality amethysts. Oh, and your blue feathers aren't the sapphire I'm used to seeing but that of a rare blue diamond. When I look upon them, it is as if the sea and sky have melded, your wings their immaculate conception."

Minty only half understood Mistress Essodel's words, but she knew a compliment when she heard one. She did not know whether she should be pleased by the unexpected attention. Minty had seen what Mistress Essodel's notice had meant for Rit.

Is she planning on plucking my feathers? Momma pretends it don't matter, but I'm old enough to know better. These are my feathers. Mistress Essodel has no right to them.

"But the pink feathers are my absolute favorite."

Minty had heard many sounds come from dragons. All of them sounded like a variation of a growl to her, but she'd never heard a dragon ... purr? Yet, the old dragon emitted the strangest, oddly sweet sound when she spoke of Minty's pink feathers.

"So beautiful. From rhodolite's dark hues to pink coral's wispy shades. But not on the same feather because each one stands in its own light. Magnificent in their combined individuality. You are stunning to behold."

Stunning is a good word, I think. But her attention don't feel good. She hasn't even asked me to dance. Should I bring it up? If I do, maybe this visit will end sooner. I could return to Momma and Poppa.

"Should I dance, Mistress Essodel?"

"Ah, you wish to entertain me more than you already have, do you?"

That couldn't be further from the truth, but Minty nodded, not above a silent lie.

"Well, then. Climb up here."

Minty couldn't help herself; she grinned on the inside. Mistress Essodel's hoard might not be a black walnut tree, but she would never reject an opportunity to climb, not even glistening piles of unimaginable gemstones.

Tentatively, Minty moved toward what seemed like endless hills and valleys, suddenly afraid to touch a single piece of the dragon's coveted hoard. But when her taloned feet grazed against something sparkly and transparent like water from a stream, she decided this would be a once-in-a-lifetime experience.

"Perhaps I've given you too much credit, after all. Do you not know how to climb?"

"I know how, Mistress Essodel."

"Good, then make haste. You are such a small, frail-looking thing. My great hoard will hold your meager weight easily, so come, fledging, come."

From the base of Mistress Essodel's significant hoard, she eyed as much of it as possible, determining the best route up to the scaly beast. However, it didn't take her long, and then she was off. She plodded up the nearest pile, stepping on jewels and gold nuggets that would never be hers but that held her weight.

Considering she could not see all of Mistress Essodel's body, Minty concluded she walked on not only priceless gems but also tough dragon skin. She had never been so far from the ground, not even during her most courageous climbs. Rit's warning, "You'll break your stubborn neck if you climb too high," had been enough to squash Minty's more reckless impulses.

"Frightened?"

"No, ma'am."

"Such a pretty little liar. You have climbed only halfway."

Was that amusement Minty detected in the dragon's voice? She shrugged off the thought that this mighty dragon would find anything a little enslaved girl did as humorous.

"If you are tired, I suggest taking a break and beginning again."

"I'm not tired."

"If you are going to lie, I suggest perfecting the craft before trying it again."

Not a scold, Minty could tell, but the same amusement she'd sensed before. Even so, she had not lied. Minty had strength and wind to spare. It was just that . . . "I don't want to scratch your sparkly jewels."

"Ah, because the rest of the climb is steep, you must dig deeper to reach my head. Not stupid, then. It matters not. Your tiny talons will scarcely leave a print. I want to see how much farther you can climb before you beg me to let you down."

She doesn't think I can do it. I don't like that. But I am pretty high up already. Momma would tell me to turn back. She would say there is no shame in fear, only in not tryin' your best. But I haven't given it my all yet. I might not reach her head, but I can climb more.

"Well, look at you go. Such a stubborn little ground-scraper. I did not expect to be so entertained today. Perhaps I'll grant you a boon."

"What's a boon?" Minty slipped on a . . . she watched the gold teapot she'd uprooted from its spot tumble down the hill. But it never made it to the bottom.

"Do not touch that again."

No humor or amusement in her voice but the familiar growl of a mean, old dragon. *"Step carefully and avoid the gold lamps."* Mistress Essodel's tail was still wrapped around the golden lamp she'd caught, although Minty did not see how it was a lamp, not a teapot. It had a handle and spout. Surely, that meant it could be used to hold hot water for tea. *"Do you understand? No touching. Ever."*

"Yes, ma'am. No touchin'."

"Good. Are you tired now?"

"Yes, ma'am." A lie. But Mistress Essodel's hardened voice reminded Minty of something she should never forget. *Dragons aren't kind. I've never met a Dragonkin who didn't hurt or use Birdfolk. She's the one who lied. Trickin' me with her gentle voice.*

"Then take ahold of this."

Minty scurried onto the offered tail, careful to stay clear of the golden lamp and sharp spikes.

"I barely felt you. Tiny, indeed. Now that you have returned to the flat ground, I wish to be entertained with dance."

Minty pretended not to notice where Mistress Essodel placed the golden lamp—at the top of her highest pile. She couldn't imagine anyone daring enough to steal from Mistress Essodel, but the dragon obviously could.

"And a song."

"At the same time?"

"Can you not manage both simultaneously?"

Yet again, the dragon's voice had shifted from severe to almost playful. The longer Minty stayed in Mistress Essodel's presence, the more confused she became. Just when she thought she knew what to expect from the dragon, she would do something different, forcing Minty to reevaluate.

She didn't like it. Not one bit.

"I only know a few songs." All of them she'd learned from Ben, but none Minty thought Rit would approve of her singing for a dragon, much less their dragon master. Still, she had to sing something, so Minty selected the first song that came to her mind.

She sang a song about a balm in Gilead. Minty emphasized certain words like "discouraged" and "Holy Spirit" because Ben always did when he sang the song. She didn't know the song's meaning or even most of the words she sang, but her voice was "pleasant," she'd been told, so she sang the same way she danced—with everything inside her.

When Minty finished, she opened eyes she hadn't realized she'd closed. Her chest expanded, and her breaths came faster than they should've. But she felt invigorated, having, for the minutes that she sang and danced, forgotten she'd done so inside a dangerous predator's mountain home and not in her safe cabin with her family.

The beast that was Mistress Essodel did not watch Minty as she'd done before, with great stomach-churning intent.

Her eyes are closed. Is she asleep? Her head is still high, but she isn't movin'. Was my performance bad? Will she punish Momma for trainin' me poorly?

Without conscious thought, Minty stepped backward, stopping only when she felt the soft cotton of her new dress. Still, the dragon had not stirred, so Minty shifted into her human form and dressed.

Unsure whether she should stay or leave, Minty considered the ramifications if she left without permission. However, if she stayed and the dragon slept long, she would miss dinner with her family. Sunday was their only free day, and her siblings weren't granted permission to return home every Sunday.

I don't know what to do. I don't want to get a whippin' for disobeying Mistress Essodel. She told Momma she would call her when she was done with me. I don't think one song and dance is enough for me to leave. Should I do more? But what if she wakes up, angry that I disturbed her rest?

Minty's mind whirled on and on, unable to settle on the safest course of action.

"*You are a tiny speck of nothingness.*" Mistress Essodel's large lids parted halfway, revealing a sliver of gold. "*Your wings are mere decoration. A distraction from their uselessness. A mockery of God's brilliance. Yet, your voice echoes through time, a call for healing but tinged with judgment to the one who failed to offer the much-needed treatment.*"

Minty fisted the sides of her dress, wanting to run away but fearing the dragon might give chase and, in annoyance, gobble her up. So, she planted her feet on the ground, feeling every bit the stupid girl Mistress Essodel had questioned if she was earlier.

"Your singing will be a beginning but also an end. A balm to some but a prickly burr to others. I see that I have frightened you. Normally, I would enjoy the scent of your fear. But today I only feel tired. Tired and so very old. So, go. But know no one is to touch even one of your feathers. They all belong to me. Now go. Run back to Rit."

Minty turned and ran. She didn't stop running until she reached the mountain's mouth. As Rit had promised, her family was there, offering her smiles and hugs. A week later, however, only Rit, Rachel, and Ben Jr. were at the cabin when Minister Breembat came for her.

Staring down at her from atop a dark bay horse whose coat glistened like a lake during a sweltering day, Minister Breembat grinned from Minty to Rit, looking more like a hungry wolf than a civilized dragon.

Minty winced at how hard Rit gripped her hand. Sensing she held on too tightly, Rit eased up but maintained a firm hold.

"Mistress Essodel told Minty she ain't to be defeathered by anyone but her."

"I make excellent contracts, Rit. Jolara Calis and his wife, Theria, will take good care of Minty. After all, she is a rare beauty, and Mother agrees. Besides, your precious little Minty will only be two farms over. Not far at all."

When Rit didn't reply, she glanced up at her mother, only to find her looking down at her with eyes so dark brown she didn't know whether Rit would rage or cry.

"It's okay, Momma. I'll have a grand adventure."

"A grand adventure, huh?" Rit knelt. Her eyes were no less stormy for the beautiful smile she gifted Minty. "Be a good girl."

"Yes, ma'am."

"Always mind your manners."

"Yes, ma'am."

"We'll be here when you're allowed to come home."

"Rit." Minister Breembat's thinly veiled impatience was obvious even to little Minty.

"You're takin' another one of my babies away from me. You could at least give me time to say goodbye."

"You've had six years to prepare. Unless you want me to return next week for those two"—Minister Breembat nodded to where Ben Jr. and Rachel waited behind them on the cabin's steps—"you'll give Minty to me so I can be on my way."

Minister Breembat's words landed in a way Minty did not comprehend because the storm she saw brewing in her mother's eyes turned to rain clouds.

Rit hugged her tightly and kissed her cheek before jumping to her feet. Then, in a fast motion—Minty barely registered the movement—Rit lifted Minty and handed her over to Minister Breembat.

The Dragonkin settled Minty in front of him; her short legs stretched wide on the large horse.

"Bye, Bennie. Bye, Rach."

"Bye."

"Bye."

Minty returned her siblings' waves, her grin as big as she could manage. But the image of her mother standing beside them, hands fisted in her dress, delivered a different farewell because Minty knew what that gesture meant when she did it.

Momma is afraid for me. But she needn't worry. Minister Breembat said my new owners would take good care of me. And I won't be gone long. I'll be back on Sunday for service and dinner with the family. Momma will see she has nothin' to worry about. Nothin' at all.

Chapter 8
SHE'S JUST A SCRAWNY SLAVELING

Berzogtown
Calis Farm

Two farms away turned out to be farther than Minty thought, not that she'd ever been anywhere other than Mistress Essodel's aviary, no more than she'd ever had reason to ride atop a horse. But she'd done both in a single day, a feat that had a happy, silly grin plastered on Minty's face the entire ride to the Calis farm.

However, she stood barefooted and before strangers in a dining room that was neither her cabin home nor Mistress Essodel's big white house Rit helped to maintain for their master's kinfolk. Minty had never felt more nervous. Her stomach fluttered, and her heart pounded.

She wiggled her toes against the cool, wooden floor, the grain so smooth Minty did not fear getting a splinter. Hands at her sides, she gripped her dress so tightly she felt capable of tearing the garment in two. Not wanting that embarrassing fate, she quickly released the soft, reassuring material, but not the anxiety that kept her head bowed and eyes lowered.

"Minister Breembat said your name is Araminta Wren. He even seemed proud to have remembered the mouthful. Araminta Wren is a big name for such a little slaveling."

The woman's voice, as sweet sounding as the milk Minty had spied the family drinking when she'd entered the dining room, drifted to her like the sun's brilliant rays cutting through her cabin home on a sweltering summer's day—harsh despite its beauty.

"What does your ma call you?"

"M-Minty, ma'am."

"Minnntyy," the woman said, stretching out her name beyond anything that made sense. "Minntyy. It has a ring to it. What do you think, Jolara, dear?"

"We should introduce ourselves to the poor slaveling. If we do, perhaps she'll cease admiring our floor and her toes and give us the respect we paid for and look us in our eyes."

Minty's small shoulders trembled, but she did not run or cry, although she desired little more than to do both. Her new owner's tone had started as sweetly as his wife's but ended with the same undertone of biting meanness.

Breathing deeply, Minty lifted her head and forced her eyes to meet the four gazes that stared at her as if she would make a better meal than the roasted piglet on a serving tray in the center of the dining room table.

Minty slammed her eyes shut, feeling out of depth in her new home and with these people who looked nothing like anyone she'd ever seen. Slowly and with cautious effort, she opened her eyes. The gathered group watched her with an intimidating mix of smugness and mockery.

Minty did not understand their unkind attitude. Nothing she'd done in the short time she'd been in their home warranted the mistreatment. What she did grasp, however, was that Minister Breembat hadn't prepared Minty for her new living situation, no more than he had revealed to Rit to whom he had hired her out for the foreseeable future.

Momma wouldn't have agreed to this. Wait, what am I thinkin'? Minister Breembat didn't give Momma a choice. I could tell she didn't want me to leave with him. To be away from her like the others. But she always told me where dragons were pompous and powerful and gryphons sneaky and greedy, harpies were jealous and cruel.

"Look, Ma. I think the slaveling is gonna vomit. Hey, slaveling, never seen a harpy family before?"

The young harpy garnered her attention. The male sat next to another young male harpy. Considering she'd never seen a harpy before, only heard about them from bedtime stories, Minty could only guess at the boys' ages. But, from how their taloned feet swung from the chair, unable to reach the floor, and the small size of the clawed hands that gripped the glasses of milk, she assumed they were about her age.

Like their parents, their faces were human enough, except for brown and black streaked feathers where normal hair should be and birdlike eyes she only ever saw when family or friends were in their complete bird form.

I don't understand them. They're a confusin' mix of bird and human. And why do they have so many clothes on? They dress fancy like Minister Breembat and Master Gyzad, even though their brown wings hang over the back of their chairs and their feathered legs peek out beneath their pants.

Minty's inquisitive gaze traveled to the woman of the house, wondering if her feathers were visible below her long black dress. But she only saw taloned feet and large ruffles nearly to the floor.

"I-I w-won't vomit," Minty said, replying to the boy in a voice she wished hadn't shaken because his self-satisfied smirk couldn't have been more human if he tried.

"Well," the male harpy said as he stepped forward, "that is something. I'm Master Jolara Calis." He laid a hand on his chest as if Minty required the gesture to know he'd introduced himself. Hand pressed to a button-up vest that appeared more constricting than comfortable, Master Calis lifted his left wing, settling it behind the woman beside him. "This is my wife, Mistress Theria Calis. And these are our sons"—he nodded to the boy who'd mocked Minty and then to the other child—"Typhalle and Urasis. You will refer to them as 'Young Mister.' Do you understand?"

Minty also heard the unspoken dictate. "Yes, sir, Master Calis." She curtsied to the sole female harpy in the family, remembering her manners as Rit had cautioned. "Yes, ma'am, Mistress Calis."

Lowering his wing and straightening his tie, Master Calis nodded to the pitcher beside the roasted piglet. "Sweet milk?"

Minty would love a glass . . . or three of the milk, along with a thick slice of the piglet. At the thought, her stomach rumbled, but not too loudly to give away the extent of her hunger.

I can't eat or drink in front of these people. They've already judged me as lower than dirt. I've never been called a slaveling. For some reason, it feels worse than being called a ground-scraper.

"No, thank you, Master Calis."

"You don't like sweet milk?"

"No, sir."

"The slaveling thinks she's better than us," Urasis said, abolishing any hope that there was one member of the Calis family who would show Minty kindness. "Dragonkin think they're better than Harpyfolk. I bet they train their slaves to think that way, too, Pa."

"Perhaps," Mistress Calis agreed, retaking her seat and downing the glass of sweet milk Minty wanted desperately to coat her empty stomach. "But her kind isn't better than us. Thanks to your pa, we're moving up in the world." A taloned finger pointed to Minty, whose thin shoulders had slowly hunched to her ears. "We can finally afford to hire our very own slave. And not just any slaveling, but one from the coveted Essodel aviary. Everyone knows that Essodel breeds the finest Birdfolk in all Miadar."

The Calis boys did not appear impressed, but they rolled little dark birdie eyes at Minty before resuming the meal her arrival interrupted.

"She's just a scrawny slaveling too stupid to like sweet milk." Typhalle cut into the piglet with his talon, then, as if he knew she was starving, wagged the delicious-smelling meat at her before devouring it in two gluttonous bites.

"Not only that," Master Calis said, steepling his long, taloned fingers, his elbows going to each side of his dinner plate and his words for his wife. "Minister Breembat not only assured me that the girl can dance and sing but also that she is one of Essodel's rarest Sankofa bird shifters."

"No," Mistress Calis said, a happy squeak of sound that had the harpy pushing to her feet and, once more, reminding Minty that she stood on display for this harpy family who obviously admired the Dragonkin as much as they despised them their high societal status. "This slaveling is a Sankofa bird shifter?"

Mistress Calis stalked up to Minty, and she told herself not to flinch, no matter how long the female stared at her. But when one of her rough-taloned fingers touched her chin, Minty vomited a little in her mouth.

"Show me."

She swallowed her vomit, disliking that the brat Urasis had been right about her, but not as much as she hated the whipping sound of Mistress Calis's command.

No wonder Momma looked at me the way she did. I thought this would be a grand adventure. I'm such a stupid kid. A baby who keeps forgettin' her place. A slaveling. A ground-scraper. I'm anything but a person with feelings. Why don't they see that? Why are they all so mean?

Slap. "I said show me."

Eyes filled with stunned tears, Minty looked up at Mistress Calis from her place on the floor. She sat on her bottom, her new dress up to trembling thighs and sweaty palms flat against the hardwood floor. A wet trickle ran from her cheek to her chin, and Minty did not need to wipe the moisture away to know she bled.

Before she could catalog the fullness of the moment that she'd been struck without cause or warning, she was suspended in the air, the front of her dress fisted in Mistress Calis's hand.

"I do not want to repeat my command when I tell you to do something. Do as I say the first time and be quick about it. Or I'll offer more than a slap to your tender baby face." She dropped Minty, who stumbled but managed not to fall. "Now, remove that dress before I rip it from you. I want to see what my husband paid for."

"Quite right, dear. Undress so I can see how well I invested in you or whether Minister Breembat was all boasts. I had to rent you sight unseen, trusting that drunk to keep good his side of the contract."

Shuffling away from Mistress Calis and hoping her retreat wouldn't encourage another attack, Minty grabbed the hem of her dress and pulled it up her body and over a wooly head of human hair that would one day save her life. But nothing and no one could protect her from the Calises. Not on this day, nor in the two years she would live with them.

So, Minty laid bare her little girl's body before an adult male, not her father, and in front of two boys who were not her brothers. Ben, Robert, and Ben Jr. only ever looked at her with love. They certainly never laughed at her nude form, making her the brunt of a secret joke.

"She's scrawnier without her dress on, Ma." Typhalle cut another slice of piglet and shoved it into his big mouth, the same way Minty wanted to punch the young harpy.

Unlike Mistress Calis, however, Minty had never struck anyone, not even Ben Jr., when he pulled her hair feathers.

"That's fine because this isn't the form that matters."

Minty knew she had better shift before the harpy decided her statement was actually another command for her to transform. She'd never needed the focus that closed eyes afforded the change than she did on this day. If, even for too-brief seconds, she could free herself from the sight of the Calis family, Minty was grateful for the reprieve.

Even nervous and sick to her stomach, Minty never forgot one of Rit's lessons, including how to quickly transform.

I survived doin' this in Mistress Essodel's lair. I can do the same here. She was impressed. I hope these harpies will be, too. If not, I must brace myself for a whippin'. I've never had one before, but I've seen them. Minister Breembat and Master Gyzad make us watch. It's a horrible sight. I don't want to end up like that. Skin sliced open, and rivers of blood everywhere.

At the awful memory and a successful transformation, Minty shivered.

Master Calis whistled. "Well, look at you."

Minty opened her eyes, taking in the small dining room and family with a keener sight than her human orbs. Everything was sharper and brighter. The brown-black of the harpies' feathers appeared more vibrant, with Minty capable of discerning their feathers' different shades of brown. Through her transformed eyes, she could see the many nuanced differences between the brothers. Whereas Typhalle's eyes were a dull greenish-white, his brother's carried a blue undertone not present in either of their parents' eyes. While Mistress Calis's dress was the darkest black Minty had ever seen, the ruffled trim was more of a dark purple, the fresh stitching and newer material different from the older, more worn parts of the dress.

Minty saw it all in crisp colors. Her perspective did not alter, not even when Mistress and Master Calis flanked her.

"Well done, husband. She is absolutely gorgeous."

"She is. No wonder Minister Breembat raised the rental price on her. I thought he was putting me on. But, no"—one hand, then two stroked her left wing—"he simply knew this slaveling's worth."

"Indeed. I can't wait to show her off. We'll be the envy of our friends and family. I almost don't care if she can sing and dance."

"I bet she can run fast in this form, too."

"Ha, ha, ha." Mistress Calis's laughter stung almost as much as her slap had for all the vile intent Minty could detect. "But not too fast."

"Just fast enough to make it fun for our guests." The taloned hands that stroked her feathers moved slowly, possessively, from her upper wing coverts to her underwing coverts.

Yank. Off came a feather, a stinging assault that had Minty jumping away from her assailant.

"Don't," she said instinctively. "You aren't allowed to do that. Mistress Essodel said so."

Slap.

Minty crashed to the floor, head spinning and mouth filling with blood.

"She talked back, Ma. Hit her again." Urasis.

"You not so pretty now, are you, slaveling?" Typhalle.

Master Calis crowded her where she sat, hunched in on herself and daring not to meet the harpy's eyes. "You'll learn how things work around here, Minty. My wife and I are your new masters. Do you know what that means?"

She didn't answer, afraid she'd splatter his taloned feet with blood. Bad decision.

He lunged for her, and she scooted backward.

"Wait. Wait. It means I answer only to you now."

"Our house, our rules."

"Yes, sir, Master Calis. Your house, your rules." She bobbed her head but regretted the movement when a sharp pain exploded behind the eye Mistress Calis had struck when she'd slapped the side of her face.

"That's right. I paid good money for you, and I'll do what I please with you. When I tell you to dance or sing, you'll do it until told to stop." Two long strides had him over Minty again, she between mighty legs and taloned feet capable of slicing her as easily as Typhalle had cut into the roasted piglet. "And when I decide I want your feathers to sell, bringing in extra cash from my rental of a pricey Sankofa shifter, I better not hear any backtalk from you."

"Y-y-yes, s-sir, M-Master Calis. N-no backtalk."

He patted her head. "That's a good little slaveling. Now get up and dance while we eat."

Pushing to her feet, no pride to support her wobbly legs, Minty shrugged off her pain and tears.

She danced.

The harpies ate.

She sang.

The harpies ate.

She danced and sang.

The harpies ate roasted pork, corn, potatoes, and green beans.

She twirled, dipped, and jumped.

They ate sliced cheese on bread.

They refilled glasses with sweet milk.

She twirled, dipped, and jumped.

The adults ate apple pie with cinnamon, and the children scarfed down two helpings of almond custard.

None of the food went to Minty, who provided the evening entertainment.

Not a crumb or a sip.

At the end of the night, Minty's first evening away from her mother and home, she curled into a ball under the dining room table. Her sleeping quarters, Mistress Calis, had told her.

"This dining room floor or the kitchen floor. Pick one and be happy we didn't make you bunk in the barn with the cows."

Minty had chosen the dining room, hoping to find dropped food under the table. She did; she found a tasty piece of pie crust she wolfed down, but the taste of it on her tongue increased her hunger pangs instead of alleviating them.

As she drifted off, she imagined the comfort of her mother's arms surrounding her in a hug, only to be jolted awake the following day. She was pulled out from underneath the table by a leg, claws cutting into her ankle.

"We didn't buy you for sleeping, slaveling. Get your lazy butt up and help me cook breakfast."

Theria Calis.

Minty's mistress.

HARRIET'S ESCAPE:

Minty's tormentor.

Chapter 9
I Want to Go Home

1830

Berzogtown

Calis Farm surrounding property

Minty bolted into the woods. Not once did she look back because she'd done this too many times not to know what slowed her down. Worse, she understood what defeat felt like. Minty did not want to lose again despite never winning this so-called game. So, she ran as fast as she could.

Darting around trees, she recalled taking this route last month. It led to the marshy wetlands where she'd been forced to set muskrat traps. Despite having caught dozens of them for the Calis family, she had yet to taste even a morsel of the semiaquatic rodent.

Come on, I gotta keep runnin'. If I make it to the wetlands, I have a chance of survivin' this hunt. If I don't... no, no, I won't think about what happened those other times. I'm two years older and a little taller than the first time the Calises made me do this. I'm stronger, too, whenever I can get a bit of food. But the scraps Mistress Calis gives me aren't enough. That ain't fair because I do most of the cookin'.

Minty rounded another tree, slipping on moist leaves and blood from reopened cuts on her feet. She paid neither any heed, no more than she did her nude state. To her way of thinking, she ran faster naked, and her brown skin blended better with the slowly darkening sky than her bright Sankofa wings would. As far as camouflage went, she possessed nothing more effective than her sweaty brown skin, bushy black hair, and head feathers almost as dark from days without a good wash.

It would have to do, so Minty prayed night would soon fall and that she would not.

She ran and ran, leaving a trail of blood any fool, much less skilled harpy trackers, could follow. But Minty did not care because the Calis's hunting party gave her no good options.

"Run or die," Master Calis had told her about a week after her arrival. "Typhalle, Urasis, and the other children will lead the hunt. If they find and corner you before the adults catch up to them..." He'd shaken his head as if he cared about Minty's fate at the taloned hands of harpy children. But she'd seen the anxious gleam in his eyes, and the look had not changed with each of these "slaveling hunts," as the Calises called them.

Mouth hanging open and chest heaving, Minty pumped her arms and legs harder. She could smell the fresh water and decayed vegetation muskrats used to build burrows—two signs she neared her goal. It was a goal in her mind only because she'd never lasted this long without being caught. Making it to the stream would change nothing, however. Her arrival there would not end the slaveling hunt. But it would be a personal best for Minty, so she worked hard to turn the awful hunt, the grueling race to avoid another beating, into something she had control over when little in her life belonged to her.

Even this, the nasty wetlands, had become more of a home to her than the one she shared with the harpy family.

Skin slick from perspiration and heart raging in her chest, Minty stepped into the shallow water, carefully avoiding the traps she'd set on the bank.

Her teeth chattered, and the cuts on her feet stung. Neither prevented her from wading deeper into the stream and away from the familiar footfalls she'd refused to admit drew ever closer.

Crossing her arms over her chest, Minty dragged her legs through the water, wincing with each step. She could no longer feel the difference between the water's wetness and that of her blood.

Winter had set in with a biting chill. She felt every temperature drop as the sun faded behind the trees, and she crawled onto the bank farthest from her pursuers. As she did each night under the Calises' dining room table, Minty curled into a tight ball.

No pillow.

No bedcovering.

No fire to keep her warm or even bedclothes to protect her from the elements.

Each morning, she would make Typhalle's and Urasis's beds, clean the fireplace in their bedroom, and wash their urine-stained sheets and undergarments.

A cold breeze encircled her, and Minty would give anything to be wrapped in one of the Calis children's sour-smelling sheets.

"You can't hide from us, slaveling."

If Typhalle wants to rout me from my hidin' spot, he's gonna have to come over here. I won't make it easy on him and his cousins.

"We're gonna get you, slaveling. Don't think we're afraid to cross this stupid little stream."

"Or that we're afraid to fly in the dark," Urasis said, sounding more fearful for having claimed otherwise. "We'll do it, too, Minty. We'll get you before Ma, Pa, and the other adults arrive."

"Yeah," said a girl whose voice she'd come to recognize and loathe as much as she did the Calis brothers. Norveis, at eleven, was one of the many Calis cousins she'd met. At various times, they'd all hunted and beat Minty upon finding her, generally up in a tree. But none enjoyed the beatings more than Norveis. "We're gonna come over there and . . . huh? What, Typhalle, I'm talking."

"I know . . . just . . ."

Minty strained to hear the harpies, but they no longer yelled. If they didn't already know where she was, their silence would've pleased her, but it only heightened her anxiety.

They're plottin' somethin'. Typhalle is as mean as his ma. But he likes to show off when he's with his older cousins. That means bossin' me around more than usual. That also means him forcin' me to shift and allowin' his cousins to pluck my feathers. This time, I won't shift. I'm sick and tired of the Calises sellin' my feathers to feed and clothe them while lettin' me starve.

Knees up to her chin and arms covering her head, Minty waited for the inevitable *thud* of harpy children landing around her.

She waited.

And waited.

Nothing.

Sliding her arms apart, she peeked across the stream to the bank where she'd been and where the other children should be.

Nothing.

Minty calculated the odds of her making it to the nearest tree undetected. Determining the odds were favorable, she slid on her belly, like a silent snake in the grass, to the closest black walnut tree. As they did each year, the black walnut trees were the first to lose their leaves come fall, making them a less-than-ideal hiding spot for Minty. But she didn't plan on climbing the tree she'd crawled to, no more than returning to the Calis farm that night and straight into whatever trap Typhalle and Norveis had prepared for her.

Large brown leaflets surrounded the base of the tree. However, mixed in with the leaves were round fruit with a thick and green husk.

These aren't ripe. Some are rotten. They taste better when they're yellow or tan.

Hauling herself up, she leaned against the tree, knowing, from this position, no one could see her from the bank where the harpy children had called out.

Master Calis would make me throw these away if I brought them back after one of my harvestin' days. Even when he don't want them for his family, he still won't give them to me to eat. Unripe and rotten ones don't taste good, that's for sure. But it's better than goin' to sleep with nothin' in my belly but cramps.

She decided to spend the night there rather than willingly return to the Calis farm for another beating. Minty pretended the fruit was sweet, the leaves were blanket soft, and the temperature was warm kisses.

I'm so lonely. I want to go home. Go home to Momma and Poppa. Bennie and Rach. I haven't seen them in a long time. I bet chubby Kessiah is so big. I bet I can't pick her up now. Will Poppa still pick me up and swing me around now that I'm eight? Will Linah still look and smell like our momma? Will Robert and Soph tell me stories?

Tears tracked the canvas of Minty's face, warm where every other part of her was chilled to the bone.

Will my family remember me? Will they want me back? I'm not the same. I look different. Feel different on the inside. Maybe Momma won't recognize her little Minty. Maybe...

Arms wrapped around raised legs and forehead on knees, Minty wept. She didn't know for how long. But her time in the woods faded to quiet blackness.

Bleakness.

A month and two slaveling hunts later, flat red spots appeared on Minty's face near her hairline. The next day, the red spots had spread to her neck, but small raised bumps accompanied them.

"I feel sick. Warm," Minty told Mistress Calis, trying not to cough on the platter of eggs she held. She placed them carefully on the dining room table and looked up at the scowling harpy female.

"You better not have gotten snot in those eggs, Minty."

"I-I didn't. It's just..." As if her nose knew it was the subject of Mistress Calis's ire, it leaked snot, which she quickly wiped with the collar of her dress. "I don't feel good."

A hard shove had Minty stumbling toward the kitchen. "What you are is a lazy slaveling. There's nothing wrong with you that hard work can't fix. Now get back in there and finish breakfast. After that, the boys' room needs cleaning, and the muskrat traps require checking and resetting. Master Calis expects more muskrats from your traps so he can sell their pelts." Another hard shove had Minty in the kitchen doorway and Mistress Calis looming above her. "You know what it means when you don't meet your quota."

Minty coughed but nodded because she knew the ramifications of her failure to meet her daily muskrat quota. Not that, until moving in with the Calises, she'd learned what the word "quota" meant.

Now, she could summarize the definition in two words: beatings and defeatherings.

Mistress Calis's threat, however, did not change the truth. Minty was unwell. Her apparent sickness, however, neither moved Mistress Calis to sympathy nor altered the family's expectations of her. So, she trudged along with her days, completing chores from sunup to sundown, all the while feeling worse and worse.

Until one day . . .

I can't breathe. C-can't breathe. Can't . . .

Calis Farm

Ben had never had any use for harpies, no more than he did for gryphons or dragons. He knew not all of them were self-absorbed, cruel people who cared little for Birdfolk except as a means to their selfish ends. In his mind—hell, in his heart—Ben knew this to be true because every group member couldn't be a vile, unconscionable piece of rodent droppings.

Yet, as Ben opened his feathered arms to take his child, his Minty, whom he hadn't seen in two years, he cursed the unrepentant harpy male before him and his entire race. Wrapped in a ripped piece of sheet that barely covered Minty's naked body, his daughter slept too deeply for his comfort.

Sweat beaded every part of her he could see. However, as plentiful as the beads of sweat were, they could not conceal the raging red spots that began at Minty's forehead and covered the entirety of her face, neck, and chest. Ben did not need to pull back the cloth wrapping to know the red spots continued onto her lower half. He could see them dotting the limp feet that hung below the piss-scented material.

"She has measles." It was all Ben dared to utter. Anything else would've had him strung up and whipped to death after he murdered Jolara Calis and his wife, who glared at Ben from the open front door of the farmhouse his daughter had been forced to slave in since she was a girl of six.

I missed her seventh and eighth birthdays. Worse, I couldn't protect her from the Calises. I gotta take her home to Rit, but, my God, I don't want my wife seein' our child like this. Especially not after what Minister Breembat did to Mariah. My poor Mariah. My poor Minty. They don't deserve this harsh world. None of us do.

"She got it on her own. We aren't to blame."

Heat radiated above Ben, and he knew the minute the Calises realized a lowly enslaved bird shifter father hadn't come alone to retrieve his sick daughter.

Theria Calis stumbled backward, all but falling in her effort to put a house and a meager closed door between her and the creature who hovered in the sky.

Jolara Calis did not retreat into his house along with his wife, but Ben did not deem that action as a sign of bravery or even of bravado. From his slack-jawed expression, the male was too frightened to do anything as reasonable as flee. Not that, when a dragon had prey in their sight, escape was possible.

"Rit was right. Birdfolk mother's intuition. From the look of her, they've done nothing to treat the child's symptoms. I've only seen measles this bad once or twice before."

So had Ben; both were enslaved adults. They'd survived despite being forced to work during their illness. But children as young as Minty weren't as durable as adults, their bodies not meant to withstand the abuse the Calises had obviously inflicted on her.

Ben stepped away, cradling Minty in his wings, and knowing what would come next.

"Something is wrong with our Minty," Rit had told him that morning. They were the first words she'd spoken to him when he'd arrived home early Sunday morning for his weekly visit.

"A dream?"

Rit had nodded, but Ben hadn't placed much stock in her dream. Not the one about Minty or any of their other children. As far as Ben was concerned, Rit's dreams were manifestations of her fear for their children and being powerless to keep them safe.

"I've already spoken to Mistress Essodel about Minty."

"You what?"

When Mariah was first sold, Ben and Rit had discussed the possibility of raising the issue with their dragon master, assuming, but perhaps only hoping, that Minister Breembat had acted without her knowledge and that their accusation of Mistress Essodel's youngest son would not inflame her anger. In the end, they'd decided even if Minister Breembat had acted without his mother's knowledge, the blowback from him against their other children could be worse than losing Mariah.

Their decision hadn't gone down any better for Rit than for Ben. No more than Ben could stomach what would what have happened to Rit if she'd been wrong about Minty and the Calises.

"Mistress Essodel said she would command Master Gyzad to escort you to the Calises to check on Minty. If she is sick, to bring her back here."

"What else?" he'd asked, knowing Mistress Essodel did nothing out of the kindness of her questionable heart.

Rit had hugged him, but her voice held absolute certainty. "If you don't bring our Minty home to me, Ben, she'll die. I saw it. Feel it in my soul. I don't care about Mistress Essodel's threat to sell me away from here if I'm wrong about the harpies breakin' the contract. I know they've done more to our baby than take her feathers without Mistress Essodel's permission."

And that was all the old dragon cared about, Ben knew. Not Minty's overall welfare. Not her mental and physical health. But whether the Calises had disobeyed her orders.

Master Gyzad landed in front of a still, unmoving Jolara Calis. If Ben hadn't shifted to the left, Master Gyzad's massive body would've concealed what he wanted to witness.

"Mistress Essodel expects her rental contracts to be followed to the letter. No deviation."

"I-I . . . I mean, we didn't do anything or—"

"There are endless reasons why dragons are superior to harpies. Your ignorance is as appalling as you are pathetic. Everyone knows that defeathering a Birdfolk under ten makes them weak and susceptible to illnesses like measles and pneumonia. Her rapid, shallow breathing is enough for me to know you and your wife have subjected the child to many defeatherings. Otherwise, despite your disregard for someone else's property, she would've recovered from the illness soon enough."

Property. A more accurate word than servant. Property is all my family has ever been to Mistress Essodel and her kin. Born into slavery and dying a slave. Between the beginnin' and the end, we try our best to eke out what happiness we can. What God and our dragon masters will allow. My family is all I've ever needed to be happy. But havin' a child sold away and the others forced to labor too few years into their fragile lives is a hell I don't have to die to experience.

Deciding that returning Minty to Rit for care, as quickly as his bird feet would take him, trumped him living vicariously through Master Gyzad, Ben forwent seeing the execution of Mistress Essodel's dictate and the Calis family.

So, whereas Minister Breembat excelled at breaking his mother's rules, Master Gyzad reveled in reminding everyone, even a harpy with only enough financial means to rent a young slave girl, of Mistress Essodel's might and, by extension, Master Gyzad's.

A *whoosh* of sound was followed by a *hiss*, *pop*, and *crackle*.

It's done. No sound other than Master Gyzad's fire. If I turned to see, there would only be charred wood where a farmhouse had been. Not even my keen bird sight would be enough to find the ashes of the Calis family. Master Gyzad told me the couple had two children. Boys. I didn't want their deaths. Children are always innocent, even when they do awful things. They only imitate what they witness adults doin'. But I knew what Master Gyzad was ordered to do when I saw Minty covered in red spots. There was nothin' I could've said, nothin' I wanted to say, that would've prevented what happened. I shouldn't take pleasure in the Calises reapin' what they sowed. But God help me, I do.

Leaving Master Gyzad to revel in his kill, Ben took off, a barely breathing Minty pressed to his chest.

The Sankofa bird ran faster.

Chapter 10
We Can't Keep Them Safe

Essodel Plantation

Rit refused to cry, but God knows she wanted to cry herself dry. However, Minty did not need a weeping mother, no more than she wanted to fall apart in front of Ben Jr., Rachel, and Kessiah.

"I'll help you with her." Harkless, an enslaved Birdfolk male Linah met when she was hired out to a shrewd harpy female who'd won Harkless in a card game, extended his arms to Ben. "I'll take her so you can shift and dress. I got her. Good Lord, she's so . . ."

"It's fine, Harkless." Rit stood beside her son-in-law, focusing on her daughter and not her husband, who'd moved behind the privacy sheet and into their bedroom to do as Harkless had suggested. "We see what's been done to our little Minty."

"Minty?" Rachel said, going on tiptoe to see her older sister.

An awful realization struck her, making her sick to her stomach. *Minty's been gone for two years. Does Rachel remember her? My God, does Minty remember Mariah? She was the same age as Rachel when Mariah was sold. Both three. I can't lose another one of my babies.*

Rit kissed Minty's forehead. It felt hot and tasted salty. "It's okay, Araminta, Momma is here. You'll be fine. I'll take care of you." Lifting her gaze to those gathered, Rit corrected. "We'll take care of you."

They all knew Mistress Essodel had granted only Rit permission to cut back on her chores to care of Minty.

A shifted and dressed Ben came up behind Rit, his chin going to her shoulder and wide fingers to her protruding belly. "It won't be long before this little one greets us."

The pending birth of Rit and Ben's eighth child was Mistress Essodel's true motivation for limiting Rit's slave duties to a few hours of domestic chores a day. Once the baby was born, Mistress Essodel would only get a little work out of Rit for several months. So, having Minty home at this time was a blessing in disguise.

"You and the baby will be fine. Minty is past the contagious stage."

He sounds winded. I bet he ran all the way here. I can see why. Our child looks like she's knockin' on death's door. I can't have that. Not now. Not ever.

"Harkless, Ben Jr. added a second board box in my room."

"With plenty of straw and two nice, warm blankets." Ben Jr. appeared on the opposite side of Minty and beside Rachel, who stared at her sleeping sister with a furrowed brow that could've meant anything to the five-year-old.

Whereas she might not have known Rachel's thoughts, Rit knew her son had stolen the blankets from Mistress Essodel's big plantation home. She didn't abide thievery but made an exception in this case.

Ben Jr.'s gaze shifted between Rit and Ben. "Will she be okay?"

With the same faith she had that Ben would bring Minty home, Rit felt Ben's words, "She's in your momma's good hands now," just as keenly. "Harkless, I believe Rit was about to ask you to take Minty into the bedroom. I'll go with you."

A gentle rub to her belly preceded Ben's exit.

Then Linah was there, hugging her from behind with one hand while holding six-year-old Kessiah's hand with the other. "I'll come by as often as I can to help with Minty."

At twenty-two, Linah had her own family to see after, but Rit wouldn't deny her eldest child her desire to care for a sister young enough to be her daughter. Marriage extended a family. It did not replace the existing one, so Rit nodded, wishing a family event other than bad tidings had brought them together.

Soph and Robert were in the winter wheat field but would return home in a few hours. Despite what lay before her in nursing Minty back to health, Rit took solace in having most of her children near enough to touch. Or, in Linah's case, a daughter capable of giving unaided support.

"She's home now, Momma."

"I know."

"And she's as stubborn and strong as a mule."

The characterization brought a laugh because Minty stayed inside the longest of all her children but was the first to talk and walk.

"The water you boiled earlier should've cooled enough for you to use on Minty. While you wash harpy filth off her, I'll take the children from underfoot. We'll go down to the lake. Let Ben Jr. try his hand at catchin' somethin' for dinner."

Rit thought Ben Jr. would whoop, excited his older sister had acknowledged his fishing ability. Instead, she spotted him and Rachel by the sheet, hesitant to push it aside and enter.

"Grandmomma," Kessiah said, releasing Linah's hand to stand before her, "will Aunt Minty play with me when she's feelin' better?"

Rit smiled down at her granddaughter, pleased at the thought of Minty being well enough to play with not only Kessiah but Ben Jr. and Rachel, too. "You girls always played nicely together. Maybe you and Ben Jr. could show Minty that new game you two created. I'd bet she'd like that."

Kessiah's return grin reminded Rit of Mariah that it sometimes hurt to see so much of her daughter in Linah's child. But on this day, with the return of Minty, Rit chose to believe that wherever Mariah had been taken, she'd met people who made her happy, bestowing them with her warm, beautiful smile.

"Harkless," Linah called, already pulling away from Rit and gesturing to the closed cabin door, "let's take the kids down to the lake. My brother said he could catch more fish than you."

"Did not." Ben Jr. swung away from the privacy sheet and toward his eldest sister. He narrowed his gaze at Linah, but humor played around the edges of his twitching lips. "But, yeah, I bet I can catch more fish than your old husband."

"Old?" Harkless, only two years older than Linah at twenty-four, grabbed Ben Jr. from behind and tossed him over a brawny shoulder. "You hope to be as strong and good-lookin' as me when you grow up."

"Get off me, old man. I'm gonna be like my poppa when I grow up. He's plenty strong and good-lookin'."

"That's right." Ben gently smacked the back of Harkless's head, and the younger man laughed, then placed a grinning Ben Jr. onto the floor.

"Come on, Rach and Kess. I bet we can beat Linah and Harkless to the lake." Not waiting for the girls' assent, Ben Jr. grabbed their hands and pulled them outside. Clearly, neither minded because Rit could hear their retreating laughter.

Linah patted Rit's belly again. "That was easy. Come on, Harkless, if Ben Jr. beats us there, he'll never let me live it down."

"You started it."

"I sure did." With a playful shove to her husband's chest, Linah took off out the open door. "Race you to the lake."

Knowing no goodbye was necessary, Harkless ran after his wife, leaving the door open and Rit amused.

"I miss this when I'm away." Ben closed the door, denying the winter chill easy access to the cabin.

The lit fireplace helped chase away the harsher bites of winter. But slave cabins offered far less insulation than any dragon home Rit had worked in, cleaning and cooking but never reaping the benefits for her endless hard work.

"I removed that nasty sheet she was wrapped in and tucked her under the blankets. But she needs a good washin'."

"I know." Rit nodded to the bowl of warm water on the table. "Bring that into the room for me, please."

"You go on in and get yourself comfortable, and I'll be right behind you."

Sure enough, Minty slept soundly, two blankets pulled to a chin dotted with red spots.

Rit knelt, elated to see her child after so long despite the circumstances of her return. "I missed you, my little Araminta Wren."

"You called her by her full first name earlier, too." Ben joined her beside the board box, the water bowl with a floating rag on the floor between them.

Rit grasped his unspoken thought. Despite them having given Mariah two first names, no one called her Mariah Ritty. Yet, in the days and weeks after her sale, the few times Rit could bear to utter her lost child's name, it was said in its glorious fullness.

"I know she looks bad. But I meant what I said. With you takin' care of her, Minty will recover."

"Physically."

"Are any of our minds right after what we've endured?"

Pulling back the blankets, Rit winced as if struck by a corded whip. Red spots were everywhere. If the damage ended there, the tears she'd fought since Ben's arrival with Minty would've stayed away. But they formed, warm and angry, and then fell down a face that couldn't look away.

Minty had grown a couple of inches. The difference in height between her six-year-old self and the eight-year-old before Rit was negligible but noticeable. The heels of her feet were hard like a pebble, grayish-black and cracked. The soles, softer and more vulnerable than heels, were a tree branch of cuts in varying healing states. Caked dirt prevented the cuts from bleeding onto heels forced to battle the cruel elements, but some had forced their way to the surface, congealing around the edges.

"They never even got her shoes, and Minister Breembat only brought her a single dress so she would look good when he presented her to the Calises."

Ben covered the hand that trembled above feet that told the awful tale of her time away from home. Rit wished the evidence of Minty's mistreatment began and ended with her feet.

"If it helps, Master Gyzad torched the house she slaved in." His hand lowered hers into the bowl of water. "Along with the Calises. He killed the entire harpy family."

"Children?"

"Two."

"That's terrible."

"Maybe."

Rit squeezed the excess water from the rag, a silent acceptance of his perspective. *No child deserves to die, especially not by fire. Yet, every slave owner or aspirin' slave owner started as a child who grew into an adult comfortable with denyin' Birdfolk their freedom while also doin' all manner of villainy to keep them in line.*

Rit began with Minty's feet, slowly washing her daughter's body.

All the while, Ben held Minty's hand, his face as grim as each layer of dirt Rit removed. "She's nothin' but skin and bones. If Jolara and Theria Calis could be killed a second time, I would . . ." Bringing Minty's limp hand to his mouth, Ben kissed her palm. "Is it wrong for us to continue to bring life into this world, knowin' they could end up like this or worse?" The hand not holding Minty's settled on Rit's six-month pregnancy belly. "We love our children and grandchild, but I hate addin' to Mistress Essodel's human hoard."

Rit knew Ben did not regret marrying and having children with an enslaved woman. Yet, if he'd chosen differently, a free Birdfolk woman, his children would've followed the legal status of their mother, making them free and bound to no dragon or harpy master.

She did not have a good or even soothing response to give her husband because their children's brilliant light made her enslaved existence bearable. They brought her joy and laughter, even enlightenment, with their intelligence and ingenuity. They were her greatest achievements, her indomitable heart, and her courageous spirit.

Her children gave her life purpose and meaning beyond endless years of servitude. The truth of that felt selfish, to want physical manifestations of her inner need to love and be loved in return. An emotional juxtaposition to a life where personal choices and desires mattered to no one in power to grant what should be a right but were, in reality, a privilege for the rare few.

Minty stirred, saving Rit from her thoughts. Eyelids parted but only enough for Rit to glimpse a dull sliver of brown instead of the vibrant chocolate that had sparkled when Minty had left with Minister Breembat. Rit had tried to muster a return smile for her daughter back then. She'd failed, fearing every awful experience that could befall a young, enslaved girl on her own for the first time. Only future conversations with Minty would reveal all she'd suffered.

Yet, with Ben beside her and Minty home where she belonged, conjuring a genuine smile for her little girl was easy.

"Welcome home." Ben kissed Minty's hand again, his voice thick with an emotion greater than a parent's desire for revenge. "We got you, Minty. You're safe."

They were the right words for the situation. But after two years of living with cruel harpy masters, their child had learned a lesson every enslaved parent wished their children would not.

We can't keep them safe. As long as we live under a slave master's yoke, there is little we can do to protect them. But we can try.

"S-s-safe."

"Ben," Rit said, not needing to utter more than his name for him to know what Minty needed.

"Drinkin' water. Be right back."

Minty's eyes slid closed again, and, for a second, Rit wasn't sure if Minty knew who'd spoken and where she was.

But then tears slipped from under her eyelids, followed by a soft "M-momma" and "Home."

Minty leapt from the cabin steps, convinced she'd catch her younger siblings or niece in five long, fast bursts of speed. Well, perhaps not Ben Jr. since he was only a year younger than Minty and had grown to her height during her time away from home, but certainly Rachel and Kessiah, who she was taller and older than.

But they were quicker than she remembered them being, and Minty wasn't as recovered as she liked to believe. Still, she was home and feeling better than she had since being sent to live with the Calises.

Tripping over her feet, Minty righted herself as she darted around a tree, laughing as she reached for little Rachel.

Her sister ducked, avoiding Minty's tag and denying her victory. "Too slow, Minty."

She was too slow, but that truth did not halt her pursuit or limit her fun. *I'm home. I'm finally home where I belong.*

Minty ran as fast as she dared, unwilling to do anything that would cause an injury and make her mother more worried. But before she knew it, and without conscious thought, she'd shifted into her Sankofa bird form.

She ran faster still, buoyed by the false sensation of freedom and the glorious ripple of winter wind sliding over her feathers.

Minty ran and ran, forgetting the game.

Minty ran and ran, remembering when she'd been chased... hunted.

Minty ran and ran and ran. Because she could. Because the transformation from human to bird had become a matter of survival.

Easy.

Swift.

Vital.

So Minty ran, taloned feet taking her from one end of Mistress Essodel's aviary to the other. On each trek around, she was met with smiling, familiar faces, waving hands, and heartfelt greetings.

"Stronger every day."

"You got big, girl."

"That's right, run, little Harriet. Run."

Harriet is Momma's real name. When an elder calls me that, it's meant as a good thing.

Minty ran, grinning on the inside because she loved being compared to her mother.

"Miiiinty. Miiiiinty."

Skidding to a halt at Linah's booming voice, Minty nearly tumbled face-first into the nearest sweet gum tree. Its yellow-brown branches and twigs were a depressing, wintry sight. However, come spring, vibrant green leaves with a light gloss would transform each sweet gum in the aviary, nature's reminder that nothing, good or bad, lasts forever.

"Cut all of that runnin' out and get in here."

I'm too far away for Linah to see me. Someone must've told her I was runnin' around like a wild thing. Probably Kessiah.

Despite the chill of the day and the growing lateness of the hour, Minty wasn't yet ready to shed her feathers like sweet gum trees their leaves, so she took her time answering her sister's continuous calls for her to "Hurry up."

Five minutes longer than it should've taken Minty to return to her cabin home, she slinked up to Linah, feathery head lowered.

"If I weren't so exhausted from helpin' Momma give birth, I'd swat your little behind for keepin' me waitin'. You got me out here callin' your name like some kind of . . ." Linah trailed off, her eyes sharpening on Minty as if seeing her for the first time. Reaching for her, Linah's gentle hand lifted Minty's head to its proper place upward. "How have I never seen your bird form before? I mean, I kind of assumed you were a sight because Momma and Poppa never talk about it. That's never a good sign because they know what pretty and unique Sankofa shifters mean to Mistress Essodel and others."

Despite Linah's demand for Minty to return home "Now," the sight of her feathers, jade, amethyst, and blue diamond, as the Calises had taken to describing them to feather buyers, had overridden the urgency of greeting the newest member of the Wren family whose cries had reached Minty the moment her cabin had come into view.

"You have pretty feathers, too," Minty said.

"I do, but not like this. No wonder Minister Breembat . . ." Linah's hand drew Minty close, and, despite her being in bird form, Linah's human one still towered above her. "They take somethin' beautiful that God has given us and abuse it to the point of turnin' a blessin' into a curse."

"A blessin', not a curse. I'll remember."

"Good. Now go find wherever you dropped your dress and put it on. Henry is waitin'."

"Who's Henry?"

"Our new baby brother. Now get."

"First come, now get." Chuckling in the only way a bird could, ineffectually, Minty trotted away, pretending to leave in search of a dress she only now remembered lay in bits and pieces of torn cotton because she'd shifted without first removing the garment. "Make up your mind, Momma Linah."

Her sister laughed.

Henry shrieked again, the sound of a wail of hunger she knew well from caring for Ben Jr. and Rachel.

Minty felt at peace. Safe.

For a while. For precious months.

Then Minister Breembat returned with a pretty new dress, scuffed shoes that rubbed her heels and pinched her toes, and a smile Minty knew better than to trust again.

This time, when she was placed atop his big horse and waved goodbye to a frowning Rit, she knew what awaited her, and it wasn't a grand adventure.

Chapter 11
Don't You Ever Forget Me

1832
Berzogtown
Hinizi Farm

Minty's bare, sweaty feet glided effortlessly around the dining room. Broom fisted in slick palms, Minty swept the floor with so much strength that no sooner than she rid the floor of dust, it settled on the furniture like a second layer of cotton and wood. Even the black piano, which Mistress Sorekoh claimed to love but rarely played, received the full brunt of Minty's vigorous approach to the mindless task.

She swept, aggressively displacing dust in a plume of fine particles she could never quite manage to prevent from cascading onto chairs, tables, and Mistress Sorekoh's piano like snow forced from naked tree branches by a fierce winter wind. The side-to-side movement was still ineffective despite the months she'd labored in the Hinizi household.

This is nothin' like dancin'. But I feel better when I pretend it is. My body responds, goin' where I want it to go. Light, when I want it to be. Fast when I want to go that speed. But also strong and fast when I rush through cleanin' to make breakfast. I can see Momma and Poppa when my eyes are closed like this. Poppa's warm smile. And Momma's big belly. The baby should be here. I wanna see it. Do I have another baby brother like Henry and Ben Jr? Maybe I should've prayed for another sister. Would God have answered that kind of prayer?

Opening her eyes, Minty grimaced, unsurprised by what she saw. Leaning the broom against the back of a wooden table chair she knew better than to scratch with her "dirty slaveling nails," as Mistress Sorekoh had repeatedly snarled, much less sit on to take a meal, Minty snatched up the dusting cloth from the table and went to work clearing away the mess she'd made.

Minty attacked the furniture in the room with the same fast fervor she'd used to sweep the floor. Moving from one piece to the next, well-worn, and not nearly as exquisite as the furnishings in Mistress Essodel's plantation home but still in good condition, Minty ignored the pang of envy that crept up her stomach and stuck in her pulsing throat each time she cleaned up behind a slave owner too privileged to appreciate their good fortune.

No, not just envy. Mixed in with that traitorous emotion was the bitter taste of anger. Minty did not simply want what people like Mistress Essodel and Sorekoh Hinizi took for granted, a home to call their own, food to slake their hunger, the humane comfort of clothing, shoes, and furniture, but the legally sanctioned right to lead a life unburdened by the will and control of others.

With each passing day, each beating and whipping, the twin blades of envy and anger churned in her head, having already settled firmly in her heart—a heavy weight challenged only by the love for her family. She would never leave them behind, seeking freedom in a place far away from Mistress Essodel's aviary and her despicable sons.

Finished with the table, chairs, and piano that, in Minty's unschooled opinion, should've been in the living room where entertaining took place instead of in the dining room where any family member or guest could spill a drink on its shiny finish, she snapped her dusting cloth, prepared to wipe down the fireplace mantel. Instead, her eyes settled on a familiar length of leathern thong. Platted and tapered at one end of the handle, the silvery-gray whip, dirty in parts and worn in others, matched both Mistress Sorekoh's eye color and her brutal personality.

Minty didn't dare voluntarily touch the piece of cowskin hide, so she cleaned around the whip in the same way she avoided fire ant mounds—carefully but quickly. Fear, then a sense of powerlessness, threatened to overtake her, but she pushed the vile sensations down. She was used to both. They were life lessons she had been forced to learn that kept her sane and alive.

But no strategy, no amount of self-control, and no level of obedience ever proved enough to ward off the violent villainy that was Dragonkin Sorekoh Hinizi.

Minty smelled the cloying thickness of her perfume mere seconds before the dragon female entered the room—a tickle of a breeze capable of transforming into a dangerous windstorm in a single exhaled breath.

Hands dropping to her sides, she turned to face her temporary owner. The sight rarely changed. If the woman's pale, smooth face could form a smile, Minty had never witnessed the feat, not even when Mistress Sorekoh held her plump baby boy.

Silver-gray eyes roamed the room, landing on a piece of furniture before jumping to another and then another before finally settling on the black piano in the corner. Mistress Sorekoh's eyes swung back to Minty, a torrent of displeasure leaking from them.

Minty stepped backward.

"What have I told you about getting dust everywhere?" A long, pink tongue licked lips so red if Minty did not know better, she would've sworn the female had burst into the living room after devouring a dairy cow raw. But no, like her perfume and penchant for anger, Mistress Sorekoh went overboard in everything she did, including the makeup she refused to leave the house without applying in great detail and quantity. "I said," she moved toward Minty, "what have I told you about getting dust everywhere?"

No answer would suffice. This Minty knew from experience. She also understood what would come next and could do little to nothing to prevent the inevitable. So, she pivoted just as her mistress grabbed the whip from the fireplace mantel, giving the suddenly enraged dragon shifter her back.

Whack. Whack. Whack.

Head and neck.

Whack. Whack. Whack.

Head, neck, and, despite Minty's best efforts, the cowskin whip slashed across her face, leaving marks that went deeper than her fragile flesh.

"You'll learn to sweep properly or, by God, I'll . . ."

Whack. Whack. Whack.

Whack. Whack.

Minty heard the Dragonkin's child crying somewhere in the distance. Hungry, most likely, but perhaps also soiled and uncomfortable. Usually, Minty would go running, tending to Brikog's every whimper and need.

Whack. Whack. Whack.

Hunching in on herself, Minty crouched, covering her head with her arms and hands. She knew better, but survival instinct wasn't easy to overrule.

The protective posture angered Mistress Sorekoh even more, prolonging the cruel punishment beyond anything warranted by specks of dust in an otherwise tidy dining room.

Decades later, Minty would tell the story of her time with cruel Dragonkin masters like Sorekoh Hinizi, claiming they never made her holler. Minty would never know why anyone would believe a child capable of such unbridled strength. But she lied anyway because she wished she hadn't given the brutes the satisfaction of her tears and screams. She also lied because sometimes, legends were more powerful weapons in the fight for freedom and justice than harsh, ugly truths.

Whack. Whack. Whack.

Minty cried. Hollered.

But Sorekoh Hinizi did not break her spirit.

Fact. No legend.

1833
Berzogtown

Hitching her skirt to knees dark from scrubbing floors on all fours, Minty sprinted away from her master's home. She loved to run, and this night proved no different, despite the winter chill and her bare feet hitting the ground the way her master would certainly whip her if she were caught out without permission.

But Minty had no intention of being caught, so she ran without looking back and with determination.

Momma is close enough for me to sneak out, visit for a while, and be back before sunup.

Minty rounded a towering tree, its branches full and heavy with leaves. She didn't know what it was called when a tree didn't lose its leaves during the cold months, but she preferred trees that way because it made hiding behind and on them easier. But Minty did not plan on taking advantage of any trees on this night because she was sure no one tracked her, and she was too close to her goal to stop and hide.

So, she ran with a controlled glee that always overcame her at the thought of seeing her family again. She knew they wouldn't all be at her mother's temporary cabin home. She'd heard through the slave rumor mill that Linah was sick, so she didn't expect to see her oldest sister and her family. It was too bad because Minty had missed playing with Kessiah, and she hadn't seen Linah's youngest daughter, Harriet, in months. Minty also missed how Linah would both baby and boss her around, but she hadn't revealed that secret to anyone, not even to Rachel or Ben Jr.

Still, some Wren were better than none, and Minty had never been an ungrateful girl. Tempted to transform but unwilling to slow her pace to remove the first dress she'd owned in a long while that wasn't too tight, short, or long, Minty shrugged off the desire to break free of her human confines.

But she was still Birdfolk; no matter her form, she needlessly reminded herself, she didn't need a pointless excuse to run wilder, faster.

Minty zigzagged between trees, arms stretched out as if capable of taking flight.

I don't care nothin' about those mean slave owners. They can't deny me this. I dance for them. Clean their homes. Nurse their babies. And what do I get in return? Nothin'. That ain't right. Ain't right at all. But this here is all mine. The outdoors. The wind on my skin. The grass and dirt under my feet. Even my kinky hair feathers. All mine.

Footsteps sounded behind Minty. Quick. Hard.

Her wayward thoughts stuttered to a halt. A cold sweat broke out on skin moist from exertion. A foot slipped on fear as she rounded another tree, a flat dark road ahead of her but the slave cabins and safety farther still.

As if the rigorous sprint had reared its exhausted head, an awaking snake slithering from under a rock, Minty gulped in lungfuls of air. But she didn't stop running.

Neither did the person who pursued her.

She refused to look back.

She ran. And ran. And ran.

Until she didn't.

Yanked from the road and off her feet, Minty sailed into the air and over a wide, stiff shoulder.

"Get off me. I said get off—"

"Hush, girl, before you get us caught." A hand swatted her bottom. Not hard or rough the way she'd become accustomed to being touched, but still a stern warning to do as she was told.

"Robert?" Minty whispered, recognizing her oldest brother's deep, rough voice in a way she hadn't his footfalls behind her.

"Who else?" He swatted her bottom again, but just as gently he lowered her to the ground and behind a tree. "What are you doin' out here? Somebody could've seen y—"

Minty crashed into Robert, burying her face against his chest and hugging him with all her might. He smelled of greasy fatback and days-old sweat. But he felt like safety and home.

She sobbed like the child her owners never treated her as. Minty's tears wet an already sweat-stained shirt, but despite Robert's taps to her bottom, he rarely scolded and never raised his voice to her.

Tonight proved no different. But he did lift her into his arms and carry her to Rit's cabin home.

Legs wrapped snugly around Robert's waist, Minty breathed her brother in, unashamed of her reaction to seeing him after nearly a year. With her family, she never wondered if they missed her just as much as she did them because they made up for what they lacked in material possessions with unconditional love and affection.

Robert ruffled her hair and kissed her cheek the entire walk to the cabin, steering clear of the road the way Minty had not.

She tucked that bit of common-sense wisdom away for future use because, as long as her mother and siblings were within running distance, Minty would make it her mission to sneak away to visit as often as she dared.

"Is that my Minty you got there?"

At the sound of her mother's warm voice, happy surprise in each word, Minty wiggled out of her brother's arms. Minty vaulted up the three cabin steps without thinking and heedless of what her mother held. She flung herself at Rit.

Rit's laughter filled something profound inside Minty like a bowl of warm porridge. But she couldn't hug her mother the way she liked, the way she needed because . . . "You had another boy," she groaned involuntarily, then snapped her mouth closed, surprised by her reaction.

Laughter rippled from Rit. "Don't sound so disappointed. This is Moses."

Realizing she'd ignored everyone on the porch except for her mother, Minty stepped away, embarrassed but not to the point that she would alter her future reactions to seeing her mother again after so many months separated from her. Still, she wasn't a baby, small and needy like her two youngest brothers. She would remember at least that much.

"I guess the rest of us don't matter, Momma." At twenty to Minty's ten, Soph's delicate features reminded her of a doll gifted to a child too young to understand how to care for delicate items. Catching her in a bear hug, Soph spun Minty around. "Don't you ever forget about me."

"Never." The simple five-letter promise hit Minty harder than it should have. Years later, she would understand why, making her even more determined to keep her long-ago vow.

After that, Minty was given hugs and kisses from everyone gathered on Rit's cabin porch—Ben Jr., Rachel, and Henry, who clung to Rit's side as if uncertain of Minty's place in the family. At three, Henry hadn't seen much of Minty, so she didn't take his shyness personally, no more than she thought her failing to notice him at Rit's side registered with the toddler.

Minty didn't mention the absence of Ben and Linah. She knew he would have been there if her father could've joined them. Still, it felt wrong to be gathered like this without everyone present.

Minty was convinced Moses had been swapped at birth when she took her youngest brother from Rit. He was a chubby eight-month-old with bright, brown eyes and even darker skin and hair. "He doesn't look nothin' like you or Poppa."

"Told you, Momma." Ben Jr. stood beside Minty, examining their brother as if he hadn't seen him every day of his young life. "His nose is wider than ours."

"And his chin is rounder."

Rachel joined them, running work-calloused fingers through Moses's mass of feathery hair. "Too curly."

"Yup." Minty handed Moses back to her mother, deciding having another baby brother wouldn't be all bad, even if a new sister would have been better. "But he's cute."

"I was cuter," Ben Jr. said loud and proud, thumping his chest like he would take on all challengers to his bold assertion.

They laughed, except for the newest member of the family, Moses Wren, who shoved his fist into his mouth; drool was Moses's response to Ben Jr.'s proclamation.

Minty held Moses again while Rit claimed the single chair on the porch, a rocker that looked pieced together from the branches of a dying tree. But it held Rit's weight well enough, so Minty returned Moses to her mother when she reached for him.

Everyone else settled on one of the three steps, with Robert on the bottom landing and Ben Jr. on the second step directly behind Robert. He craned to look over Robert's head instead of moving to either side of him. Another self-imposed challenge, Minty concluded, happy to sit beside eight-year-old Rachel on the third step.

The cold feel of winter joined the affirming sight of darkness, neither capable of overpowering the other in a relationship of independents and equals. But whereas darkness would return each and every night, a reminder of its permanence, winter and coldness eventually retreated, giving way to the sensations of other seasons.

Minty supposed life under the whip of enslavement was like seasons. Freezing like winter. Blistering like summer. Rainy like spring. Unpredictable like autumn. But nighttime, the darkness that returned regardless of the season or even a Dragonkin's privileged will, was like a homecoming.

Trusted.

Faithful.

Reassuring.

Robert jumped to his feet, pointing to the sky. "Did you see that?"

Minty parted her lips to ask: "See what?" but something bright and fast streaked across the sky. Before she knew it, everyone was on their feet because the once dark sky, her familiar calm that offset her turbulent days, beamed unfathomable light.

She shielded her eyes with hands that trembled from the ungodly display of dominance. No longer were the winter chill and the dark night equal. The sky had seized power and control, raging in the sky with an intensity that left them all silent.

The light fell like fiery snowflakes from the sky, beating back cold with its strange, thick warmth. Undoubtedly, the shower of fire was an omen of bad tidings. What else could it be? Minty had no idea, but the phenomenon lasted well into the morning, making her return to the Hinizi household fraught with danger.

Minty did not like the fiery snowstorm. She knew no good would come from it. The end of the world, perhaps, she concluded. If not that, then another awful event would occur.

Two years wasn't long to wait before Minty's fears became prophetic.

Chapter 12

I Am the God of Justice

1835
Pelduth Neck

Mudspike did not know why the ground-scraper bothered fleeing. Hell, why any slave would think themselves faster and more intelligent than a gryphon slave catcher of his caliber, he couldn't reason. But Drake, one of Gyzad's hired-on slaves for his mine camp, had done precisely that, slipping away when Mudspike had been preoccupied with the new harpy cook who, thankfully, wasn't averse to interracial sex play or a quickie behind a shack.

More amused than insulted, Mudspike tracked Drake from a sky the bird shifter could never fly through, not even one that smelled like freshly washed linen on a line. Keen brown eyes nearly twinkled with mirth, enjoying the silent chase and the subtle battle of warm versus cool as fall fought summer for dominance.

The new season would prevail, just as Mudspike would have his prey. So, he watched the enslaved male jog through a busy downtown Pelduth Neck. Slipping and sliding between late-afternoon shoppers and early-evening drinkers, Drake hustled up a street that would take him to the town limit. Even if he crossed into the next locality, he would still be in Dralox County, so Mudspike had plenty of time if he chose to extend the game.

But Gyzad was slated to arrive tomorrow morning. After all these years, Mudspike still despised taking orders from a slave overseer. Ben Wren knew his master's comings and goings better than anyone at the mining camp. But that did not mean he trusted either of them, especially Ben, who was too friendly with the workers—enslaved and free.

Drake stuttered to a stop, glanced around but not up, then darted to his right. He rushed toward a dry goods store, kicking up dust. Landing on the step of the store with a hard *thud*, Drake crashed into a young Birdfolk female who wore a woven paisley shoulder shawl incongruent with the one-piece faded gray frock slaves wore. He knocked her into another female slave a few years older and several inches taller than the one who, despite being nearly run over by a thirty-five-year-old muscular male used to the rigorous demands of mining, fell back with a dancer's grace typical of many Birdfolk women.

"Sorry, sorry," Drake said, then leaned closer and whispered something to the females Mudspike couldn't hear.

But the taller of the two slaves cast her gaze upward, and he knew he'd been made. Just as quickly, she lowered her eyes, linked her arm with the young slave, and followed Drake into the dry goods store.

Mudspike had no idea why Drake would corner himself in a store or why he would reveal himself to two strangers. But the game of gryphon and bird would soon come to its inevitable end. He would drag him back to the camp long before Gyzad's arrival tomorrow. Then he would toss the runaway at the dragon's feet, tell all, and then glory in the punishment, not just Drake's but Ben's for his carelessness. Or maybe, Mudspike thought, landing in front of the dry goods store, his yellow-gold coat still tingling from his harpy lover's taloned touch, Ben's duplicity.

Whether true or false, Gyzad only needed to believe the accusation Mudspike had every intention of leveling against Ben. But first, he needed to catch Drake.

He entered the store, never having a good enough reason to do so. Gryphons did not play dress-up like harpies and shifters, so they had no need for textiles and clothing, which filled most of the shelves in the store. From neutral blacks, blues, and browns in wool and linen, to polychromatic cotton patterns, to decorative silks he'd seen on pompous Dragonkin and pretentious Harpyfolk, be they wealthy or wealth-seekers, the store catered to a clientele far above what Gyzad paid him to track down the likes of Drake Alouette.

But there the runaway was, staring at him with beady bird eyes from the opposite end of the store.

I'll give him credit for having some smarts. Shifting in the middle of a busy street would've brought unwanted attention from more than just me. He also has a better chance of evading me in his bird form. He won't, but it'll make reminding him of his place much more fun because ripped feathers taste better than shredded skin.

Mudspike scanned the store, taking stock of the customers. Twelve of them, including the two females from earlier. From their tattered clothing, rundown shoes, and wide, brown eyes, he concluded they were slaves running errands for their masters.

The subtle shifting of the person behind the sales counter caught Mudspike's attention seconds before the male said, "I don't want no trouble. Take it out of here."

In a threat the speaker would do well to heed, Mudspike opened and closed his eagle's beak at the store owner, a stout harpy male who'd squeezed himself into the same constricting clothing he sold, including a vest and trousers that, if he did anything more vigorous than breathe, would rip from seam to button.

Returning to his quarry, Mudspike caught when Drake glanced behind him to a closed black curtain.

"Ain't nothing back there, boy, but a storage room." The store owner nodded to the door Mudspike stood several feet in front of. "One way in, one way out. No back doors on this side of the street. You chose poorly. Now get on. Leave with that gryphon slave catcher. Runaways and his kind ain't welcome in here."

Mudspike cataloged both the insult and his advantageous position. Drake had indeed chosen poorly, and the harpy's linen would soon meet flint and steel. But that fun excursion back into town wouldn't happen for another night or two.

As much as a gryphon could, he smiled at Drake before planting his big, wide feet on the smooth wooden floor. "Come on, ground-scraper. Let's see how strong Gyzad's mine has made you."

Drake rushed him, and Mudspike wished the male's unflinching reaction hadn't surprised him, yet it had.

He knew Drake was strong, but the collision still knocked Mudspike off his clawed feet. They tussled on the floor. Wings whipped and snapped. So, too, did their beaks—slicing, ripping, and puncturing.

They knocked into shelves, and linen fell like clouds from the sky. Soft and silent.

Mudspike stabbed his beak into Drake's multicolored neck but was unprepared for his quick retaliation.

Slash. Slash.

Talons across his face. Eyes.

Mudspike refused to lose this fight, even if he had to . . .

Slash. Slash.

Slash. Slash.

Blood filled Mudspike's eyes, dulling his vision but not the pain. Worse, the taloned attacks had him on his side and a frothy-mouthed Drake atop him. Barely able to see through the curtain of thick crimson, Mudspike bucked. He managed to displace Drake from above him using his much larger body.

Later, he would admit that the Sankofa shifter had been more interested in escape than a death fight.

In that moment, however, all Mudspike saw was a slave who'd dared to defy his orders. A runaway he would rather see dead than have his perfect slave catcher record sullied.

Adrenaline propelled him from the floor like a lightning spark, and after the retreating Drake. The rational part of Mudspike knew he should tend to his wounds and then renew the hunt. His eyes felt like Drake tried to claw them from the sockets, an excruciating mix of pain and humiliation.

"Stop him," Mudspike yelled to the blurry image of a short, slim form near the door. "Stop him. Don't let him leave."

The small form did not move to intercept Drake. Instead, it shifted away from the open door, providing Drake with an unobstructed exit.

"No, no, no." Mudspike reached for a weapon, anything to stop the fleeing Drake. His wing landed on something small but hard. Very hard.

An iron weight. Perfect.

With an intense wing fling, he heaved the two-pound weight in Drake's direction.

It landed, but . . .

A female screamed.

Mudspike wiped his stinging eyes, sure he'd. . .

The girl from earlier lay crumpled on the floor, her friend beside her. The shawl Mudspike had known belonged to the slave's master stuck to the girl's head, embedded in her skull by the iron weight that had struck her.

I did that. I didn't mean to. Nothing would've happened if she'd stopped Drake like I told her. These slaves need to learn their place, or they'll all end up like this stupid ground-scraper.

Mudspike shoved past the bleeding slave's friend, his mind no longer on the girl he'd injured but on the prey she'd helped him lose.

"Oh, no, Minty," was all he heard before taking to the sky.

Minty knew she'd been hurt. Badly.

She recalled walking to the dry goods store with the cook, Piper, a chatty woman around Soph's age of twenty-two. Minty enjoyed Piper's company. Her sweet nature made their time in Mistress Naddra's aviary bearable.

She also recalled a husky Birdfolk male, a runaway, he'd told them when Minty paused at the entrance to the dry goods store, causing the man to knock her into Piper. Despite having taken Mistress Naddra's shoulder shawl to cover her bushel basket–looking hair, Minty was ashamed to be seen in town with slave rags and hair that had never known a comb's touch. But Mistress Naddra had placed an order at Orveis Dry Goods, so Minty and Piper had gone with a strict directive to "Get my new frocks and return home with haste."

The "Or else" had gone unsaid. But Minty had interpreted the warning correctly, just as she had the runaway's advice when he'd told her, "Gryphon slave catchers don't like to run. Big temper but little breath. Remember that."

At the time, she had known better than to follow the runaway into the store. But once Piper had crossed the threshold, she knew she couldn't allow her to go in there alone. Minty should have, though, because when that gryphon slave catcher had yelled at her to "Stop him," a nauseating wave of banked urging flooded her small body.

She yearned for the freedom the runaway dared to claim for himself. For bright, blissful seconds, she envisioned herself joining the older man, taking her life in her hands for the first time, and fleeing captivity.

Minty hadn't, of course. She couldn't. So, she moved from in front of the door instead of making herself an unwilling barrier to the bird shifter's mad dash for freedom.

Yes, Minty remembered everything that proceeded the pain . . . and the blood. So much of both. But the minutes that followed, the hours, the days, and the weeks were not tracked as easily. They threaded together like a virtueless tapestry of wicked inhumanity and cruel apathy.

Split skull. No medical attention.

She danced.

Split skull. Bloody sweat.

She cleaned.

Split skull. Pounding headaches.

She danced.

Split skull. Sleeping episodes.

Split skull. Sickness. No energy.

Wasting away.

No medical attention. No medical . . . returned to Mistress Essodel's aviary.

Minty despised giving her mother reasons to weep over her, yet in less than a decade she'd been returned to Rit in a near-death state twice. A parent shouldn't have to nurse their child back to health only to have them ripped from their protective embrace repeatedly.

No, Minty recalled very little of the time immediately following her head injury, and the aftereffects would plague her for the rest of her days.

But she finally understood God's will, and it wasn't for Birdfolk to be slaves. God's message was clear, and Araminta Wren would heed the divine decree by any means necessary.

My children, I have ordained the path of liberty for all souls. It is my will that the shackles of servitude be broken so the oppressed may rise to embrace their freedom. Let this message resound across the ages: slaves shall find their rightful place in the sunlit realms of liberation, for I am the God of Justice, and in my name, they shall be free.

PART III

"I HAD REASONED THIS OUT IN MY MIND; THERE WAS ONE OF TWO THINGS I HAD A RIGHT TO, LIBERTY, OR DEATH; IF I COULD NOT HAVE ONE, I WOULD HAVE THE OTHER; FOR NO MAN SHOULD TAKE ME ALIVE; I SHOULD FIGHT FOR MY LIBERTY AS LONG AS MY STRENGTH LASTED, AND WHEN THE TIME CAME FOR ME TO GO, THE LORD WOULD LET THEM TAKE ME."

Chapter 13

I Hate Them with Everything I Am

1836

Essodel Plantation

"You shortsighted piece of worthless dragon scale." *Whoosh.*

Breembat stumbled backward, falling on his backside and barely avoiding Gyzad's fist. A tic in his jaw twitched, and his nostrils flared. Breembat glared at his older brother, letting him see every inch of his anger.

"Stay down and don't say anything, or I'll pummel your stupid scale-brain from here all the way to the other side of Mother's mountain."

The tic in his jaw spasmed harder, faster, just as his heart raced with thudding humiliation so fierce it tightened his throat and stilled his tongue.

Breembat's darkened mood matched the blackness of the cave's walls that led him to Essodel's lair. But the magnificent brightness of her hoard showed the way as clearly as last night's luminous full moon did when he was in downtown Berzogtown stumbling toward his favorite saloon and searching for a less-than-genteel Dragonkin female to share more than drinks.

Before him, Essodel reclined, surrounded by a hoard wasted on an old dragon who cared more for her solitude than wielding her power and wealth. One of these days, Breembat told himself, he would be rid of his family. All that stood between him and getting everything he deserved in life, including from underneath Essodel's gray, clawed feet, was a solitary dragon.

Gyzad.

Breembat snarled at Gyzad but knew it wasn't time to challenge his brother, especially not in front of their mother. But that didn't mean he would permit Gyzad the high ground, so he jumped to his feet, dusted himself off, and took solace in Essodel's silence at their unscheduled visit.

"Gyzad dragged me in here after the slave service. I reminded him that you like to take a nap afterward, but . . ."

A pile of gold coins that shouldn't have been large enough to accommodate the massive chin of a dragon held firm when Essodel raised her head—a graceful yet terrifying motion. Twin gray eyes watched him with a cold mix of disinterest and disappointment.

"What has Breembat done this time, Gyzad? Come closer, son, and tell me all."

She watches me but also acts as if I'm not here. One of these days, Mother, I'll come to you with news that will break your putrid heart. What will you do then? Who will you turn to? Who but me will you be able to trust then?

As compliant as ever, Gyzad did as told, a chilling reminder that little had changed since they were hatchlings. Gyzad reported all Breembat's misdeeds while hiding his own so well that Breembat was always the one caught out. Even when they plotted together, Gyzad knew Breembat well enough to trust that he wouldn't put himself on the wrong side of Essodel's anger just to bring hell down on him.

As always, that left Breembat to stand behind his smug brother as he snitched his way deeper into Essodel's clutches.

"As you know, there isn't always enough work around here for the number of ground-scrapers we have. But that doesn't stop the bills from piling up."

Breembat felt Essodel's unwavering gaze as if there were volcanic-hot pokers wedged under his scales. When her voice sounded in his mind, her tone was like a lance of impatience across the edges of his brain.

"I am aware, Gyzad. We've had this discussion before. But I will not part with a piece of my hoard, including my ground-scrapers. Make do with what I have already granted you both."

"Yes, of course." Gyzad shifted even closer, stepping on fine jewels that, if Essodel got her way, would never again see the light of day. "But you granted us permission to rent out the ground-scrapers, which we've done to keep the estate and aviary going."

"Do get to the point of your intrusion. And do not dare step on that feathered crown before you. I ripped it off the head of a Sankofa king from a Birdfolk kingdom in west Sika. I can no longer recall how he tasted. But I remember every transparent diamond and golden weaved band in his crown."

Breembat felt as grateful as a fox who'd escaped a gryphon bored with the hunt when Essodel peeled her eyes from him. They traveled to every inch of her sprawling lair, and he knew she searched for the other crowns she had claimed, precious spoils of war for a Dragonkin as ancient as Essodel.

Gyzad halted, lowering his foot to avoid contact with the Sika crown. But Breembat tracked his mother, chronicling each time she settled on a spot in the cave, emitting a low hum of sound when she located something that pleased her.

Breembat might have wanted Essodel's entire hoard, but he would settle for a few curated pieces, especially the jinn lamp she coveted most of all.

If I possessed that lamp, I could rule this entire continent. I would be King Breembat, The Powerful One. Yes, that has a nice ring to it.

"My point, Mother, is that Breembat chooses poorly." An accusatory thumb pointed over Gyzad's shoulder and toward Breembat, who'd peeled his eyes from the tenth Birdfolk royal crown he'd spied in time to witness his brother's betrayal. "Whether dragon or harpy, every rentee fails to grasp what will happen to them if they break your rules."

"I'm not responsible for what happened to your precious Ben's daughter." He used his foot to shove a cluster of golden nuggets out of his way, secretly hoping he would catch a glimpse of the jinn lamp. "It was your incompetent gryphon slave catcher who hit the girl with the weight."

"Mudspike was doing his job. I've never had a successful slave escape. My mine brings in a profit every quarter, and my ground-scrapers know what will happen to them if they break the rules." Gyzad shoved Breembat, a physical assault to match his arrogance. "But your lowly rentees can't do something as basic as taking care of someone else's property."

"My contracts are—"

"*Quiet!*" The single word boomed in the cavernous space like foreboding thunder on a clear summer's day.

Breembat shook his head, feeling a stream of wetness flowing from both ears. Looking at Gyzad, he noticed Essodel's loud command had a worse effect on him because of his closer proximity. Blood trickled from Gyzad's ears and nostrils, but Essodel either didn't notice or care because she repeated the command.

Louder. Fiercer.

Breembat dropped to his knees, covering his ears and wishing, not for the first time, that his mother had grown less formidable in her old age instead of unaccountably stronger.

Gyzad collapsed beside him, and the child dragon inside Breembat, who once revered his older brother, felt sorry for him because Gyzad had spent his entire life seeking Essodel's respect. He hadn't earned it and never would, yet Gyzad hadn't accepted that unfortunate but obvious truth.

But not Breembat. No Dragonkin amassed a hoard the size of Essodel's or her warrior titles without also having defeated beings of immense strength. He couldn't imagine what respect would look like to someone of Essodel's caliber, but he sure knew it did not take the face of a no-title dragon like Gyzad.

"Tell me who."

Breembat understood the simple sentence to mean which of Essodel's Birdfolk had been injured. If it had been one of her plain bird shifters, even Gyzad would not have bothered revealing the injury to Essodel. But they both knew the high value Essodel placed on servants like the Wrens.

It was why he could charge so much for each Wren rental, especially for the Minty girl. But Gyzad's reckless gryphon slave catcher had made Minty virtually worthless. Breembat had even tried to sell her to recoup his losses. However, no one would take her off his hands. One prospective buyer even went so far as to tell him that the girl wasn't "worth a sixpence."

Laid out on the floor in Essodel's lair, his fuming mother above him, aware one of her prized Sankofa Birdfolk had been injured and ignored, Breembat was grateful he hadn't been able to sell the girl. Essodel didn't like the tiny ground-scraper so much as she fancied anything rare and lovely.

Minty Wren was both. In time, Breembat thought the girl would heal, but with the severity of her head injury, he doubted she could ever again be used as a dancer.

That wasn't something he wanted to confess to Essodel. Instead, he unfurled from the tight ball her stomach-clenching command had forced him into and stared up at her with concealed detestation but open fear.

"One of Rit's. The prettiest of her flock," Breembat swiftly added before Essodel roared the natural follow-up question in his head.

He saw Gyzad roll away from him from the corner of his eye. He wouldn't have known where his brother had moved if it weren't for the clinking sound of gold coins being shifted.

Gyzad had moved to the opening that led to Essodel's lair.

He started this. Now he thinks he can leave me here to deal with Mother alone. But she isn't paying Gyzad any mind. As always, all her ire is for me. Go on then, brother. But I'll be seeing you again soon. Just know that you've earned what you've got coming.

Heavy footfalls raced away, a thudding punctuation of revenge years in the making.

However, Breembat shouldn't have shifted his attention away from Essodel and to Gyzad. Not even for a second. He knew better, but the taste of retribution had been so strong on his tongue, like 200-proof whiskey straight out of the bottle, that he'd forgotten.

Smash. Smash.

A heavy-clawed foot slammed onto his head, forcing him under pounds of suffocating gold and jewels.

Smash. Smash.

His eardrums burst, his jaw cracked, and his skull split. The brutal attack forced his transformation.

Breembat shifted into a dragon form, barely a third of Essodel's. Bigger and stronger, he stood on four legs. But they trembled like dragon fire caught in a deadly hurricane.

Smack.

Breembat went flying. The rugged, crisp flick of Essodel's wing sent him across the cave. He slammed into the opposing wall, whimpering on impact and gasping for breath.

He didn't dare move. He wasn't sure if he could.

"When I see you thus, I regret not devouring your egg. Gyzad is little better. Smarter and more obedient, yes, but no less weak for having me as your scale donor. Keep to the sermons. Make sure my ground-scrapers understand their place. Make sure they worship God the way we see fit."

A large gray wing covered half of his body, from an aching head to a constricting stomach, like a frozen blanket in winter. Essodel didn't push down, but it was unnecessary because the sheer weight of her thick wing reinforced her point well enough.

Breembat got it. He was weak, but she was strong.

Still, he was neither unintelligent nor without cunning.

"From this day forward, Gyzad has full control of my aviary. Sales, rentals, and punishments are all his responsibilities. Yours is the ministering of my Birdfolk's souls. Keep them compliant. Ignorant. The divine hereafter will be their reward for serving us well." The wing pressed ever so slightly, but enough for an already throbbing rib to crack. *"Do you understand?"*

He did. Breembat understood the pecking order, and his place was barely above that of Essodel's favored ground-scrapers.

"Yes, Mother, I understand perfectly," Breembat responded with every ounce of feigned obedience he could muster. But deep in his heart, where envy and greed coiled like a venomous snake waiting to strike, Breembat's true reply dwelled.

Vengeance is mine. I will repay, saith the Lord.

"I can help." To prove her point, Minty leapt to her feet only to feel a firm hand yank her back to the cabin steps.

Linah's warm but resolute "Be still" should've had her obeying without question.

"I can—"

"You can't."

"I'm fourteen," Minty grumbled, as if the twenty-eight-year-old mother of two was the one whose skull had been split, fracturing her memory along with her head. "Kessiah is at the big house, so she can't help you with little Harriet. But I can. I can show her the simple dance steps. I remember them," she added with a look that dared her eldest sister to insult her again.

Minty sat beside her sister on the second step of Linah's family home. She wore one of Soph's hand-me-down dresses, which she didn't mind because, when the wind blew just right, Minty could smell Soph's reassuring scent—earthy oakmoss after a warm rain shower.

"Momma, watch me."

Three-year-old Harriet twirled and twirled, her gap-toothed smile growing each time she performed the move correctly, and Linah nodded her approval.

Minty remembered when she used to do the same with Rit, loving the feeling of her mother's praise. Nothing in life compared to making her parents happy. She would do almost anything to have them grin at her like Linah did little Harriet. But lately, their looks were tinged with concern wrapped in anger.

"You're still healin'," Linah said, surprising Minty when she resumed their conversation. "Being fourteen just means Minister Breembat might now consider you for breedin' since you're no good to any of them dragons as a dancer anymore."

"Momma. Momma."

"I'm watchin', baby. I see you. Don't forget to bow at the end of the third twirl. Good. Do that move ten more times."

"She can't count to ten. And you're tryin' to scare me. I won't be nobody's breeder." Sucking in a deep breath and praying her bold seed words would sprout into the truth, Minty crossed her arms over her chest.

"Harriet is named after our momma, so she can do whatever she puts her mind to."

"But not me?"

"Especially you, but not until you fully heal. You haven't, so you can't help me teach Harriet to dance for Essodel or anyone else. I won't have you passin' out on me again. I won't do that to Momma, and I won't allow you to do that to yourself."

"Master Gyzad is in charge, not Minister Breembat."

"That's your response to everything I've said?"

"Yes, ma'am. I won't be no breeder. You just tryin' to scare me."

Minty didn't protest when Linah tugged her arms from where she had them crossed over a chest that had grown noticeably larger. Last year, she bled for the first time, even more evidence that she was no longer a little girl.

But why did she still feel like one, especially with Linah and her parents?

Minty sank into her sister's embrace because she desired it as much as Harriet craved Linah's appreciation.

"I'm not tryin' to frighten you but to prepare you for what could come. I know Master Gyzad is in charge now, but I don't trust Minister Breembat to do right by any of us." Linah kissed the side of Minty's head, a warm breath inches from her injury. "It's not an insult to say you aren't the same after what happened to you. It's not your fault, and nobody blames you. But Dragonkin only cares about what we Birdfolk slaves can do for them."

Despite her protestations to the contrary, Minty's days of twirling, dipping, and jumping with anything resembling grace were behind her. She'd tried and failed. Repeatedly. Still, she refused to accept whatever Master Gyzad or Minister Breembat had planned for her. Surely, there was something she could do that did not involve her supplying Mistress Essodel with the next generation of Sankofa slaves.

Linah kissed her head again, closer to the injury that nearly claimed her life. "Choose your fate, Minty, before they choose it for you."

"I get to choose?"

Slaves don't choose. Wait, that runaway at the dry goods store did. He decided to be free. God wants us all to be free.

"Minister Breembat tried to sell me." Minty spoke against Linah's shoulder, accepting her sister's babying despite their adult conversation. "He kept bringin' people to Momma's cabin to examine me. But they all left after gettin' a good look." Before she could stop them, tears fell, and the pain she'd been holding inside flooded from her, too. "They said mean things, Linah. Called me ugly, skinny, worthless."

"Momma? Minty?"

"It's all right, baby. Aunt Minty is a little sad, but she'll be fine. Come give her a hug."

"Lies," Minty heard Linah whisper in her ear a second before tiny feet thudded on the step beside her. "Vile lies."

A forehead fell against the center of Minty's back, and two tiny hands fisted the sides of her dress. "Vile lies," Harriet said, repeating Linah's words with a child's loving innocence.

"They think they can take everything from us. But where would any of them be without us? Our labor? Our skills? Our smarts? Nowhere, that's where."

As if choreographed, Linah's and Harriet's holds on Minty tightened.

"Don't cry, Aunt Minty."

She didn't want to, but . . . Minty clutched Linah close, truly afraid of the unknown but grateful she wouldn't have to face the future alone. Linah would be there, as she always was when Minty and the family needed her. The least Minty could do, she reasoned, withdrawing from Linah and wiping her wet nose with the back of her hand, was to become stronger so she wouldn't be a burden.

"Maybe Poppa could use me in the mine."

Mine work wasn't performed by someone of Minty's small stature, which everyone, including Linah, knew. So, her sister's words surprised her.

"Good idea."

"Really?" Minty perked up, displacing Harriet, who she had a sneaking suspicion was about to turn her hug into a piggyback ride.

"You're small enough to fit into tight places the bigger Birdfolk can't. You're also reliable and smart, meanin' you'll learn quickly and well."

"I am?" Whatever tears she'd shed, defining herself as worthless because she'd listened to the heartless opinion of others, retreated under Linah's honest assessment of Minty.

"You're a Wren; of course you are." Linah's hand settled beside Minty's injury, and she knew she placed it there deliberately. "You are small, Minty, and you'll likely always be shorter than the average Birdfolk. But that doesn't mean you can't strengthen your body and your mind. Mine work will be unlike anything you've done before. You'll also be farther away from Momma and the rest of us."

Minty didn't like that idea despite spending extended time away from home throughout her childhood. But if she went to live with Ben, she would at least be near her father and the free Birdfolk community in Pelduth Neck. Perhaps that was part of what Linah meant by strengthening her mind.

"Let's play, Aunt Minty." Harriet tugged her hand until she gave in and stood. Then the three-year-old was off, naked and unbothered by her nudity as Minty had been at that age.

"You used to run just like that. A wild thing without a care in the world."

Minty could hear the wistfulness in Linah's voice as clearly as she could feel the emotion throughout her battered and scarred body.

"Were we ever children?" she asked Linah.

Grasping her about the waist and pulling Minty to her, Linah kissed her cheek and held her close. Like Soph, her scent reminded Minty of earthy oakmoss, not the way it smelled after a cleansing rain shower but during a hearty snowfall instead. "Barely."

Much went unsaid with the six-letter word, but more wasn't required. Life of an enslaved Birdfolk left little room for the privilege of being a child.

"I love you, Linah." Minty didn't say those words enough, but she meant them from the depths of her soul.

Another kiss on her cheek was Minty's soft, warm reward. "I love you, too. You've grown up nicely, and I can't wait to see what you become in full bloom." Linah swatted her bottom, two playful taps that had Minty giggling. "Now go get my wild child and bring her back here. It's time for her nap." Linah paused. "And yours."

"That's not fair. You said I was a grown-up. Grown-ups don't take naps."

"They do when they're sick."

"I'm not . . ." Minty lifted her head from her chest. A great weight of exhaustion had her stumbling to the cabin steps and sitting before her knees gave out.

"Minty. Minty." Linah's voice was lower than a scream but louder than a conversational tone.

"Did it happen again?"

"Two minutes, this time. Maybe three. You just stopped talking, and your head fell forward. I thought you would drop to the ground, but you just stood there like you were asleep."

"I don't feel rested." Minty never did after one of her "sleeping" episodes. "I feel achy like I've been up all night working. I guess you're right about that nap. I need one." With Linah's help, Minty got to her feet. "Sorry I couldn't help with Harriet, but I know if I tried to get her now, you'd have a fit and start actin' like Momma Linah."

"You almost died."

The gravely whispered fact hung between the sisters like a fly caught in a spider's web.

"Some days, Minty, I hate them with everything I am."

Minty's response, though spoken softly, came quickly and was deeply felt as the weight that had nearly stolen her life. "So do I."

Chapter 14

A Sweet, Honest Girl

1837
Pelduth Neck

"Where are you off to in a hurry?"

At the sound of Ben's deep, inquisitive voice, Minty halted. Hands fisted in her dress pockets, and mere inches from making her escape from their cabin home, Minty shuffled her feet to face her father.

At forty-nine, Benjamin Wren's intelligent eyes were as dark as any bay horse Minty had seen Minister Breembat ride, showing off in a way her father never did. But whereas the rich darkness of his eyes once matched the thick onyx of his hair, the decades-long unforgiving sunup to sundown labor that marked his life as a slave had produced patches of persistent gray at his temples.

While his body appeared as strong and fit as ever, with defined muscles that flexed with the simplest of tasks, Minty's time away from her parents meant that at each reunion, she saw them with both old and new eyes. The former image would be replaced by the recent truth of the limping passage of time.

Growing older wasn't the domain of the young, Minty reminded herself, and neither was hunger. So, Minty cataloged the rapid beating of her heart and willed it to slow to a staid pulse.

"I'm gonna help Ms. Dorane with the evenin' meal."

"You've been doin' that a lot lately. Work all day in the mine, then cook with Dorane." Ben reached for Minty, and she went, forever grateful to Master Gyzad for permitting her to live with Ben and work in the mine despite her petite stature and sleeping spells. Ben's warm lips settled against Minty's cool forehead. "Don't think I haven't noticed you bringin' home food from Master Gyzad's kitchen." Another kiss to her forehead. "It ain't your responsibility to make sure your old man gets enough to eat."

"I know, Poppa, but . . ."

Ben pulled Minty to him, his hug of gratitude as fierce as Minty's desire to help and protect her parents. At fourteen, and with the lingering effects from her head injury, Minty knew she was limited in many ways but that she was also neither weak nor helpless.

"Watch out for that harpy, Minty. Anybody who voluntarily spends time with Mudspike has questionable judgment and can't be trusted."

Pulling back to look up at her father, Minty wondered if Ben had noticed what else she'd taken from the mine. When he didn't confront her, she considered unburdening herself and telling him the truth.

"Poppa, I—"

Ben's stomach growled. Loudly. He stepped away, laughing and shaking his head. Both were signs of embarrassment she knew well.

"What were you gonna say?"

"Ummm, only that I should get goin'. Ms. Dorane is waitin'."

"Yeah, you best get. Master Gyzad likes his dinner on time and pipin' hot."

"Yes, sir." Minty darted out of the cabin, hating deceiving her father but despising the inadequate weekly food rations Master Gyzad granted the hard-working Ben even more. None of the mine workers were compensated with enough food to offset their grueling labor.

The biting wind hit Minty the second she exited the cabin, sending a blast of cold air through a dress made more for frolicking in a summer garden than fighting back what smelled like the first snow of winter. Grateful for the pair of boots Ben had scavenged for her, Minty decided that having warm, protected toes was preferable to returning home to retrieve her shawl and hat only if it meant risking the lie she'd spent two months reinforcing. Crossing arms over her chest and running from the aviary of the mining camp and toward Master Gyzad's two-story home, Minty reasoned that, for her lies of omission, she deserved to suffer winter's wrath.

From one step to the next, Minty prayed she wouldn't black out or, worse, have another seizure. With how fast she ran, she feared she'd fall, adding another injury to a body that needed no more evidence of the horrors of slave life. But no sooner than she had the thought to slow down, lest she give Ben another medical reason to worry about her, then she . . .

Oomph.

Minty stumbled backward, yet her too-big but sturdy boots helped her regain her balance before her soft bottom met the hard ground. "Sorry," she said, looking down at her feet instead of at the person she'd plowed into. "Sorry, I didn't mean to—"

"Well, look who it is. Ben's worthless fledgling."

Minty recognized the rough, cruel voice as much as she did the stench of sulfur and feces that clung to his matted lion's fur. She refused to look at Mudspike, much less give him a reason to extend his verbal insult to outright physical bullying. So, Minty clamped her mouth shut and waited for him to either step out of her way and let her pass or continue with his usual curses and complaints.

"Every time I see your worthless hide, I'm taken back to that day at the general store." Mudspike's golden-brown tail swung around, snapping so close to Minty's face that she feared he'd take an eye along with her pride. "Thanks to you, I almost lost my quarry and my job that day. The arrogant Master Gyzad would've fired me if that ground-scraper had gotten away."

The dark, hairy tuft of his tail slid across Minty's cheek. While Mudspike hadn't pressed hard enough for her to feel the spur, Minty knew his tuft concealed a clawlike nail sharp enough to slice open her delicate skin.

She planted her feet, relaxed her shoulders, and prayed the onlookers would not try to help her by seeking out Ben. The other enslaved Birdfolk were older than Minty. Surely, they knew any confrontation between Ben and Mudspike would end badly for her father, even if he managed to defeat the gryphon.

Twisting her head slightly to the right, she caught the dark, piercing gaze of the twenty-nine-year-old Barbury. He leaned against the side of the wagon Ben used when he went into town for supplies. The general store where Minty had that fateful encounter with Mudspike no longer stood.

Apparently, soon after her incident, the building caught fire and burned to the ground.

While Minty held neither fondness for the general store nor its owner, she did care what happened to the good Birdfolk of this mining camp, including Barbury, who watched Mudspike with open hatred.

The dark tuft swatted across her face, drawing her attention back to Mudspike instead of to a bloody wound the spur was capable of inflicting.

"Barbury is the strong silent type." Mudspike lowered his eagle's head, his long, sharp beak inches from her ear. "He couldn't get away from me either."

Minty's gaze shot back to where she'd last seen Barbury. But darkness threatened to consume the space where he'd been.

Mudspike's beak opened, a silent threat to slice her neck the way someone had Barbury's, leaving the man mute.

"Sixteen, if a day, when he ran. I caught him before he reached Pyzai. I'll catch you, too, if you ever try the same. Even if you try to kill yourself the way he did, I'll still drag your body back here to claim my bounty." Mudspike's beak snapped closed, and Minty nearly wet herself. "Dead or alive, little ground-scraper. Whether dead or alive, I get my money. Remember that the next time you stand between me and my prey."

Tears filled eyes that were still cast to where Barbury had been. Minty blinked away the traitorous tears, yet they returned, even as Mudspike shifted around her, finally giving her leave.

Minty took it.

She ran. A constricted sob escaped, a stuttering hiccup of sound given free rein. It galloped around her, gaining momentum until . . . Minty rushed through the back door and into Master Gyzad's kitchen.

The flicker of candle flames bounced off the walls and onto Dorane's partially feathered face; her feather-winged brows were pinched, and her thin human lips tight. Bright golden eyes blinked down at Minty as if deciding whether her sudden appearance was a welcome to be accepted or an annoyance to be tolerated.

"What have I told you about running in here like a chicken with its head cut off?"

Minty never liked that saying because it was too close to how some slave owners treated captured runaway Birdfolk when they cared more about sending a threatening message to the other slaves in their aviary than sparing the life of a rebellious runaway.

Deciding Dorane's question was more of an invitation to stay and proceed as they did most nights, Minty removed her dirty boots. This subconscious habit had been beaten into her by unremarkable yet unforgettable temporary masters.

Minty sat at one of two stools at the butcher block table. She no longer required a stool to reach the table, as she had when she was six and cooked for the Calis harpy family. But the blue-winged harpy before her exhibited none of Mistress Theria Callis's cruelty or pretension. So, Minty relaxed atop the stool, confident she wouldn't be whipped for taking such a liberty.

She glanced around the kitchen, spying several waning candles and two oil lamps, but little evidence that she had interrupted Dorane's meal prep.

"You're a smart girl." Dorane joined her at the table, careful not to sit on her long wings when she claimed the stool at the opposite end of the table. "Smart and observant." A single finger, more human than a bird claw, pointed to a cloth-covered basket in the center of the table. "It ain't much, but there's bread, cheese, and a few leftover apples. I planned to give you more fruit, but Master Gyzad commanded I cook two apple pies for a Dragonkin wench he's courting."

Minty glanced around again, realizing she neither smelled Master Gyzad nor heard anyone else in the home.

"Just us girls tonight."

Any day she could stay off a Dragonkin's radar was a good day, Minty thought, so she nodded, already planning what meal she'd make Ben and herself with Dorane's gift. The thought of the exchange reminded Minty she hadn't upheld her part of the bargain for the basket of food.

Digging into her dress pockets, Minty extracted two items, handing both over to Dorane.

Minty rarely thought much about another person's physical appearance. Their level of attractiveness wasn't nearly as important as their degree of kindness. But each time Minty presented Dorane with a piece of layered mineral from the mine, her smile could only be defined as beautiful.

"You're gettin' better at this. Choosin' with a bird's keen eyes." Dorane held up one of the mineral chunks, displaying it in her open palm. "When I first asked you to retrieve these, you would bring me whatever you could find."

"Dragon Liver mineral." Minty had never heard of it before moving to the mining camp and meeting Dorane.

"An odd name, I know. To most people, includin' to young Dragonkin like Master Gyzad, this mineral is worthless."

Again with that word. Minty did not understand why anyone thought it necessary to define things in life by their subjective standard of worth.

"I learned much at my grandmother's clawed feet. See here, Minty. This first layer, the red one, is called Demon Fire. The black and gray second layer is known as Hellhound Fur." Dorane used the pointed nail of her left index finger to touch the red-black spotted third layer. "This one is Ghost Heart."

Minty enjoyed learning new information, and she found Dorane to be an endless source. Yet, most of what she shared went over Minty's head, especially when her stories turned wistful. Dorane's focus was primarily on harpy culture and not the Dragonkin lifestyle that dominated their lives.

"Why are they called that?"

"They aren't. But that's my best translation."

"Oh, I see." She didn't, but Dorane either didn't notice or mind because the harpy continued to smile at the mineral chunk, fueling Minty's pride in how well she'd chosen. She scooted to the edge of the stool, grateful for this quiet time yet anxious to return home to Ben. Between Minister Breembat and Master Gyzad, they'd robbed Ben of much of Minty's childhood, forcing him to live apart from his family and her with the likes of the Calises.

"I see you squirmin' over there." Dorane's oddly conspiratorial laughter rippled over the basket of food. "Give me what else you have for me, then you can go."

"Right." Minty dug into one of her dress pockets again, fingered the final item to make the bread, cheese, and apples all hers, and then handed it to Dorane.

"One of your blue feathers." The grin that seemed fixed grew that much larger. "My favorite color. Thank you."

"Are you gonna sell that one, too?"

For the briefest of moments, Minty swore she saw Dorane's smile falter.

"They are quite valuable. What else would I do with them but sell to the highest bidder?"

A part of Minty wanted to think of the older female as a trusted friend. But each time she traded one of her feathers for food, she was reminded of her true worth to Dragonkin and Harpyfolk.

Minty sensed there was much left unsaid with Dorane's answer, just as she knew there was a reason the harpy wanted the Dragon Liver mineral chunks that had little to do with them being "rare" and "beautiful," as

Dorane often mused when she spoke of her desire to have "as many as you can bring me."

Stowing her curiosity and deeming the knowledge dangerous to a long life expectancy, Minty jumped from the stool and snatched up the basket.

"The next time you come, bring me more chunks like these two, and I'll refill that basket with twice as much."

"Another blue feather?"

"No. The balance needs to be perfect. Three pink ones should get me there. At least for now."

Minty did not want to know what she meant by that, no more than she relished plucking her feathers and bartering them away. But survival came before pride, so Minty nodded, accepting Dorane's terms.

The harpy pushed to her feet, her blue wings a lush magnificence that had likely never been used to fill someone else's pockets with coins.

Dorane lowered her eyes to Minty's head, and she was reminded that everyone in the mining camp knew what had transpired between her and Mudspike.

"I'd say that bushel basket hair saved your life."

Minty agreed, but Dorane wasn't entitled to any part of Minty other than the bartered feathers, so she placed the basket on the floor, pulled on her boots, and didn't reply.

"I like you, Minty. You're a sweet, honest girl. But being too much of either will have you in an early grave or a slave for the rest of your days."

A cold shudder of dread passed through Minty, stilling her fingers on the bootlaces.

"One of these days, I'll show you how to make a special concoction."

"Concoction?" Compelling her fingers to work, Minty tied her laces and then rose, making sure to grab the basket of food.

"Maybe it's better for you to think of it as special seasoning used in food for Dragonkin."

Minty had no interest in learning how to make food taste better for Dragonkin, so she again chose silence over a reply. Besides, the day grew long, the evening colder, and Minty's patience short.

"Until next time, little Minty."

"Bye, Miss Dorane." Unlike the mad rush into the house, Minty exited with calm, measured steps. However, she took but a few before someone joined her on the path. One hand settled on a shoulder, while the other held a knife he should not have. "Evenin', Barbury."

As protective as her oldest brother, Robert, Barbury walked Minty home, and Mudspike was nowhere to be seen.

Minty had many questions for Barbury, none of which she was bold enough to ask or him capable of replying. Still, he'd run away and survived the ordeal. There had to have been glory in the effort, an affirmation of self even in the face of capture and punishment.

In the following months, Minty looked forward to their silent walks and his reassuring presence at her side. Dorane even kept her word to teach Minty how to make the special Dragonkin seasoning. It was then she realized the harpy had lied about more than selling Minty's feathers.

But some secrets should never see the light of day.

Chapter 15
You're a Cruel Harpy

1837
Pelduth Neck

Until several weeks ago, Ben never had a reason to enter Master Gyzad's bedchamber. However, the first time he did, he wasn't surprised by the furnishings because they matched the rest of the home—a hodgepodge collection by a several-hundred-year-old Dragonkin with an insatiable need to hoard.

However, unlike Mistress Essodel's carefully curated hoard, Master Gyzad's tastes seemed less exacting. Or rather, he had a penchant for paintings of old-world dragons, handwoven carpets with fire motifs, and books about Dragonkin lore that overflowed his library. For an unknown reason, Master Gyzad also collected decorative teapots from around the world and from different periods.

While Ben knew Master Gyzad was fond of showing off his teapot collection to his current lover, affecting a false air of civility, he rarely saw the male with a book.

Master Gyzad's chosen hoard, Ben realized, was subjective to the beholder, making them either a wasted purchase or a brilliant investment. Although, with what Ben knew of Master Gyzad, he doubted the dragon shifter had engaged in an honest exchange to acquire a single piece in his collection. Even Ben himself had been gifted to Master Gyzad.

Ben leaned against the doorframe of Master Gyzad's bedchamber, staying out of the way but near enough to assist if needed.

"His liver has ruptured." The Dragonkin physician, nine feet tall and dressed in a perfectly fitted black suit with a white shirt, looked over his shoulder at Ben, who promptly pushed from the doorframe, awaiting the male's command. But only a pained expression crossed his face, a stubbled rigid jaw set against narrowed green eyes and a pinched brow. "Mistress Essodel won't be pleased with my report."

Ben knew that much but did not understand the reasoning behind Master Gyzad's failure to shift into his more potent form. Surely, if he did so, the might of his dragon body would fix anything ailing his human one. That was true even for Birdfolk, despite the result being less potent than the Dragonkin's.

"He should shift." The moment the words exited, Ben regretted uttering his thoughts aloud.

Dr. Vairco swung to face Ben. His irises turned a darker green, revealing more of the reptile hidden inside the human facade. "Birdfolk know nothing of Dragonkin physiology. In what part of your insignificant brain do you think your master wouldn't transform if it were in his power to do so?"

Ben's gaze lingered on Dr. Vairco but slowly shifted to Master Gyzad's prone form in his bed. The physician had asked a rhetorical question, even if it was valid. Of course, Ben hadn't appreciated the insult, no matter how commonplace.

Despite his sizeable human body, Master Gyzad appeared smaller than he'd ever seen the male. Bundled under layers of bedcoverings as exquisite as the carpets he collected, Master Gyzad shivered like a baby bird cast out of its nest onto a frozen lakebed. Smeared, dried blood stained his mouth, and the part of the bedcovering he held clutched in his hands.

Ben had never seen a Dragonkin sick, much less vomit blood and groan in pain the way Master Gyzad had these past few weeks. He wasn't immune to the occasional thought of using violence to exact revenge. He'd desired to kill Minister Breembat for selling away Mariah. He felt the same when he'd learned that Mudspike was responsible for harming his Minty.

Even as he listened to Master Gyzad's wheezing breaths, his pain evident with each forced exhalation, Ben felt a sense of rightness being played out before him. He wouldn't attribute Master Gyzad's illness to the Dragonkin's God because the God whom Minister Breembat preached about was merciful and forgiving of slave masters instead of unsympathetic and vengeful.

"Considering I have no choice but to perform emergency surgery here, I hope you aren't as stupid as you look because I'm going to need your help."

"There's no drug or alcohol I'm aware of that will subdue a Dragonkin." Ben returned his attention to a frowning Dr. Vairco. "I suppose you want me to hold him down."

"You aren't that strong, but you're essentially correct. Go and get help. I'll prepare while you're gone." Dr. Vairco shooed him out of the room with a haughty impatience rivaled only by Mistress Essodel.

Ben went, grabbing the first two people he saw—Dorane and Barbury. They returned with him to Master Gyzad's bedchamber. Ben was grateful it was too early in the day for Minty to have been in the kitchen when he had gone searching for assistance.

Ben had accepted Barbury's glower without insult. Still, the younger man had joined him anyway because they shared the same understanding. A master they knew was better than one they did not. If Master Gyzad died, Ben had no idea what would happen to the enslaved people at the mining camp. Would they be sent to Mistress Essodel's aviary? Be sold to another Dragonkin living in Pelduth Neck? Or worse, shipped off to the Deep South, where slaves were treated even worse.

Dr. Vairco had used Ben's time away to prepare for surgery. He'd stripped Master Gyzad out of his nightshirt, pulled back each window curtain, and lit every candle and lamp in the room. He had also removed every item from the nightstand beside Master Gyzad's bed, replacing them with an assortment of medical tools Ben had no names for other than the basic term of a knife.

The physician's black suit jacket had been hung on the chair's armrest. The sleeves of Dr. Vairco's white shirt were cuffed at his elbows, revealing muscular forearms and veins as thick as a giant garter snake.

Fresh blood ran from Master Gyzad's parted lips, and Ben wondered if he should mention turning the dragon onto his side so he wouldn't choke on his blood. However, unlike his previous unasked-for opinion, Ben kept quiet and waited for the physician to direct him.

Dr. Vairco's commands came fast and furious. He pointed to Dorane first. "Harpy, hand me what I tell you to and sop up the blood when and where I tell you. Got it?"

"Whatever you say."

"Ben, climb onto the bed behind your master. Cradle his head between your knees. Keep him as still as you can. But I also want you to hold his arms down. When I make the first incision, he'll likely react the most. Don't let him buck you off."

Ben didn't waste words on a reply. Instead, he set about securing Master Gyzad the way Dr. Vairco had ordered.

"And you," Dr. Vairco said, speaking to Barbury without looking at him, "keep Master Gyzad's legs still. If you must, use your weight to keep him down by sitting on his thighs. That will leave his middle open and ready for my scalpel."

As if he were breathing for them all, Dr. Vairco inhaled deeply and exhaled slowly. In and out. In and out.

He had mentioned making a report to Mistress Essodel before deciding to operate on Master Gyzad, a telling admission of the severity of Master Gyzad's medical condition.

Perhaps the physician feared, as Ben did, that Master Gyzad wasn't much longer for this world. Certainly not strong enough to last the time it would take for him to travel to Berzogtown to speak with Mistress Essodel. Despite Master Gyzad being his patient, Ben knew, like everyone in the room, that Dr. Vairco would have to answer to Mistress Essodel.

He didn't envy the male that conversation. If he were lucky, Master Gyzad would survive the operation, leaving Mistress Essodel forever in Dr.

Vairco's debt. If he weren't, Ben doubted there was any place the Dragonkin could flee that would protect him from Mistress Essodel's wrath.

Again, he was grateful Minty worked in the mine today instead of in the household. He'd never been able to shield her from much, but he would've from this had she been there.

Ben gripped Master Gyzad's wrists, pinning him to the bed.

Then, the first incision was made.

Master Gyzad's scream was like a baby ripped from its mother's womb—an unnatural wail of inconceivable pain.

Blood gushed from the opening in an erupting tidal wave bent on escaping its confines.

Dr. Vairco swore.

Barbury lowered his eyes.

Ben held Master Gyzad's wrists tighter.

But Dorane, who stood beside the physician, patiently awaiting his directive, watched the blood ooze from Master Gyzad with an expression that radiated neither kindness nor malice. Later, when he would think of the harpy's expression, the best word he would come up with was satisfaction.

While not a slave like Ben, Barbury, Minty, and the dozen more mine workers in the camp, Dorane was an indentured servant. Ben no more knew how Master Gyzad came to own Dorane's contract for her passage across the ocean from her homeland than he knew the balance of the time left on Dorane's contract. But at that moment, when dragon blood flowed over skin gone ghost white, he imagined the female contemplated her life without Master Gyzad in it the same as he did.

"This is worse than I thought." Dr. Vairco used the back of his hand to wipe the perspiration from his forehead. "He was a fool for not seeking professional medical attention because this isn't a new rupture. It's at least a month old. Stupid, prideful dragon. I can't stop the bleeding. None of this makes sense. I should be able to stop the bleeding."

Ben watched Dorane pull shirt after shirt from Master Gyzad's dresser drawers, soaking up an endless river of crimson. One by one, bloody bib shirts were dropped onto the floor, a foreboding configuration of discarded fine linen.

Bloody handprints decorated Dr. Vairco's shirt and pants, feeble attempts to remove the sticky substance.

Ben had never considered himself squeamish, but by the second hour of watching Master Gyzad bleed out, his shallow breaths slowing even as Dr. Vairco's efforts to save his life increased, Ben choked on the sickeningly metallic scent of blood.

He coughed.

The dry aroma of impending death sucked all the fresh air out of the room, leaving behind the foul stench of desperation and defeat.

Barbury climbed off Master Gyzad.

"What are you doing? I didn't give you permission to move."

Even if Barbury could speak, Ben didn't think his response to Dr. Vairco would've been different. Barbury rubbed what had to be aching knees, shrugged, and left.

"He's right." Dorane cleaned her hands with Master Gyzad's favorite brocade vest. "There's nothin' else we can do for him. He doesn't believe in my god, so my prayers won't do him any good." She dropped the once immaculate vest atop the heap of bloodstained clothes. "I'll be of better use in the kitchen."

"Why, when your master can't eat what you prepare?" Dr. Vairco sounded as if the wind had been knocked out of him, reducing the impact of his question to that of a child's petulant whine.

"It's what I'm contracted to do until I'm told otherwise. I'll leave a covered plate for you on the dinin' room table. I hope you will eat up before ridin' out."

"You're a cruel harpy."

"No, I'm an alive harpy." Dorane nodded to Master Gyzad. "But he's a dead dragon."

Dead. Dead. Dead.

The four-letter word slammed from one side of Ben's head to the other, an echo of reality he'd felt under him mere seconds earlier.

Ben stared down at where his knees held Master Gyzad's head in a vise. He relaxed, backed away, and then tried not to stumble when he stood. He could taste Master Gyzad's blood in the air, just as he could still feel the dragon shifter's human head pressed against his bent knees.

Master Gyzad is dead. Dead. Oh my God, my master is dead. Should I feel sadness? What a stupid question. If I felt that way, I wouldn't have to ask. But I've known him my entire life. In his own self-serving way, he stood between my family and the harsher realities of slave life. For that, I'll always be grateful. But I also won't shed a tear for him. Not a single one.

"I'll clean Master Gyzad up and prepare him so he can be presented to his mother."

"Y-you e-expect me to return to Pelduth Neck with the corpse of Mistress Essodel's first hatched son?"

Ben had never heard a Dragonkin stutter with fear, but there Dr. Vairco stood, bloody hands fisted at his side and eyes a putrid green. A part of Ben felt sorry for the physician, which was why he would clean and dress Master Gyzad well so Dr. Vairco could at least present him to Mistress Essodel in a dignified manner.

"But you gotta close him up first."

"I don't need no stupid ground-scraper telling me what to do. Go. Get out of here until I call for you."

Dead. Dead. Dead.

Master Gyzad was gone.

How would Mistress Essodel take the news of her son's passing?

Worse, what would Master Gyzad's death mean for Ben and his family?

Only time would tell.

Chapter 16

MANUMISSION UPON DEATH

The State of Miadar

Essodel bolted through the sky. Fire churned and raged in her belly, heating her insides and fueling her fury. The wretched day had morphed into an abysmal night, so Essodel had erupted from her mountain home, a vain attempt to flee from the very grief that had pierced her scales and burrowed its way into her heart.

"I'm sorry, Essodel, but Gyzad was too far gone for me to save him. Please accept my deepest condolences."

Broad, strong wings flapped with the force of a deafening windstorm. They snapped hard and strong, displacing the air around her. A ripple effect of wind surged outward, exploding birds on contact. Their blood, bones, and feathers disintegrated. The reverberation of Essodel's mighty wings left nothing alive within a hundred-mile radius.

How could this happen?

She dipped low, gliding over a sleeping town that did not exist the last time she'd taken to the sky like this.

How could this have happened?

Dark, quiet roads and silent, neat homes blended in a disgusting tapestry of peace and contentment.

A raging, brutal beast of fire shot from Mistress Essodel's sharp-toothed maw. Streams of molten heat poured from her, scorching roads and obliterating houses.

Why didn't Gyzad inform me of his illness?

Grief gouged at her insides, gnawing and clawing with the intensity of a thousand ravenous birds of prey intent on freeing themselves from her belly with all deliberate speed.

Why didn't anyone tell me before it was too late?

She flew, laying down unrepentant streams of murderous flames.

Grass receded to nothingness. Trees shriveled to unmemorable dark patches. Rivers, lakes, and ponds boiled, forced to relinquish their inhabitants in exploding geysers of unhinged destruction.

Gyzad belonged to me. I did not grant him permission to die. Do you hear me, Gyzad? You did not have my permission to die.

Livestock fled. Children screamed. The elderly cowered.

None were spared.

Essodel's fire claimed them all. More precise than a barbarian's longsword. More savage than a clan of starving hyenas.

She flew and flew. Into slave-owning and free states. Into the Deep South and unorganized territories.

Into Birdfolk aviaries and Harpyfolk villages. Into gryphon woods and sprawling cities.

If dragon fire were tears, Essodel wept her body weight, leaving her exhausted but no less furious. But all rampages eventually ended, and Essodel's long night of fiery debauchery was no different.

She descended into her mountain lair like a cautious spider from a tree to the ground. Essodel expected to find chunks of the mountain littering her home, but an unexpected visitor watched her land instead.

"You're back."

Finding the spot she loved, Essodel reclined atop small hills of gold coins. Tucking wings at her side, she used her tail to draw more gold coins nearer, creating a security blanket from her favorite possessions.

The cruel, grieving mother that was Essodel wanted to lash out, to brutalize the male before her because she was large and mighty and he small and so very weak. But she had already lost a son, so she would not permit grief to cause her to strike down the one that remained.

"I removed the rubble." Breembat peered up at the hole her exit had left in her precious mountain home. "You've made yourself one hell of a skylight, Mother." She detected the forced laughter in his voice. "You're so far down; it'll be no more by the time rain or snow breaches the mountain. So, a beautiful view for a mighty dragon."

To her surprise, she found herself comforted by Breembat's presence, even more so when his trembling hand touched the tip of her warm nose. Essodel could not recall the last time she was voluntarily touched, not even by one of her hatchlings.

Her large head was on the floor, and she was safe at home; Essodel's waning strength left her, and she closed her eyes.

"What's left of Dr. Vairco is in the corner to your left. A snack for when you're next peckish."

Essodel did not recall leaving any parts of the physician unclaimed. Still, she supposed that burning rage had a way of playing tricks on even the mind of a great dragon such as herself.

"I've scheduled Gyzad's funerary rites for Sunday. I'll hold the service at the entrance to your mountain so you can hear." Breembat's soothing left-right stroking stopped. "But it would be nice if you decided to join us."

She had no intention of doing any such thing. Her emotions were not for public consumption.

"I want Gyzad buried in here."

In her thoughtlessness, Essodel hadn't credited what would happen to her son's body when she smashed through the mountain. She had also made sure not to look at the potential damage upon her return. Now . . . *"Is he all right?"*

It was a foolishly worded question considering Gyzad's quite dead state. But she knew Breembat understood her poorly articulated query.

He resumed stroking her nose. The peaceful cadence settled the fire in her belly, cooling her nose and calming her rampaging heart.

"I had one of the ground-scrapers take him to the big house. He'll be properly bathed and swathed in your scales. After the service, I'll return him here for burial."

This meant she had to select and dig a hole for Gyzad's final resting place, and also craft a dragon-scale cocoon for his corpse. Unlike caterpillars who emerged from their cocoons as magnificent butterflies, Dragonkin cocoons were protective vessels that transported the deceased dragon from the living world to the world of everlasting spirits.

"When you next arrive, I'll have prepared both for you." With a gentle nudge of her nose, she displaced Breembat's hand, annoyed by her neediness.

"I guess that means you want me to leave now."

Essodel despised the dejection Breembat hadn't bothered to conceal. But she'd long since stopped caring what her actions meant for others. She thought doing so would shield her from heartache, but Gyzad's untimely death had proven her the fool of the century.

"Investigate your brother's death. I want to know everything."

"What if there is nothing to find?"

Dr. Vairco had asked the same, but she had lashed out at him without giving his question a moment of thought. There was always something to find if one looked long and hard enough.

"I am a patient dragon, Breembat. Patient but unforgiving. I want to know the truth."

Despite her silent rejection, Breembat patted her nose once more before moving to the mouth of her lair.

Breembat had been right. She'd created a stunning skylight. The sun had peaked in the sky, and shafts of its morning glory had driven deep into the mountain, settling on a cleared-away swath of cave floor perfect for her Gyzad.

"Do you need anything, Mother, before I leave?"

Eyes still closed and her traitorous nose missing Breembat's soothing touch, she replied simply: *"I look forward to your eulogy."*

"I'll make you proud."

She doubted it, but Breembat did have a way with words, and he was her only surviving offspring. They had much to discuss, and she would have to trust him more than ever before.

The thought almost unsettled her as much as the alternative of her reentering the world to care for her own affairs. She'd relied on Gyzad for mundane things but couldn't anymore. That left Essodel with only Breembat.

Well, Breembat and a final wish she'd held on to for centuries. As much as she loved Gyzad, Essodel would not sacrifice her final wish to resurrect a son who should've known better than to succumb to a pedestrian illness or, worse, to treachery.

Essodel tracked Breembat's retreat. Halfway to the mouth of the mountain, he whistled a jaunty tune.

1837

Essodel Plantation

"Stand up straight."

Despite Minister Breembat's booming voice and dictatorial presence, Minty did not shrink from the cold sound of his voice. However, she lowered her gaze because she would rather he think she was afraid than glimpse the glow of her guilt.

Feet shuffled around her, including her parents and siblings, who already stood in the position Minister Breembat demanded but, unwilling to evoke his ire, made a show of compliance.

Every bird shifter in Mistress Essodel's aviary had gathered, not at the mouth of the dragon's mountain home, as they had for Master Gyzad's funeral, and as they did each Sunday for service, but in the dirt expanse that connected the slave cabins. As a girl, Minty would run between the cabins, wild and as ignorant of the horrors of slave life as she was naked and hungry. But standing between her sisters Linah and Soph, one enslaved Sankofa bird shifter among nearly a hundred, Minty felt the shift of Master Gyzad's death in the pit of her roiling stomach.

She had no proof of Dorane's involvement in Master Gyzad's illness and eventual death. But her suspicion was as strong as her mouth was shut. Minty knew better than to share her thoughts with anyone, including about the concoction Dorane had taught her to make. Her silence also extended to her parents, particularly to Ben, who she feared would be blamed for Master Gyzad's death simply because he was the dead dragon's overseer and hadn't reported his illness until Master Gyzad was beyond medical intervention.

Minty also hadn't shared Master Gyzad's sickness with anyone, despite his weakening state being fuel for the rumor mill during the long work hours in the mine. Yet, three months later, no culprit had been arrested, Dorane was released from her contract, and Minister Breembat's investigation seemed to have stalled. Although, unlike Minister Breembat's seriousness in his scheduled meeting, Minty hadn't sensed the same focused care when he'd interviewed her about Master Gyzad's final weeks and days. His visits to the mining town and brief interviews with the mine workers seemed more performative than sincere.

But there he stood before them, hands clasped behind his back, hair slicked back with pomade, and his black suit spotless, save for the dust he kicked up each time he marched from one end of the line of enslaved bird shifters to the other.

"That's right, stand up straight. That's the way I like to see you. Strong and able-bodied. You know who is in charge now." Minister Breembat paused, and Minty raised her eyes, only to catch the Dragonkin arch an eyebrow as if waiting for someone to dispute his claim.

No one with an ounce of common sense would, which obviously pleased Minister Breembat because he grinned at them with such self-satisfaction Minty wanted to spit.

"What happened to Master Gyzad was unfortunate. Mistress Essodel and I appreciate your prayers in this time of mourning."

Oh so imperceptibly, Minty felt Soph's shoulder graze hers. While she did not see her sister as often as she liked, their separation hadn't diminished their connection, even silent ones. Minty understood Soph's message. Not a single member of the Wren family, much less the aviary, had prayed for the un–dearly departed Master Gyzad.

"But come next year, when the mourning period has concluded, changes will be made."

To Minty's credit, she followed the lead of the older bird shifters and did not openly react to what they all feared would happen to them with Master Gyzad's death. It was all everyone talked about, and the wait felt like an eternity. They had months before they would learn the details of Minister Breembat's plans.

As if sensing her fear of the unknown, Linah slid her hand over Minty's, grasping the appendage she hadn't known trembled, and squeezed.

Flanked by her sisters, Minty knew whatever would come, Linah and Soph would always be by her side. There was a mighty power in sisterhood, and Minty took strength from hers.

Clearly relishing in his newfound power, a Dragonkin youth discovering the deadly heat within, Minister Breembat breathed in deeply, spraying them with a menacing truth hotter than his dragon fire.

"Some of you are owned by Mistress Essodel, while others were gifted by your lady to Master Gyzad, making you his property instead of hers."

Minty felt Linah's grip on her hand squeeze once, letting Minty know Minister Breembat's statement wasn't news to Linah.

"While you will never be able to read it, Master Gyzad left a will. His will contained certain stipulations for the servants under his care."

Minty's gaze flew to Ben, who stood beside Rit. A minute into the meeting, her father had hoisted five-year-old Moses onto his shoulders, a surefire strategy to keep the boy still and quiet.

She did not need Linah's hand squeeze to know all the Wrens were aware of the provisions Master Gyzad had made for Ben in his will. Teaching an enslaved bird shifter to read was illegal, so they would never be able to confirm for themselves what was in Master Gyzad's will, which was not the same as them not knowing its contents. Master Gyzad had been arrogant, impatient, greedy, prideful, and violent. But when it came to his so-called servants, he wasn't a liar.

He'd dangled freedom in front of Ben like fresh meat to a starving lion.

"Manumission upon death or service until the age of fifty."

Soph's arm rubbed Minty's again, and she felt the excitement wafting from both sisters. Minty might not have known how to read, but she knew her numbers well enough to calculate her father's age. But she needn't bother because the Wrens were already planning for Ben's fiftieth birthday next month.

Whether through manumission or turning fifty, Benjamin Wren would be a free man before the end of the year.

Minty squeezed Linah's hand, proud of her father and grateful for Master Gyzad's progressive stance on enslavement. But she did not give the dead dragon too much credit because most dragons lived longer than a bird shifter's lifespan, making manumission upon their death almost unheard of, while freeing an enslaved person at the age of fifty, when they were beyond their peak working and baby-making years, was more an act of financial sensibility than moral rightness.

Still, Minty would embrace the selfish act just as she would a snake if freedom lay on the other end of its sharp bite.

Minister Breembat halted his pacing as if pulled to a stop by an invisible string from the heaven he told them they could enter if they obeyed their masters.

Minty liked the thought of a hereafter where everybody would be free. But she doubted a place the Dragonkin boasted about to the enslaved was a destination she wished her soul to travel to upon her death.

Besides, the God who entered her dreams didn't tell her to obey her master. God told her to be free. Be patient, but also be free.

Minty couldn't wait for Ben's freedom, even if she would for her own. But making it to fifty was many years in the future. Minty knew every one of Mistress Essodel's slaves over fifty. None had been released from bondage, including the enslaved women Minister Breembat had raped years ago and forced to have his children.

Abbott and Efron, Minister Breembat's twin sons from the enslaved woman Aveline, were forty-four. Considering Aveline was sixty-eight-years old but still expected to cook and clean and Mistress Essodel wasn't moved by the slightest humane practices of Dragonkin slave owners like Master Gyzad, Minty doubted when the twins turned fifty, freedom would be their birthday present from their Dragonkin grandmother.

But Ben had been blessed to be owned by Master Gyzad. Minty indulged her selfishness over her father's good fortune rather than Abbott's and Efron's.

Pulling a hand from behind his back, Minister Breembat raised it to his face and stroked his chin with his thumb and forefinger as if in deep thought. Minty had never credited the dragon for much wisdom in the past, and she did not see her opinion changing with his new status as master of the aviary.

"Until I discover what happened to Master Gyzad, I will stay the contents of his will."

"Wait. What?"

Linah's free hand covered Minty's mouth, but the act did nothing for her whirling head and stuttering heart.

Her gaze swung to Ben again, hoping her interpretation of Minister Breembat's declaration was incorrect.

But no.

She'd never seen shoulders slump while holding a child atop them. Yet, Ben's did, as if Moses's slight weight had the improbable ability of bringing Ben to his knees. Before that happened, though, Robert freed Ben of Moses.

With his youngest son's safe removal, whatever held Ben upright, disbelief, confusion, and anger abandoned him as his knees buckled and then gave way.

Minty turned away from her father and into Linah's reassuring arms. She wept the tears she knew her father never would, at least not until he was in the safety of his home, surrounded by his wife, children, and grandchildren. Because it was a rare enslaved bird shifter, who reached five decades of life without creating their own flock.

But whereas neither Ben nor Rit had ever been able to shield Minty from the fist and whip of cruel masters, she nor her siblings could compel Minister Breembat to honor Master Gyzad's will.

Linah's back rub conjured a memory of her doing the same whenever Minty struggled to sleep. "Don't worry, our poppa will have his freedom. Sooner or later, freedom will be his."

Minty was no longer that girl Linah could so easily soothe into a restful night's sleep. Back then, naïveté prevented her from detecting the undercurrents of emotions she had no names for. But fourteen brought a staggering awareness that hurt her heart and challenged her fortitude.

She pushed away from Linah, determined to face whatever else life had in store for her. But she wished she would've held on tighter.

Held on forever because life kept proving its cruelty, and so too did Minister Breembat.

Chapter 17
CALL ME HARRIET

1839
Pelduth Neck

The chill from being seated on the floor of the damp cell drew Robert to his bare feet. He hadn't appreciated being stripped of the one decent pair of boots he'd had in years, especially since he purchased them with his own hard-earned money. Unlike Master Gyzad, Minister Breembat did not care if Mistress Essodel's enslaved folk hired themselves out if he got the more significant share of whatever they made.

Long fingers ran over the rigid grooves of the moist wall, a familiar feel for the number of times he'd been in a cell like this one because Minister Breembat had no talent for finances or business.

"This is bull."

Robert smiled because, for a precious few seconds, he'd forgotten he shared the ten-by-ten-foot cell with five other men. Not all were enslaved Birdfolk like him, locked up and forced to work off their master's debt. The male who repeated the same three-word sentence from the time the cell door slammed behind him was a self-professed "abolitionist."

Not one to question a person's honesty without cause, Robert had simply nodded and then scooted over to give the newcomer room on the floor with the rest of them. There wasn't much to give, but Robert came from a family with many siblings, so he did not share the same aversion to close proximity as others.

"Shut up about it already," Lewis said to Jondrin.

Robert did not bother turning around to observe the exchange. He'd shared the overcrowded cell with the same men for two weeks, and by the third day, he could distinguish one man's voice from the others.

Daniel. Twenty-three like Robert. Blind in one eye and a new father. A flat voice.

Lewis. Thirty-eight. Crisscross welts on his back like Robert. A gravelly voice.

Edwin. Seventeen. Small boned, shy, and freeborn, unlike Robert. A modulated voice.

Mack. Twenty-eight. Unmarried but had a sweetheart owned by a different master, like Robert. A husky voice.

Jondrin. Five hundred thirty-two. Dragonkin abolitionist. A member of the Society of Friends, also known as Quakers. A deep voice.

According to Jondrin, Quakers believed in six principles: simplicity, peace, integrity, community, equality, and stewardship. Robert couldn't testify to whether the beliefs were fact or fantasy, but he and the dragon shifter had ended up in the same prison cell, so he supposed there was something to be said for that truth.

"You all know this is bull." Jondrin.

"Says the dragon." Lewis. "Like I said, shut up already. We know. We get it. We're in here with you."

"Why are you in here again?" Daniel. "I mean, I get that you were talkin' about freein' people like us from slavery, but why did they throw you in here instead of in a Dragonkin prison?"

"Because I'm one of you. Oppressed. A free thinker in a state of the greedy and privileged."

"You ain't like us." Edwin.

"He sure ain't." Lewis.

"Quakers like me are fighting the good fight. You need people like me to stand with you."

"He ain't wrong." Mack. "But you also ain't right. Fightin' to free slaves ain't the same as bein' one. You're in here to make a point. I don't know who to. Maybe yourself. You look like the type."

"You made the same observation the first day we met. Care to explain?"

"Don't have to," Mack said. "Listen to how you talk. Just like one of them. Better than the guards who dragged us in here."

"The institution of slavery won't end because the Dragonkin were beaten into submission. Good talk is the best strategy for my kind. To end enslavement, you need true religious folk like me to change the hearts and minds of slave owners and supporters of the slave system."

Robert finally shifted to his cellmates. "Because no one cares what enslaved folk have to say. They won't listen to us. Don't care about our stories of abuse and cruelty because they already know it. They've written those stories over and again." Robert pointed to Daniel's unseeing right eye and then to the welts on Lewis's bare chest. "Each story is etched into our minds as much as they have been carved onto our bodies."

"That's why it's important for Dragonkin to stand up and speak out. They'll listen."

Edwin lowered his forehead to his raised knees and mumbled, "You're right. Someone did listen. That's why you're in here. They listen, but they do not care to hear."

"You're wrong. They'll come around. You'll see. Don't turn away from me. Trust me. You'll see. One day, slavery will end."

Robert believed Jondrin. Slavery would eventually die out because everything had an inevitable end. But a five-century-old dragon's concept of time did not match that of the Birdfolk, who struggled to survive to see the ripe old age of seven or eight decades. Still, Robert would not begrudge Jondrin's efforts just because he doubted he would see the fruits of the dragon's labors during his lifetime.

Silence descended between the men again, a healthy difference of opinion that hadn't devolved into violence. It wasn't fair that his life held less weight in society than the likes of Minister Breembat, Mistress Essodel, and the countless other Dragonkin who kept his people in bondage.

From his experience, Dragonkin like Jondrin were a rare, silenced breed. Imprisoned, fined, and shunned

"No, no, get off me. I don't want to go in there."

The sound drew Robert's attention to the closed cell door. Heavy and inches thick but not soundproof, Robert could hear all comings and goings.

"No, no, please. My children. What about my poor children?"

Robert rushed to the door, nearly falling over Mack in his haste.

"Shut up and get in there."

"No, please. My children. My poor children."

Robert knew the voices of his cellmates. But the voices he knew deep in his soul, the voices he could detect in the middle of a blizzard, were those of his family.

Ben. Resonant.

Rit. Crisp.

Soph. Honeyed.

Minty. Mellifluous.

Ben Jr. Booming.

Rachel. Ethereal.

Henry. Throaty.

Moses. Animated.

Linah. Silvery.

"You can't take me away from my girls."

Linah. Silvery.

"My Kessiah and Harriet. No, please."

Linah. Silvery.

"My Harkless. Please don't."

Linah. Desperate.

Pleading.

Tremulous.

Robert banged on the door. "Linah! Linah!"

"Robert. Oh, God, Robert."

"I said, get in there, girl."

"Robert, tell everybody I love them. Please, tell my girls and husband I'm sorry."

"Linah. Linah." Robert's vocabulary had narrowed to a single word. Before he could walk, he could say, "Linah." Linah was a mother when Rit wasn't around. She was his first friend. The holder of his secrets. The teller of truths and the giver of love. She was his big sister, and now ...

"Whatever that devil is sellin' her for, I'll pay it." Robert banged and screamed, his voice no more his own than Linah's.

"You ain't got four hundred, ground-scraper. Now shut up, or I'll come in there and give you something to really cry about."

Was he crying? Robert touched his face.

Wet. Drenched.

"I don't care how much. I'll pay. I'll work as long as it takes. Just don't take my sister away. Please. Please. Don't take her from her girls."

Thud.

The sound of Linah's closed cell door and the guard's mocking laughter triggered something feral in Robert.

He shifted.

His body re-formed in heartbreaking seconds.

Slam. Slam.

Robert rammed into the door, over and again.

"Jondrin. Help him." Lewis.

"I can't."

"You can. You're a big dragon. Shift and break him out of here so he can save his sister."

Slam. Slam.

Edwin jumped to his feet. "You're all talk and no real action. If you won't help, then we will."

Slam. Slam.

Four shifted Sankofa birds joined Robert, adding their might to his own.

Slam. Slam.

Slam. Slam.

Through it all, the brutal, bone-breaking effort to break down a prison cell door, a physical representation of the impenetrable institution of slavery, Linah wept and wept and wept.

Bird clawed, and blood decorated, the cell door remained.

Scream exhausted and soul bereft, Linah quieted.

There was no silvery voice for Robert to detect, an emotional tracker between Wren siblings.

The following day, she was gone.

Linah Wren.

Born in 1808.

Sold in 1839.

Fate unknown.

1840
Pelduth Neck

Eyes widened, and mouth fell open with an awestruck country girl slackness that would've embarrassed Minty had anyone in the bustling crowd paid her the slightest attention. But none were, so Minty breathed in the dark, rooty scent of horses, heard the *clippety-clop* of overladen carriages rocking down the dusty street, and listened to grunts and foul curses of dockworkers heaving wooden barrels and crates down boat ramps and off barges. Above those near sensory overloads was the sight of merchant ships of all sizes, most with two to five masts Minty imagined would whip like sheets on a line when surrounded by nothing but water and wind.

Closing her mouth, Minty inhaled through her nostrils. She enjoyed the wondrous scented mix of salt and seaweed, making her new work location the best yet. As far as Minister Breembat's leases went, Minty had come to expect little from them except for inadequate pay for her hard work and temporary masters who were kinder to an annoying gnat at dinnertime than they were to the enslaved Birdfolk under their charge.

"Impressive, aren't they?"

Minty nodded, feeling like the speaker had plucked the thought from her mind.

Two males around the same seventeen years as Ben Jr. but not as stocky as her brother lost control of the four barrels they'd been maneuvering onto a flat trolley with two wheels on one end. They scrambled to secure the barrels, catching up to three but temporarily losing the fourth in the crowded dock.

Minty's shoulders were hunched, and her jaw tightened as if she were about to be beaten for mishandling her owner's cargo. But as the two young Birdfolk slaves retrieved the barrels intact, the cargo within safe, she released a sigh of relief.

"You're kind. I could see your worry for those boys. It's gone now, but you still look ready to jump into action. Or maybe run. Which one is it?"

Despite having provided a nonverbal response to the stranger's initial question, Minty hadn't bothered with the basic courtesy of granting him her full attention. He'd invaded her thoughts with his nearness, but his unsolicited observation made her uninterested in matching a face to a voice.

Minty turned to her right and looked up. She'd seen handsome Birdfolk males before. Muscular and fit ones, too. Dark of complexion, light of complexion, and the beautiful range of browns between the two. Cocky smiles, knowing smiles, confident smiles, even smiles her sister Soph had called sexy. Soph had also told Minty that men with sexy smiles made for good bed partners but not trustworthy husbands.

She wasn't ready for either, so she was as intact as the four barrels the young dockworkers had wrangled back onto the trolley and as untouched as the cargo within.

The stranger smiled down at Minty, not with a cocky, confident, knowing smile capable of knee-weakening sex appeal but with a warmth unbefitting a first encounter.

Minty stepped back but kept her gaze trained on the male. He was as tall and lean as Robert, but whereas her older brother was clean-shaven, the stranger's chin, cheek, and upper lip were dotted with patches of hair that seemed incapable of deciding whether they wanted to grow into a full beard and mustache. Apparently, the hair had given up, yet the stranger hadn't on the hope of developing the last outward sign of manhood. If he had, Minty reasoned, thinking his complexion as gloriously dark as any Wren, he would've removed the patches and been done with it.

As if swallowing bitter lemonade, Minty clicked her tongue. She should stop comparing every Birdfolk male she met to the men in her family. Soph had told her the same, but her sister's husband could not have been more similar to their father than if Ben and Rit had created him. So, maybe there was something unstated yet important about using her father and brothers as reference points.

Soph and Walter had a good marriage, just as Linah and Harkless's marriage had been. Minty scrubbed her hands over her face, a small act of self-harm that changed the route her mind had taken. She did not want to think about Linah. Not in front of a stranger who looked as if he would understand all too well the pain of losing a sibling to sale. Although, the stranger gave off the same aura as every freeborn Birdfolk she'd met.

It was one of those sensations Minty had no words to describe. It couldn't be summed up so shallowly as the difference in speech pattern or dress because sometimes the lived experience of a freeborn Birdfolk and an enslaved one was a measure of small degrees, like the difference between the colors of ebony and charcoal.

The stranger laughed, giving her a thorough up-and-down regard before he said, "You would help if you could. But you're also smart enough to know when to run and hide." Wiping his right hand on his pants, he extended the appendage to Minty. "I forgot my manners. I'm John Cassin, and you must be Araminta Wren, Ben's daughter."

Oomph.

A passing dockworker pushed past Minty, shoving her into John, who caught her by her arms.

"Are you okay?" John glared over his shoulder after the man, but he'd been swallowed up in the crowd. "He didn't hurt you, did he?"

"It'll take more than that." Minty squirmed enough in John's hands to make her point without being rude. He released her, and she stepped back, grateful that his action matched his kind smile. "No one calls me Araminta, not even my father."

"That's fine. What should I call you, then?"

Years later, Minty would reflect on this day as one of many turning points in her life. She had always been Minty to her friends and family. On occasion, even her Dragonkin owners referred to her as such instead of ground-scraper, slaveling, gal, or girl. But there was something about John Cassin, the man she'd traveled there to meet on the first of many days as a dockworker.

He knew nothing about her beyond whatever her father and her new lessee, Master Nirvode, had shared with him. At eighteen and finally having a paying job, even if she had to turn over most of it to Minister Breembat, Minty felt like a real grown-up for the first time. Grown-ups did not carry childhood nicknames with them into adulthood. And while her parents had lovingly gifted her with the name Araminta, in honor of both her mother and her sister, Linah, who had paid homage to Rit in the naming of her second daughter, she would do the same.

Beginning a new phase in one's life wasn't on par with creating life, as Linah had done, but every decision needn't be grandiose, only fitting and proper.

"Call me Harriet."

John inclined his head, no fanfare for the bold step she'd taken toward a future where too many legends were forged from the rot of society. Forced to bloom without the benefit of rain showers or sunshine.

"Good to meet you, Harriet. I'm sure Ben told you I'd meet you at the dock today."

"He did. So did Master Nirvode."

"I'll be your trainer. I hope that's fine by you."

Harriet did not see why it wouldn't. But she did wait for him to mention her gender and size. John was unaware of her headaches and sleeping spells, so he wouldn't know to use those to question her suitability for such labor-intensive work.

Awkward seconds grew between them, and still, John said nothing Harriet could use to dislike the man. So, she stumbled through a pointless statement, referencing something he'd said earlier. "You called those two dockworkers 'boys.' But you can't be much older."

Harriet didn't think anything she said warranted the toothy-mouthed smile John granted her, but she could not deny the flutters they produced in her stomach.

"I'm twenty-eight. But thank you for the compliment."

Harriet did not give compliments to people she barely knew, especially not to men a decade her senior.

"You're four years older than my brother Robert." Too late, Harriet slapped a hand over her mouth. She really needed a frame of reference other than her family. Shaking off the embarrassment, Harriet walked toward what she knew to be Master Nirvode's ship, a three-mast schooner, fully fore-and-aft rigged, not that she understood what any of that meant. But Master Nirvode had told her to look for a "three-mast fully fore-and-aft rigged schooner with a flag the same color as my dragon scales. The colors you see at sunrise and sunset."

Red and yellow. Harriet quickly spotted the ship. But it would take considerably more effort to understand the annoyingly strange reaction her body had to John Cassin.

Wishing, not for the first time, that she could talk to Linah, relying on her sisterly wisdom, Harriet shoved the odd sensations away. She focused on learning all she could about being a dockworker.

"Where do we begin?"

Chapter 18
Caring Can Be Painful

1842
Pelduth Neck

The sky bled molten fire. Raging streams of unrepentant heat consumed the night sky, stealing fresh air and thousands of years of serenity.

Of freedom.

Ancient empires and birthplaces of civilization vanished, were destroyed, and obliterated by unquenchable greed. Claws claimed what remained.

HARRIET'S ESCAPE:

Families were torn asunder, yanked from the rich soil where their ancestors once tread. Forced to leave the fertile land from which trees of life had bloomed long ago, the strength and breadth of their roots unseen yet mighty.

Enduring. Like the people.

No choice but to start anew.

They were compelled to work, obey without question, and fear the whip's sting.

Trauma was passed down from one generation to the next, an oppressive poison with a singular antidote.

Emancipation.

Harriet rolled onto her side; her crooked fingers clutched around coils of thick, coarse feather hair. Bright, white lights flashed behind her closed eyelids, celestial bioluminescence capable of transmigration, her spiritual form weightless and free.

White lights merged with the blackness of the heavenly body, an intimate foreshadowing of the immaculate conception to come. The womb fluttered and clenched, ever-tightening contractions meant to prepare but never to forestall.

Harriet's back bowed, her neck arched, and her mouth opened on a wordless scream.

Life came forth, a rushing, velvety tide of iridescent auras: pink, blue, green, and purple. Three-dimensional holograms, prayerful projections that reverberated, creating a chorus of harmonic flapping wings.

The sound grew and grew.

Just as quickly, it receded like air from a burning barn.

"No! Don't go. Don't leave me here."

"I'm not goin' anywhere."

Farther away. Colors dulled, dimmed, and then disappeared.

"I've got you."

Farther away. Gone. Silence.

Except.

Harriet accepted the familiar hands that shifted her from the prickly, summer-hot grass onto a steady lap and against a sturdy chest whose heart pounded as vigorously as hers. "John?" she whispered, her tongue thick and her mind questioning.

"Yeah, it's me. I'm here." Arms tightened around her waist, and, for a shameful fleeting moment, Harriet cursed the human shell of her body that kept her tethered to this place and the immutable reality of her enslaved life. "I'll always be here."

Harriet accepted John's truth with the same intense affection she felt for the male blessed to be born free.

"I'm sorry."

"No need to apologize, Harriet." John chuckled, a sound halfway between forced humor and dwindling fear. "You sure do make an evenin' stroll interestin'. Come here." With one strong arm wrapped around her waist, John scooted backward several inches, stopping when his back met the rough bark of a tree. "That's better. Are you okay? You're sweatin'."

Harriet knew her body had done more than sweat when she had one of her more "worrisome episodes," as her mother had taken to calling what happened to her body when she fell into a fitful sleep.

"I can't help it. I'm sorry." Harriet disliked apologizing for something she had no control over. But John wasn't family, and while she'd revealed much about her condition to him, she held on to a sliver of hope that he would never witness one of her spells.

"Don't do that." Two fingers went to her chin and lifted. "I didn't know the Harriet before your head injury, but I know the one who agreed to let me court her. And there ain't nothin' wrong with her that she should feel any cause to apologize for bein' who she is." The two fingers slid across her jaw and up to her right earlobe, caressing. "I accept who you are, just as I like to believe that you accept the man I am. Or at least the man that I try to be."

"What kind of man do you try to be?" Knowing she should move off his lap but enjoying the feel of his muscular legs under her bottom nearly as much as she reveled in the warm sensation of his calloused fingers grazing her damp skin from chin down the column of her pulsing neck, Harriet stayed right where she was.

"It's hard bein' a Birdfolk man in a land dominated by Dragonkin, Harriet. It's equally difficult for a Birdfolk woman, I know. But it's different."

Harriet thought she understood the difference because she'd seen the defeated look of banked anger on her father's face more times than she cared to recall. She'd felt the same frustrated helplessness as Ben whenever a master took a whip to her, and she was unable to do more than bear the lash.

Then there was Linah. Harriet would rescue her sister if she could. But she knew that will alone wasn't enough. Skill and knowledge were needed, none of which she possessed in great enough quantity to find Linah and bring her home.

"I'll never be able to protect you the way I want. That keeps me up at night. So, I try to be brave. I pray that my bein' a freeborn Birdfolk can be enough for the woman I see you growin' into. Even when you're in human form, I see your wings. They are always in motion, anxious and ready to fly away." John hugged her, and she thought he would crush her with his strong embrace. "You aren't the only one who dreams, Harriet."

"I don't need you to protect me. My God will see to that. I just need you to lo—" Harriet clamped her mouth shut and buried her face against John's neck, cursing how close she'd come to revealing her secret. "You don't have to be brave alone. We can be brave together. Pretend together until it's truer than not."

"You aren't a shy woman, Harriet Wren, but when it comes to me and our relationship, you're like a cute, little meerkat who peeks their head from their burrow, makin' sure everythin' is safe before venturin' out."

Harriet didn't see the problem in exercising caution, especially when surrounded by fire-breathing predators. But she did not argue John's point because she had no interest in lying to him, much less herself.

"I've never done this before." She'd spoken against the soft skin of a neck that would no doubt taste salty. But the shy, cautious meerkat John likened her to kept her tongue in her mouth and the confirmation of his taste unanswered.

"Don't I know it."

At a decade her senior, John exceeded her experience in a multitude of ways, which did not equate to him treating her as an inconsequential girl or to him pressuring her into intimate acts she was not ready to engage.

Harriet appreciated John's patience, but on days she felt especially insecure, she wondered why he had chosen to court an enslaved woman instead of a free one.

He kissed her cheek. "You think too much."

"What makes you think I was—"

He kissed her cheek again. "You aren't stuck on a farm anymore. You go into town all the time now that Minister Breembat has taken to hirin' you out. You've seen the free Birdfolk community. A good half of them is either courtin' or married to an enslaved person."

Harriet had, but something was disconcerting about a non-family member's capability to discern her thoughts before she gave them a voice. John had proven his ability to read her the first time they met, and his aptitude for doing so had increased since becoming a couple.

John lifted her chin so their eyes met. Soft, gentle lips brushed against hers. "I don't care about your legal status."

Harriet believed him, but surely, he had to see how simpler his life would be with a freeborn mate. While they hadn't talked about marriage, John's intention was as clear as the gaze that held hers. And whenever he got around to proposing, Harriet didn't doubt what her response would be. Still, one of them needed to think about the potential pitfalls of such a union. If it wouldn't be John, then Harriet would accept the responsibility of keeping them grounded.

He kissed her lips again, longer than a graze, but with a controlled restraint to which she'd become accustomed.

Harriet returned the sweet embrace because John had taught her well, and she desired him more with each passing day.

"That was nice," John said against her tingling lips. "You've become good at that."

Harriet laughed, knowing he complimented his teaching skills as much as he did her ability to take his instructions to heart. She jumped to her feet, steady despite the heady way John's kisses made her feel.

She loved Sundays because it was the one day of the week she could relax and spend time with family and friends. Like every other enslaved Birdfolk, Harriet worked the other six days of the week. But Sundays were for the Lord and family. While she would never look forward to Minister Breembat's mandatory religious services, she did to the communal gathering of the Sankofa people.

Sundays were even more special because she had John to share them with her.

Harriet offered him her hand, secretly pleased when he'd accepted it and permitted her to help him to his feet the way he always did for her. Like much of John's character, Harriet found many reasons to appreciate the man. More reasons to love him.

He really did see her. Accept her. Harriet's small stature, enslaved status, sleeping spells, religious fervor, and propensity to shyness when insecurity got the better of her hadn't sent him running.

Like her father and brothers-in-law, John Cassin would make a fine husband. If they married, and Harriet prayed Mistress Essodel would permit the union, she wouldn't allow anything or anyone to come between them. She would never leave him as long as he wanted to be by her side.

Never.

1844
Berzogtown
Essodel Plantation

After so many years, Harriet hadn't gotten used to visiting Mistress Essodel's lair. Little had changed since the last time she'd been there. Not the heaps of gold coins and priceless jewels enslaved Birdfolk were forced to shine, the same way they were compelled to deliver Mistress Essodel's meals and muck out her inner chamber as if she were a horse and her lair a stall. Nor had she forgotten the unbridled magnitude of the Dragonkin.

She knew the massive dragon hadn't grown, for if Mistress Essodel had, she wouldn't have been able to fit what Harriet knew to be Master Gyzad's belongings into her chamber. Oil paintings of Dragonkin in the air, on the ground, and even under the ocean occupied a corner of the inner chamber, along with piles of tea sets. Some she'd seen Master Gyzad drink from, others she'd helped Dorane wash, while even more, she'd spied in one of Master Gyzad's many bedchambers.

But Harriet had never seen a single piece chipped, which many now were, she assumed, during the packing and relocation. Still, she wondered about the carelessness, especially considering the items comprised Master Gyzad's precious hoard. And while Harriet did not shed a tear at the news of his death, she credited the Dragonkin for building a non-Birdfolk collection.

She eased farther into the chamber and told herself she played no part in Master Gyzad's death, not even unintentionally. Mistress Essodel had no reason to seek revenge against her because ignorance and hindsight protected the youth from the consequences of both.

Harriet halted, having gone as close to the dragon as she dared. Her back was as straight as a pole, her neck craned back, and her eyes cast upward. She cleared her mind of everything except for the reason for her visit and the deadly beast that loomed above her.

Had Mistress Essodel's eyeteeth always hung so menacingly below her upper lip? Sharp and with . . . Harriet blinked, knowing that no matter how many times she did so, the sight would not vanish. Blood stained one of the eyeteeth, around which a twisted Birdfolk intestine was lodged.

Harriet wasn't assigned to food prep and delivery or waste disposal during her time in the aviary. The former involved serving up a fellow enslaved Birdfolk for Mistress Essodel's meal by any means, including trickery or violence. The latter chore was a reminder that the life of the enslaved was a crappy existence that too often ended as a pile of manure to be hauled away.

"Breembat tells me you wish to wed."

Harriet knew better than to interpret that simple statement as a question needing an answer. So, she said nothing and waited for Mistress Essodel to continue.

"Linah came, then Soph came, and then Kessiah. All smelled of their men, but you do not."

Again, Harriet refrained from replying despite knowing the inevitable question. Perhaps this was why Minister Breembat laughed when she'd asked permission to speak with Mistress Essodel about marrying John. She obviously smelled the same to him that she did to her owner.

Who knew virginity had a scent?

A fog of hot air surrounded Harriet, and she closed her eyes. Afraid but well-versed in dragon behavior to not encourage their predatory instincts by fleeing, Harriet locked her body in place and willed her stomach into feigned calmness.

"Unions between my ground-scrapers are for the purpose of increasing my hoard. What good is an untouched servant?"

Despite their differences, Harriet agreed with Mistress Essodel, but not in precisely the same way.

Every married Birdfolk in this aviary has stood where I am today. And every female of the unions has added to the aviary. Kessiah was pregnant before marriage, and any day now, Soph will be a mother and Kessiah one before the end of the year. I want to be one, too, but that would mean ... Maybe John should've chosen a freeborn woman to marry. It ain't too late; he still can if he wants. I wouldn't be mad at him if he did, although he'd be furious if he knew I was havin' these thoughts again.

"I understand that marryin' John means I must bear him children."

"Bear me children. Nothing that comes from my property will ever belong to another. Do you understand me, child?"

The heat of the fog intensified, a heavy weight that sent Harriet crashing to her knees. She coughed over and again, working hard to breathe and expel whatever had taken up residence in her lungs.

Blood flew from between dry, cracked lips and onto the ground in front of fists that clenched spasmodically with each ragged cough.

"Your mother bore me nine servants, but your sister, Linah, only two before she ran away. Soph, Rachel, and Kessiah must do better. I have no tolerance or use for a childless female servant of breeding age."

Harriet didn't know what was worse, Mistress Essodel's ability to inflict harm with the might of her dragon's breath alone or the ancient creature's ignorance of her son's deceitful nature. Not for the first time, Harriet wished that the same toxic mix that had taken Master Gyzad's life had also claimed Minister Breembat's and Mistress Essodel's.

She knew it was wrong to wish, much less pray, for vengeance. But surely a just God would punish the wicked and protect the innocent.

"Do you understand me, ground-scraper?"

The debilitating heat withdrew, releasing her from its oppressive weight. But the insult washed over her instead of landing like an arrow into a bullseye, as it had for most of her life.

Harriet stood, spat blood from her mouth as if it were a wad of tobacco, and then wiped what remained from her lips with the back of a shaky hand.

"Yes, I understand, Mistress Essodel. Thank you for your permission to wed."

The Dragonkin may not have forced the words of permission into Harriet's mind, but her parents and experience had taught her that Mistress Essodel submitted to no one's will. She delivered orders and commands. Simply put, she hadn't forbidden Harriet from marrying John, which was Mistress Essodel's way of approving the union. Specifically, she expected Harriet and John's union to add more enslaved Birdfolk to her hoard.

Selfish, as all Dragonkin she met were.

But Harriet had achieved what she'd gone there for, so she backed away with cautious slowness.

"So much potential."

Harriet halted her retreat.

"Beautiful and rare. I have never seen feathers as vibrant and gorgeous as yours. But with your head injury, you are all but worthless now."

Offended but too intelligent to show it, Harriet stared up at the dragon, who was impossibly large and unfathomably heartless.

"Such a disappointment. Now, you are only suitable for the docks and the fields. Between pregnancies, you'll work one or the other, paying Breembat sixty a year for the privilege of hiring yourself out."

Harriet dropped her gaze, knowing better than to stare too long at the scaly beast lest she interpret her boldness as disrespect. But also to hide her shock at how a near shut-in could be both accurately informed and utterly oblivious of the goings-on beyond her mountain home.

"Yes, Mistress Essodel. Thank you for your kindness."

"I am a kind master, indeed. Now, go. Your brother nears the mountain, running as if chased by a pack of hungry gryphons."

Dropping a quick curtsy, Harriet turned toward the mouth of the chamber and then quickly ran through it, wondering which brother had come for her and why. Everyone knew her goal for the day, and no one could help her achieve her task, so most had gathered in the old Wren slave cabin, waiting for news but also for . . .

Harriet crashed through the opening to the mountain, nearly running into twelve-year-old Moses.

Her youngest brother skidded to a stop. His chest heaved, and nostrils flared, but he grinned at Harriet in that way of youth with plenty of energy to spare.

"What's wrong? Is it Soph?"

"Baby comin' now, Minty. Momma told me to come get you. She figured you'd take your sweet time gettin' home if I didn't."

Harriet's smile felt good after being in Mistress Essodel's lair, like the feel of sunshine and the smell of flowers after a long, moody winter.

Moses grabbed her hand and tugged. "Come on, Minty, let's go."

Harriet allowed herself to be pulled along by Moses, just as she permitted him to call her Minty. It took a bit of getting used to referring to her as Harriet after she had been Minty for so long, so she didn't fault her family when they fell back on old ways.

But that did not mean she wasn't above reminding her baby brother that twenty-two wasn't old and she incapable of carrying her own.

Harriet bolted away from Moses and toward the old Wren cabin.

Laughter rippled behind her, and feet thudded, drawing ever closer. "I'm gonna catch you."

She knew he would, but not without a hearty chase.

No darting around or hiding behind trees. No glancing backward or spying upward.

Harriet ran flat out. No spell overtook her, no illusions blurred her vision, and no heavenly music impaired her focus.

Moses caught up, his face glistening and his smile an ever-present warmth unrivaled by the sun's heat that beat down on them.

Side by side, they ran the rest of the way home, a prelude to future life changes for the Wren family.

But first . . . Harriet burst through the cabin door, Moses right behind her.

Ben and Rit only stared at Harriet and then shook their heads as if expecting nothing less from their fifth-born child. But it was their third child whom everyone else crammed into the cabin had eyes for. Or rather, the squalling newborn Soph held against her chest.

Ben Jr. patted Harriet's back like she'd won a grand prize. "Another niece. Healthy by the look and sound of her."

A healthy baby was a prize indeed but also a reminder of Mistress Essodel's expectations for Harriet.

She wouldn't steal her sister's moment, so Harriet tucked away her good news for a later family reveal.

The old sheet from her childhood still separated the main part of the cabin from the area her parents had carved for themselves. That tiny bit of privacy had led to three generations of Wrens, the newest edition to the family a living, breathing symbol of resilience in action.

Kessiah, Linah's oldest daughter, and a niece barely two years younger than Harriet, would be the next to add to the Wren family and Mistress Essodel's hoard.

No one who knew Linah would think she could run away and leave her family behind, especially her daughters.

But the thought of fleeing bondage was never so close to Harriet's consciousness than when she glimpsed new life tied down by old, rusty chains of subjugation.

"Ann" reverberated through the crowd of Wrens, the three-letter name spoken with love.

By the time it was Harriet's turn to meet Ann and congratulate Soph, they were both asleep.

Peaceful, even if not free.

Harriet lay beside them, careful not to awaken either. Giving birth and being born was hard work, and while Harriet did not remember the latter, she wished to experience the former.

With a tenderness she learned from Ben and Rit, Harriet kissed Soph's moist forehead. Her sister didn't stir, so she drew closer and kissed her cheek, pouring all her love into the simple gesture.

She had done the same to Rachel and Kessiah, gifting them the love she could no longer offer Linah.

"Harriet," Rit said, sounding more motherly with the birth of each of her grandchildren, "get out here and tell us how it went with Mistress Essodel."

Kessiah poked her head into the room, the sheet hiding what Harriet knew to be a round belly. She whispered, "Another wedding?"

Unable to contain her happiness, Harriet let her smile serve as an answer enough.

Kessiah whooped, followed by a flurry of excited but hushed sounds.

Rit tossed the sheet aside, and Ben stood beside her. Harriet didn't know what she expected them to say or even what she needed to hear. But they watched her in a way that revealed their feelings more than she cared to know.

Twice, she'd nearly died. Both times, only Rit's care had prevented Harriet from meeting her heavenly maker sooner than she wanted.

Now, she would marry, a milestone her parents likely feared Harriet would never experience. She had no words to take away her parents' old worries, but she offered them the only reassurance she could give.

"I'll always return home. I promise."

Chapter 19
With All My Heart, I Do

1844
Berzogtown
Essodel Plantation

Rit's voice cut through the silence. "The moon is full and bright, Harriet. It's time."

"I know, Momma." Instead of obeying Rit's unvoiced directive to exit the old cabin, she stared out of the side window, watching naked Birdfolk leave their cabin homes and walk toward the ancient woods that buttressed Mistress Essodel's property.

Arms seasoned by five decades of toil wrapped around Harriet's waist, and naked breasts that had nursed nine Wren babies pressed against her back. Slick and sweaty, despite the chilly autumn air, Rit's hug had never felt better. "I know what you're feelin', baby. Special days like today pierce the heart more deeply. Birthdays. Births. Weddings. Each life event is a cruel reminder of what was taken, but also that life endures. We move on because we must. Because livin' is the greatest way to honor those no longer with us."

"Momma is right." At nineteen, Rachel, taller than Harriet but equally lean and strong, moved to stand beside her. "We still got our momma, but Kessiah and Harriet don't. But we stood by our niece when she gave birth. Not replacin' Linah because can't nobody do that. But we were there for her as we always are for each other."

"Kessiah cried a lot that day."

"We all did." Rit squeezed Harriet tight as if the might of a mother's love could shield her from the fate that had befallen Linah. If that were true, if Birdfolk mothers had such wondrous but unnatural power, none of their families would have been dislocated, and people cast to different corners of the world. Their fates were unknown, but their absence left a gaping hole incapable of being mended.

As if Rit's body was the softest of pillows, and Harriet a newborn seeking warm shelter, she sank into her comforting hold. "If Linah were here, what would she tell me, Momma?"

Rachel yanked the end of one of Harriet's braids. The braids went from the forehead to the nape and between feathers, around which a scrap of material was tied in a bow. It was a simple hairstyle Rit would do for Harriet and her sisters when they were girls and time allowed. But Rit's workload seemed endless, and Harriet was tender-headed, disliking even the gentlest hair wash. Still, on this special day, Harriet hadn't complained when Rit pointed to a chair beside a table with bacon grease and said, "Sit. Ain't no way I'm gonna let you get married with your hair lookin' like a bushel basket."

Rachel pulled the end of another braid, but Harriet wouldn't be moved from her spot until she was good and ready. "You're such a baby."

"That's what Momma called me not five minutes ago." At twenty-two, the baby that had been Araminta Wren was buried beneath years of labor and abuse. But also the natural maturation of life, the coming into her own skin, and the breaking in of a new name that would soon match the adoption of a new role.

Wife.

Rachel tugged her hair again. "That's what she calls all of us. Linah would've told you the same. She would've also told you to not be afraid of steppin' from the shadow and into your own light. Robert told us Linah fought, screamed, cursed, and prayed. She didn't want to leave any of us." Rachel slid between Harriet and the window. "John loves you."

"And I'm grateful for it."

"And you love him."

"With all my heart, I do."

Rit's soft chuckle reached inside Harriet and stroked the young bird poised to leave the nest; its talons sharp but its wings like leaden weights. "Simple but good vows right there, my Minty, who honors me with the name Harriet. You kids are my joy. Nothin' as inhumane as a dragon's livin' hoard but people with hopes and dreams. But also genuine fears. Yes, your sister would've told you not to be afraid because you need to hear it more than the truth that marriage and motherhood can be frighteningly hard. Nothin' in our lives has ever been easy, not even lovin' another."

Rit slid from behind Harriet, taking her warmth with her but not her support. Then, with a mischievous grin, she tugged one of Rachel's braids. "Were you listenin' to what I told Harriet?"

"Yes, ma'am."

"Good."

"But you'll say it again when it's my turn, right?"

"Just as my momma did for me, and you'll do for your future daughter."

Harriet accepted Rit's kiss on her forehead, secretly pleased that she'd kissed her before she did Rachel, but knowing her mother did not have a favorite child.

The door creaked open, letting in the moon's glow and a familiar sight.

"What's this?" As naked as them all but with no baby Ann in her arms, Soph stepped fully into the cabin. Her sister scowled, a strange reaction to the sight before her. "Daughters-momma time without me? That ain't right."

Because Harriet had felt the same when Minister Breembat forced her to live with one temporary master after another, and her siblings were allowed to see Rit, but she was not, Harriet rushed to Soph's side and tugged a braid.

Behind her, Rachel and Rit laughed, and she swore she heard Linah's rich laughter, too.

"What's that for?"

Going on tiptoe, Harriet kissed Soph's forehead.

"What did I miss, Momma?"

"Nothin', baby."

"Everything," Rachel said, and Harriet nodded because Soph had always been an easy target. Being thirty-one and a new mother hadn't changed that about her.

"Stop messin' with me, Rach. Anyway, everybody is at the big old tree in the woods. John is like a nervous cat surrounded by rocking chairs. Get changed, put that man out of his misery, and marry him already."

Rit ran her hand over Harriet's braids, laying down whatever stray strands she saw that Harriet could not. "We've been tryin', but Harriet was missin' Linah. You should've come sooner, but I suppose Ann needed feedin' before you could leave her."

"John's mother has taken a shine to my baby. But Mrs. Cassin ain't family yet, so I don't feel right leavin' Ann with her for too long."

Harriet supposed that was a new mother's reaction because over a dozen Wrens were also in the woods. Nothing would happen to little Ann, even if Mrs. Cassin wasn't a lovely woman.

Soph turned away to leave, but just as quickly, she faced Harriet again. "I don't like bein' left out."

"We didn't mean to."

"I know. But it still doesn't feel good. I know I'm makin' a big deal about nothin'. But—"

Harriet tugged Soph to her instead of continuing the sisters' game of hair pulling. She smelled of fresh breastmilk, waning autumn, and realized fear. Soph's anxiety didn't have the same scent as Harriet's: rotten meat on a muggy summer's day, but with the hint of overripe apples before they fell from the tree, still edible but only briefly.

"It's fine. We can blame our ragin' emotions on the full moon like a couple of wolves." Harriet howled softly in Soph's ear, pleased when all three Wren women laughed at her silliness. But she soon sobered. "We better get goin' before John thinks I've changed my mind."

Soph returned Harriet's kiss, pressing soft, full lips against her cheek. "Let's get you married, little Harriet."

Rachel's hand crashed down on Harriet's shoulder, its sharp sting a playful continuation of their hair-pulling game. "Finally, because I can't wait to shift."

Soph backed away, and Harriet couldn't help but marvel at the changes to her post-birth body. Her hips were rounder, her breasts fuller, and her stomach bore the dark but slowly fading marks of skin stretched taut.

Does she know how much she glows since givin' birth to Ann? I'll tell her later. If I do it now, Rachel will make fun of me, and Soph won't believe me. She's the only big sister I have left. Even when Linah was around, Soph took her role as big sister seriously. She's goin' to make a great momma. I'll tell her that later, too.

Harriet felt her mind wander even more, flittering from one thought to the next like a hummingbird flying from flower to flower, filling up on nectar.

"Come, Harriet."

Her mind snapped to attention, focusing on Rit's voice and words. She hadn't noticed her mother and sisters had moved to the open door. *It's time to step from the shadow and into my own light.*

Harriet followed her family out of the cabin and closed the door behind her.

Rachel's longing sigh reached her before the sight of the offerings did. "Seein' so many of them never gets old. I can't wait until it's my turn. Look, Harriet."

Five Sankofa Birdfolk feathers, a vibrant range of blues and greens, had been placed on the porch. Harriet bent, inspecting each one with both eyes and appreciative fingers that slid over the smooth offerings. She picked up the bluest feather and sniffed. *I knew it. This one is from Poppa. I know the others, too. Robert, Ben Jr., Henry, and Moses.*

Tears threatened, but Harriet forced them back.

She gathered the feathers, feeling the first stirrings of excitement for the wedding ceremony. When Harriet took the first of the three steps off the porch, she understood Rachel's awe. Perhaps it was the glow of the full moon casting its mystical light, or the excited butterflies fluttering about Harriet's stomach, but she'd never seen a more beautiful display of family and friendship.

Feathers of varying shapes, sizes, and colors—from long, rich reds; to wide, refreshing greens; to curved, ambitious purples—had been left as an offering. They hadn't been dropped aimlessly or tossed one on top of another in a heap but left in a neat row that led from the Wren cabin to the woods where she would find the community of Birdfolk awaiting her arrival.

Her community. *Her* family.

Few traditions had survived the transmigration of Birdfolk from their native land of Sika, but the gifting of feathers as part of the wedding ceremony hadn't been lost to memory or master.

Harriet collected each precious feather as she went, freely given instead of forcefully plucked by Mistress Essodel. Their value viewed through the prism of greed and power instead of legacy and love.

Her mother and sisters walked behind her as she followed the trail of colorful feathers. They led her into woods she'd run through as a child, playing tag with Ben Jr. and climbing trees. She would leap from a tree on multiple outings, arms flapping. Each time, she would drop to the ground like a stone sinking to the bottom of a lake. Inevitable because she could no more fly than a stone could float.

But on Harriet's wedding day, she felt capable of taking flight and riding the waves.

She stopped at a clearing, but her mother and sisters continued, joining those gathered to witness her marriage to the man she'd spied the moment he'd come into view.

In the center of an open circle was John. He wasn't naked, as she was, and neither was anyone else, despite her having seen most of their glistening nude bodies walk past the Wren cabin.

True to the spectacular array of colorful feathers she held in her arms, so too were the avian forms of the Birdfolk before her. John Cassin was in the middle of the magnificent bodies of beaks, talons, and feathers.

Like most Sankofa males, John's plumage and feathers lacked females' more vibrant, rich colors. No reds, pinks, or purples. Harriet stepped forward, eyes misty for how handsome John's bird form was, a magnificent canvas of bright blues he'd kept from her until this day.

"Some things are better left for our wedding night." John had been right.

Thank goodness John was born free. The bright blue feathers are as pretty as any I've seen. The color and shade suit him. Loyalty, confidence, and security are what I see when I look at him. Momma said weddings are a special day. She was right, and there's more left to go.

Despite what she'd initially thought, not all present were in their bird form. Those too young to shift were not, and neither were new mothers like Soph and Kessiah, who held their babies in arms no more protective than a parent's.

Somewhere between leaving Harriet and joining Ben's sapphire blue bird in the circle, Rit had shifted. At fifty-seven, Rit's pink and peach form still radiated like a warm sunset.

It's time. Everyone is here because of John and me. This ceremony will be the only one that matters. Among my family and friends, I'll marry the man of my heart. I don't care about the wedding service Minister Breembat will make me submit to. These woods here are the closest we have to what my ancestors experienced in Sika. This is God's will.*

Harriet stepped entirely from the shadow of the trees into the full moon's light. The feathered offerings fell from her arms. With each step toward her future husband, she transformed, challenging the invisible manacles that held both forms in bondage. However, she detected a subtle grinding of metal as if being pulled by a growing power.

"You're finally here."

"Sorry for worryin' you."

John's beak lowered to her head, gently touching a wound that had forever changed her life. *"You're as beautiful as I knew you would be. I've never seen that shade of pink before. I'm lookin' forward to cleanin' each feather. Thank you for agreein' to be my wife. Ready to take me as your husband?"*

Harriet stepped closer to John, walking on her toes instead of her entire foot as she did in human form. *"If you're ready to have me as your wife."*

"It's all I've wanted since the day we met."

Touched by words meant as a slight exaggeration, Harriet decided that she would initiate for the first time in their relationship. *"I'll go first. Your blue feathers call to my beak and my heart."*

John stumbled backward as if shocked, and Harriet would've swatted him if they'd been in human form.

Instead, she strutted up to him and nuzzled his neck, beginning the mating ritual. Harriet used her beak to gather preen oil from a gland at the base of John's tail. She took her time distributing the oil through his smooth neck feathers. She drew each feather through her beak, nibbling from base to tip.

Preening came naturally to Birdfolk, even to slaves disallowed from shifting whenever they desired. But Dragonkin understood they couldn't prevent enslaved Birdfolk from practicing every aspect of their culture and heritage. So, this wedding ritual had crossed the ocean with its people, allopreening as much a part of the mating ritual as the offering of feathers, a symbol for the nest the couple would build together.

Harriet could've confined her preening to John's head and neck, the loving act an ample acceptance of him as her husband. But the need to express the depth of her affection for him and the hope for a long, happy marriage had Harriet extending the ritualized preening to the rest of John's body.

Her efforts had John chirping a one-two note with a burbling sound that both pleased and encouraged. She continued, gathering oil and spreading it through his feathers with the same care Rit had taken when she'd washed, greased, and braided Harriet's hair for the ceremony—a different kind of familial preening.

Ben's familiar chirp joined John's, followed by her brothers, then every Birdfolk male in attendance. They chirped and chirped, accepting the freeborn John into their community.

But on this moonlit night, when Harriet fluffed out her feathers and enjoyed being preened by John, accepted as his loving and devoted wife by his family and friends, she felt transported beyond Mistress Essodel's aviary and the institution of slavery.

The land of her ancestors beckoned, and she went, following each unique chirp and whistle.

"Harriet. Are you all right?"

She was fine, but why did John sound . . . Harriet opened what should not have been closed eyes.

"Good. Welcome back."

Welcome back! What does he mean? Oh, no. I hope I didn't. Not during our wedding. Harriet shot up, only then realizing she was in human form and had been placed on a bed of feathers. Her head fell into her hands, embarrassed, if not ashamed. "I'm sorry. I ruined our wedding."

Unknowingly mirroring Rachel's actions from earlier in the evening, John tugged the end of one of her braids. "You did no such thing, Harriet Cassin. Now stop hidin' from me and let me see my wife's beautiful face."

Harriet Cassin? That's who I am now. Harriet Cassin. Harriet Wren Cassin. I like the sound of that. I'm someone's wife. No, not someone's wife, but John's wife. We finished the ritual. I remember now. His female family and friends chirped for me during John's preenin' of my feathers. But I don't remember anything after that.

"Where did everybody go?" Harriet lowered her hands and raised her face to meet John's. She expected a frown, maybe even worried eyes, but not the wide-toothed grin that greeted her. John had never smiled at Harriet in such a way, and for a dizzying second, she wondered if she'd fallen and knocked her head. Unless the trees were the pearly gates to heaven, she still lived, and John was indeed her new husband.

John's arm went around one of her thin shoulders and tucked her against his side. The soft press of his warm skin against hers revealed a very obvious but belatedly recognized fact. They were both naked. "They left to give us privacy." He patted a section of greenish-blue feathers in front of them, spread out like peafowl elongated upper tail coverts. The Sankofa feathers were equally as lovely but without the eyespots. "If you are feelin' unwell or a little nervous about the physical consummation of our marriage, we can wait."

The ritual of consummating Birdfolk marriages on a bed of feather offerings had also survived the brutal passage from Sika. This ritual was still essential to the bonding process, even for couples who shared intimacies before the wedding ceremony.

"I'm fine." Harriet twisted to face John, needing him to see the truth of her words. "I don't want to wait any longer." Because she wanted every part of him, including his body inside of hers. But Harriet wasn't brave enough to speak such explicit words. Instead, she took ahold of his dark, strong hand, calloused in spots and smooth in others, and placed it over a breast. "I'm sure."

Harriet had long ago come to terms with the scars on her body, including on the breast John's fingers caressed with a gentleness her mistresses had never shown her when they forced Harriet to remove her coarse frock for a whipping. But John didn't seem to mind; his touches were loving, if not reverent.

She kissed him because she desired her husband and because he was hers in all ways but one. But that would soon change, so Harriet followed John down onto the feathered bed, touching and being touched.

"I love you, Harriet."

She loved him too, but John had claimed her body and her lips, leaving her breathless.

Chapter 20
I Can't Save Them

1845
Pelduth Neck

"Yeah, kill her. Kill. Her."

"You dirty, ground-scraper."

"They got you, girl. Now you're gonna get it good."

The crowd around Harriet swelled. They pushed and shoved, jockeying for position to better see the further demise of humanity.

A burly Dragonkin who smelled of tobacco and impatience knocked into Harriet. "Watch it, ground-scraper, or you'll be the next one in the noose." He raised a meaty hand to Harriet, ready to strike her the way she imagined he'd done to many Birdfolk, but . . .

John stepped between them, giving the Dragonkin his back with a quick "Apologies." As swift as a pickpocket, they were off. John all but carried Harriet through the ever-growing crowd.

"Are you all right?" John's fingers slid over her shoulders and down her arms. "You're tremblin'." He leaned in even closer, inspecting her face and head. "And sweatin'." Lips found her cheek and kissed with such slow tenderness Harriet did not have to touch his chest to know John's heart raced, but she did anyway.

"Tremblin' and sweatin'. Normal reactions to what just happened."

So was John's pounding heart, but Harriet felt no need to mention the obvious. Instead, she snuggled against his side, seeking warmth and comfort in equal measure.

The wind whipped and whistled, snaking through the bulging crowd and biting everyone as it passed.

Harriet peeked around John, seeing and hearing more of the same as before the Dragonkin had plowed into her.

More spectators.

More name-calling and spewed curses.

There were also many more Birdfolk in the crowd, likely forced from whatever they'd been doing, working on the docks or in the stores or simply walking down the street, as Harriet and John had been before being approached.

A female Dragonkin had planted herself directly in their path. Her hair was the color of strawberries, but her attitude held none of the fruit's sweetness. "You know the law."

Harriet did know because Minister Breembat had a lengthy lecture of dos and don'ts for the enslaved he permitted to hire themselves out.

"Well, go on over there."

Harriet had grasped John's hand, finding it cold and him unmoved by her subtle tug.

"I said go over there, boy." At least nine feet in her white booted heels, the Dragonkin bared the faintest elongated eyeteeth. "Unless you got freedom papers, the law says you will stay, and you will watch." Her eyeteeth had lengthened, and her lips had thinned into a smile that threatened.

"Show her," Harriet had said in a soft tone she hoped her husband would interpret correctly as, "Protect yourself. I'll be fine here alone."

"Freedom papers," the Dragonkin had demanded. She stuck her hand out, palm up. "Show me. Now!"

Harriet had made no other attempts to persuade John to prove his freeborn status. So, she hadn't been surprised when he'd turned away from the woman and led Harriet toward the crowd.

She hadn't liked it one bit, John being treated as a slave would and him complying with a law not meant for the freeborn population.

"You're my wife," he'd said to her. "Where you go, I go."

So, there they stood together, forced to witness the public execution of an enslaved Birdfolk female. Harriet knew the story. She'd heard tales of the reported crime and eventual confession after the accused woman had been dragged off to the town's prison. The old workhouse served as a jail and a holding area for saleable Birdfolk.

Harriet never wanted to see the inside of the building for either reason.

John's arm settled around her shoulders, holding her close, but he lowered his mouth to an ear. "I heard she used an axe on the harpy family. Got them when they slept. Husband and wife. Even the baby."

HARRIET'S ESCAPE:

Gossip traveled fast, especially in a town where different types of people were more likely to mix than they would in rural areas like Mistress Essodel's aviary.

"The wife got it the worst. Her head was nearly cut off."

Harriet closed her eyes, not because John's retelling matched what she overheard everyone else around them say but with less graphic details, but because she understood all too well why the convicted woman had committed the foul deed.

I bet her harpy mistress mistreated her as much as mine did me. Cleanin' and cookin' on top of takin' care of a wailin' baby. We work and work, and they treat us like we're less than dirt. And they don't give us enough food to fill our bellies after a long day of tendin' to them. It ain't right. I feel bad for the child, I do, but not for the master and mistress. Retribution was hers that day. Now she's to be hanged. That ain't right, either. But it's what they do. Kill us when we dare to resist. Hell, even when we don't openly resist. For sport or because some are just plain ole mean.

John maintained a stream of whispered chatter, telling Harriet all he knew and everything she'd tried hard to not think about because she saw too much of herself in the woman who would hang for the audacious crime of self-defense.

"You know she didn't receive a fair trial. A Dragonkin judge and an all-Dragonkin jury. Harpy neighbors testified against her, whether they knew anything or not. Some did, I suppose, but probably not all."

Harriet shifted to stand in front of John, deeming the location safer from being pushed against by the swelling, angry crowd of Dragonkin and harpies.

"Kill her, kill her."

The chant began somewhere far in front of Harriet but soon spread like a deadly virus to the rest of the crowd.

I know this is the reason why John wouldn't leave me. But I hate the way bein' married to me has left taints of slavery on him. It isn't fair. It isn't like bein' freeborn in a slave state is the best life a Birdfolk could live, but it is a shield from the harsher parts of Dragonkin rule. I wish we could leave this place. Just run away and be free together.

Harriet slumped against John's hard, protective chest, reeling in her irrational thoughts.

"Kill her, kill her."

Grasping the arms around her waist, Harriet closed her eyes again. She refused to watch the execution of a woman who should've been able to live a normal life unmarred by the institution of slavery. Instead, the same oppressive system that held her in bondage, creating situations that led her to brood over bloody murder, sought to deny her the little life she'd been granted at birth.

I want to have John's child, I do. But what price would my child have to pay bein' born into a world that forces slaves to watch the murder of another slave as a means of deterring future acts of resistance? If anything, all the Birdfolk faces I've seen in the crowd looked more angry than cowed. Still, it's my duty as John's wife and Mistress Essodel's slave to have a child. Perhaps we will soon, like Soph. One child, then another the following year.

Harriet let her mind wander, envisioning a smiling Soph holding her second daughter. Ann appeared, too, lacing her fingers with Harriet's while reaching out to run chubby fingers through her baby sister's soft hair feathers.

Her lips lifted into a smile at the two-month-old memory. After her second child's birth, Soph glowed just as brightly as when she'd brought little Ann into the world. Soph's joy and love for her children and husband were undeniable, and Harriet had been surprised at the twinge of jealousy that had crept into her heart.

John nipped her ear. "Are you all ri—"

Harriet knew the second the trapdoor to the gallows had been released, and the convicted Birdfolk female had fallen through.

John gasped. But the Dragonkin and harpies in the crowd erupted into laughter and applause. Through the raucous cheers and vulgar curses, Harriet detected the faintest embers of weeping.

Tears stung her eyes, and she let them fall.

"And they call us barbaric." John nipped her ear again. His lips were warm, but the anger he emitted was fiery hot. "That will *never* be you. I won't allow it."

Harriet accepted John's declaration from the good place it originated, feeling no need to voice the obvious because the truth always played out whether the people involved wished it or not.

John released her waist but took ahold of her hand. "We should go. You would think these so-called religious Dragonkin wouldn't execute someone on their precious Sunday. But here they all are, in their Sunday best but doin' the devil's work."

Harriet wanted nothing more than to get away from the gallows and the vile stench of "justice" as quickly as her legs would carry her. But a deeper pull had her moving toward the wooden frame built in front of the right side of the workhouse. A flight of stairs led from the dusty ground to the platform where the executioner stood. An elevated beam with two unused nooses hung like silent warnings.

"Harriet, wait."

As if transported by one of her dreams, Harriet rushed forward.

What am I doin'? I don't want to see her. I don't want to see what was done to her. But I can't help myself. She died in a crowd of people, but she died alone. That ain't right.

Harriet stuttered to a stop, unable to get closer because . . . because . . . The first clawed strike sent the dead woman's left arm flying into the crowd. The second attack claimed both feet. The third and fourth sliced her torso in two and removed her head from her neck. Perhaps the dragon who'd done the indecent act thought it befitting since the dead woman had supposedly done nearly the same to her mistress.

Wide, wet eyes watched in horror as a group of five Dragonkin sliced the body into small pieces, then proceeded to distribute portions of the corpse to the three dozen or so dragons and harpies who had stayed, apparently, for this very reason.

John retook ahold of her waist, lifted her off her feet, and carried her away from the post-mortem carnage. "When you took off, you scared the hell out of me."

"She's a souvenir to them." Harriet craned her head backward to see John. His tight-set jaw always revealed when a storm brewed within him. "I shouldn't have run off. I'm sorry." Harriet softly tapped one of the hands holding her. "John, you can put me down now. I'm safe."

"You must make better decisions." He set her on her own two feet, his jaw as clenched as she'd ever seen it. "One day a week is all the time I get with you. Sundays are all we have because Breembat won't give you permission to live with me." John hugged Harriet to him, and she felt every bit of his anger at their situation in the tense body that draped over hers. "It's not your fault, and I don't blame you. I just hate this feelin' of helplessness when it comes to you. Even when you sneak away to visit durin' the week, I can barely enjoy our time together because I'm so afraid of you gettin' caught. You know what he'll do to you. And what the law will do to me despite you bein' my wife."

Of course, Harriet knew the consequences that would befall her if she was ever caught. They were the same penalties she risked each time she snuck away from one of her temporary masters' homes to visit Rit and her siblings.

Back then, I only thought about my own possible punishment. I didn't think about Momma's. The law protects a master's rights over their property. John could be fined or imprisoned for havin' me spend time with him without permission. I should've known better than to risk his safety.

John released her, his sigh a soft sound of controlled frustration. "You wanted to offer that poor woman a prayer, didn't you?"

Perhaps one day, Harriet would cease being surprised every time John seemed to read her mind with unnatural precision.

Harriet was tempted to glance over her shoulder, still feeling the need to offer the dead woman the respect she hadn't found in life.

Heaven will be her salvation, I'm sure of it. Her pain is over. She's finally free. Lord, thank you for guidin' her home and keepin' her forever in your eternal care. Amen.

That would have to do, so Harriet laced her fingers through John's. "I'm so tired, and we have half the day left."

"Soul weary." John's large hand squeezed hers, and she knew she'd chosen well because he understood her in a way she often did not comprehend herself. "Me too, Harriet. But that woman wasn't alone when she died. We Birdfolk were with her. In her final moments of life, she saw who she needed to see. Heard the voices that most mattered. No doubt, she already came to terms with her death when she decided to kill those who hurt her. Cause and effect. That's all life is, Harriet. Let's go home. I regret comin' into town today."

So did she.

As if public executions were a regular occurrence, and Harriet supposed they were, the crowd had finally dispersed. People continued on with their day as if the brutal loss of life warranted no more of their precious time.

Perhaps she was little better because while she was indeed soul weary, Harriet could not wait to return home with John and have him remind her of all the ways they were both very much alive.

"We better get out of the road, Harriet."

John was right because she could hear the *clip-clop* of a horse-drawn wagon behind them. She followed John and others to the left side of the road so the driver could pass. Harriet watched the wagon approach, suddenly taken in by how much the beautiful dark horse reminded her of the bay Minister Breembat had ridden her atop of when he'd taken her away from Rit and to the Calis household.

John pointed at the wagon. "Caged cart. It must've come from the workhouse, but I don't think it's a prisoner transport wagon. It's too beat up for that, and the driver don't look like law."

Harriet agreed on all accounts, but something unnameable drew her attention away from the horse, past the grisly-faced driver, and to the wagon that was indeed a cage with scratched wood for bars that looked strong enough to withstand whatever had caused the damage.

A baby cried from somewhere inside the caged cart, but all Harriet could see were the backs of three seated men.

"Birdfolk," John whispered. "Runaways, likely."

"But I hear a baby. Who runs away with a baby?"

"Somebody desperate."

Harriet agreed with John again, but something about the baby's wails struck a chord with her. "What if they ain't runaways, John?" Harriet stepped into the street. She wouldn't run away from her husband again, no matter the unexplainable urge to understand the source of the dread she felt the moment she heard the baby's cries.

"What's wrong, Harriet?"

She wasn't sure, but she'd never heard a baby cry with such ear-piercing intensity.

Where's the baby's momma? The poppa? Why ain't anybody tendin' to the child? Are the parents hurt? And why does the baby sound like...?
"John, I know that cry."

"You what?"

"So do you."

The caged cart passed, and Harriet realized more than the three men and a baby were inside. The human transporter was full of Birdfolk, mostly seated, but some stood, holding on to bars so they wouldn't fall. She still couldn't see the baby, but it cried something fierce.

Harriet's feet moved without conscious thought. Before she knew it, she chased after the caged cart, following the baby's shrill sounds. She knew that sound. Dammit, she knew the baby to whom that cry belonged. And if the baby was in there, her mother had to be as well.

"No, Soph." Harriet screamed her sister's name over and over again. But she prayed more. "Please, God, not again. Not again."

"Harriet?" John had caught up to her in no time at all. "Tell me."

She didn't want to say the words but denying them wouldn't make what she knew any less true.

"Soph's baby is in there."

"That's Modesty crying?"

The second John said Soph's baby's name, given in honor of Rit's mother, Harriet realized that she'd subconsciously prevented herself from personalizing the sound with the slim hope that doing so would make her wrong.

"Go." John removed his freedom papers from a pants pocket and showed it to her in a way he'd refused to do earlier for the Dragonkin female. "I can't risk losin' or ruinin' this by shiftin'. Go, Harriet. Do your best. Let your sister know you're here for her."

Harriet didn't need more support than that. She transformed and chased a horse no bird could ever catch. But Harriet ran and ran.

"Soph. Soph. I'm here. I'm here." Harriet stumbled over her fear of losing another sister. The emotion was heavier than all the gold in Mistress Essodel's lair, and Soph and Modesty more precious. "Soph. Soph."

Harriet screamed over and again, still not spotting Soph. Until she did.

Like a sun rising over a mountain, Soph appeared from behind the depressed bodies of Birdfolk intended for sale. If they were lucky, they would be sold to a local buyer. If they were not, an out-of-state owner awaited them, ensuring they would never see their family and friends again.

"Soph. No, my sweet, loving Soph."

Holding Modesty with one arm, Soph shoved her free arm through the bars of the caged cart, reaching for Harriet. "It's okay, Minty. It's okay."

No, it isn't. She's tryin' to protect me. Still bein' my big sister when her heart must be breakin'.

Harriet ran even faster. But what would she do if she reached the driver? Would she commit murder like the poor executed woman? She didn't have an axe or any other weapon to force the driver into releasing her sister.

Not that it mattered because Harriet was too slow. Even in her avian form, her two legs were no match for a horse's four.

I can't save them. How did this happen again? How? What am I gonna tell Momma and Poppa?

With her heart in her throat and gasping for air, all Harriet could do was watch the diminishing forms of Soph and Modesty.

Soph still reached for Harriet, and Modesty still wailed.

Soph Wren.

Born in 1813.

HARRIET'S ESCAPE:

Sold in 1845.
Fate unknown.

Chapter 21
A New Day's Comin'

1848

Essodel Plantation

Untying the faded strip of material from around her neck, Rit used it to wipe away sweat from her face, neck, and cleavage. The August heat at midday was brutal, and Rit wasn't a young woman anymore. At sixty-one, she shouldn't still be toiling in Mistress Essodel's tobacco fields, but Minister Breembat cared little for anyone besides himself.

Lifting her moist face to the sunny sky, Rit continued her work, singing as she carefully removed hornworms from the already primed and topped tobacco leaves.

"At the break of dawn, bathed in the sun's greetin' light,
Waitin' fields of tobacco remind me of our plight.
Hands are sore and soft, yet sturdy and strong,
In the green field of our blues, we croon our song.
God's daystar ascendin' to a great height, its heat a cruel friend,
With every sweaty step, our destinies blend.
Recollections of our ancestral land, now too distant and grim,
In every rhythmic movement, we stomp our hymn."

The troublesome insects, brownish, with a wormlike shape and a small, pointed red "horn" at their posterior, could cause significant defoliation. If Rit and others didn't do their job well, a plague of hornworms could destroy a crop in a week, giving Minister Breembat another excuse to sell off more of Mistress Essodel's slaves.

"Though our wings earthbound, our dreams take flight,
With each melodic song, our hopes we light.
Prayin' for the day when we'll all be free,
Till then, on bended knee we'll be."

Nothing but even rows of tobacco lay before her, a duller shade of green than some Birdfolk feathers. But tobacco had grown more valuable than even the rarest Sankofa feather to everyone other than Mistress Essodel. Even so, Minister Breembat still sold members of slave families, treating them like tobacco leaves in need of priming.

At the thought of the daughters chopped away from her family, sold off, and she left wondering if they were safe or even still lived, Rit's hand trembled. The shaking started at the tips of her ragged nails, and like a hornworm infecting one leaf and then another, the shaking moved down to her dark fingers with fine lines and healed cuts.

The hornworm she held dropped to the overworked soil, and she followed the insect down onto her knees.

Rit's mind whirled and raced. Images of Mariah, Linah, and Soph crackled and popped, a grueling emotional mix of love and grief. With each passing year, Rit struggled to recall Mariah's sweet, smiling face, the sound of her voice, and the scent of her skin.

Hands pressed against her stomach, and Rit was convinced the painful clenching she felt wasn't a sign of hunger but a mother's remembered birth pains. She fell onto her side, arms wrapped around her abdomen.

Rit's days of having children were over. She would never again experience the guilt of leaving one child home to tend to an even younger sibling while she worked the field, tended to the house, or danced for Mistress Essodel's selfish entertainment.

Unable to change the past but holding on to hope for a better future, Rit sang and sang.

". . . someday we'll be free."

"Rit. Rit."

Ashamed she'd let grief overcome her in a field where anybody could see her break down, Rit wiped away her tears with the back of her hand.

"Hey, Rit."

Usually, if Gabbe worked beside her when she sang, she'd join in. But Gabbe should've been in her cabin with her newborn son and three-year-old daughter, not calling for Rit in the tobacco fields.

Suddenly worried about the baby, Rit pushed to her feet, tension in every stiff movement.

"What's wrong, Gabbe? Is it little Oscar?"

"No, Rit. The baby is fine. It's just . . . well, I was sittin' with the cabin door open. You know how hot it gets this time of year. So I was sittin' there and fannin' myself when Minister Breembat rode up. With a young one and it being so hot, I don't have time for that dragon."

God loved her, but the younger woman never could get straight to the point. Rit took ahold of Gabbe's hands and squeezed. "Focus on me and tell me what that horrible man is up to now."

Gabbe nodded, and her light brown eyes twinkled with an unspoken understanding. "Yes, ma'am. I'll get straight to it. Minister Breembat is lookin' for Moses."

The weak, grieving mother of a minute ago, body racked with ghost-birthing cramps, withered on the vine at the news that her nightmare in dragon scales had made a special trip to the aviary in search of her youngest child. A different mother surged forward.

When that horrible man took my girls from me, he was sneaky about it. He went behind my back, and I didn't learn about what he'd done until it was too late. Now, he comes here looking for my Moses. I won't let him have him. Not today. Not ever, so help me God.

Rit hugged Gabbe, grateful for her quick thinking and kindness. She'd left her three-year-old daughter alone with an infant to come find her. Rit had known Gabbe since the girl was a child, and she loved her, so she hated asking her to do more.

"Moses is tendin' to the cows. If you run fast, you should catch him before he sets out with whatever fat calf he's picked out for Mistress Essodel."

The cow pens and barns were on the other side of the aviary and in the opposite direction of the slave quarters. If Rit thought herself capable of making the trek before Minister Breembat stumbled upon Moses, she would've already headed in that direction.

Gabbe glanced over her shoulder and toward the slave quarters where she'd left her children. "Soph was a good friend to me." She refocused on Rit. Her warm brown eyes were a wet shimmer, but her chin was set. "You stall that heartless dragon, and I'll go warn Moses."

Rit would do more than redirect Minister Breembat. She would stay with Gabbe's children until their mother returned, even if the Dragonkin objected to her not being in the field where she belonged. "Tell Moses to hide in the woods until I send someone for him. No matter how long, tell him to not come out until I tell him it's safe."

Rit took off, waving and calling, "Minister Breembat, Minister Breembat."

As she hoped, the Dragonkin stopped and waited for her to approach.

Rit's knees ached on her best days and throbbed on her worst. But she felt no pain as she ran from the tobacco fields and up a small hill to a dirt path that connected the slave quarters to the cow pens and barns.

"Minister Breembat." She sucked in deep lungfuls, and her heart beat so fast she feared it would explode before she ensured Moses's safety.

"You run like an old woman, Rit." He leered down at her, licking his lips and smiling. "Still pretty, though. But not enough to get me in trouble with Mother. For whatever reason, she still favors you."

Disgusted by his attention but grateful for small blessings, Rit bobbed a curtsy she knew Minister Breembat would interpret as gratitude for his reluctance to violate Rit for fear of his mother's wrath.

She truly despised the dragon and would happily spit on his grave whenever the devil got around to recalling him to hell.

"I'm glad you're here, Rit. I'm looking for Moses, and nobody seems to know where that boy has gotten off to."

Rit stared up at Minister Breembat. The Dragonkin exuded every basic right he limited to others. His full belly hung over his belt while his black suit fit him with a tailor's precision. The red and black snakeskin boots were the fourth pair she'd seen over the past two months, and she assumed that when he sold this year's tobacco crop, he would show up with even finer footwear.

"What do you need with my son? He ain't done nothin' wrong, Minister Breembat."

"There you go, thinking the worst of me."

With good reason, you lyin' dog. I won't let you have more of my children. I'll kill you first. I don't know how I'll manage it, but I'll take you from this place.

"There's some work I need done at the mine my brother left me." Sun-kissed hands moved to rest on the nape of the horse's neck, and Rit marveled at how casually the dragon lied.

"I thought the minin' camp was closed."

"Well, it's not, and I don't answer to you, ground-scraper."

The horse shifted at his raised voice, and its ears twitched.

"Go get your boy or tell me where to find him."

Rit shrugged and returned Minister Breembat's lie with her own. "I haven't seen him since this mornin' and don't know where he is."

Minister Breembat turned the horse until it faced Rit, and she accepted the small display as the act of intimidation it was meant to be.

But she wouldn't be cowed, and she let that truth seep through every pore of her body. "You ain't sellin' my Moses the way you did my Mariah, Linah, and Soph."

"What are you talking about? Your girls up and run off. Everybody knows that." He moved the horse closer, forcing Rit to retreat for each step forward the horse took. "Now, I better not hear you say that again. They ran away. Do you hear me?"

Rit swallowed hard, and sweaty hands clenched and unclenched. "They didn't. They wouldn't."

Minister Breembat vaulted from his horse and grabbed Rit by her shoulders, shaking her with so much force she bit the inside of her cheek and tongue. "I said those worthless daughters of yours ran off. And I better not hear you say otherwise."

The metallic taste of blood coated her tongue and fortified her resolve. "I ain't gonna never tell you where to find my Moses. You can kill me, Minister Breembat. Right here and now. I'm prepared to die. But I won't help you take another child from me. I'd rather die. What will you tell Mistress Essodel then? She won't believe I run off. She'll see through that lie."

The hands on her shoulders tightened, and his fingernails lengthened into claws. Rit had never been more afraid of meeting her maker before she was ready. But the pain of losing first Mariah, then Linah, and finally Soph was a devastation so deep and wide that no fear Minister Breembat could evoke within her would compare.

Prayers hadn't returned them to her or softened Minister Breembat's cruelty. What else did Rit have to fight with but a mother's undying love? She couldn't defeat him in a physical battle. How the delicate bones in her shoulders snapped under his rough handling proved that point well enough.

But at his core, Rit believed Minister Breembat to be a coward. So she didn't wince at the pain, nor did she retreat from her stance.

"You can't have Moses. I won't give him to you." The threat to tell Mistress Essodel hung on the tip of her tongue, held back by warm blood and cold common sense.

Mistress Essodel might punish her son for lyin' to her for years, but she'll do worse to me and mine because she wouldn't want any slave knowin' she'd been made a fool. If nothin' else, I can trust a dragon's arrogance.

Minister Breembat shoved Rit away from him, and she couldn't have prevented the hard fall if she wanted. "You speak nonsense. I have no need to sell off your kinfolk, Rit." With a clawed hand, he waved it in the air, gesturing to the tobacco fields behind her. "This is my hoard. Abundant and valuable. I have no need to sell off your worthless children."

Rit didn't believe a word that spewed from his mouth because the only hoard he'd accumulated were debts. According to Ben, Master Gyzad's mining camp closed months ago after years of poor management, confirming Minister Breembat's business acumen as uninspired as his sermons.

She had challenged the dragon beyond anything she'd ever dared, so Rit kept her mouth closed, seeing no benefit to pushing him into a pride-saving action. A life-changing injury would likely be the result. He'd already broken several bones in her shoulders. Rit could heal from those well enough, even if slowly.

Rit pushed to her feet, neither with grace nor without pain. But she would endure more if it kept her family off the auction block. Still, dragons did not have a monopoly on pride, so she stood straight and swallowed the blood.

She watched as Minister Breembat drew himself back onto his horse. Rit couldn't care less that he all but growled at her, no more than she gave two wits about his threat.

"I'll be back tomorrow. Moses better be here or else." Perhaps expecting silence to be her response, which it would have been, he turned his horse away from the path that would've taken him deeper into the aviary and toward the cow pens where Gabbe had gone after Moses.

Rit narrowed her gaze at Minister Breembat's retreating back. With each step his horse took, taking him farther away from Moses, Rit's breathing evened, and her heart slowed. But it was too soon to rejoice. Her Moses wasn't yet safe because, in this instance, Minister Breembat had not lied. He would return. When he did, what would Rit do?

She was then reminded that she wasn't alone. She had family and friends. More, Rit had an entire Birdfolk community. They had each other.

"Listen up, listen up, children of Sika,

From the Southern plains to the Northern mountains.

Listen up, listen up, children of Sika,

From the Western deserts to the Eastern forests.

Listen up, listen up, children of Sika,

We are one."

Rit turned to see every tobacco field hand looking up the hill and at her.

"Listen up, listen up, children of Sika," the field hands sang.

"We bear the load; we brave the lash.

Listen up, listen up, children of Sika,

We feathered friends, fortified souls.

Rit caught sight of Gabbe down the path. The younger woman waved, and Rit released the last of her tension. They both succeeded in their missions. Moses was safe, and with the help of her Birdfolk community, he would stay that way.

Forever grateful, Rit closed her eyes and added her voice to the song.

"Birdfolk we are,

Birdfolk we'll forever be.

From the Southern plains to the Northern mountains,

From the Western deserts to the Eastern forests.

We are one.

United. Strong.

HARRIET'S ESCAPE:

Feathered friends. Fortified souls.
Meant to be free.
Take my hand. Walk with me.
Into the forever light.
Freedom. Freedom. Freedom.
Awaits.

Chapter 22
I Can't Stay

1849
Pelduth Neck
Tozor Plantation

"She's been sick since Christmastime, Ben. It's the first week of February."

Did I fall asleep again? John and I were talkin' and . . . I don't remember much of what we talked about after he arrived. I guess that's why he and Poppa left the cabin to talk. But if they didn't want to disturb me or want me to overhear their conversation about my poor health, they should've gone farther than the porch.

Harriet rolled over, snuggling deeper under the cover, grateful for the new straw-filled bed tick she made last December before the worst of her sickness set in. She hadn't known she would spend most of the winter days on the bed tick, recovering for a short spell and then relapsing.

"John, you're tellin' me what I already know. I've been through this and worse with Harriet."

It hurts to hear the worry in Poppa's and John's voices. I don't mean to make my family worry about my health. I try to work when I can. Show everybody, especially Minister Breembat, that I'm okay. That I'm not as weak and useless as I appear. On my good days, I can use those oxen I bought to tend fields as good as any male. But then I get tired and find myself back in this bed.

"She always bounces back, my Harriet. Trust her."

"This isn't about trust, Ben. You may have known Harriet her entire life, but I also know the woman I married. She's as stubborn as a mule and as fearless as a honey badger. If reincarnation were possible, Harriet would wish to live again as the same beautiful Sankofa bird she is but with wings that would take her anywhere she desired. The same Harriet but not quite."

"We all want to be free, John. Each of my children is special in their own way. But Harriet wantin' her freedom isn't what makes her special because every slave dreams and prays for the same."

"That's not what I'm sayin'."

Harriet didn't need to see John to know his jaw was tight and that he likely paced, requiring a physical release of his pent-up frustration.

In the five years we've been married, John has worried about me more than any husband should. In that, my parents and husband have a lot in common.

Harriet laced her fingers and pressed her palms together. Lowering her head, her chin close to her chest, Harriet prayed. "Oh, Lord, help me. Make me stronger. Give me strength. My Lord, you know my heart. And it's here with my family and friends. But, Lord, gracious Lord, I got to be free. If you can't free me, soften Minister Breembat's heart. Soften his heart, Lord, so I can stay here. Please, soften Minister Breembat's heart."

"Two weeks after Soph and Modesty were sold away, Harriet gave me a handmade tin box. When we were chasin' after the caged wagon, I was so afraid of tearin' my freedom papers that I didn't shift. I left Harriet to go it alone, knowin' her chance of success was zero. When I caught up to her, she was so inconsolable that her heartache brought on an episode. I felt helpless to protect my wife for the third time that day."

Three times. The first had been when that Dragonkin female forced us to watch the hangin'. John hadn't been able to think of a way to get the both of us out of it. But what he doesn't realize is that if not for me bein' there, I would've missed seein' my sister one last time. It hurts, it does, but that final glimpse of Soph and Modesty is more than anybody else in the family has. I still dream of them sometimes. Linah, too. I hope I always will because that's the Lord's way of lettin' me know they're safe and thinkin' of me, too.

Palms on the bed tick, Harriet slowly pushed herself upward, hoping she wouldn't be overcome with another bout of nausea or dizziness. Feeling steady, she scooted backward a few inches, sighing when her back touched the wall. Harriet spied the rumpled cover tangled around her feet and swore under her breath.

Keeping her neck and head as still as possible, Harriet yanked until she dislodged the material. Satisfied with the small win, she covered herself from stocking feet to waist. Despite the logs burning in the fireplace, the winter chill had seeped into her bones, and refused to leave. So, she wore a loose-fitted frock stuffed into an old pair of John's trousers. The less-than-flattering look matched everything else about her these days.

But she was clean, thanks to Rit, and her plaits were only a week old and lint-free. That would have to do for John, Minister Breembat, and whomever else the foul Dragonkin decided to bring by to inspect her.

Harriet's eyes drifted closed at the thought of yet another humiliating inspection. She shut out John and Ben's conversation. Harriet didn't want to listen to men lament her poor health or which of them was better capable of protecting her from the ills of slavery, all the while knowing neither had nor could.

Of course, Harriet didn't blame them because the unequal system was built to yield these very results. Where, then, did that leave Harriet and John?

Comfortable and tired, Harriet stayed put at the sound of the door opening and then closing. Heavy, booted steps drew nearer, and Harriet's lips quirked into a weary but genuine smile.

"You weigh less than Poppa, but he's a lighter walker." As if her eyelids were weighed down by the same worries John carried, Harriet slowly opened her eyes. "I didn't mean to fall asleep."

John wore an overcoat patched at the elbows and trousers held up by suspenders he'd had since before they married. The way he stared down at her, brow furrowed and lips downturned, he'd brought in more than the winter chill.

"You look better than when I saw you two days ago." He walked over to the fireplace and tossed the last log onto the waning fire. "I'll help Ben chop more wood before I go." He turned back to her, grumpy but trying to conceal his feelings.

The sick and tired part of Harriet appreciated John's effort, but the soaring bird within her found his actions grating. "Sit." She patted the small space beside her, making it clear she wanted him to sit next to her and not at the table on the other side of the cabin.

"Has Breembat come by today?" John knelt before Harriet, removed his overcoat, and tucked it around her before complying with her request.

The second he sat beside her, she collapsed against his supportive shoulder. "Not yet, but he doesn't come every day."

"He shouldn't come at all." He lifted her face to his with a finger under her chin, and she accepted his kiss. "I don't expect much conversation when I visit, so I don't care that you nod off. I just want to spend time with you however I can." John caressed the feathers that protruded between the rows of plaits. "It's sad that I'm allowed to spend as much time with you as I want when you're sick because you can't work. But as soon as you are back on your feet, not quite healthy but strong enough to make a good show of it, we're back to seein' each other on Sundays only."

An arm snaked around her waist and pulled her closer to him. With John so near, warm and smelling of cinnamon, she wouldn't be awake much longer.

"Did you bring me a cinnamon stick?"

John reached into the resewn front pocket of his overcoat, readjusted it snugly around Harriet, and then handed her his gift.

"There's more to life than oxen, boots, and whatever supplies you think you need to hire yourself out." John tapped the end of the cinnamon stick that hung from Harriet's mouth. "It's okay for you to treat yourself sometimes, Harriet. All you do is work, work, work."

They'd had this conversation before, and Harriet had no interest in repeating her stance until the back-and-forth morphed into a full-blown argument. John's continual caresses to her feathers revealed he felt the same, so Harriet enjoyed the cinnamon stick. So, too, did the child Minty, who always went to bed hungry and whose masters never gave her a morsel of dessert.

Harriet didn't want to ruin the mood with harsh facts, but avoiding discussing the bigger issue wouldn't make the problem disappear.

"With my poor health, I struggle to pay the sixty annual fee to Minister Breembat for him allowin' me to hire myself out. I convinced Dr. Tozor to hire me to work with Poppa on the timbering. But most of the time, I'm in the wheat field."

"You're overworked and exhausted. I don't see that changin', although something must because you can't go on like this." John's gentle strokes ceased, causing Harrier to peer up at him. "I know what you're gettin' at, but I haven't changed my mind."

Harriet lowered her gaze, feeling the slicing cut of another rejection to a heart wounded in so many other ways long before she met and married John. But no matter how many stabs to the organ she received, taking the blow never got easier.

She lifted her eyes, determined to meet his fear and their future head-on. "Minister Breembat *will* sell me, John. Just as he sold my sisters and tried to sell Moses. Bein' sixteen, Moses would've fetched a good price for him. Sellin' Soph and Modesty together was like guaranteeing a buyer that Soph was fertile and unlikely to run off and leave her child behind."

Harriet sat up straight, long since finished with her cinnamon stick, and suddenly energized by its sweet, woody flavor. Hand warm from John's overcoat, she placed the palm on his stubbled cheek.

"I've heard the rumors, although I've tried to ignore them. Every time I'm laid up for longer than a few days, they start up again."

John's headshake rubbed his coarse stubble across her calloused hand, sendin' a trickle of sadness through her for the truth he refused to admit.

"I've given him no reason to keep me. It's more expensive to keep a sickly slave than it is to buy a new one." Underneath John's overcoat, Harriet touched her flat stomach. "Five years and no baby to show for our marriage."

"Don't." John pulled away from her hand, which she allowed to drop to his shoulder, maintaining the barest of contact.

"You know it's true. Money for labor or children used for labor is all we mean to Dragonkin. Birdfolk capable of both are highly valued. But older Birdfolk ain't worth much to Dragonkin like Minister Breembat and Mistress Essodel. And those who can't bear fruit ain't either."

Her hand slid from his shoulder, down his arm, and onto his fisted hand. She wished they could have lighthearted discussions, that every day of their married life wasn't impacted by her legal slave status and John's freeborn one that still left him with little recourse where it concerned her.

"Some things just aren't meant to be, Harriet. Not everyone is a parent."

True, but even her youngest sister, Rachel, had given birth to a daughter, Angerine, two years after Harriet's marriage and was pregnant with her second child.

No other Wren female has reached my twenty-seven years without becomin' a mother. I've never even gotten with child. After five long years, John has stopped expectin' it of me. I guess I have, too. But it doesn't feel good admittin' that. Too many whippins as a child, maybe. Or it's just my worn-out body like John said.

The fist beneath her hand relaxed, spreading out and turning over to hold her hand. "I know you want to run. You're afraid of bein' torn from us, of your parents forced to grieve the sale of another daughter."

Harriet was, but John had it wrong. She didn't *want* to run. What she wanted was to be free with her husband and family. Mistress Essodel had finally permitted Ben to buy Rit. Her father had saved for years, working for Dragonkin like Dr. Tozor, ever since Minister Breembat recognized his manumission.

Minister Breembat had to escort Ben to the courthouse, present Master Gyzad's will to the judge, and then register Ben to receive his Certification of Freedom document. Minister Breembat had to do the same after Mistress Essodel agreed to Rit's sale. Harriet had also made her parents a tin box for their freedom papers.

No, Harriet didn't want to run, but circumstances made it nearly impossible for her to stay.

"But if you run, you'll either never see any of us again or be killed for defyin' whichever slave catcher Breembat sends after you."

Despite her small stature and frequent bouts of sickness, the freedom fighter slowly growing inside Harriet was touched by how well John understood the depth of her desire to be free.

I'd rather die seekin' freedom than live out what's left of my life, regrettin' havin' never tested the true might of my wings. But I won't think of never seein' my family again. Or leavin' John behind.

Despite the consistent tug of fatigue, Harriet sat up straight and faced John. More than her illness dimmed the eyes that met hers, and not for the first time since meeting John, she wished their love and commitment to each other wasn't constantly challenged by society's rules.

"Stay with me."

"Run away with me."

They'd spoken at the same time, but they'd voiced the same requests before. With each prospective buyer Minister Breembat brought before her, hoping to palm her off on someone else, Harriet's request of John became more desperate.

Her head fell against the wall, and whatever warmth John's overcoat had granted Harriet evaporated with her husband's counter request.

"I can't stay."

"You're askin' me to leave everybody I love and know behind."

"I'll be sold away from everybody I know and love if I stay."

"A warrant for my arrest will be issued. You're my wife, but I'll be labeled a thief if I take you away from here."

Eyes cast to the flicker and crackle of burning wood in the fireplace, Harriet reached for and found John's hand. "I've prayed for the Lord to soften Minister Breembat's heart. But no matter how hard or often I pray, I feel it deep in my bones. I'm gonna leave this place one way or another. Either by sale or by stealin' myself. For once in my life, John, I'd like to control what happens to me."

John's large, strong hand held Harriet's so tenderly she wanted to cry. "You're askin' me to choose between you and the rest of my family. Between stayin' safe here and risk bein' killed out there. That isn't fair."

"I know, but . . ." *I have a right to two things—liberty or death. If I can't have one, I'll have the other.*

PART IV

"... THERE WAS NO ONE TO WELCOME ME TO THE LAND OF FREEDOM. I WAS A STRANGER IN A STRANGE LAND; AND MY HOME, AFTER ALL, WAS DOWN IN MARYLAND, BECAUSE MY FATHER, MY MOTHER, MY BROTHERS, AND SISTERS, AND FRIENDS WERE THERE. BUT I WAS FREE, AND THEY SHOULD BE FREE."

Chapter 23

Farewell, My Dear Ones

1849

Dralox County

"What do you see?" Palms pressed to the base of a one-hundred-foot sycamore tree, Harriet strained her neck back to see Ben Jr. "Well?"

Henry clamped a hand over her mouth. "Hush before someone hears you."

She ripped her mouth away, appreciating her younger brother's caution but not the taste of sweat and dirt.

"I can't see him," she whispered. "It's too dark, and he went up too high."

As if his human eyes were sharper than hers, Henry stretched his tall self in front of Harriet and stared up into the same darkness but with no more vision than she. "Yeah, I don't see him either."

Harriet pushed Henry, wishing it had more effect than a glare.

"Don't be mad at me because you got us lost."

"I didn't get us lost. I told you I didn't know my way." She pushed Henry again with the same impact as shoving the sycamore tree.

"Quit that, Minty. I ain't done nothin' to you to get you all riled up and layin' hands on me."

Henry wasn't wrong, but that did nothing to stop Harriet. She shoved him again. "Don't call me Minty. I've been Harriet for five years."

"You ain't my momma, so stop it."

"I'm your big sister, but you don't listen to a thing I have to say."

Harriet was tempted to push Henry again but accepted she'd taken it too far, even if she'd put no strength behind her unjustified attacks. Instead, Harriet shoved chilled fingers into her coat pockets. She should've offered Henry the apology he deserved, but Harriet felt mulish about more than having spent the past two weeks wandering the woods and countryside with brothers needing a good soak in a lake.

Harriet raised her arm and sniffed, a silent admission that she smelled little better.

"I would listen if you did more than shrug whenever I ask which way."

Harriet opened her mouth to reply, tired of being blamed for the mess her escape had turned into, but she snapped her mouth shut at the sound of booted feet above her. Taking hold of Henry's arm, she tugged him away from the big tree that would likely be their bed for the night.

Ben Jr. landed with a soft *thud*. Dark eyes swung from Harriet to Henry, then back to her. "I can't believe you two are arguin' again. With the way you bicker, I'm surprised we ain't been caught."

Neither could Harriet, but not for the reason Ben Jr. had given. She was certain Minister Breembat would send Mudspike after them, or a slave catcher like the gryphon, when he realized they were gone. She also assumed that would take a few days since Minister Breembat only checked on them at the Tozor Plantation when he needed something or wished to remind them who was in charge.

For Harriet, that would give them a few days of lead time. Add a couple more days due to Minister Breembat's arrogance that none of Mistress Essodel's slaves would dare run away, and Harriet estimated they had about a six-day head start. They'd exhausted that time and more. Surely, even the miserly Minister Breembat had sent someone after them. He might have even paid to run wanted ads in newspapers from Dralox County to Pyzai. Pyzai was the closest free state to Miadar, so it wouldn't take much for Minister Breembat to determine their intended destination.

The problem, unfortunately, was that Henry was right, and Harriet was very much wrong.

"I didn't ask the two of you to run away with me." Despite her uncharitable behavior, she was grateful for the company.

Ben Jr. leveled a long, accusatory finger at Harriet, reminding her of the few times she'd been scolded by her father. "You didn't have to ask." All six feet of Ben Jr. marched up to Harriet, and had he been a Dragonkin, she would have been terrified.

But he was her loving, devoted brother, so Harriet gave him the same treatment she had given Henry. She shoved him in the chest.

Henry smacked her upside her head, and the Wren siblings laughed. After the stressful weeks they'd had, the release was overdue.

Harriet had indeed gotten them lost, not that she'd ever claimed to know the route to Pyzai. She'd assumed the Lord or instinct would show her the way. Neither happened.

Harriet pointed to the tree behind Ben Jr. "What did you see?"

"Farmhouses, like before. Should we risk it this time?"

Asking strangers for help did not sit well with Harriet. It was one thing to play with her brothers about them being lost or even displaying a level of stubbornness that wouldn't get them any closer to freedom than they were. But it was something entirely different if Harriet chose the wrong person to ask for assistance, causing their capture, maybe even their death.

Henry's hand slid into hers, a subtle reminder they were in this together. Where one went, the others would follow. But all her brothers had to show for following her lead were blisters, dehydration, and hunger pains.

"I don't know if we should." Harriet ran her tongue over dry, cracked lips, ashamed of her poor planning but hopeful they could find their way to Pyzai. If she'd learned nothing else from meeting all kinds of free and enslaved Birdfolk when hired out to docks and farms, it was the importance of the North Star. She might not have reached Pyzai, but the North Star had guided them this far. "But I don't think we should quit. We're close. I can feel it."

The hand she once held when it was small and fragile, the boy to whom it belonged blindly trusting that she knew what was best, released her hand and moved to stand beside Ben Jr.

Two against one. I should've known this was how things would end. I just need them to give me another day or two. I know I can do this. The Lord wouldn't have brought us this far otherwise. I haven't had one episode. That must mean somethin', right?

"I can do this. I can."

Ben Jr.'s headshake hurt as much as Henry's withdrawal of his hand had.

"I want freedom as much as you. I do. But I left my family behind, Harriet. What is Ruth gonna do? It ain't fair puttin' raisin' our little ones all on her. Them bein' freeborn is better than not, but I want Ann Marie and Benjamin to know their poppa. They won't if I leave."

Harriet wanted to scream that everything Ben Jr. had shared was why she had tried to keep her plan to herself. When Ben Jr. and Henry visited her in March after a nearly three-month sickness, Harriet had no doubt that Minister Breembat would sell her as soon as he could find a buyer. By late August, he had begun bringing around potential buyers again. Luckily for her, all the offers were below Minister Breembat's selling price. Despite his claim that she was "worthless," he'd set a respectable selling price of $400.

She'd wondered if he sold her sisters for the same amount.

But Ben Jr. had taken one look at her and said, "You're gonna run, and I won't let you do it alone."

Henry had mumbled something similar, and, just like that, a daring escape plan for one had turned into a haphazard plan for three.

With a mind full of questions and a heart filled with self-doubt, Harriet turned away from her brothers and toward the farmhouses Ben Jr. had spied from the sycamore tree.

Ahead could be freedom, but it could also mean capture. If we're caught, Minister Breembat will have us whipped. Like that poor hanged woman, he'll use us as examples of what happens to runaways. He might even give us over to Mistress Essodel for dinner or wash his hands of us totally and sell us into the Deep South. All bad options.

"I'm not sayin' you don't understand my worry because you ain't a parent."

Harriet did, but it hurt because Ben Jr.'s valid concerns were not hers.

John refused to run away with me because he didn't want to leave his parents and friends behind. So, I left him before Minister Breembat could force us apart. The result is the same. Me here and John there. If I go back, nothin' good will change for me. But if I don't, what kind of big sister would that make me?

"It's two against one. You don't need my approval to go back. I ain't the one in charge out here. I no more know what I'm doin' than a babe can walk." She turned to face her brothers, unsurprised by Ben Jr.'s headshake and Henry's frown. "What?"

Henry reached out and held her hand again, igniting her primal instinct to protect. "We Wrens might disagree, but we ain't never against each other. I know you want to push on, but I'm afraid of losin' what we left behind. We tagged along because we couldn't imagine bein' anywhere you weren't." Henry pulled her to him, and Harriet happily accepted her brother's heartfelt embrace. "Come home, Minty." He kissed her cheek, melting what was left of her resolve. "Please. Please."

Harriet could deny her siblings nothing. In twenty-seven years of life, she'd never been inclined to try. She did not recall giving her brothers a verbal reply, but she remembered each weighty step away from the promise of freedom and back toward the peril of slavery. Her legs had never been heavier or her feet slower.

She had struck out with her brothers on September 17, 1849, and returned the first week of October. The homecoming, while sweet, was also short-lived.

Rumors of her sale intensified. Minister Breembat had finally found a buyer.

Harriet was out of time.

❖ ❖ ● ❖ ❖

Pelduth Neck

Tozor Plantation

"Come on, Momma, let's get you home." Harriet looped her hand in the crook of Rit's arm, leading her mother away from the big house and toward the slave cabins, where a surprise warm meal awaited Rit's arrival.

Harriet hadn't cooked for Rit in too long, and circumstances would likely prevent her from doing so again even longer. She also placed her favorite quilt in her parents' cabin to keep them warm during the cold winter nights. When Harriet settled and found work, she would make herself a duplicate, a soft reminder of home.

"What's gotten into you?" Rit patted the hand linked at her elbow, and Harriet feared her mother would see through the pretense. "You don't have to do my chores, but I appreciate it. I don't know the last time I had an evenin' to myself." Rit's smile cut through Harriet.

The guilt that had never left Harriet since running away with her brothers tightened like an executioner's noose around her neck. "You always take care of me and everybody else, Momma. I'm gonna walk you to your cabin so you can get a good long rest. I made sure the fireplace was poppin' hot, and I fixed you a bowl of somethin' nice and warm that'll stick to your ribs."

Harriet had inherited her body shape and size from her mother, so when Rit hugged her, she never felt engulfed by the embrace. "What's wrong, Momma?"

"Nothin'. It's nothin', baby."

A lie, but Harriet harbored her own secret. She had no right to call Rit on hers. Besides, any conversation about the state of Rit's heart would inevitably lead to Harriet confessing her sins and revealing her plans. As it was, Rit had broken down in tears when Harriet, Ben Jr., and Henry returned. She'd hugged and kissed them like she hadn't since they were children.

Ben did, too, but her father was harder to read than Rit, so Harriet couldn't tell if he was proud of her attempt, disappointed she'd failed, or hurt she'd left without a word.

When she had lain with John the second night of her return, Harriet concluded all three were true.

"I'll come back for you," she'd told John. "Not right away because it'll be too dangerous, but I'll come back. I promise."

Harriet wanted to make Rit the same pledge, although she didn't think Rit would believe her any more than John had. While her intentions were true, Harriet wasn't yet sure how she would keep the promise to her husband.

I'll find a way to do it. John just needs to have faith in me and the Lord.

Harriet stopped at the porch of her parents' cabin.

"Aren't you comin' in?"

She wanted to, but Harriet feared her resolve would crumble if she dragged out the goodbye. The invisible noose around her neck had tightened with each step, threatening to strangle her before her heart exploded from already missing her mother.

"No, Momma. I better get to the big house and do those chores." Usually, Harriet would turn away and hustle to wherever she needed to be. This time, however, she threw herself at Rit, hugging her longer than a normal goodbye warranted.

But Harriet managed to keep from weeping, even when Rit laughed and said, "You're a good daughter, Minty. See you later."

With a final wave to Rit, Harriet rushed toward the big house. Sentimentality, more than forgetfulness, had her family calling her Minty sometimes. Minty would've caved at the loving way Rit had said her name, staying in Dr. Tozor's aviary while knowing Minister Breembat would come for her. But she was no longer Minty.

Minty Wren had been a survivor, though. She'd been battered and bullied, and still, she stood tall, allowing the birth of Harriet Wren Cassin.

I won't let Minty's strength in the face of so much abuse be wasted by waitin' to be sold away from all I know and love. My fate won't be unknown because I will not allow it.

Harriet reached the big house, rushing through the gate and around to the back of it. Many Wrens worked for Dr. Tozor's family in the main house and other homes on the fourteen acres of Tozor land. But Harriet wasn't in search of a Wren. She spotted Mary the second she strolled into the kitchen.

Luscious golden-red head feathers grew alongside dark brown human hair. The combination always made Harriet think of a halo of raging fire. Harriet hadn't met many Birdfolk slaves whose ancestors were stolen from western Sika. But the vibrant color and shape of Mary's head feathers was an inheritance that transcended time and place.

Harriet would've struggled to find her in the crowded kitchen without the brightness of Mary's head feathers. Thankfully, no Wren was in the room, but plenty of other Birdfolk were there, so she couldn't risk them overhearing her message to Mary.

How am I gonna give Mary my message to pass on to Momma? I didn't promise I wouldn't run again. But Momma will have a fit if she can't find me tomorrow. I can't wait another day. Mary's my only hope.

As if she'd stopped by to say hello to a friend, Harriet skipped up to Mary and grabbed her hands. She spun Mary around, who parted her lips to say something, likely curious about Harriet's strange behavior. Instead, Mary grinned down at her, an eyebrow quirked upward, and nodded.

Perhaps Mary caught on that she wanted her to play along, or maybe she thought Harriet had juicy gossip to share. Whatever her reason for going along, frolicking with Harriet until they were outside, she was grateful.

Rit liked and trusted Mary, and Robert was sweet on the seventeen-year-old. She couldn't think of a better person to deliver her secret message to her mother.

Harriet danced around and around, strategically pulling Mary farther from the house and prying ears, and closer to the front gate.

"Listen, Mary, I need you to . . ."

The *clippety-clop* of hooves sounded behind Harriet.

Grabbing Mary's hands again, she twirled as if she were in avian form and performing for Mistress Essodel.

Dr. Tozor, clean-shaven and primly dressed for whatever evening festivities the slaves in the kitchen were preparing for, sat atop his favorite horse. Black with patches of gray at the neck and on the front legs, the horse had the same stoic air as its rider.

What should I do now? Dr. Tozor doesn't like us singin' and dancin' when we're supposed to be workin'. Wait, where is Mary goin'? No, Mary, don't go back into the house.

Unsure of what to do next and not wanting to raise Dr. Tozor's suspicions, Harriet plastered on a smile, curtsied, and sang a song that had to be delivered to her by the Lord because each chorus was new to her.

"So long, my sweet friends, I gotta leave here.

So long, oh, so long.

In the sun's first light, I'll take that steady step.

So long, oh, so long.

In the moon's beautiful glow, we'll see each other again.

So long, oh, so long.

On the trail to freedom I'll be, my journey overdue.

So long, oh, so long."

Dark Dragonkin eyes bore into Harriet, but she continued to smile and twirl as if she had no better sense than a cat chasing its tail.

But Dr. Tozor didn't stop, much less question her for being where she shouldn't be. He rode toward the back of the house, and Harriet made a show of going toward the open gate, singing all the while.

However, once Dr. Tozor was out of sight, she slowed, waited several minutes, then headed for the kitchen and Mary.

She skidded to a halt, surprised to see Dr. Tozor at the back of the house instead of on his way to the stable.

Is he waitin' for me? He told Minister Breembat that he wouldn't pay good money for damaged goods, sparin' us from the whip. But he knows I ran away. Probably knows, too, that I'm about to be sold. He can't trust I won't run again. But he ain't said nothin'.

Harriet studied the ground as if she'd dropped something earlier. She made a show of getting on her hands and knees and crawling in every direction as if what she sought was important.

Sighing with regret at not having found what she'd been looking for, Harriet jumped to her feet and shrugged, pretending to be unbothered by Dr. Tozor's steady gaze.

I can't come back here a third time. Dr. Tozor is suspicious. If he sees me around here again, he'll know I'm up to somethin'.

"So long, my sweet friends, I gotta leave here.

So long, oh, so long.

In the sun's first light, I'll take that steady step.

So long, oh, so long.

In the moon's beautiful glow, we'll see each other again.

So long, oh, so long.

On the trail to freedom I'll be, my journey overdue.

So long, oh, so long."

I want to leave Momma a message. If I sing loud enough, maybe Mary or a Wren will hear me. They won't know what it means now, but they will come tomorrow and I'm nowhere to be found.

"So long, my sweet friends, I gotta leave here.

So long, oh, so long.

In the sun's first light, I'll take that steady step.

So long, oh, so long.

In the moon's beautiful glow, we'll see each other again.

So long, oh, so long.

On the trail to freedom I'll be, my journey overdue.

So long, oh, so long."

Harriet closed the gate behind her, not confident her message reached the right ears. But there was nothing to do but push on with the rest of her plan. The sun would set in an hour, and if the good Lord saw her through, she would be beyond Dr. Tozor's property and on her way to the small Dragonkin Quaker settlement without anyone spotting and questioning her.

With her typical long, fast gait, Harriet walked to her cabin and grabbed the satchel she'd packed earlier. She paused, breathed deeply, and placed her sweaty, shaking hand over her pounding heart.

"This is it, Lord. You told me I had a right to liberty, and I'm gonna take it now. I'm puttin' my faith in you. I didn't trust in you enough the last time, Lord, and I didn't deliver my brothers to the freedom land. I didn't do right by them or you, Lord. But I will this time. I'll trust the people you steer me to. I'll trust your servants the way I didn't before. Thank you, Lord. Thank you."

Harriet closed the door to a cabin she hoped to never see again. Her stomach twisted into knots, cramping as if she'd eaten spoilt food. She had, many times, when scarfing down a slave master's discarded leftovers was preferable to going to bed on an empty stomach. But the wretched sensation of battered pride that had turned her stomach after consuming moldy food had sickened her body and her spirit.

Get yourself together, Harriet. Now ain't the time for nerves or even for guilt. I told John I'd return for him, and I will. He knows my heart. He knows I love him but that I also got to be free. He understands. He does. I know he does.

Harriet refused to entertain any other thought about John and the future of their marriage. So, she envisioned herself putting all doubts about John into the same handmade tin box she'd gifted him for his freedom papers and tucked it away for later examination.

Then she was off, as prepared as she would ever be. Harriet wore a well-worn ankle-length overcoat and comfortable boots she had purchased three years ago. She was overdue for a new pair of boots, but the ones she wore had seen her through three winters. Harriet had faith they would take her all the way to Pyzai.

Harriet walked Dr. Tozor's acres of land with the same confidence she did when on legitimate business. She came and went often, hiring herself out between performing enough chores that kept her on with the Tozors. It wasn't unusual for Harriet to be seen carrying her satchel of unseen supplies or even taking advantage of the night to sneak off to visit John.

From the look of the kitchen, many slaves who might be out at this time of the evening were up at the big house preparing for tonight's festivities. If drinking was involved, and she assumed it would be, her absence might not be discovered until midday tomorrow.

Still, Harriet would breathe easier once she was off Dr. Tozor's land and on her way to the Quaker settlement.

But there were small farmhouses between the two that Harriet would have to navigate. Most of the owners either couldn't afford a slave, or they managed just enough to own one or two, typically a husband and wife or a mother and child.

Harriet stepped carefully, avoiding downed twigs and protruding roots. The sun had set, for which she was grateful. But the woods were even darker at night, and her human-level vision was less ideal.

She rounded a tree, her hand gliding over the rugged bark. Soft leaves squished underneath her boots, and Harriet thanked the Lord for giving trees a life cycle. Autumn had come, and leaves changed colors, but many also tumbled to the ground.

Harriet slid around another tree and another. She peered up at the sky and smiled. *I can see the North Star even better than last time. Thank you, Lord. Thank you for helpin' to guide my way. Thank you, Lord, for keepin' me safe. Thank you, Lord, for givin' me the strength to see this through. Thank you, Lord, thank you.*

She kept a stream of silent prayers with each step, an internal rhythm that helped pass the time and settle her mind. Harriet didn't think about the husband she'd left behind. She didn't brood over whether Mary had heard her message to Rit in her song. Harriet didn't worry about sickness, fatigue, or even hunger slowing her down. She accepted the quiet chill of the woods but warmed herself on the hot embers of the righteousness of her quest.

Harriet stopped at the edge of the woods. Before her lay a clearing of open fields marked by wooden fences and wood-burning homes.

The last time I was here, I was with Ben Jr. and Henry. We were too afraid to ask for help, so we took the long way around this little farmin' community. The modest homes remind me of my time with the Calises, those harpies who tried to live like greedy Dragonkin.

Harriet relieved herself of her satchel. Dropping it behind the tree where she hid, she observed as much as she could see from this distance. If she walked beyond the woods' edge, nothing would shield her before she reached one of the four farmhouses she spotted from her hiding spot.

I don't know who lives in those houses. They might sooner attack me than give me safe passage. I won't make the same mistake I did the last time. My brothers trusted me to lead the way, but they have nothin' to show for joinin' me in my escape. If I can't do better by them, I can at least do better by me.

For the next two hours, Harriet watched the four homes. The farms were too meager to have slave cabins on the land, but she watched for telltale signs that slaves resided in the homes.

No one exited to fetch water or retrieve eggs from a henhouse for tomorrow's breakfast. No one swept the porches or pulled clothing from the line. No haggard slave ran after children who should be asleep. None snuck out for a secret meeting with a friend or lover.

By all accounts, the farmers either didn't overextend themselves with slave labor or, if Harriet was lucky, they did not believe in the institution of slavery.

Believin' slavery is wrong isn't the same as helpin' a slave run away. I won't turn back, but I don't want to get lost again.

Harriet stood, yanked up her satchel, and swung it over her shoulder. *Trust in the Lord. That house right there. The one with the burnin' candle in the window. Other than the moon, it's the only light in the dark. I'm gonna take it as a good sign and put my faith in that one.*

As if surrounded by God's angels, their fluttering wings drawing her away from the woods and down the hill to the closest farmhouse, Harriet walked with the same absolute confidence in her decision as she had the day she took John as her loving and devoted husband.

She stepped onto the porch and winced when the wood whined and creaked, alerting the homeowner to her presence before she had the good manners to knock on the door. She knocked anyway because Ben had taught Harriet that first impressions mattered.

"Who's that?"

Harriet knew enough harpies to recognize the chirpy inflection softened by the smooth contours of the human throat.

The Calises had mistreated her terribly, and Dorane had used her. But harpies were indigenous to this land, having a claim long before the Dragonkin congratulated themselves on a false discovery. Harpies' fate hadn't been much better than the Birdfolk.

"My name's Harriet."

"I don't know any Harriets. Go away."

She glanced around, feeling the tightening of her chest and a slow throbbing behind an eye. "I'm seekin' help. I'm hopin' you can point me in the right direction."

"Help, you say?" The voice sounded closer to the door, which Harriet took as either a good or bad sign if the harpy drew nearer to only shoot her through the door. "Where are you trying to go?"

The sensation of fluttering angel wings prodded her to have faith and to tell the truth. "Pyzai, ma'am. I'm lookin' to go to Pyzai."

The door swung open. Harriet had been right. A harpy female stood opposite her with a rifle in her hand. But the weapon hung downward instead of pointing at her.

Harriet squinted, thinking the faint glow of the moon and her fatigue were playing tricks on her eyes. The harpy looked familiar. Bronzed from spending time in the sun without a proper hat, the harpy's dark brown hair was pulled into a tight ponytail, making her appear more severe and older than her years. But the face reminded her of a harpy she would rather forget.

"Mistress Calis?" Harriet stumbled backward. She despised the taste of that harpy's name on her tongue almost as much as she did the deceased woman. "Why do you look so much like her?"

The rifle clattered to the porch, and the harpy stepped forward. Dark eyes bore into Harriet, taking her in as if she were on an auction block.

A repulsed chill ran up her spine. *Did I choose wrong? The Lord sent me to this farmhouse. This is where I need to be. But I don't like the way that harpy is lookin' at me. Maybe I misunderstood the Lord. Got his message wrong.*

"Minty?" The harpy stepped over the rifle and closed the small distance between them. "It is you. My God, I can't believe it's you." The harpy reached out, grasped Harriet's shoulders, and smiled at her with a warmth that hadn't been present seconds earlier.

Harriet wanted to shove the strong, clawed-fingered hands off her. She wasn't inclined to mood swings and did not appreciate the trait in others. But there was something in the way the harpy said her name that niggled at a long-ago memory.

Like a knot of a whip crashing down on her head, Harriet remembered. She pushed the harpy's hands away and the child Minty wanted to vomit at the strange fate that had brought them face-to-face. Harriet turned away, no longer feeling the security of angel wings.

"Minty. Minty."

She stepped from the porch, wondering how she'd ruined another escape plan. Minty would've sworn her soul had left her body if not for her thudding heart.

"Minty."

How could I have forgotten that voice? Older and deeper, but still the same voice that tormented me during those slaveling hunts.

"You're a runaway, aren't you?"

I dreamed of knockin' her, Typhalle, and Urasis over their heads. So much of my childhood is defined by what those three did to me. Why, Lord? Why would you lead me to this harpy? Why her? Haven't I suffered enough at the hands of her family?

A sudden wind blew in from the north, reminding Harriet of her mission.

I'm not a child anymore. Even then, I fought back the best way I knew how. I was hunted. I made myself forget those awful years. I ran and ran. I got good at that. Real good. How is this any different? I shouldn't have forgotten. I won't ever again.

"I was hoping to see you again."

Harriet spun to face the harpy. She hadn't been big or brave enough to do this as a child. While the confrontation would likely see her shot or returned to Minister Breembat, she wouldn't go meekly on her way without first saying her piece.

"I hate you, Norveis." Well, no one ever accused Harriet of having tact. "You look even more like your aunt. May God have mercy on Mistress Calis's wretched soul."

Chapter 24

As Fearless as a Honey Badger

Dralox County

The devil is at work today, and he has a wicked sense of humor. I ain't seen Norveis in twenty years, but she, Typhalle, and Urasis haunted my dreams years after Poppa took me away from the Calis farm. Of all the places we could have met again, it's when I'm lookin' for a savior, not a sinner.

Eyes locked on Norveis, Harriet backed away. She'd been chased and hunted by her in the past. Back then, she'd waded into swamps and climbed trees to avoid capture. But Norveis and her cousins always caught her.

With each capture, a brutal beating followed.

Harriet refused to run from Norveis again.

"If you come after me, this won't end like it did when we were children. I ain't that weak girl anymore."

"You were never weak, Minty." Instead of moving toward her, as she assumed she would, Norveis returned to the porch, slid the rifle into her house, and then shut the door.

"What are you doin'?" Harriet continued her slow retreat. She didn't detect anyone but the two of them outdoors, but that did not mean a curious neighbor hadn't spotted her. "I don't want any trouble, Norveis. So, I'm gonna be on my way."

Harriet calculated how long it would take her to return to the relative safety of the woods while keeping Norveis in sight. She then wondered at the harpy's odd behavior. The Norveis she remembered would've attacked first, taunting Harriet while leveling devastating blows.

"I'm leavin'. This was a mistake. Just let me leave in peace."

Harriet paused, convinced Norveis had something terrible planned. Her waist-length wings were at rest, and while she wore nothing more than a sleeveless nightdress, the harpy appeared calm.

I don't trust her. She'll come after me when I'm up that hill. That's what this is about. She wants a good chase. I'm too close to give her one right now. But why is she lookin' at me like that? The girl I remembered had cold, hard eyes. Her mouth laughed, and her eyes twinkled like stars dancin' across the sky when she hit and cut me. I still have scars from her claws. If she tries to touch me again, I'll give as good as I'll get.

Harriet resumed her retreat, walking slowly and watching Norveis.

"I'm sorry, Minty."

She stopped.

"For every mean thing I did to you when I was a stupid girl, I'm truly sorry." Norveis sat on the porch, not primly, the way she remembered her being, but with a rugged air of tranquility. "You have every right to hate me. The things I did to you . . . what my aunt and uncle allowed and encouraged us to do was cruel. Inhumane."

Harriet prided herself on trusting her instincts. It's how she survived as a child living with the Calises and then with other temporary masters who were no less cruel than Theria and Jolara Calis. But she hadn't trusted her instincts when she fled with her brothers.

Norveis's words ring true. She could've shot or attacked me, but she didn't. She's seated there, lookin' too much like Mistress Calis for comfort but with none of her aunt's nastiness. No sneers or curses. No insults. Her eyes are different, too. Still hard, but with a soft insight that can come with maturity and experience. My instincts say she's tellin' the truth. But . . .

"You were pretty sick the last time I saw you—measles. You looked awful, and I didn't want to catch it. I remember pitching a big ole fit until Aunt Theria took me home. I was mad at you for ruining my sleepover with my cousins." Norveis's chuckle slammed into Harriet, but not because the harpy's laughter resonated with cruel recollection. The sound was that of sad irony.

"Everybody knew Master Gyzad set the Calis house on fire and killed everybody inside. They all knew why, too. You were so young back then. So was I, but I was self-aware enough to know how hard slaves had it, even enslaved kids." Norveis's gaze lifted to the sky, but Harriet kept hers trained on the harpy. "I think back on those times, seeing the burnt remains of a house I should've been in. Knowing I tortured you as badly as Typhalle and Urasis. They died for their sins, yet I was spared." She lowered her eyes to Harriet. "Why do you think that was?"

HARRIET'S ESCAPE:

Harriet had no idea, especially since the child Minty wished Norveis had burned with the others. She wasn't proud of the thought, but she also hadn't taken an axe to her tormentors like some Birdfolk women did, the noose the ultimate price for their bloody act of vengeance.

Norveis chuckled the same sad laugh. "It's not for you to know. For years, I asked myself the same question. One day, I was in town. A woman was being dragged away by the sheriff. But she screamed about freeing slaves and that we were all going to burn in hell for going against God's will. Believe it or not, that woman was a Dragonkin. I followed her to the prison and returned every day until she was released."

Despite herself, Harriet had been drawn into Norveis's story. "Then what?"

"Then this." Norveis pointed with her thumb to the farmhouse behind her, then used her index finger to gesture to the woods behind Harriet. "Any runaway heading north from the southern counties of Miadar will likely pass through those woods back there. Looking for, well, more like praying for, a kind-hearted soul to help them along the way." Norveis pointed to her home again. "A safe stop for runaways and my redemption."

As if realizing she sat on a cold wooden porch in only a thin nightdress, Norveis stood and rubbed her hands together. She peered at the sky again and released a third chuckle before resettling her dark eyes on Harriet. "This was harpy land long before the different Dragonkin kingdoms fought over it. Those of us they didn't kill, they added to their hoards. But it's hard to enslave people who know the land and can fly away." Norveis gestured with her chin to Harriet. "A dragon will always catch a flying harpy, but why bother when there is an entire land of flightless birds? Still, some harpies have forgotten what it's like to be the lowest on the food chain. And we've become slave owners even though some Harpyfolk are kept in bondage. Treated no better than Birdfolk. Wanting their freedom and willing to do anything to get it."

Dorane came to mind, and Harriet wondered how freedom born of murder tasted to the harpy. As sweet as heaven or as bitter as hell?

"You're an a-a-abolitionist, Norveis?" Harriet whispered, stumbling over a word she knew better than to utter in mixed company.

"You said that with a fair amount of shock." Norveis looked down at herself and shrugged. "That's probably a heavier word than I deserve. But I help whoever is brave enough to come knocking on my door. Small but brave. That's the Minty I remember. You are the face of my redemption." Norveis stepped to the side. "I have food, water, and a fireplace that'll heat you up. I also have good friends who have good friends."

She stepped onto the porch, and with a hand steadier than Harriet's pounding heart, Norveis opened the door to her home. "I'm not the girl I used to be, Minty, but she did make me the woman I am today. I can't change what my family did to you, but if you choose to trust me, my home can be the first safe stop on your journey to freedom." Norveis chuckled again, and Harriet interpreted the physical response to their unintended reunion as the emotion it was.

Guilt. Genuine, heartfelt guilt.

She ain't the same. I can see that as plain on her face as she can see I'm a runaway needin' her help. Trust and forgiveness ain't the same. I ain't ready to forgive, but the Lord and my instincts tell me I can trust this grown-up Norveis.

Harriet readjusted the satchel on her back and strode toward her tormentor-turned-ally. When Harriet entered Norveis's home, the distinctive scent of roasted chicken reminded her of too many days she'd slaved in the Calis household preparing the same but never once offered a morsel.

"Thank you. I appreciate your hospitality."

"You're welcome. You'll rest tonight and eat, but come sundown tomorrow, I'll deliver you to the next safe house."

"I'm lookin' for a Quaker named Jondrin." Robert had relayed the details of his time in the workhouse, including Linah's sale and the men he'd shared a cell with. Jondrin hadn't helped Linah when Robert had begged him to, but he was a Quaker abolitionist, and Harriet thought her best chance of success would rest with finding the Dragonkin Quaker settlement.

"While you eat, you can tell me how you know Jondrin. His house is a little farther than I think it safe for us to travel together without me pretending to be your master, but my friend will get you to him if that's the route you want to take."

"You're gonna take me to another safe house?" *She makes it sound like there are plenty of others like her. God-fearing people who are willin' to help runaways get their freedom. Is this what it means to be an abolitionist? Ain't she afraid of gettin' caught? Of bein' punished by the law?*

"We have all night for questions and answers. I'll tell you everything I know. God willing, it will be enough."

"Like followin' the North Star?" Feeling strangely protected in Norveis's home, Harriet dropped her satchel beside the rifle the harpy had picked up and placed on the table nearest the front door. Harriet removed her overcoat and knelt by the fireplace, feeling safer inside. "And the burnin' candle? Was that a sign for runaways like me?"

"You were always smart. I cursed that about you whenever you found a good hiding spot."

Harriet turned to see Norveis staring past her and into the leaping flames. When Harriet looked at the fire, she saw the family she'd left behind and the many nights they'd gone to bed cold and hungry. Harriet didn't want to know what other sins Norveis had committed before she'd taken the righteous path toward redemption.

"Do you know why we always caught you?" Norveis pointed to a towel-covered plate on a wooden end table that was beside a rocking chair. "Go on. It's untouched. I'll make my own sandwich later."

Harriet had packed a few food items in her satchel—two-day-old cornbread, three hand-sized sweet potatoes, and a thick slice of salted pork. The other food she'd managed to squirrel away after her return, she'd packed up and taken to her parents' cabin.

At the thought of having fresh chicken, Harriet's stomach grumbled and growled, but she didn't move toward the offering. "I don't eat on Fridays. But I'll gladly have it come mornin'."

She waited for Norveis to mock her for willingly abstaining from eating when much of a slave's life was spent in the pursuit of their next meal. But the harpy merely nodded and claimed the rocking chair, careful to tuck the lower half of her wings through the chair's broad wings slot.

She really has changed. I don't think she made that sandwich for herself. I think she added fresh logs to the fire, made the sandwich, lit the candle, then sat in the rockin' chair and waited. She waited for somebody like me to knock on her door, whom she could offer that sandwich before takin' them to one of her friends' homes. One rockin' chair. She lives alone.

"We never really talked when we were children. My fault, I know."

Like a cat settling in for the night, Harriet reclined on her side in front of the fire. From that angle, she could only see Norveis's clawed feet, but the hearing mattered the most to Harriet. "You, Typhalle, and Urasis always caught me because I was smaller and slower."

She watched the subtle back-and-forth rhythm of the rocking chair, listened to the soft *tick, tick* of harpy claws against the wooden floor, and felt her heart squeeze for how deeply she'd failed Ben Jr. and Henry.

"That's Dragonkin talk. Compared to them, we're all small and slow. So what?"

Harriet remained quiet because that's when she learned the most, even if she disagreed with the speaker's perspective.

"There's a reason why slave owners don't want Birdfolk to shift without their permission."

"Sankofa bird shifters can't fly, Norveis. You know that."

"So what?"

So everything, Harriet screamed in her mind.

"My point is simple. Don't be afraid to use everything you know and be all you are. That looks different for all of us. And sometimes, we don't know what we're capable of until a situation demands it from us. I knew you would survive that illness. Smaller and slower than harpies and dragons but as—"

"Stubborn as a mule and as fearless as a honey badger." Harriet turned onto her back, hearing John's voice when he described her to Ben.

The smooth glide of the rocking chair resumed. "That pretty much sums it up. Have more faith."

"I have absolute faith in God."

"I'm sure you do. But I meant in yourself. Always in yourself."

Harriet didn't know what she expected when Norveis told her she would take her to a friend's home. But hiding under piles of foul-smelling blankets in the back of a wagon hadn't come to mind. Curled in a ball, her satchel clutched to her chest, Harriet felt every dip and jostle as the wagon rattled along.

Please, Lord, don't let anybody stop Norveis. Thank you for softenin' Norveis's heart. She grew up, Lord, and turned into a good person. Upstandin' and moral. Righteous in your light. I wouldn't have thought. Her turn of heart gives me hope, Lord. One day, all my people will be free. Until then, I'll do whatever I must. My life is in your hands. Use me how you will.

Through every tumble and turn of the wagon, Harriet prayed. Her pounding heart and sweaty, taut skin kept sleep and an episode at bay, and her mind and ears alert. There was a hair-raising tranquility of experiencing the silence of the night without also seeing the beauty of its darkness.

"We're almost there," she heard Norveis say in a voice pitched barely above a whisper. "No one wants to check under piss-scented sheets, so if you must go, do it on one of the bedcoverings. That'll just make the ruse better for the one who'll come after you."

She's thought of everything. I never asked how long she's been doin' this, but I suppose awhile. Lord, please keep Norveis safe. Lead many runaways to her farm. Fill their hearts with trust and their souls with courage to keep pushin' on. Mine, too, Lord. I ain't to the promised land yet, but I feel it gettin' closer and closer. Thank you, Lord, thank you.

With a final jerk forward, then backward, the wagon stopped. Harriet didn't dare move. She hardly breathed.

The front of the wagon shifted, and seconds later, a familiar voice sounded to Harriet's right. "Don't move an inch until I say."

Harriet strained to hear, but all she could make out were retreating footsteps and the faint sound of male laughter. She wondered at the time and how far they'd traveled. A handful of hours, she speculated. They'd left half past midnight, so maybe three hours had passed, giving them a few more before sunrise.

She felt Norveis had made good time, quicker than if Harriet had been on foot. But she'd rested well the night before and during the ride, so she was prepared to walk the rest if needed.

A soft tap sounded against the right side of the wagon. "I'm going to lead the horse into a barn. Only on my signal should you reveal yourself."

It wasn't lost on Harriet that she had placed her life in the clawed hands of a person who'd once bullied and beaten her. God was forgiving, and Harriet would do well to follow his example.

"Is anybody else here?" Norveis said.

"Just the farmhands out front." A man with a voice that sounded like thick molasses answered Norveis's question, letting Harriet know they weren't alone in the barn. "Once they finish their last round of drinks and play the final hand of cards, they'll head home. It's Xielborod's birthday, and I couldn't very well send them home too early without raising their suspicions. Not that I always know when you'll have a new delivery for me."

Xielborod. That's a Dragonkin name. The Lord really does work in mysterious ways. Mistress Essodel would kill this male if she knew he was helpin' Birdfolk run away from the likes of her.

"Come on out, Minty, it's safe."

While Minty heard Norveis, her body didn't automatically reply. Between the weight of the blankets and the stiffening of her limbs, the transition between stillness and motion was a slow, embarrassing process. But Harriet managed to push to her hands and knees. As if she were a dog drenched from an early morning downpour, Harriet shook off the blankets.

"Deghor, this is Minty."

Deghor, a ten-foot Dragonkin with straight, shoulder-length blond hair ending in midnight black tips, likely the same color as his dragon scales, moved to the back of the wagon. A healed claw slash that looked years old and likely bled like a river when new bisected his left cheek and the flat nose that twitched.

"Nice to meet you, Minty. Sorry about the accommodations."

She felt he meant how she had to travel, and the barn was likely to be her resting place for the night. Harriet wouldn't be so ungracious as to complain, no matter the lodging.

"Come on, gal, let me help you from there."

Stunned by a Dragonkin's humane treatment, as if she were a lady instead of a slave no better than a mule, Harriet's shaking hand settled in Deghor's. The appendage swallowed her own, but he held it as if it were a delicate feather, helping her from the wagon with the same care she imagined he showed any female of his acquaintance.

Harriet looked around. The barn was like other agricultural barns she'd seen at home. It was a simple and open structure made of clapboard, with a gabled roof, two small side doors to the right and left of her, and a large carriage door at the end of the barn. She supposed his cattle were housed in another barn because this one was stacked full of bound hay and bags of feed ready for sale and use.

Deghor gestured with his chin to the back of the barn. "Behind that big stack of hay is a blanket and water canteen in the corner. Once the boys leave, I can bring you something to eat." His soft laughter touched her heart as much as his kindness did. "They're a greedy, rowdy bunch, so much might not be left."

While Harriet may have eaten Norveis's chicken sandwich earlier that morning, washing it down with a delicious cup of milk, she'd gone longer than a few hours between meals before. Besides, she still had the food she'd brought with her in her satchel, and circumstances had taught enslaved Birdfolk how to stretch the food they had.

"Thank you, sir. I appreciate everythin' you and Norveis are doin' for me." They were heartfelt words but ones she never thought she would have reason to say to Norveis, much less to a Dragonkin.

"We're doing God's work. Now go hide while Norveis and I pretend to be a strange but devoted courting pair."

Oh, that is their scheme to explain Norveis's comins and goins. Dragonkin prefer to mate with other dragon shifters.

Norveis's clawed hand settled on Harriet's shoulder. Their eyes locked, and Harriet knew they both recalled the last time the harpy had laid hands on her. Back then, Harriet had flinched but was too afraid to fight back, so she'd taken another beating.

"I'm sorry for the pain I caused you in the past. One night and a day in my care can't make up for what I did to you. But I truly regret the girl I used to be. You know where to find me if you ever need me again. Safe travels, Minty."

Norveis's hand fell away, and she turned to leave.

Harriet could've let the harpy go, granting her the final word. But kindness given was kindness returned. "Thank you, Norveis. I accept your apology. You have my forgiveness, so free yourself from your past sins."

Norveis did not face Harriet again, but her entire back and wings shifted downward as if freed from a tremendous weight.

"If we ever meet again, Norveis, call me Harriet."

When Norveis and Deghor left the barn, and Harriet settled in her hiding spot behind tall, wide stacks of hay, she could have never imagined the even greater role a redeemed Norveis would play in the lives of so many runaways, including many members of Harriet's family.

When Sunday night came, Harriet was off toward the north and the Quaker settlement. She moved quickly yet cautiously. Whenever possible, Harriet stayed away from main roads and wide-open fields. Woods and swamps were her friends. She'd spent enough time in both to know their rhythm and flow.

Harriet could see a settlement from a tree she'd climbed. The bridge by the river she'd spied earlier would take her into the farming community of plain wooden and stone buildings, along with crop fields smaller than the ones she was used to tending. But it all looked neat and tidy, perhaps even welcoming to a runaway.

The sun's gonna rise in a couple of hours. What should I do? Pretend I know Jondrin? What if he doesn't live around here?

Concluding it would be best to rest before making a life-or-death decision, Harriet lowered herself onto the fat branch below her perch, propped her back against the tree trunk, held her satchel firmly in her arms, and closed her eyes.

Harriet rested neither deeply nor comfortably, but the good Lord had seen her this far. So, she accepted each backache and leg cramp as the price she'd have to pay to earn her freedom.

She felt, rather than heard, someone approach.

Harriet's eyes snapped open. The sun had risen fully, beaming through the canopy and onto bare branches like a warm omen. She sat straight, glanced around, and then craned her head upward.

Wings flapped overhead. Fully awake, she could hear what she hadn't seconds earlier—the telltale beating of wings against the air.

Large wings.

Dragon wings.

Harriet didn't dare move again. Despite Deghor's kindness, Harriet thought it best to assume that every Dragonkin was her enemy until proven wrong.

If I stay nice and quiet, I won't attract its attention. It would've swooped down and got me if it knew I was here. It's just a dragon out enjoyin' the first mornin' air. Except for ancient dragons set in their ways like Mistress Essodel, most of them live and eat as humans. That dragon ain't out this early in the mornin' lookin' to hunt for food.

At least, Harriet hoped that was the case. She lowered her head and closed her eyes, seeing no better time for a silent prayer.

Harriet prayed and prayed. Even when the sound of snapping wings beating against the air ceased, Harriet continued to pray, offering her Lord thanks for keeping her safe.

She settled against the tree trunk again, feeling exposed and threatened. *I should stay here awhile. Wait for darkness before movin' again.*

The day passed with Harriet in the tree, but she lowered herself to the ground when day gave way to night. Harriet sucked in a groan. Her lower back and shoulders had corded into tight knots, and she thought she would double over in pain.

She dropped her satchel to the ground. Going on tiptoe, Harriet raised her arms high and stretched. The throbbing pain remained, but the stretch had released enough tension that walking would be bearable. Still, Harriet carried her satchel in her right hand instead of slinging it across her shoulders.

As if she belonged and knew where she was going and was expected, Harriet strolled across the bridge and into the Quaker community. Even though darkness had set in, it was still early, so some were still out.

She saw neither harpy nor gryphon. But five Dragonkin children in dragon form played inside a fenced front yard. A Dragonkin female watched them from the quiet of her porch.

Harriet never caught the female's eyes on her, but she felt her gaze. The same was true for the two Dragonkin males on the roof of the longest church she'd ever seen. Their hammers were in steady motion, but so too were the eyes that tracked her every movement.

But most had settled down for the evening, returning to their homes when the sun set, and little could be done outdoors when not in dragon form with night vision.

No one has attacked me or sounded an alarm. I might not find Jondrin here, but this settlement isn't openly hostile to Birdfolk. Maybe it's as Norveis told me that night in her home. There are more abolitionists than Birdfolk know and that slave owners want to admit.

"Times are changing, Minty. Slowly but steadily. It might not be next year or even a decade from now, but slavery will end. I'll fight for that day, and I know wherever you find yourself, you will, too."

Harriet stopped before a stone home with a lit lantern in the window. Unlike when she'd unknowingly approached Norveis's farmhouse, Harriet's heart did not feel like it would escape her chest. But it still raced at the negative response she could receive from the unknown homeowner.

She knocked, cleared her throat, and spoke the words she'd learned from Norveis. "I'm lookin' for a station. Might you point me in the right direction?"

Harriet heard nothing on the other side, not even playing children or a startled pet.

But a gruff voice was suddenly at the door. "Are you a parcel?"

"Yes, sir."

"Just you?"

"Yes, sir."

"Go 'round back."

Harriet hid in the Dragonkin's fruit root cellar that night and the following day. Wedged in a space barely large enough to accommodate a child Minty, Harriet made do and gladly helped herself to a few apples.

Under the cover of darkness, Harriet left the Quaker settlement, without crossing paths with Jondrin. Even so, she'd stayed at another "station" and had met another "conductor." Having never ridden on a train, Harriet didn't understand the use of such terms to describe helping and hiding runaway slaves. But she grasped the word "underground" well enough, as in secretive.

So, Harriet continued, determined to make it to Pyzai.

Most days, she hid in swamps and wooded thickets. Come nightfall, she'd hunt a critter, a squirrel, or a small rabbit. A fire would've been nice, but Harriet feared it would attract unwanted attention. So, she would shift into her bird form and devour her catch.

Harriet plowed ahead, staying out of sight and walking with a purpose that came with being the daughter of Benjamin and Harriet Wren. She might have left them behind, but she refused to let the pain of losing another child be wasted on her failure.

I'll survive for everybody back home. I'll get my freedom. Everything I've done, every house I've worked in, every backbreakin' field labor I've endured has prepared me for this. I don't see any railroad tracks, but I feel every mile of my journey. The passage has marked my blistered feet, set a fire on my swollen tongue, and danced a jig in my growling stomach. But...

"*There is an invisible line, Minty,*" Norveis had told her the day they'd set out for Deghor's station. "*I've seen it myself. It's the dividing line between Miadar and Pyzai. On the other side of the line is freedom.*"

"I can't see no invisible line. How will I know when I get there?"

"*There are stone markers up and down what's known as the Mutoath-Dupa Line. Those are the names of the two dragons who helped settle the dispute between Miadar slave owners and Pyzai residents after they abolished slavery. It's an eighty-three-year-old history that has to do with border disputes. All you need to know is that the other side of those markers is freedom.*" Norveis had removed a piece of paper from between the pages of a book. "*This first image is a crown. Some markers will have this at the top, but not all. This letter is an M for Miadar, and this is the letter P. The P will be on the Pyzai side of the marker. That's it, Minty. I've told you everything I've learned from being a conductor. The rest is up to you."*

The rest was up to her.

Harriet couldn't read. She'd never been taught because it was a crime to teach a slave to read and write. But she remembered much and forgot even less.

She dropped to her knees. Trembling fingers lifted, paused, and slowly touched the stone marker before her. Her fingers ran over the smooth grooves of a crown carved into the stone. Below the crown was the letter M she'd learned from Norveis. Scooting to her right, she allowed her fingers to graze over the indentation of four numbers—1766.

Tears filled her eyes, and she thought her fingers would fall off for how hard they shook. On unsteady hands and knees, Harriet crawled to the side of the stone opposite the large M. There, more beautiful than anything she'd ever seen, was a solitary letter.

P.

P for Pyzai.

P for freedom.

Harriet collapsed onto her back, crying. She wept for the girl who'd endured unimaginable mistreatment and for the wife, daughter, sister, aunt, and friend who'd been forced to abandon her family.

I'm free. Thank you, Lord, I'm finally free. I'm finally free.

But Harriet's freedom came at a tremendous personal loss. Her soul wouldn't rest until she brought every family member north. Because what was freedom without loved ones to share in God's emancipated glory?

Chapter 25

Harriet Will Show Us the Way

1849
Pelduth Neck
Tozor Plantation

Ben stepped between the towering Minister Breembat and a glowering Rit. This standoff had been years in the making, ever since the Dragonkin had tried to sell Moses. Rit had their youngest child hide in the woods until Minister Breembat turned to other pursuits.

"Rit has told she knows nothin' about Harriet runnin' away."

They stood in the middle of Ben and Rit's cabin, Minister Breembat having barged in with every ounce the conceited, privileged slave master he'd been for all of Ben's life.

"She knows something, Ben. Mothers always know."

"I don't know. I've done told you that before. Harriet walked me back here and left."

John rose from the table where they'd been seated for a late Sunday meal when Minister Breembat had arrived like a dreaded snowstorm. "Come sit back down, Momma Rit. Whether seated or standin', your answers won't change. But this is your rest day, and nobody has a right to keep you from it."

"You got a smart mouth, boy."

"What I got is a free mouth." John moved to stand beside Ben, and he was as grateful for his son-in-law's support as much as he'd been surprised by John's appearance at the cabin. He supposed the day was meant for unexpected visitors. "Ben and Rit are also free. You don't have a right to boss them around anymore. It ain't right. They're just tryin' to get on with their lives as free people in a slave land."

"You know, boy, it's a felony to help a slave run away. I could have you sold into slavery for the crime of helping your wife escape."

Ben opened his mouth to reply, but John barreled forward, a lit candle with a dwindling wick.

"My wife ran away because you were gonna sell her. What did you think she would do? Even on her sickbed, you brought men into this very cabin. Gawkin'. Assessin'."

"I'm Minty's owner. It's my right to do whatever I want with my property." Minister Breembat raised a hand as if he would strike John.

For anyone other than a Dragonkin, three-against-one odds wouldn't favor them. But dragon shifters were formidable, and Ben didn't own a rifle or revolver. Even a Dragonkin in human form could be hurt and killed by munitions.

"I will strike you down if you aided Minty's escape." The threatening arm lowered, but Ben remained alert for a sneak attack, which was more in line with Minister Breembat's personality. A direct assault was Master Gyzad's approach to conflict. If nothing else, Ben could trust Minister Breembat to devise a scheme to make them pay for Harriet daring to defy him.

Ben hid a smile behind a hand and a fake yawn. He was so proud of his Harriet for claiming her freedom with both hands.

"I'm boring you, Ben?"

"Long, tiring week, Minister Breembat. That's all. My Rit ain't never lied to you." Ben shifted just enough to his right to draw Minister Breembat's attention away from John and his short fuse. "We ain't happy about losin' another daughter. Every time one of our girls goes missin', you tell us she up and run away."

Ben slid farther to the right, subtly encouraging the Dragonkin to follow him to the door.

"We believed you each time, but maybe you really sold them off. You did bring strange men around here when Harriet was laid up from that head injury she got when workin' with that family you hired her out to."

As if he'd been out in freezing weather, Minister Breembat's cheeks reddened. "I didn't sell them off. You don't question my truth, Ben. I know what Rit thinks, and she's wrong. I didn't sell your girls. Minty ran off."

"If you say so, Minister Breembat." Shift to the right.

"I do say so."

"You're a man of God. You wouldn't lie to lowly slaves, I know." Shift to the right.

"At least one of you got your head on straight. What I say is gospel. Do you hear me, Rit?" Minister Breembat said, his voice pitched as if Rit were three cabins away. "My word is gospel. I didn't sell your girls, but I'm sure as hell going to catch Minty, or whatever the name she goes by now. Mark my words, I'm going to hire a slave catcher who'll drag her back here. A little worse for wear, but Mudspike will find her."

Ben stepped aside, permitting Minister Breembat to stomp from the cabin with the same fury he'd entered. But he'd left with no more information than he had when he arrived, so Ben considered that a win.

He blew out a slow breath, suddenly exhausted and feeling every bit of his sixty-two years. Ben's lower back tightened, and his knees ached, but he managed to claim the rickety wooden chair beside his wife.

Rit slid close and kissed his cheek. "You did good." She nodded to John and then to the chair across from Ben. "You, too. Harriet would be proud."

"Harriet ain't here to be proud." John sat on the only other chair in the cabin.

The fourth had broken months earlier, and Ben hadn't gotten around to the repair. He'd meant to ask Harriet for her help. But time had gotten away from them both. Now, well, he still had a broken chair but no Harriet to enjoy doing a good deed for her parents.

Ben's heart squeezed, but he refused to go down the same angry road as John. "You know she had no choice but to run."

"Knowin' don't make her abandonin' me hurt less."

Rit scooted closer to the table that separated her from John. But the old, scuffed table alone couldn't measure the gulf between them. "Not to be unkind, John, but you could've gone with her. She asked you, didn't she?"

Ben leaned back in the chair, not the least bit embarrassed when his stomach grumbled. But he wished John would leave so he and Rit could have dinner or cease whining about a decision that cut them all, including Harriet.

It wasn't that Ben did not sympathize with John's hurt feelings. After all, Harriet hadn't shared her plans with Ben and Rit either. The difference was that he understood Harriet had kept her secret to protect them from Minister Breembat's wrath. It was one thing to feign ignorance and stroke a Dragonkin's massive ego, but it was something entirely different to tell a lie over and again. Ben would rather leave that level of deception to the likes of Minister Breembat.

"This is my home, Rit. And you heard Breembat. If we were caught, he could've had me sold into slavery." John's shoulders slumped, and his eyes lowered to the table. "I sound like a coward. I didn't want to lose my wife. But I was afraid of what would happen if we were caught. I ain't built to be a slave."

Ben's barked laughter had John's head snapping up, his eyes filled with a shame Ben knew well. "Nobody is built to be a slave, John. But you married one. What did you think your life together would be like?"

"I-I don't know, Ben." John pushed from the table and stood. "Not this. God knows I didn't want her sold off. I wanted to keep Harriet right here with me. For five years, we saved to buy her freedom. Between her bouts of sickness, we couldn't save as much as we wanted. But you managed to buy your wife."

"It took Ben years of beggin' and pleadin' with Minister Breembat just to get him to mention it to Mistress Essodel. Our Harriet did what she must." Rit got to her feet and walked around the table to stand in front of John. Grasping his hand, she squeezed, offering their son-in-law the only comfort they had to give—the truth. "Kessiah married a freeborn man, too. Oddly enough, his name is also John."

"I know, Momma Rit. And Kessiah named her daughter Araminta. I've never known a closer family. I know it hurt Harriet to leave us behind. Are you tryin' to tell me that we shouldn't have married?" John glanced at Ben, who hoped his opinion on the matter didn't show on his face.

Still holding John's right hand, Rit smiled and shook her head. "Harriet loves you, and I know you love her. But sometimes love ain't enough, especially when you're a slave. It ain't for anyone to tell you how to feel, though. You feel how you do. The fact is that she's gone, and you're still here. What are you gonna do about it?"

Ben grabbed a couple of peanuts from the table, cracked them open, and shoved them into his mouth. Rit had fixed vegetable stew, and he didn't think he could wait much longer to dig in. Deciding it would be rude to begin without his wife, Ben cracked more peanuts and waited for John to go home or sit down.

"There's nothin' for me to do. Harriet is gone. I don't even know if she made it to Pyzai. None of us do."

John had hit on the very detail of Harriet's escape Ben had avoided discussing with Rit. Ben didn't know how much more damage his heart could sustain before it faltered and finally failed. Three daughters were sold to only God knew where, and one run off to the North. Out of five daughters, Ben only knew the whereabouts of one. Rachel had a son a few months before Harriet's escape, making Ben a grandfather again and honoring him by naming her son Benjamin.

Rit's hand slipped away from John, and Ben wanted to tear the foul institution of slavery to shreds with his bare hands. From the moment Birdfolk villages were raided, and they were marched to the Sika coast and boarded onto slave ships, their families were broken and left to the mercy of unscrupulous Dragonkin. Little had changed since the awful days of the slave trade, with enslaved Birdfolk families strong yet fragile.

Ben recalled how he'd felt when Master Gyzad forced him to leave Rit and his young children to oversee the work of his silver mine.

I cried my first night alone. I'd never felt so lonely. Is that how Harriet feels so far away from home? Does she cry herself to sleep missin' us as much as we miss her? John doesn't have enough faith in our Harriet. I ain't worried she didn't make it to Pyzai. I know she did. I trust the good Lord saw her through. I trust that he also watches over Mariah, Linah, and Soph.

Ben lowered his head, breathed deeply, and forced thoughts of his sold girls out of his head. Ben had no interest in ruining what was left of the evening with tears, especially in front of John, who'd clearly shed his own angry tears over losing a wife he could've held on to if he'd decided differently.

But John hadn't, and neither had Harriet.

Rit straightened her spine as if the possibility of Harriet's failure was a personal affront. "She ain't here, and Minister Breembat hasn't seen hide nor hair of her. If his visit here ain't enough to convince you of Harriet's success, then I feel sorry for you, John. I guess you did give up on Harriet along with your marriage."

Ben felt he should intervene, but he didn't have any words of wisdom for John. Good reason or not, Harriet had been the one to leave. He wondered if they had a plan for John to join her later or whether she promised to return for him after she got settled. But returning for a free man and risking being captured seemed foolhardy to Ben. He couldn't see Harriet taking such a risk. Then again, love did make people do strange things. So, too, did fear.

Maybe they shouldn't have married. A freeborn man like John can only see what he has to lose. But slaves live for whatever we can gain. Little bits of freedom we can eke out for ourselves, even when the real thing seems so far away. But fear can stop us all in our tracks. Fear can save our lives but also prevent us from followin' our heart. John isn't just angry with Harriet; he's also upset with himself because when Harriet needed him, he couldn't match a wife's courage with a husband's bravery.

"I haven't said anything about givin' up on Harriet and our marriage. That's not fair."

Rit shrugged. "Only you know if you have or haven't. I trust Harriet will find a way to get a message to us when she can. She was smart about that song. Mary didn't know what to make of it, but she told me when we realized Harriet was gone. If she could do that right under Dr. Tozor's nose, she will find a way to get word to us. I believe in my daughter." Rit reached up and hugged John.

"Thank you, Momma Rit." John kissed Rit's cheek.

Ben had never doubted the younger man's love for his daughter. No more than he'd ever had reason to question the strength of his spine. He still didn't, but a man needed a reason to stay committed to a woman he didn't know the next time he would see. Considering Harriet and John had no children to bind them, he wondered if five years of marriage was long enough to survive Harriet's absence.

"Thanks, Ben. I didn't mean to interrupt."

"You ain't stayin'?"

John shook his head. "I got things to do."

Ben wiped his hands on his pants and then extended his right hand to John for a shake. "Don't be a stranger. Just because Harriet ain't here doesn't mean you aren't welcome. We still family. Don't forget."

"I won't, Poppa Ben. But I should be goin'."

Ben didn't watch John leave, but he did push Rit's chair in after she sat, and the door closed behind his son-in-law.

Rit kissed his cheek again, but Ben needed more. So, he grabbed his wife by her waist and slid her onto his lap.

"What's gotten into you, Benjamin Wren?" Rit's voice was buttery smooth with surprise but also filled with the kind of love that comes with over forty years of marriage, nine children, and several grandchildren.

"I want our Harriet to have this with John. But I worry."

Rit wrapped her arms around his neck, and Ben wasn't ashamed to sink into his wife's embrace with childlike comfort. "And I worry about Harriet out there alone. Free but without family and friends. I know she'll be fine, but . . . she and Rachel are all the daughters we have left, Ben."

He hugged her tightly to him. Ben wanted to reassure Rit in a way he hadn't John. But couples married as long as they were valued silent agreement of shared pain over feel-good words that held no weight and power to alter the facts of life.

Apparently, Rit disagreed. "Love means lettin' them go. Encouragin' them to fly without the benefit of the sky."

Ben pressed his forehead to Rit's. "But still soarin'?"

"Yes. That means we can't be afraid to soar, too."

"What does that mean?" Ben asked.

"I don't know yet, but I have a feelin' Harriet will show us the way."

Chapter 26
I'VE MISSED YOU

1850
Miadar Province
Dralox County
City of Cosaru

"One hundred."
"Two hundred."
"I bid two fifty. What a fine gal."
"Three hundred."

HARRIET'S ESCAPE:

Arms crossed in front of his chest, Minister Breembat observed the spirited auction. He stood in front of the steps of the Cosaru courthouse, watching a small but anxious crowd of Dragonkin bid on what should be a big payday for him after the auction.

The Dragonkin auctioneer cupped his hands around his mouth and shouted over the clamoring crowd. "We have a bid of two hundred fifty dollars." The auctioneer had streaks of gray in a braided beard and an unfortunate limp that likely occurred in a battle against one of their kind because Minister Breembat couldn't fathom the male sustaining such an injury by any other means.

"Can I get three hundred?"

"Three hundred."

"Three twenty."

Minister Breembat's smile grew with each bid, as did his self-satisfaction at pulling off yet another sale under Mistress Essodel's nose. Better still, this sale would remind Rit that no matter her free status, the fate of her family rested in his hands.

Look at her up there. I was told her mother screamed and cursed and eventually cried when reality set in. She hasn't done any of that. But she's no less afraid than Mariah, Linah, and Soph had been. Look at how she clutches her infant with one hand and holds her son close with the other. She's terrified. If I opened my mouth, I bet I could taste her fear. Here it is, late December, and I can see the sweat on her forehead.

"Three seventy-five."

"Three ninety."

Rit thinks I'm an idiot. She knows more about Minty's escape than she's said. I'll sell off her entire family. Children, grandchildren, and great-grandchildren—all belong to Mother, which means they are also mine to do what I will. I'll show Rit what it means to defy me.

"I have four hundred. Four hundred going once, going twice—"

"Four twenty-five."

Minister Breembat stepped aside as a young Dragonkin couple elbowed their way down the courthouse steps. The female's belly protruded almost as much as her bottom lip did.

"She's just a country slave from Berzogtown. She and her brats aren't worth more than three fifty."

Minister Breembat said nothing when the disgruntled woman passed, but he did lift his lips in a sneer when she glanced at him.

Taking hold of her mate's hand, she scurried away, and Minister Breembat breathed in the cool winter air. He didn't always bother traveling beyond Berzogtown to sell off one of his mother's slaves. But since learning of Minty's escape, Mistress Essodel had questioned him more.

"Four hundred eighty."

Allowing Ben to buy Rit was a stroke of genius. Not only did I make money from the purchase of an old, worthless slave woman, but I also got Rit away from Mother. They think I let them talk me into asking for Mother's approval. No, but one of these days, Rit would've told Mother every awful thing she thinks I've done. Mother may have killed her afterward, but she would also believe her. Better gone than a viper waiting to strike.

"Five hundred fifty going once, going twice, going three times. Sold." The auctioneer grinned and nodded to Minister Breembat as if he expected to receive more than the customary payment for doing his job. "Congratulations on making a fine purchase, mister. As I said at the opening, this here is Kessiah, age twenty-six. Her son is six, and the baby girl is just a few months old. This young, healthy Birdfolk is worth every cent you'll pay to the owner."

Dragging his right leg as he walked, the auctioneer opened the courthouse doors and shoved Kessiah and her son inside. "That's all for today, folks. Come back tomorrow morning." The auctioneer shook the winning bidder's hand.

The Dragonkin male was two inches taller than Minister Breembat and broader across the shoulders. He wore an ankle-length overcoat fitting for this time of the year. There was nothing noteworthy about the man. Minister Breembat imagined the other male could blend in among a group of Dragonkin; few would recall his presence afterward.

But Minister Breembat saw no need to remember anything about Kessiah's buyer. As long as the man paid his bill in full, that was all he required to know about him.

"That's a fine gal you're getting, mister. Come back in an hour or so, and I'll have her ready for you. Go fill your belly, and then we'll finish our business."

Moving in the opposite direction of the grumbling crowd, Minister Breembat joined the auctioneer in front of the courthouse doors. Kessiah still did not scream or curse as her mother Linah had, but he detected soft, hiccupped tears.

Take that, Rit. Mudspike might not have caught Minty yet, but I've taken someone just as precious from you. I'll have Moses, too. I haven't forgotten about him.

"Why did you send the buyer away? When do I get my money?"

"Patience. You interrupted my lunch earlier; now it's dinnertime." The auctioneer opened the right side of his overcoat, revealing a bottle in an inside pocket. "Care to join me for a meal and a drink?"

Already knowing the answer but unwilling to appear too anxious, Minister Breembat paused with feigned contemplation.

"Don't worry. This is how we do things in the big city. The buyer isn't going anywhere. He'll have dinner too, and then we'll come back here to settle everything."

The city of Cosaru might be fancier than Berzogtown, but it wasn't a big city by anyone other than the auctioneer's stretch of the imagination. Even so, dinner and a few drinks sounded like a good idea, and Minister Breembat's suddenly growling stomach agreed.

The auctioneer laughed, and so did he because his pockets would be filled with five hundred fifty dollars in an hour. Since the city boasted several nice hotels with a convenient bar and restaurant, he thought he might stay the night and head home tomorrow.

Maybe in a week or two, I'll return to Rit's tiny cabin and ask about Kessiah. I want to see the look on her face. The raging pain and her muted anger. Besides a good drink and even better sex, nothing compares to witnessing the utter helplessness of Birdfolk in the face of Dragonkin dominance. I'll remind Rit of her place and enjoy every second of her hurt.

"Lead the way."

The auctioneer did, and Minister Breembat had to admit that the city of Cosaru boasted fine chefs who cooked the most succulent steak he'd ever had. But he limited his drinking to three shots of whiskey. There was no need to get too comfortable until the sale was finalized, and he found a woman to spend the evening with.

Ninety minutes later, Minister Breembat was back in front of the courthouse. Unlike before, there was no crowd waiting to exchange money for bodies.

He looked around, seeing plenty of people doing their business on a Friday, but not the highest bidder.

"Where is he?"

The auctioneer shrugged, seeming unconcerned. The man's nonchalance put Minister Breembat at ease. He would admit that he knew little about how things worked in Cosaru, so if the auctioneer wasn't worried, he would follow suit. But ten minutes turned into twenty and then into thirty.

"He should've arrived back here by now." The auctioneer pointed to the setting sun. "All sales close by sundown. If he doesn't return soon, that gal and her children must stay the night in the courthouse. I'll hold her over for the bidder's return or for a new auction tomorrow."

"This is inconvenient." It didn't matter that he'd already decided to stay the night. Minister Breembat wanted money in hand and one less Wren for him to worry about gone. "Go get my property. I want to have a word with her."

"Of course. Right away."

Minister Breembat had nothing important to tell Kessiah. But since he was annoyed by the delay, he wanted to soothe the emotion in Birdfolk tears. Surely, the agony of waiting to be taken away from everything she had known would've set in deeper during the ninety minutes he'd been away enjoying a delicious meal.

Kessiah and her children would be hungry, too. He hadn't given her more than two slices of bread since forcing her onto his wagon. He intended on breathing in her face, permitting her to smell the remnants of his meal. Then he would list every person she would never see again, beginning with her husband, John. Finally, he would threaten to visit her at the courthouse that night. It would be a hollow threat because a wailing baby did not make for good background music. But Kessiah would spend the entire night waiting for his arrival, frightened because there would be nothing she could do to stop him.

At the thought of the mental torture, he tingled in the place in need of a female's touch. Maybe he would seek Kessiah out after all.

The courthouse door swung open. "They're gone."

"What are you talking about?"

"The gal, the baby, and the boy are gone."

Minister Breembat swore.

"Momma, where we goin'?"

"Hush, baby, and keep up."

Kessiah held a sniffling Araminta in one arm and James's sweaty hand in the other. She followed behind a Dragonkin dressed in an overcoat as smoky gray as his eyes.

"Come with me if you don't want to be sold," he'd told her.

He'd entered the courthouse after the auctioneer had left. When Kessiah saw the dragon shifter, as tall as Master Gyzad had been but with wider shoulders and scarier eyes, she shrank against the cell wall. But then he'd broken the lock and opened the metal doors.

Kessiah hadn't questioned his motive or his intent. But she did grab her son's hand and rushed from the building.

In silence, they walked down the street. She passed white house after white house. Each home had a small but functional front yard, identical except for the numbers on the homes.

Kessiah had worked in places like the ones she saw. They were owned by Dragonkin with only enough money to afford one, maybe three slaves. Older couples tended to work in such homes, or women like Kessiah, mothers tied down with young children.

The Dragonkin stopped in front of a home. "This is where we part ways."

Kessiah glanced over her shoulder. They hadn't traveled that far from the courthouse. Surely, this close, someone would find her.

"But, ah, sir. We can't have walked more than five minutes."

"Exactly. No one will look for you this close to where slaves are sold." With a meaty hand larger than her face, the Dragonkin opened the white, wooden fence. "Now get. Someone is waiting for you inside."

Waitin' for me? I don't know anybody in this city except for mean, old Minister Breembat. But somebody must've sent this dragon to help me and my children.

"Thank you, sir. Thank you."

Without a backward look, Kessiah hustled through the gate and to the front door. Like every home she'd seen on the street, this house also had a door so white she imagined a slave had painted it that morning.

The curtains on the window to the right of the door shifted, but Kessiah couldn't see more than the subtle movement. Seconds later, the door opened, and a full-bosomed, wide-hipped Birdfolk woman in her late sixties stood before her. A mixture of gray and graying black hair curled around yellow and black feathers that would never be gray. The intricate wavy designs of her feathers ran the length of both cheeks, ridged markings of a Sankofa bird shifter from eastern Sika.

"Momma?"

"It's all right, baby." *I hope. I don't know her. But I got two good eyes, and this woman is freeborn through and through. What does she want with me?*

"Get in here before somebody sees you."

In less than fifteen minutes, Kessiah put her life in a stranger's hand for the second time.

She followed the older woman into a living room. The curtains were closed, but the room was lit by two bright oil lamps. A small, circular table was underneath a window, likely the same one the older woman had peered through before opening her door to Kessiah and the children. The rest of the room was decorated with simplistic but well-maintained wooden side tables and chairs.

Embarrassed she tracked dirt from her ratty old boots into the woman's home, Kessiah released James's hand and bent to a knee. If she held Araminta just so, she could remove her shoes and clean up her mess.

"Momma."

Head lowered, Kessiah focused on untying her boots without dropping her baby.

"Momma, it's, it's..." James burst into tears.

Kessiah's head snapped up, and she was suddenly afraid she'd made an awful decision trusting the Dragonkin male and the freeborn Birdfolk woman.

Her son rushed from her side to the opposite end of the room. The living room led to the kitchen, which Kessiah could see from her kneeling position. But she saw more than the kitchen the homeowner had walked into with a softly spoken, "He's been on pins and needles waiting on you and the children."

"Poppa." James wept and wept.

"It's okay, my boy." John scooped their six-year-old into his arms, hugging and kissing James. "Poppa is here now. Sorry I'm late."

"Poppa, I thought... I thought..."

"I know. So did I. But I'm here now." Their eyes met, and John's were as wet as hers. "Kessiah, I'm here. Come closer so I can see you and our little girl."

Recognizing her father's voice, Araminta's eyes opened wide, and she twisted in John's direction.

Unconcerned that her shoes were untied and she'd likely trip in her haste, Kessiah rushed to John. Despite holding a child each, they managed to embrace each other.

Kessiah hadn't cried when Minister Breembat had forced her and the children into his wagon. She had refused to give him the satisfaction. But she broke down after the auction. Thoughts of Linah had crowded her mind, and all Kessiah could think was that she was grateful she wouldn't be separated from her children.

"Mrs. Ziet will allow us to stay here until it's time to leave."

Face pressed against her husband's shoulder, Kessiah's mind whirled with questions. But all she could manage was, "How?"

How was he there? How did he arrange to have the Dragonkin help her? How did he know Mrs. Ziet?

"He bought me. I saw him. Heard his winnin' bid."

"We'll have plenty of time to talk while on the boat."

"Boat?" James squeaked.

Untangling themselves from each other, Kessiah handed Araminta to John. The baby cooed, sweet and innocent, like all babies should experience life.

"Kessiah," Mrs. Ziet called from the kitchen, sounding too much like her grandmother Rit, "once you wipe your tears, bring your boy in here and eat. Then you can feed the baby. She still takes milk from you?"

"Yes, ma'am."

"Good. Then she'll grow big and strong as long as you get enough and the right foods in you."

Kessiah slipped from her boots and placed them near the front door. She had a thousand questions for John but was more hungry than curious.

Unable to believe her blessing, she hugged John again. "I love you."

"I love you, too. That low-down dragon thought he could sell my family, and I wouldn't do anything to stop him. We didn't have much time. We worked fast. Our family still has a hard journey ahead of us. But together, we can do it."

Kessiah still didn't grasp the fullness of John's plan. But it was clear as day that he had one. "You mean to take me away from Miadar?" She gently pushed James's back and encouraged him to join Mrs. Ziet in the kitchen. If she were anything like Rit, she would already have a plate waiting.

John readjusted Araminta on his shoulder, rocking her in a rhythm that always relaxed the baby into a peaceful sleep. "I mean for you and our children to be as free as me."

"I'll be a runaway."

That wasn't the same as being freeborn like John. But it was certainly better than living under the control of a Dragonkin master.

"You look ready to drop. Eat, feed little Minty, and then sleep. We have a long night and day ahead of us."

Having John with her, Kessiah could let down her guard and relax. When she realized Minister Breembat meant to sell her, she had been coiled as tight as a rattlesnake.

Whatever energy she'd had while standing before the crowd of buyers, her back straight and tears held at bay, abandoned her the second she felt her husband's firm, protective arms around her and their children.

So, Kessiah submitted to John's and Mrs. Ziet's urgings. The food was warm and well-seasoned, and the pallet was soft and welcoming.

When night came, Kessiah and her family thanked Mrs. Ziet. Then they were off. Kessiah wrapped Araminta in the knitted quilt Mrs. Ziet had gifted her, but there was something oddly familiar about the quilt's design.

Once more, Kessiah followed, but with absolute certainty the person leading the way could be trusted.

Kessiah was used to Dralox County's fertile shoreline, but she'd never seen Calgro Bay this far north and under a glowing full moon.

John helped her and James into a fourteen-foot, two-person log canoe. Despite being married to a skilled sailor, Kessiah had never traveled in a boat.

"Do you want me to help you paddle?"

"You'll have your hands full with the children, especially Minty. James, sit between your momma's legs."

John looked over James's head to Kessiah, who understood the position would help balance a boat not meant to hold four people. However, Araminta and John didn't weigh much, so Kessiah assumed John's plan included the correct calculations.

"Wrap that quilt around you and the children. It'll keep you warm."

Not warm enough, with it being late December and them on the water. But Kessiah would rather be cold in a log canoe with her family than in a warm home owned by a new master.

She covered herself to her neck. James reclined snugly between her legs, holding his sister against his chest. Like most babies, Araminta slept best when tucked close.

"There are Birdfolk communities up and down the Calgro Bay. Some free. Others are fugitive communities. We'll stop so I can rest. We'll stop at a safe house if the water gets too choppy. It won't be easy, but I'll get us to Bodan."

"Bodan City." It wasn't a question but an awed repeating. Kessiah had never traveled beyond Berzogtown and Pelduth Neck. Come tomorrow, she would be even farther from her family. "After Momma was sold away, I did my best to help Poppa raise Harriet. Momma used to say that's what big sisters were for."

Like Kessiah, her sister Harriet had two children. Both were girls. They'd been pregnant at the same time, with Araminta born a couple of months before Sarah.

"Will I see Harriet and Poppa again? My grandparents?"

Kessiah maintained a stream of chatter. She didn't expect John to have answers or to even reply. He needed to conserve his energy and keep his focus. But he also couldn't afford to fall asleep, so Kessiah chatted away.

Time wore on. Darkness surrounded them as much as the bay did. Each time Kessiah had to relieve herself, she envied her husband and son.

"What are we gonna do when we get to Bodan? It's still in Miadar."

They'd stopped at two waterfront homes. The owners of the safe houses, as John had called them, were as gracious as Mrs. Ziet. No one had remarked on their odor or seemed offended by how fast they'd scarfed down the food they'd been given.

Their hosts didn't seem to have much, but they shared with a nod and a knowing smile.

Then, they were back in the canoe. The sun was out, warming chilled bones, and the children were awake but sluggish.

"How much longer?"

"Not much more now." John pointed to the golden horizon. "Keep lookin' there. You'll see soon enough."

"How did you plan all of this?"

"I had a lot of help. Some of us can write, but most can't. But these waters and communities talk, Kessiah. Up and down this bay, we travel. Sendin' word from north to south and back. All the way down to Dralox County and up to northern parts of Miadar like Cosaru and Bodan. Farther north than that, if you can believe it."

Kessiah's heart melted when John looked at her over his shoulder. His smile was brighter than the sun. He had to be exhausted, but nothing in the way he looked at her, bedraggled and smelling of urine and James's vomit, reflected the physical toil the last day and a half had taken on him.

"Dragonkin masters want to keep slaves ignorant to the vast network of free and fugitive Birdfolk communities along these waters and in free states. But she learned. She's still learnin'. I couldn't have saved you without her help and the help of her friends."

"John, who are you talkin' abo . . ." Kessiah looked down at the quilt. She'd never seen it before. But the craftsmanship looked familiar. No, it couldn't be.

"Momma, look." James sat up straight. His hair and feathers were sticking every which way, and his breath smelled as bad as her tongue tasted.

"I see it, baby." Kessiah couldn't yet make out the land but sails from boats much larger than the log canoe whipped like beacons of salvation.

They were still a ways off, but being so near their destination had her heart racing.

"It won't be long now."

Oddly, the last few legs of the journey felt longer than all the miles that came before. But when they finally reached Bodan's dock and climbed from the log canoe, Kessiah dropped to her knees and kissed the ground. It wasn't free land, and John hadn't said where they'd go or what they would do once they arrived. But for the first time in her life, she had no master to answer to. That singular truth doubled her over in body-racking tears.

She felt a gentle hand touch her shoulder. Small yet strong, so not James's. A second hand settled against her wet face and wiped away tears with a calloused thumb.

"Cryin' already? I ain't even gotten you to the promised land yet."

With her heart in her throat, Kessiah opened her tear-filled eyes. She took in the small figure that knelt in front of her. Two birth years separated them. They were as close as sisters. They climbed trees together, waded in creeks without permission, and snuck food from the big house when no one was looking. And they'd cried together when Linah was sold. Kessiah had lost a mother, while she'd lost an older sister.

"Minty." They were so close that Kessiah named her daughter after her aunt. She would always be Minty in her heart. But the woman who stroked her face, freeing it of tears, was also Harriet.

"I was afraid we'd be too late." Harriet wrapped her arms around her, the same way Kessiah had swathed her children in a quilt she now understood Harriet had sent to Mrs. Ziet for the long, cold ride up the Calgro. "But the good Lord has seen you through." Harriet hugged her tighter. "I've missed you. I've missed you all."

Chapter 27

What You're Plannin' is Dangerous

The State of Miadar
  Bodan City

As if he were a man of leisure instead of a hardworking stevedore, John's brother, Majors, leaned against the living room wall opposite where Harriet sat. At five six, he matched his younger brother's height and coloring. Grayish-blue feathers dominated his head. His black human hair blended into the feathers like a seamless body of water swept away in a current that swooped up at his forehead. "You're a natural at that."

Seated in a rocking chair, Harriet hummed a lullaby she'd learned from Rit. Harriet had spent much of her childhood tending to babies not much older than Kessiah's daughter. Back then, she thought it unfair. As a twenty-eight-year-old childless woman, she also felt that was unfair.

But the good Lord hadn't seen fit to answer every prayer, so Harriet had chosen to be grateful for the prayers he did answer.

Nuzzling the baby's cheek, she indulged in the feeling of her petal-soft skin. "If I have my way," she said, speaking in low tones, "and I intend to, she won't know a day of slavery."

"Thanks to you, she's here with us."

"Not me alone. None of this is all me. Thank you for hidin' us."

Majors quirked an eyebrow, and Harriet ignored the subtle objection. "Everything ain't about doin' on your own, but about bein' the one to act. To set things in motion." Majors nodded to Harriet. "That's you." He pushed from the wall and smiled down at her like a cat who'd caught a mouse. "Still married?"

"Ain't you got a woman?"

His shrug was as devilish as his grin. "Sometimes I do, sometimes I don't."

"I told you before, I ain't in the market to replace my John."

With a single long step, Majors stood before Harriet. Perhaps sensing she did not appreciate having him loom over her, he knelt. "You're too good for a man who wouldn't run away to save you from the auction block."

Harriet wouldn't have this conversation with Majors, not with him, not with anyone. What she had with her husband was private, and no one had a right to her deepest feelings about John and their marriage.

"It ain't none of your business. Now stop talkin' foolish."

"It ain't foolish, and you know it." Majors lifted his hands in surrender. "But fine. Keep this in mind, Harriet. You've been gone for a year. A man can always find someone to warm his bed." He intentionally grazed his hard, muscular chest against her knees when he stood, a subtle reminder of how long it had been since a man had touched her. "And so can a woman. I respect your loyalty. But there's a fine line between bein' loyal and bein' a fool in love."

Harriet closed her eyes and let Majors's harsh words wash over her. She was a guest in his home, so it wouldn't do for her to get into an argument with the man. But he'd deliberately stepped over her well-established boundary, and she had no kind words to match his insensitivity.

"The baby is asleep." Halting her rocking, she stood slowly so as not to awaken her niece. "I'm gonna take Minty back to her momma."

"You're mad. Don't be. I didn't mean nothin' by what I said."

"We both know that's a lie. Loyalty and trust given is loyalty and trust returned. Don't mention John again."

"That mean tone sounded like a threat, Harriet Cassin. Don't shoot me for worryin' about your tender heart."

A soft laugh escaped, and Harriet couldn't help but shake her head at Majors's strange apology. "I would never shoot family." She stopped at the threshold. "I don't even own a gun."

"I can take care of that. It ain't safe for you to travel between Pyzai and Miadar alone."

Until slavery was outlawed in all states, no place would be absolutely safe for fugitive slaves. Despite the adoption of the 1850 Fugitive Slave Act, Harriet would feel securer once she crossed back into Pyzai.

"Thank you, Majors. You're a good man."

Harriet thought he would use the compliment as an opportunity to flirt again, but he only stared at her until she walked away.

He pities me and thinks I'm a fool for holdin' on to John. Momma and Poppa weathered storms in their marriage. They were forced to spend time apart. But Poppa always returned to Momma, and she welcomed him back home each time. John just needs more time to wrap his mind around movin' away from his parents on the Eastern Shore and joinin' me in Pyzai. It ain't like he doesn't also have family outside of Dralox County. His brothers are here.

Harriet refused to follow her thought through to its most logical conclusion. Instead, she crept into the bedroom where Kessiah's family slept. After helping Kessiah bathe the children in a basin large enough to fit James, she'd left the room so John and Kessiah could take their turn. When she'd returned, only Araminta had been awake.

She didn't think Kessiah would mind, so she'd taken the baby into the living room.

An hour later, she stood in the bedroom again. James still slept like the dead. But instead of resting on his mother's pallet, tucked under her chin, he was sprawled across his father's chest like a newborn seeking their parents' reassuring heartbeats.

Harriet knelt at the foot of Kessiah's pallet. Holding Araminta's neck and back, she placed the sleeping baby beside her mother. Satisfied the child wouldn't awaken, she made to stand but stilled when Kessiah's eyes fluttered open. "I didn't mean to wake you," she whispered.

"You didn't. I was lyin' here thinkin'." Shifting from her side onto her back, Kessiah smiled at Harriet, and a piece of her heart clinched at the resemblance to Linah. "You must've gone to a lot of trouble to get us here."

"You know me better than to say somethin' like that. No trouble."

"I do. Still, you're riskin' your freedom for mine. John says we're gonna move to another safe house before goin' on to Pyzai."

Shifting to the pallet, Harriet lifted Kessiah's feet and placed them in her lap. She leaned against the wall and sighed. She hadn't slept much since learning of Kessiah's intended sale. Harriet was too tired to get into the details of her plan. But there would be time enough for that later.

"My John has two brothers, Tom and Evans. I've arranged for us to stay at their homes. Two or three days apiece. We don't want to stay in any one place too long. But you need a few days to rest, especially John. I'd rather not head out until John's strength has returned after all that paddlin'."

"To Pyzai. That's where you live now?"

"Pholgre. It's a city in Pyzai. I cook and clean to make ends meet. Save as much as I can."

She had also sold several feathers when she arrived. It was either that or starvation and homelessness. But Harriet had no interest in sharing those stories with Kessiah. As long as she had Harriet, her niece wouldn't have to sell pieces of herself to survive.

"What are you savin' up to buy?" Kessiah shifted until she sat beside Harriet, her back propped against the wall. "Do you wanna know about home? How Rit and Ben are gettin' on?"

Harriet swallowed a laugh. "You better not let them hear you call them by their first names. No. Not now. I don't think my heart could take it. Tell me about Minty's name."

Harriet felt a warm hand settle atop hers, holding with a familiar tenderness. She had missed her family more than words she owned to express her loneliness without them.

"Araminta was your name first."

"It's an honor. But why give it to me instead of to Linah?"

"Momma would fuss at you for bein' so thick-headed. No matter where she is, she knows all of our hearts."

"Meanin'?"

"Meanin', I love you like a sista, a momma, and an auntie wrapped in one thick-headed package. Don't think I didn't catch you not answerin' my question. What are you savin' for, Minty?"

"Don't call me that. You got your own Minty, now."

Kessiah brought Harriet's hand to her chest and placed it over her strongly beating heart. "You were first in here. You don't have to say it because I know why you're savin'. What you're plannin' is dangerous."

"I don't know what I'm plannin' yet. But havin' you and those children here safe and sound gives me hope. I won't let you down. It's not a good feelin' leavin' your heart behind."

Kessiah's gaze fell, and Harriet assumed her thoughts had settled on her sister and two nieces. Harriet wished she had enough power and savings to lead them all out of slavery. But she was one Birdfolk woman, and the system of enslavement was vast and mighty.

How much more can I do? I've met a lot of people since comin' north. Good people. Righteous people. Fighters against slavery and champions of rights for Birdfolk. I've been thinkin' on this for a long time. I ain't special. I follow the good Lord's will. And when I can't hear him clearly enough, I follow my own. Gettin' Kessiah and her family here ain't no miracle. She right, though. I worked hard to make it happen. But I ain't done it alone. Still, I think I can do it again.

"I brought you one of my dresses. Won't be a perfect fit, but it'll do until we get home."

"Home." Kessiah leaned against Harriet, and she gladly accepted more than the physical weight on her arm. "Home is Berzogtown and Dralox County."

Harriet thought the same, but only because her people were there. But she also had family and friends beyond the stifling confines of plantation life and aviary living.

Kessiah's arm snaked around Harriet's waist and squeezed tightly. "But home is also wherever you, John, and my children are. You're a blessin' from above, Harriet. I know I'll get sad sometimes, missin' my sister, father, and home."

Harriet felt the same.

"And I'll feel guilty, sometimes, because I'm free, and they ain't."

So, too, did Harriet.

"Then I'll remember every awful thing that's been done to me and even more that could've been done under a new master. And I'll cry because I'd rather have my freedom than spend the rest of my days enslaved with my family."

Again, Kessiah's feelings mirrored Harriet's.

"You ain't wrong for wantin' freedom and claimin' it for you and yours. I've had to tell myself the same. Night after night, I ask the Lord to cleanse me of my sins. Of feelin' guilty for takin' what should've been mine from birth. But prayin' ain't been enough, Kess. Havin' you here helps. It lifts my spirits."

"And gives you ideas?"

"I want my sisters back. I want everything the Dragonkin have stolen from us. But that power rests with God almighty."

"But God didn't plan my escape. You did. So, what are you gonna do?"

"I don't know yet, but somethin'."

1851

The State of Pyzai
Pholgre City

Harriet forwent the available train station benches, choosing to stand instead. Her nerves were itching her skin, and her legs twitched too much to relax. "You didn't need to walk me to the train station, but I sure do appreciate the company."

Kessiah was rarely without her children, so Harriet took extra pleasure whenever they could spend time alone. Not that their walk to the train station had been marked by lighthearted conversation and laughter.

"This would be easier if we knew how to read and write."

"It would. But we manage because we must."

The smell of coal smoke hung in the air; a lung-tightening pollutant Harriet hadn't gotten used to. There was much about city living that was acquired tastes, Harriet had learned. Some days, she could hardly hear herself think with her neighbors' fondness for late nights, loud talking, and laughter that flowed freely and often.

But people were friendly enough, even if they were more cautious of strangers than she was used to back home. However, Harriet didn't blame them because she'd developed an eye for runaways like her, particularly those fresh across the border.

"I know you did the same for me, Harriet, but I don't like it."

Kessiah slipped her hand into Harriet's free one. In the other, she held a rose print carpetbag she bought from a Birdfolk man selling wares on the street. She didn't question where he'd gotten the items, but she did say an extra prayer of repentance that night.

"You don't have to hold my hand. I'm a grown woman. I ain't gonna walk on the track."

"Hush, Harriet. You've been without family for a year. I'll hold your hand if I want to."

"There's plenty of family here and in Bodan."

"By marriage, mainly. It ain't the same, and you know it."

No, it wasn't, but Harriet had been blessed to discover a thriving Birdfolk community from Dralox County in southwest Pholgre. She couldn't imagine settling anywhere else in the big, bustling city.

However, Kessiah was also correct. Until Harriet had hugged her niece at the Bodan dock, she hadn't realized how touch deprived she'd been.

Kessiah lifted Harriet's hand to her mouth and kissed the back. "Even though I've watched you talk to people almost every day, gettin' information about home and sharin' what you know, it's still hard to believe."

Every time Kessiah mentioned the hasty plan she and John had cobbled together, awe entered her voice, producing a burn of discomfort in Harriet's stomach.

She withdrew her hand, unsure how to respond to a reverence befitting someone more important than a Berzogtown runaway who struggled to pay rent.

"I'm gonna ignore that because you're nervous about Moses."

"He only nineteen and ain't never been nowhere but home."

"Just like me." Kessiah poked Harriet's shoulder. "And just like you. He's grown. Bigger than us both and fast as lightnin'. Trust he got your message. He won't let nobody stop him from gettin' to you."

Harriet had faith in every detail of her plan. She trusted everyone she'd confided in to help Moses and his two friends make it to Bodan. From there, she trusted her brothers-in-law to keep them safe in their homes, and she had absolute faith in herself to see them safely to Pyzai.

Harriet had zero trust in Minister Breembat and the unknown. No matter how well she thought out her plan, the devil never took a day off.

As the minutes ticked by, more people filled the platform. Birdfolk, Dragonkin, and Harpyfolk waited for the train. Even three gryphons had joined the crowd, although they were the only group who seemed more inclined to travel by air. So, their presence at the train station was unusual but not odd.

Harriet had thought it strange for winged creatures to travel by train. However, she supposed the preference for this form of transportation for flying beings was similar to dragon shifters and harpies back home who chose to ride horses and drive wagons. Privilege came in all forms, Harriet concluded, for she couldn't imagine having the ability to fly yet choosing not to use her wings for that purpose.

"No, get off me. I said get off me."

"You coming with us. We got you now, ground-scraper."

Harriet went on tiptoe and tried to see what was happening at the other end of the platform. But all she could see were backs because everyone on the platform had turned toward the scuffle. Yet, icy unease went up her spine, and she feared she knew what was happening.

"Harriet?"

From the sound of Kessiah's squeaky voice, she'd concluded the same.

She grabbed her niece's hand but knew better than to run and draw attention to them.

"I said get off me. I'm free. This here is a free state."

"You ain't free, boy."

"Leave him alone," someone in the crowd yelled.

"Go back to where you came from. We don't want slave catchers around here."

"Back up. I said back up. We have got every right to be here."

Fingers laced with Kessiah's, Harriet slowly backed away as the crowd surged forward. On any other day, she would've used the distraction to make her escape. But if she missed the train, she also risked missing Moses. It had taken her months to save for the train fare, with enough left over to fund their time at the safe houses until she deemed it safe to return to Pyzai.

Harriet had yet to reveal to Kessiah all the small but essential details of her escape plan from the Cosaru courthouse, like the cost of food, clothing, and disguises. Saving Kessiah and her children from the auction block had eaten up most of Harriet's savings, but it had been worth it.

"Leave him alone."

"Get off me. I ain't goin' back. I'm free. I'm free."

Harriet retreated as far as she dared without isolating herself and Kessiah from others who hadn't joined what was quickly becoming a mob. She turned to her niece and drew the shawl from around Kessiah's shoulders up to her head, concealing what she could of her face.

Wide brown eyes met hers, and Harriet prayed her own didn't reveal her fear. She sucked in a deep breath and then slowly blew it out. "Those slave catchers ain't here for you. And they ain't here for me. I want you to walk away."

With her lower lip trapped between her teeth, Kessiah shook her head. "Not without you."

"Right here and now, I'm choosin' you. Your freedom. Your safety."

"Harriet, no."

"I need you to get out of here so I can choose Moses."

"Harriet, p-please."

"My baby brother is countin' on me, Kess, just as your children and husband are countin' on you to come home."

Someone from the gathered crowd spoke out. "We won't let you take him. We don't care about that stupid Fugitive Slave Act."

"Get back. I said get back. This ground-scraper is returning to Miadar with us."

"Go home. We don't want you here."

"Go home."

"Go home."

Harriet couldn't believe her ears. She'd chosen well when she'd settled in Pholgre, but the Fugitive Slave Act had changed everything. The law passed in September 1850 was a compromise between the politicians of slave-owning states and free states after the territory of Chonsa was admitted as a free state. The admittance of the West Coast state of Chonsa unsettled the delicate balance of slave and free states.

Now, slave catchers had the legal authority to enter a slave-free state and forcibly remove any runaway they caught. Worse, the law compelled local authorities to help the slave catchers apprehend fugitive slaves.

However, as Harriet looked around, station security guards were nowhere to be seen. She wouldn't dare guess what that meant for the slave catchers or the runaway slave. Later, she would sit down with her thoughts and hatch a plan now that the Fugitive Slave Act made Pyzai as nearly as unsafe for runaways as Miadar.

Still, no law or slave catcher would stand between Harriet and her brother. One way or another, she would bring Moses north. But first, she needed to ensure Kessiah's safety.

The chanting of "Go home" swelled, and it took every ounce of Harriet's courage to not leave the station with Kessiah. The sound of violence brewed behind her, and the station would soon be an unsafe place for any Birdfolk without freedom papers.

"You see that ferry tavern across the way?"

Kessiah nodded, but her eyes kept skidding from Harriet to the chanting crowd behind her.

"You'll be able to see me and the train from over there." When Kessiah didn't answer, the confrontation behind Harriet garnering more of her niece's attention, Harriet took ahold of Kessiah's arms. She shifted them so that Kessiah's back was to the crowd. "Go to the ferry tavern. Watch me from there."

Unlike the compromise between politicians who supported slavery and those who did not that resulted in the Fugitive Slave Act, Harriet's compromise risked no one's freedom but her own.

"Do you hear me?"

Harriet saw the moment Kessiah's resolve snapped into place.

"I do. Right, I gotta get back to John and the children." Kessiah's hug reminded Harriet of the intense way she'd embraced Rit, knowing she might never see her mother again. "Don't you dare get caught?"

"I won't."

"I'll do my best" would've been closer to the truth and the new reality of runaway life under the Fugitive Slave Act. But Harriet could feel Kessiah's need for reassurance in the taut body pressed to hers.

"Moses and I will be along shortly."

"You better. And please try not to have one of your episodes."

If Harriet knew how to prevent them, she would've done so years ago. Instead of stretching out the goodbye, Harriet turned Kessiah toward the ferry tavern. Thankfully, her niece went without another word.

Unfortunately, in the time it had taken Harriet to convince Kessiah to leave her, the situation at the other end of the platform had turned uglier. The only thing that would've worsened the brawl was if a Dragonkin had transformed.

Being owned by a dragon shifter who eschewed her human side was a different experience from living among Dragonkin with the opposite perspective. Perhaps Northern Dragonkin thought themselves more dignified and less animalistic, living in their human skin instead of scales. Whatever their reason for preferring their human form, Harriet was grateful.

The security guards she hadn't seen earlier joined the crowd-turned-rescue mob. She couldn't see the group of gryphons she'd spotted earlier but could hear the sound of pounding fists and stomping feet. Harriet couldn't muster a bit of sympathy for the slave catchers. The first time she'd met one had left her with permanent head damage.

So, Harriet clutched her carpetbag with both hands, stood straight and tall, and waited for the train to arrive as if a brawl wasn't taking place forty feet away.

She was the first to board when the train finally pulled into the station, blowing its whistle and emitting coal smoke.

A Birdfolk man plopped down on the seat beside her. His overcoat was torn at the shoulder seam, scratches marked his face, and the hand on his bobbing knee had cuts across three fingers and blood under his nails.

"Did he get away?"

The man pointed a dark finger to the window and the platform beyond.

Harriet turned to see the same group of gryphons she'd mistaken as casual travelers waiting on the southbound train. They lay on the platform, beaten and bloody but, thankfully, still alive. Returning to Pholgre after the brutal assault on federal government–sanctioned slave catchers, with three freshly runaway slaves, would make Harriet's job harder.

She relaxed in her seat, her carpetbag snug between her feet, and the man beside her an opportunity she wouldn't let pass.

"You got slave family or friends in Miadar?"

"Don't we all?"

Fair enough.

Without turning, Harriet extended her hand. "I'm Harriet."

"I'm Frederick Dou ... Frederick is fine. It's good to meet you, Harriet."

Chapter 28
Always Meant to Soar

1851
Pelduth Neck

A candle burned in the window as she remembered, warming Harriet's heart, even if the rest of her was chilled to the bone. As she'd done the last time she'd spied the farmhouse from the safety of the woods, Harriet waited until no one else was about before making her way down the hill. However, instead of approaching the front door as she had done previously, Harriet strode to the back of the house.

A stone path led to the back door, and beside the door was a window with another candle. This one was barely burned down, but the flickering light was just as much a beacon as the well-used candle in the front window.

"You're awfully loud out there. Are you trying to get shot?" The back door swung open. The owner held a rifle in her clawed hands and wore a frown instead of the smile Harriet had expected. "Get in before someone sees you."

Harriet hustled inside the farmhouse, relieved at having made it this far without being caught. "Thank you, Norveis."

"Don't thank me because you shouldn't be here."

Harriet looked around Norveis's kitchen. It hadn't changed in the two years since she'd last been in the harpy's house. A square table with four chairs in the center of the room occupied most of the space. But only the floor underneath the chair at the head of the table had deep scuff marks no amount of polish could fix or hide.

"Still livin' alone, I see."

Norveis leaned her rifle against the back door and gave Harriet a once-over, her eyes so disapproving that she felt judged to the depth of her soul.

She dropped her satchel, sat in the chair to the right of Norveis, and removed her overcoat. Considering the chair had the only placemat on the table in front of it, on top of which a covered plate had been placed, Harriet assumed she'd either been waiting for her or whichever runaway she'd been expecting hadn't arrived yet.

"Smells delicious." Harriet plucked the sleeve of Norveis's lilac and white plaid dress. "This is better than that nightgown you came to the door wearin' the last time. If you don't mind, I'm gonna eat this."

"You are an idiot, Harriet Cassin."

Mouth full of tender turkey meat, Harriet glowered at Norveis.

"Don't look at me like that. I sent a message for you not to come."

"And my return message said I'd be here Christmas week."

Harriet glanced around the kitchen again, seeing no sign that Norveis had decorated for Christmas. There were no adornments outside the house either, not even a wreath on the door. She remembered Norveis celebrated the holiday as a child, but she either ceased the practice as an adult or felt no need to spend time decorating her home because she had no one to enjoy the holiday with. Having run away in late October of 1849, last year was the first Christmas that Harriet had spent without family. It had also been the first Christmas she hadn't awoken in John's arms since taking him as her husband.

Harriet hoped to change that this year. If she kept to her schedule, she wouldn't be home in time for Christmas, but she could spend the holiday with her husband. It wouldn't be an ideal way to celebrate Christmas, but they would be together again, and that was all that mattered to Harriet.

"You got to be the stubbornest person I know." As if the chair had caused her foul mood, Norveis yanked it away from the table, adding more scuff marks to an otherwise pristine floor. She sat and eyed her rifle as if contemplating using it on Harriet.

Harriet ignored Norveis's less than cordial welcome. Instead, she broke a slice of cornbread in two and shoved half in her mouth. "I've come for John."

"You shouldn't have. It's unsafe for you to be here. Patrollers and slave catchers are everywhere. I can't believe you didn't get caught."

Neither could Harriet, although she'd been careful not to. But she knew the terrain and the route better than the previous time. She had also spent the last two years cultivating relationships in three states: Miadar, Pyzai, and Drethos, a slave-free state to the south and west of Miadar.

Harriet wasn't the same ignorant, frightened runaway she'd been when she'd knocked on Norveis's front door in 1849, unsure if she'd be met with open hands or closed fists.

"I know comin' all this way was risky. But, for John, it's worth it." Harriet ate the other half of the slice of cornbread, wishing she had a cup of milk to wash it down. But the concerned way Norveis watched Harriet, she thought it best not to ask her for one more favor. "I'll be out of your hair soon enough."

"That's not my worry." Norveis scooted her chair until her arms could rest comfortably on the table. She hunched forward, parted her lips, and then closed them.

Harriet dropped the green bean she'd been about to eat. "Spit it out, Norveis. What do you know that I don't? Have you word about my parents?"

If either were hurt, Harriet would run straight to Dr. Tozor's plantation. Her freedom be damned.

"No, I haven't any news of your parents." Norveis took ahold of one of Harriet's hands, unfurling fingers she hadn't realized had seized at the thought of something awful having befallen Ben or Rit. "As far as I know, they're fine. Don't get yourself worked up. You haven't even rested yet. You must be exhausted."

Harriet was, but she wasn't too tired to force out of Norveis whatever news she didn't want to share. The harpy's response to Harriet's inquiry about John had worked its way from a trusted Berzogtown freeborn Birdfolk dockworker up the Calgro Bay, to Bodan and then on to Pholgre and a Dragonkin train conductor she met through her friend Frederick.

"Whatever it is, just tell me."

Norveis grasped Harriet's other hand, and her gaze lowered for a soul-shattering heartbeat before lifting.

Before Norveis shared what she clearly did not want to tell, Majors's words echoed in Harriet's mind.

"A man can always find someone to warm his bed."

"Before you left, I promised to send news if I heard anything about your kin. You have got a big family, so it's hard keeping track of them all."

Harriet disliked a person taking the long route when a more direct one would've better served all involved.

"I got lucky with Kessiah because a bar owner friend overheard a drunk Minister Breembat complain in one breath about needing money but brag in the next about having a plan to sell a slave from one of his mother's prized Birdfolk families in a Cosaru auction. No offense, Harriet, but everyone knows that means the Wrens. My aunt and uncle used to brag to family and friends like Minister Breembat. They were so proud of themselves, so they showed you off every chance they got."

The painful years of living with the Calises hadn't faded from Harriet's mind, much less from her body. Even during the early, more desperate days and weeks in Pyzai, where food was scarce and shelter insecure, Harriet would rather starve than risk having a bad episode performing one of her old dance routines. The decision wasn't a difficult one to make. But Harriet hadn't achieved freedom only to die of starvation, so when she sold her feathers to Dragonkin who did not own slaves but who understood the value of having Birdfolk feathers the vibrant color of Harriet's in their hoard, she soothed her pride with dreams of saving enough money to bring her family to the North.

"Old, painful memories, Norveis. I don't like beatin' around the bush any more than I enjoy talkin' about the past. Just tell me. Please."

"Right, I'm sorry. People in town know your family, so it was easy for me to find and get to know them. At least the ones hired out have more freedom to travel. Moses pointed out your husband to me one day when they both were hauling crates onto a merchant ship. I've only seen him a handful of times since that day. The last time I did, he was with a woman. Walking close and smiling at each other. I asked around about her. Her name is Caroline, and she's freeborn."

Harriet made to withdraw her hands, but Norveis wouldn't release them.

"A man can always find someone to warm his bed."

"You wanted to know, now I'm telling you."

Harriet did, but... "Friends?"

"More. Much more. I'm sorry."

Harriet yanked her hands from Norveis and jumped to her feet.

"A man can always find someone to warm his bed."

"This is why I didn't want you coming back here. John has moved on."

"He wouldn't."

"He's with someone else."

"Can't be. You're wrong."

"I wish I were. I wouldn't have said anything if I weren't positive. I'm sorry. But John married that freeborn woman. Caroline Cassin. That's the name she goes by now."

A year ago, Harriet had promised Kessiah that she wouldn't have an episode. She'd traveled by train to Bodan, collected Moses and his two friends, stayed with family, and then safely returned to Pholgre. Harriet had done all of that without a single episode. She didn't know how she'd managed it then or how she'd traveled from Pholgre to Dralox County without blacking out a single time.

Yet, news of John's remarriage had her stumbling backward. Darkness threatened, and she felt herself falling.

Norveis caught her, and she fell limply in the harpy's strong arms. "I got you. This is why I'm still single."

Harriet didn't recall much afterward, certainly not Norveis carrying her upstairs and laying her in a bed. In Harriet's twenty-nine years, she'd never lain on a bed with a mattress.

"G-go to him, p-please." Lord, her tongue felt twice its size, and her eyes wouldn't focus.

"No."

"Please. Tell John I'm here. Tell him I've come for him."

"I won't."

"Please. He'll come. I know he will."

"Harriet, you got to let him go."

Harriet wouldn't. She couldn't. She had spent two years nursing the dream of being reunited with her husband. She'd been faithful of heart and of body. But she wasn't a naïve woman who didn't understand carnal needs. She might not have liked Majors's statement of a year ago, but she hadn't disagreed with him.

But she could forgive John because she believed in his love for her.

"If he knows I'm here, he'll come."

"He married someone else, for God's sake."

"No, he's still *my* husband. In front of our family and friends, we took vows."

The side of the bed dipped, and Harriet couldn't bear to see the pity in Norveis's eyes as she had in Majors's, so she closed hers.

"If I go, promise me you'll accept whatever happens."

"He'll come. I know he will. John loves me."

"I'm sure Caroline believes he loves her too. But you think he'll choose you because you've still chosen him. That's not how it works." Harriet felt Norveis's strong, warm hand on her shoulder. "It's late, I'll go down to the docks tomorrow."

Harriet wanted to demand Norveis seek John out that night. But she had neither the energy nor the right to demand anything of the harpy. "Thank you."

"This won't end well. But you came all this way for John. You might as well learn the truth of his feelings. Either way, he will break a heart tomorrow. The question is whether it will be yours or Caroline's." Norveis patted her shoulder and then stood. "Get some rest. This is the guest room, so you aren't putting me out tonight by sleeping in here."

Harriet forced heavy eyelids to open. As she knew she would be, Norveis stood beside the bed, staring down at Harriet with a look that called her a fool.

She didn't care what Majors or Norveis thought, no more than she cared for the unasked-for opinions of Kessiah and Moses. Neither had approved of her decision to travel to Miadar for John. She'd suspected Moses had known more than he'd shared about John, but nothing on the scale of her husband having remarried.

Her brother would not have kept that a secret from Harriet, especially if the knowledge of John's second marriage would have prevented her from risking re-enslavement by returning to Dralox County.

"Thank you, Norveis. You're a good friend."

"Remember that when I don't return with him."

"I have faith in John and the Lord. He'll come. You'll see. You'll see."

John couldn't believe his eyes. He'd worked with harpies on the dock. Occasionally, he'd even had drinks with them on his days off. But he wasn't friendly enough with any of them to extend an invitation to his home, or they so enamored with him to visit without so much as a by-your-leave.

He closed the door to his cabin but didn't move beyond the porch. "Who are you, and what do you want with me?"

A harpy female watched him from the foot of his porch. How human a harpy's face appeared varied, with some more birdlike. But the harpy who'd knocked on his door and then retreated to the steps wore the face of a lovely human woman. He couldn't detect a single feather on her face or neck. Her upper body, including her arms, was that of a human woman. John supposed most of her legs were human, too, although her ankle-length dress and open overcoat shielded the rest of her. But not the clawed feet or the large, brown wings pushed through slits in her clothing, or the spiky mix of feathers and human hair that reminded John of Birdfolk.

He didn't know the harpy, but she frowned at him like a woman scorned. "I said, who are—"

"I'm a friend of your wife." A bushy eyebrow quirked up. "Your first wife, considering you have two now."

"What?" John looked around. The sun hadn't yet set, and if not for a chill he hadn't been able to shake the last few days, he would've still been in town working. The nearest cabins were quiet, but wouldn't be once the sun set and his neighbors dragged themselves home from a long day of work. "You mean Harriet?"

"It's nice to know you remember her name."

John recalled everything about Harriet, including the two times she'd left him. The second time, she hadn't returned, not that John expected her to or even wanted her to if it meant being sold by Minister Breembat. But the stranger wasn't entitled to any of his memories.

"Harriet ain't here. But you know that already since you know I have a new wife. You been followin' me?"

If she had, John hadn't noticed. That thought sent a tingle of unease through him because the harpy could've killed John without him realizing he'd been in danger.

John stepped forward but with no intention of leaving his porch. Standing where he was placed him at eye level with the tall harpy. He already felt at a disadvantage; he wouldn't give the female another.

"You're two years late if you're lookin' for Harriet."

"Aren't you curious why a stranger would track you down to ask about a wife who's been gone for two years?"

Of course John was, but it wasn't the first time someone had come looking for Harriet. Admittedly, only Minister Breembat and Dr. Tozor ever had, and that had been within the first two months of Harriet having run away. After being away from home for so long, no one expected to see Harriet again, including John.

So, why, after so long, had this harpy sought him out, asking about a wife who'd abandoned him, along with her parents and siblings? Still, if the harpy intended him harm, she would've done more than knock on his door and give him space.

"How is she doin'?"

"You actually sound concerned."

"Harpy, you don't know me to judge my feelings for Harriet."

A small, irrational part of John had thought Harriet would return. He'd worried she'd been caught, hurt, or worse when she didn't. But news on the docks traveled far and wide. His brother Evans had sent him a message about Harriet, which he'd dutifully passed on to Ben and Rit. She was safe in Pholgre, and the tight knot his stomach had become after Harriet left slowly uncoiled. But the pain it had left behind remained.

"If you have news of Harriet, tell it, then go before Caroline gets home."

"Don't want the new wife hearing about the old one?"

"That ain't none of your business."

From the darkened look on the harpy's face, John thought she would fly at him. But her wings only fluttered, and her clawed feet stayed put.

"I told her this was pointless, that you've moved on with another woman, freeborn. That bit of truth hurt her almost as much as your betrayal. You shouldn't have married Harriet if you wanted a freeborn wife."

Wait. What is she talkin' about? It sounds as if she's done more than receive an oral message from Harriet. It's almost as if she's spoken to her personally. That's impossible. That would mean the harpy's been to Pholgre or Harriet is here. Harriet wouldn't do somethin' so reckless and stupid. Would she? For me? Lord, please, no.

"I see you get it now. Guilt and dread are an ugly look on you, John Cassin. I don't care how you're feeling. But Harriet wants to see you, so I need you to come with me." The harpy gestured with her thumb to the wagon she'd parked several feet from his home.

John stepped backward, and his mind reeled. *Harriet is here. I can't believe she returned to Dralox County. Two years and no message from her, and she thinks to stroll back into my life like nothin' has happened.*

"No."

"What do you mean?" The harpy's wings fluttered again, this time with stronger intent. "You won't go see your wife?"

"Harriet stopped being my wife when she ran away. It was her choice to go. To leave me."

"This is the reason I'm single."

"What?"

"You. Her. Even knowing you remarried, she thinks you'll drop everything and run away with her. She thinks she believes in your love for her. But what she doesn't realize, or maybe what she doesn't want to admit, is that she is viewing you through the lens of the love she holds for her husband. And you were a stupid freeborn smitten by a cute and smart enslaved woman, and you gave yourself way too much credit."

"I'm not stu—"

"I don't need to know the details of your marriage to know whatever you envisioned life would be like married to a slave wasn't the reality. Harriet wouldn't have been able to live with you. Most anything she did, she would've had to get permission from her master. And her decisions without Minister Breembat's approval risked you and her. For Harriet, hell, for most slaves, getting one over on their master is an act of survival and resistance."

John did not require the harpy to explain married life to Harriet to him. He'd lived it, and while John loved Harriet, being married to her wasn't easy. Not only because she was enslaved, but Harriet always had one foot planted northward, her body primed to go places John did not wish to go.

"I've learned a lot helping runaways. I listen to what they say but also to the pain that's left unsaid. Harriet is waiting for you in my farmhouse. She's hopeful you'll choose her over Caroline, while you're still hurt and angry that she chose freedom over you. Irrational, the both of you, but that's where we are."

John wouldn't bother pretending he hadn't courted both of those emotions. He also wouldn't deny that part of Caroline's appeal was her freeborn status. Caroline lived with John when all Harriet could do was steal moments to be with him. The children from his union with Caroline would be free like their mother, which eased John's mind in a way it hadn't each time he thought Harriet might be with child. He wanted at least that tiny recognition of him as her husband, but the good Lord hadn't seen fit to answer that prayer either.

"I've moved on, and Harriet should too. I'm sorry, no good will come from seein' each other after all this time." John stepped backward again, done with the conversation. Before Caroline returned home, he needed time to sit with his thoughts and feelings.

The harpy grabbed something from the back of her wagon instead of leaving the way he hoped. She tossed it to him, and he caught it.

He frowned at a wrinkled pair of black dress pants and a matching jacket. "A suit?"

"Harriet saved for months to buy that for you. Instead of packing enough food and water to make the trip back here, she squeezed that stupid suit into her satchel. She showed it to me, assuming her thinking of you meant that you also thought of her. Harriet doesn't know I took it, but it proves she never abandoned you in her heart."

John never doubted Harriet's love, and it made him sick to his stomach to have hurt her. She wouldn't take the news of his refusal well, but Harriet harbored an unmatched resilience that made John an incompatible partner. He'd always felt that everyone except Harriet viewed them in that light.

I'm bein' a coward. She came all this way for me. But seein' me won't make my decision to stay hurt less. I'm with Caroline now, and I love her. A part of me still loves Harriet, too. She'll see that if I go. But I can't be with her anymore, not in Berzogtown or Pholgre. It's best we leave it where we did two years ago.

"Take it back. I don't want it."

"You certainly don't deserve her gift, that's for sure. But it was given with love, and she doesn't need a physical reminder of your rejection." The harpy, who hadn't bothered with a proper introduction, climbed into her wagon, and grabbed the reins with an expert hold. "Be a better husband to your second wife than you were to your first. Bravery comes at a cost, and

Harriet's been paying for it for two years. And now she'll pay even more. I hope to never see you again, John Cassin."

John stomped into his cabin and slammed the door. He could also see why the harpy was single. She didn't understand a thing about marriage. John slid down the door, the black suit clutched to his chest.

"I'm sorry, Harriet. God knows I am sorry. But you'll be better off without me keepin' you grounded when you were always meant to soar."

John Cassin never saw Harriet again, and although he never wore the suit, he also couldn't bring himself to throw it away. It was all he had left of an enslaved woman he loved but ultimately had to set free.

Chapter 29

Start Believin' in Myself

"I wish you hadn't given John that suit." Harriet contemplated taking her satchel but decided she could move quicker without it. Instead, she dropped it beside Norveis's back door.

"It made a perfect guilt gift." Norveis leaned a hip against her kitchen table, exuding a false calm.

"I could've used it as a disguise or gifted it to Moses or Kessiah's John. But since you all but sat on me when I would've gone to John's cabin, full of piss and vinegar, I guess a guilt gift will do."

"I'm proud of you. You made the right decision."

"No point allowin' my temper to make mischief." Although Harriet still wanted to confront John and see the woman he had chosen over her. "No good would come from feedin' my anger. I won't let a broken heart see me back in shackles. If John can do without me, then I can do without him." Much easier said than done, but Harriet had never been one to cry over spilled milk. In time, her feelings for John would fade, and she prayed she could drop him out of her heart as quickly as he had her out of his.

"Tomorrow is Christmas. It's a good day to flee. Smart choice. Slaves are off, and everybody is celebrating. Masters. Slave catchers. They would rather be drinking and caroling than paying attention to their slaves. If you're going to do it, now is the best time of year. That still only gives you tonight. Which plantation are you going to sneak onto?"

When Harriet had planned her return trip to Dralox County, it had been to spend Christmas with John. Instead, she'd spent the last three days plotting a bigger escape plan with Norveis. Harriet had no idea if she could convince anyone to take the risk of running away. But she'd come too far to leave Dralox County empty-handed. She might not have fulfilled her dream, but she hoped she could help others obtain theirs.

"I won't go to Dr. Tozor's plantation. But there are others close by. I have a friend from my silver mine days who lives on a plantation not too far from here. He has a wife and adult son."

Norveis nodded, but she also frowned and pushed from the table. "This is your first time being a conductor, Harriet. Don't fill your train car with too many passengers."

A conductor? Me? No. I returned here to fulfill my promise to John and myself. Families should be together. It ain't right that so many aren't. Nothin' about slavery is right. Since runnin' away, I've met many people who help slaves and who fight to end slavery in their own way. Maybe this is my contribution. If I can't bring John north, why not someone who wants to go?

It's too soon to try to free another member of my family. Minister Breembat is probably expectin' somethin'.

"I'll take whoever wants to come and figure out the rest on the way." Harriet snatched up her satchel, deciding to alter her plan. "I've been here more days than I should've. It's too risky comin' back here so soon. I'll head north after I've gathered Barbury and his family." Harriet hadn't told Norveis about Barbury. If all went well, the next time she saw the harpy, she'd have quite the story to share.

"In that case, I have a gift. Be right back." Norveis darted from the kitchen, and Harriet swore the harpy flew up and down the stairs because she didn't hear a single creak or thud. A minute later, Norveis returned with something wrapped in a hand towel. "Here. It'll keep you safe."

Harriet took the gift, surprised by the heavy weight. She flipped the towel to the side, revealing Norveis's present. Her mouth fell open.

"I was hoping your time in the north included how to use one of those. From the look of you, it hasn't. That there is a revolving-cylinder handgun. It's old, but it'll get the job done."

"I've never held a gun before." Harriet disliked needing a pistol, but if Majors had his way, she would be a sharpshooter. "Is this necessary?"

"If you will be taking on passengers now, it is. Understand this, Harriet, once you start out, you can't let your train run off the track. That must be the deal. They promise to stay until you reach the final stop, or you don't take them. Runaway slaves who are so afraid that they want to go back are dangerous. They can get everybody caught or killed. You can't let that happen. All runaways aren't built the same. It's up to you to determine which can make the trip and which are better left behind. You can't save them all, no matter how much you might want to try."

Harriet ran a finger over the gun's smooth, cool barrel. A well-placed bullet to the heart or head of a Dragonkin in human form could kill a dragon shifter. Luckily for Harriet, most Dragonkin preferred their human form. Still, even in that weaker state, they were strong and fast. If Harriet had any chance of successfully using the weapon against a Dragonkin or gryphon pattyroller, she would need to rely on stealth more than speed.

"A quick lesson, then you can be on your way."

Harriet would need more than a rushed tutorial to feel confident using the weapon. But Norveis's "Take a steadying breath, aim for the biggest part of the body, and pull the trigger" would have to suffice.

Harriet rewrapped the gun in the hand towel and secured the weapon in her satchel with a brief prayer that she would never have reason to point it at anyone, much less shoot a scared runaway or even a threatening pattyroller.

"Be safe, Harriet, and good luck."

Going on tiptoe, Harriet hugged Norveis. She couldn't afford a Christmas gift for the harpy. But she had left four of her feathers on the guest room bed. Supplying food and clothing for runaways was a costly undertaking. She hoped selling her feathers would offset some of Norveis's abolitionism bills. Harriet also trusted Norveis to choose an out-of-county buyer, minimizing the chance of someone recognizing Harriet's feathers from Mistress Essodel's hoard.

"Thank you." With her satchel across her shoulders and her destination clear, Harriet took off toward Mistress Shandoth's aviary. The Dragonkin wasn't nearly as old as Mistress Essodel or as solitary, but she was no less covetous of her hoard.

Harriet had never thought much about her memory. She'd neither credited herself with having great retention, no more than she lamented for having a subpar one. There were simply life events that she recalled with greater detail than others, and some she'd forgotten altogether. But when she had struck out for Dralox County and Norveis's farmhouse, the extent of Harriet's recollection made for a less stressful journey.

The same was true as she marched through the woods toward the Shandoth Plantation. This was her home, and she knew it well: the vile and vicious alongside the bountiful and beautiful.

She stopped. Listened.

No pattyrollers. Thank the Lord. Mistress Shandoth's place ain't much farther. Better leave this satchel here. My overcoat, too. I got to look the part.

Harriet walked a few more minutes, scanning each tree she passed, looking for... "There's one." Harriet knelt in front of a sixty-foot black cherry tree. She wouldn't have noticed the two-by-two hole in the tree's base if she hadn't spotted a red ribbon tied around one of the tree's thick branches. She cleared away fallen leaves and stuck her hand inside the hole, pleased when she felt supplies she could later use but also room to conceal her satchel and overcoat.

Removing both, she folded them as small as possible and then shoved them into the hole. Harriet gathered fallen branches and leaves and placed them in front of the cavity. She didn't conceal the space completely, though. Her memory was good, but it wasn't perfect, so she might need assistance finding the tree again.

Satisfied with that part of her plan, Harriet was also pleased to confirm what she'd learned from abolitionist friends about secret strategies they used to help runaways along their journey, such as using trees to hide maps, shoes, and clothing. Food would've been great but impractical, so Harriet didn't expect to find that level of support. But it was a rare Birdfolk slave who didn't know how to hunt, so she and her passengers wouldn't starve.

Harriet continued on her way, undoing her braids with each step she took. Since going north, Harriet had taken more care with her hair, no longer able to rely on Rit to do it for her. But most enslaved women rarely had time to indulge in the same beauty rituals as free women, so Harriet used her fingers to pull her hair this way and that until it looked as if she'd spent a long, hard day laboring in the field or on the docks.

The subtle transformation from the lifestyle she'd led of a free woman in Pholgre for two years to the twenty-seven years of enslaved living in Berzogtown unsettled her spirit but fortified her determination.

Slowing her gait to that of an exhausted, overworked enslaved woman, Harriet strolled onto Mistress Shandoth's property as if she belonged. Because she entered from the north instead of the south, she avoided the tobacco fields and placed herself directly inside the aviary. The saying, "If you've seen one slave aviary, you've seen them all," sadly applied.

But Harriet had heard of a 30,000-acre plantation in Domusku, North Cevno, a southern slave state not far from Miadar. The Dragonkin master owned nine hundred slaves who were forced to build their aviary, each home designed with four rooms. Harriet couldn't imagine living in a cabin with so much space, much less slaving on a 30,000-acre plantation with two states between lifetime enslavement and a stolen life of freedom.

Dark bodies dragged themselves from the fields. Some chatter drifted on the cold night air, but no laughter warmed the space between involuntary servitude and the Christmas season that would grant them a small respite.

Hands in her dress pockets and head lowered, Harriet shuffled along from one cabin to the next until she spotted a familiar face. At twenty-two, Jack was half his father's age, but he walked with the same unbroken determination as the Barbury she remembered meeting in the mining town.

Harriet increased her speed, wanting to catch up to Jack but without drawing attention to herself. She might have known some of the slaves on this plantation, but most were strangers. Until proven otherwise, Harriet wouldn't trust any of them.

"Jack," she called in a voice barely above a whisper. "Jack."

Foot inches away from the cabin porch he was headed to, Jack paused and turned in Harriet's direction. The sun may have set, and the man might not have been in his avian form, but Jack's human vision was as keen as any Birdfolk shifter. "Harriet, is that you?" He glanced around, as aware as she was that she shouldn't have been there and, being out in the open, could see them both punished. "Get in, quick."

Jack proceeded up the steps to his cabin and entered as she imagined he did every evening. However, instead of closing the door after himself, he left it open.

Harriet quickly joined Jack inside the cabin, closing the door from prying eyes and ears.

She turned, only to be engulfed in a tight hug. "You come to set us free?"

Harriet had no idea how Jack could've reached that conclusion, even if it were true.

"I can't think of any other reason you'd be here." Jack stepped back, and his youthful, trusting grin reminded Harriet so much of how Moses had looked at her when she'd met him at the Bodan dock. "I heard about Kessiah and Moses. Our parents are still friends. Oh." Jack stepped aside, and Harriet realized they weren't alone in the cabin.

The sight reminded her too much of home and the fragility of slave families.

"You remember my wife, Eliza, from our weddin'."

Harriet did, although she did not know the woman well. She plastered on a large grin because, despite Jack's enthusiastic hug, Harriet had blown into their home like the wind battering against their windows.

Jack had moved to stand beside his family. "This is my son, Will. He's four. And this is Fanny. She's two. This is Harriet. She's gonna set us free."

Only Jack had smiled at his bold declaration. Eliza's pinched brow was her only response, and the children, who stared between Jack and Harriet, appeared more confused than excited.

She didn't blame them.

"I, ah, I was hopin' to talk with Barbury and Priscilla first. But I don't believe in breakin' up families."

Jack is willin' to place the safety of his family in my hands. I'd forgotten the couple had children. Young ones, too. It's cold out and dangerous. Kessiah and her children had a shorter distance to flee. But they made it.

"Harriet," Eliza said, hands fisted at her sides and voice a soft quaver, "did you really help Kessiah and her children escape the auction block in Cosaru?"

"It wasn't just me, but I did."

"And they safe in the North?"

"By the grace of God, they are."

On her way to the Shandoth Plantation, Harriet decided it wasn't her role to convince slaves to run away but to guide those to safety who chose to go with her. If Eliza agreed to stay, regardless of her reason, Harriet would bid the younger woman farewell and be on her way.

She wanted to give the couple privacy to discuss the most significant decision of their lives. But Harriet would rather not be seen outside their cabin again until it was time to leave.

Luckily, her response must've been enough for Eliza because the woman blessed Harriet with the same bruising hug as Jack.

"Don't go anywhere. I'll be right back."

"You've done it now, Harriet. My Eliza is on a mission." Jack lifted his two-year-old daughter in his arms, kissed her nose, and then handed the child to her. "This is Aunt Harriet."

The girl stared at her with bewilderment befitting the situation, and Harriet passed on that look to Jack.

"Savin' a child makes you family. That's how it works. Come here, Will."

Harriet watched as Jack lifted his son and handed the four-year-old to Harriet, too.

"Suits you. You're a natural."

Harriet was tired of men projecting a motherly sensibility onto her when all she'd been able to do was care for other women's children. Yet, she couldn't deny the sense of rightness that washed over her when she held a Birdfolk child, even if that child wasn't hers.

She placed Fanny and Will on their feet, unnerved by how much they reminded her of the children she and John would never have and the unexpected dissolution of her marriage.

"I'm sorry. I wasn't thinkin'."

Harriet was unsure if Jack's apology stemmed from him belatedly recalling Harriet's difficulty getting with child in the five years she and John were married or if he knew John had taken another wife during her absence. Either way, Jack's insensitivity had been unintentional, but the impact was still keenly felt.

Harriet waved off Jack's apology, unwilling to be waylaid by thoughts of John and their failed marriage. "Gather what your family needs but keep it light. And bring whatever will keep the children quiet when we need them to be."

"Right. Tomorrow is Christmas. I couldn't have given my family a better gift."

Jack had spoken more to himself than to Harriet, but she understood the feeling. Being there had solidified within her the importance of freeing those who she could, even if they were not her blood family.

The cabin door behind her opened, letting in the cold. A breeze blew through Harriet's dress, chilling her bones and reminding her she had an overcoat waiting for her just beyond the Shandoth Plantation.

Harriet turned, coming face-to-face with a man she considered an older brother. If she couldn't free Robert on this trip, Barbury's freedom would be nearly as sweet.

The forty-four-year-old opened his arms and, like a child seeking comfort after a nightmare, Harriet filled them. If she sobbed once or twice, no one would've blamed her.

Barbury's wife, Priscilla, rubbed circles on Harriet's back and kissed her temple. "Moses delivered his people from slavery. Masters don't want us to know that biblical story. But we pass it on durin' our secret church meetins. We know about the prophet and what he did for his people." Priscilla's hand stilled on Harriet's back. "You came for us. Thank you. Tell us what we need to do."

Not for the first time that night, Harriet felt humbled but also overwhelmed by the weight of responsibility. This was her first true rescue mission. From Dralox County, Miadar, to Pholgre City, Pyzai, Barbury's family's safety and freedom were her responsibility.

Harriet hugged Barbury tighter but forced herself to release him. He was a little older than the last time she'd seen him. There were a few more gray hairs in his beard and along his hairline, but nothing to take away from the resilience that all but glowed through his dark brown eyes.

Three more people appeared before Harriet, bringing the count to nine. Norveis had advised Harriet to keep her train car small since this was her first escape mission. Nine people, two of whom were young children, didn't qualify as a small party of runaways. But they'd come voluntarily, and Harriet wouldn't deny them.

Barbury touched the shoulders of the three other people Eliza had brought with her, and Priscilla introduced them for her mute husband.

"This is my sister, Amanda, her husband, Caesar, and their thirteen-year-old son, Nathan."

Harriet didn't know the three, but she trusted Barbury's judgment, so she smiled and prayed she wouldn't run her train off the track.

Amanda bobbed a curtsy as if Harriet was Dragonkin. "Thank you. We appreciate what you doin' for us."

Harriet was about to say it was nothing but closed her mouth before she voiced something so foolish. Running away wasn't nothing. It was everything; she wouldn't minimize the high stakes or sell herself short.

I gotta start believin' in myself as much as these people do. I ain't no Moses, but that doesn't mean I can't see these people to Pholgre and then on to Cothru. With the Fugitive Slave Act in effect, the North ain't safe for runaways anymore. So, we got to go even farther north to the country of Cothru. No need worryin' them about nothin' they can't control. First I must get them far away from the Shandoth Plantation and Dralox County. I didn't bargain on nine people, but I can still make it work.

"Pack what you need but keep it light. We'll set out before midnight. Until then, rest because you'll need every bit of your energy for the journey."

Chapter 30

I Ain't Got You to the Promised Land Yet

Dralox County

Barbury was every bit the loving, protective male as he had been to Harriet when he'd taken it upon himself to walk her to and from Master Gyzad's home whenever he suspected Mudspike was out and up to mischief.

At twenty-two, Jack could've easily carried his son, Will, on his back, but the moment they'd entered the woods, Barbury had bent to a knee in front of his grandson and tapped his back.

The four-year-old hadn't wasted any time taking advantage of the offer, and all Harriet could do was smile and nod. Will was as brave as Kessiah's son James had been. But children their age shouldn't have to muster such courage.

Little Fanny had started in her mother's arms before Eliza had passed the sleeping child to the forty-year-old Amanda, who settled Fanny's head against her shoulder and hummed softly. Her rhythmic humming seemed to relax more than the tired two-year-old.

Amanda's husband, Caesar, walked in front of Harriet. He was a large man, nearly six feet tall and weighing over two hundred pounds. Harriet had no idea how he'd managed it, but he'd shaved every strand of human hair from between his feathers, leaving him bald in spots.

He doesn't know the way, but that's not why he has taken the lead. With Jack placin' himself in the rear, he and Caesar must've decided this before we left the cabin. Women and children in the middle and the strongest in the front and the back. I ain't never been one to stand between a man and his protective pride, and I won't begin today.

Two hours turned into four and then into six. No one talked, and Amanda's humming had given way to heavy breathing an hour earlier.

Harriet tapped Caesar on the shoulder to get his attention, then raised her fist so the others would know to stop. "The sun will rise in an hour. We've made good time. But everybody's tired and hungry." Harriet pointed northwest. "That route leads to Citirzo Creek."

Nathan, who'd kept lockstep with Harriet, a silent companion who'd eyed her when he thought she wasn't looking, gathered Barbury's and Jack's canteens. "Ms. Harriet, I can get water for you, too." Like her younger brothers, Nathan was eager to prove himself a man capable of being relied on. He held out his hand expectantly.

In almost any other situation, Harriet would have permitted the young man to have the growth opportunity. But danger lurked, whether they could see it or not, and Harriet wouldn't let any of them out of her sight if she could help it.

"You can fill my canteen when we get to the creek. But we go everywhere together. It's safer that way."

"Yes, ma'am."

Harriet met Barbury's gaze, and he nodded. No power plays existed between her and the men. They'd agreed to the escape plan, and she promised to take them north.

No turning back.

No arguing over when to rest, eat, or walk.

No questioning Harriet's decisions.

Harriet stepped around Caesar to lead the group down to the creek. "Let's fill these canteens, then find a safe place to rest during the day."

The trees were bare in winter, which wasn't ideal for hiding. But winter also brought shorter days and longer nights, which made this time of year perfect for running away.

Harriet stopped at the clearing and raised her fist again. The group behind her heeded her directive and halted.

I don't like comin' to waterin' holes because everybody uses them. Animals and people need to drink, but seekin' out a place to fill my canteen leaves me vulnerable. Creeks and lakes are also good places for pattyrollers or slave catchers to sit on, waitin' for a thirsty runaway to stumble into their trap. But I don't see anybody. If the bare trees can't hide us, they won't hide them either.

Harriet said a quick prayer and motioned with her hand for her passengers to follow. She maneuvered around fifty-foot trees, down a hill, and toward the creek. The water sparkled with a cool cleanness that reminded Harriet how deeply she'd suppressed thoughts of her dry mouth and cracked lips.

Despite the chill of winter, green grass grew along the creek's bank, making for a refreshing sight.

"I'll keep watch." She handed Nathan her canteen, and the teen took off toward the creek.

The others followed. Shoes were removed, and feet were placed in the chilly water. Faces and hands were washed, and a chorus of "Ah, feels good" coursed through the early morning air.

Priscilla appeared beside Harriet. Her face glistened, and her eyes sparkled with a rejuvenation that came from immersing her face in a cold creek while on a family journey toward freedom. "Me and Barbury grew up on Mistress Shandoth's plantation. My momma and his were friends. Mine died givin' birth to a brother. The old midwife couldn't save him either."

For as many babies enslaved women successfully birthed, some babies did not survive. Older women helped the younger ones during childbirth. Their knowledge was old wisdom passed down from when their ancestors were in Sika. But the passage of time and the corruption of their culture were unforgiving. So much had been lost. Still, Birdfolk midwives helped to deliver healthy babies under the worst conditions every day, with most mothers and newborns surviving the ordeal.

But not all.

Harriet scanned the opposite side of the creek, searching for suspicious sights or sounds. Fortunately, she saw and heard none.

Priscilla pointed to Barbury, who stood several feet away from the creek. His shoulders were slumped, his hands were in his pockets, and he appeared strangely tense for what should've been a moment of relaxation.

"His mother killed herself."

Harriet shifted to her right to better see Priscilla. Considering the nasty scar that ran the length of Barbury's throat, Harriet had a good idea of how his mother had inflicted the self-harm.

"Afterward, Mistress Shandoth started hirin' Barbury out. But he ran away. Without his momma, he had nothin' other than anger that she'd freed herself but left him to fend for himself. I was too young to know how I could help him back then. But we all tried our best. It wasn't enough, though. After months of bein' away, workin' in a silver mine in Pelduth Neck, he returned with the same scar on his neck as his momma. Despite all that, he survived. Pieces of him, anyway."

Birdfolk were not as durable as other races, but they were a sturdy stock of people. So, for Barbury's mother to have died, she must've cut deeply or done it in a place where she wouldn't be found until it was too late.

Harriet closed her eyes, realizing where Barbury's mother had likely gone to commit suicide. A creek would've made a blissful last sight for the enslaved Birdfolk woman. The location of her death would've also almost ensured that her son would not have been the person to find her body.

Priscilla blew out a wobbly breath. "It's a brutal, sad escape to freedom."

Brutal, yes. Sad, certainly. But also more than that.

Harriet's eyes slid open, and she focused them on Barbury again. The man hadn't moved from his spot. Whatever swirl of emotions coursed through him, none were powerful enough to discourage the protective Barbury from following his family to the creek. He also hadn't inflicted the level of damage to himself that his mother had. For Harriet, that distinction wasn't coincidental but evidence of the heartbreaking degrees of slave resistance.

"It ain't my story to know." However, Mudspike had spoken of being the one to capture the sixteen-year-old Barbury enough times at Master Gyzad's mining camp for Harriet to know that part of Barbury's story. "Why tell me?"

"You as blunt as your momma."

Harriet had never minded being compared to Rit, so she didn't take offense, not that she'd interpreted Priscilla's statement as more than a friendly observation.

"Me and Barbury have our own way of communicatin'. He wants you to know so you'll understand why we are all here with you. Death ain't no way to get freedom. But, sometimes, it seems like the only way out. It must be an awful thing to want to die more than you want to live."

"Maybe that ain't the way it is for those who kill themselves. I think it ain't about wantin' to die but the bone-deep misery of not bein' able to live peacefully. Safely. Of dreamin' and prayin' for a better life but wakin' up to the same ole pain. Livin' is hard, that's for sure. But I think choosin' to die might be harder."

"You got an old soul, Harriet. Just know that what you doin' for us means everything to me and Barbury. We thank you."

"I ain't got you to the promised land yet. Don't thank me too soon."

Priscilla's soft chuckle drew Barbury's attention, but he only looked from his wife to Harriet, then back to the creek. If anyone was out there, Harriet trusted Barbury would spot them.

"An old soul but still young and unsure. We're in this together, Harriet. I thought you should know what you doin' means to us. The sun is about to rise; you want to show us where we sleepin'?"

Harriet couldn't have chosen better passengers for her first mission. Priscilla reminded her of an older sister. With how close they all were, Barbury's family could've been Harriet's.

I'd gladly risk my freedom for theirs, but I won't let this train run off the track. God is with me, and God is always good.

Harriet whistled, getting everyone's attention. She led them across the creek to the opposite side of the bank where she located a cluster of trees that would serve her purpose well. "If we set up camp between these trees, we'll see anybody who approaches. We'll sleep on the ground instead of in a bare tree that would more likely reveal our hiding spot than shield us from unwanted eyes."

Without having to direct them, Barbury, Jack, and Caesar secured the children and women between them. They also knew to position themselves in opposite directions.

Harriet dropped her satchel at the base of a tree she'd claimed because it faced the side of the creek they'd just come from. If Mistress Shandoth had discovered Barbury's family missing sooner than Harriet anticipated, her overseer would likely track them to the creek.

Nathan appeared above her; her canteen strap was fisted in his hand. "Here, Ms. Harriet."

"Thank you."

The thirteen-year-old stared down at her like a puppy wanting a treat. But granting Nathan a tasty snack would've been easier than giving him what Harriet assumed he wanted from her.

"I can take the first watch with you."

"It ain't your responsibility but thank you."

"I know, but I can still help."

Harriet considered reminding Nathan that he could help his father during his watch. But she recalled how he'd stolen glances and kept lockstep with her. It wasn't a young man's infatuation with an older woman, but respect for Harriet being an up close and personal reminder that Nathan could be more than Mistress Shandoth's field hand.

"Go get permission from your parents first."

Nathan rushed off, and Harriet prepared herself to spend one-on-one time with an impressionable teen. The thought wasn't unpleasant, but it did add additional weight to a body in need of a long rest.

The boy returned with the speed and endurance God granted to youth. "They said it's fin—"

Harriet yanked Nathan to the ground and covered his mouth with her hand the moment he was beside her. "Be quiet, but look there," she whispered. Harriet pointed to the two who plodded down the hill and toward the creek.

They wore hats pulled low, overcoats meant for cold Eastern Shore winters, and heavy boots that crunched and squished every branch and leaf they encountered. It wasn't the two Birdfolk males who had Harriet crawling backward with Nathan, but the creature that stalked them.

She smelled him seconds before she spotted the two men. Harriet hadn't seen him in years but hadn't forgotten his foul odor or nasty attitude.

Harriet glanced over her shoulder. Seven sets of dark eyes met hers. Never more thankful for a calm toddler and a proactive mother, Harriet acknowledged the hand Eliza had placed over little Fanny's mouth.

She had two options, neither of which sat well with her. One was to escape farther into the woods and leave the two Birdfolk to their undeserved fate. Two was to help the men and risk losing her passengers.

I ain't made a promise to those men. Fool on them for not knowin' they bein' hunted. Shame on me for considerin' slinkin' away and doin' nothin' to help. But nine people are relyin' on me to see them north.

In her haste, Harriet had left her satchel by the tree. She swore under her breath because the second she decided to return for her bag and the pistol inside was the exact moment she knew no part of her could abide not offering the men aid.

Harriet didn't relish the confrontation to come. But she figured it was better done on her own terms than on his.

Using hand signals, Harriet relayed her message. All but Barbury quietly gathered their belongings and crept in the direction she'd pointed. She decided it would be futile to waste time and energy on the overprotective Barbury, especially since he likely detected the stench, too. Like her, he would know the source.

She crawled on her belly to the tree where she'd left her satchel, with Barbury behind her. The pistol was still wrapped in Norveis's hand towel, and Harriet withdrew it from her bag. For some reason, the gun felt heavier now that she held it with intent.

Barbury's arched eyebrows delivered his thoughts about the turn their escape had taken with the introduction of a lethal weapon. Then he shrugged, silent support for Harriet to protect them all by any means necessary.

"It's been mildly entertaining following you two idiots, but I'm hungry, it's Christmas, and you aren't nearly as fun as I thought you'd be."

If Harriet needed confirmation that she knew to whom the stench belonged, the arrogant, gravelly voice would've solidified her conclusion.

The men at the creek's edge halted, wet hands to their faces and them on their knees beside the water.

Harriet still couldn't see the owner of the voice and smell, but he'd given away his location. She shifted her gaze to the hill above the creek, not to the sky, although he'd likely tracked the men that way before landing.

Beside her, Barbury stripped. Priscilla hadn't shared with Harriet the slave catcher's name who'd captured the young runaway Barbury. She doubted the older woman knew. Certainly, Barbury couldn't have told her. According to the older mine workers Harriet had met during her time in Pelduth Neck, the young Barbury had worked at the mining camp years before it was purchased by Master Gyzad. Along with most of the freeborn workers and slave hires, Master Gyzad had also kept on the gryphon slave catchers.

With how quickly Barbury shifted from man to bird, Barbury hadn't forgotten who had returned him to Mistress Shandoth with his throat sliced open. Harriet's temporary master hadn't treated her head injury after her run-in with the gryphon any better than Barbury's had.

The sun crested the hill, and with it the gryphon she'd hoped never to see again.

With a fully transformed Barbury beside her and a warm gun in her cold hand, Harriet stood. She'd told Norveis she would have a story to share about her first trip as a conductor the next time they saw each other. Harriet assumed most of her tale would involve blistered feet from too many miles walked, motion sickness from riding a crowded train, maybe even a story about a clever disguise she piecemealed together or an official she bribed with one of her precious feathers.

The death of a wretched gryphon wasn't the kind of story she wanted to relay, much less a situation she wanted to find herself in. But there Harriet stood, resigned to what was to come.

The two men pushed to their feet and turned to face their pursuer.

Three steps brought the gryphon into full view. Eight feet and five hundred pounds of muscle; Harriet wouldn't deny the sight of the eagle face and wings with the body, tail, and back legs of a lion sent her heart pounding like a drum. But his taloned front legs reminded Harriet that Birdfolk were mightier in their avian form.

"You want to fight him, don't you?" she whispered to Barbury.

The six-foot, two-hundred-fifty-pound Sankofa bird stepped in front of Harriet, answering her question.

Harriet's right hand clutched the pistol's handle, and she placed her left hand on Barbury's back. His greenish-blue feathers weren't so different from most of the Birdfolk males in Dralox County. They were beautiful but too common to be, by Dragonkin standards, special and, therefore, worthy of a high sale price. So, Mistress Shandoth had used Barbury for field and mine work, as Mistress Essodel had with the men in Harriet's family.

"W-where you come from?"

"Stupid runaway. Just because you can't fly doesn't mean you shouldn't look up. But you ground-scrapers always look forward and back."

The man who'd spoken stepped backward and into the creek. The other runaway followed, and Harriet wondered if they planned on making the gryphon chase them in earnest. In human form, they couldn't outrun him, and by the time they shifted, he'd be on them like a snake on a field mouse.

But Harriet and Barbury could give them time to escape the gryphon.

Harriet patted his feathered back again. "Let's go teach Mudspike a lesson." Concealing the gun in her overcoat pocket, Harriet walked behind Barbury and toward the creek.

"Where do you think you're going, ground-scrapers?"

"We ain't goin' back." The taller of the two men continued his retreat, and his voice niggled at a memory because it sounded as familiar as Mudspike's odor. "Slaves in Miadar are supposed to be set free at fifty. We fifty-eight and ain't been let go."

But Mistress Essodel thought rules that weren't of her making did not apply to her. Slaves were born and lived their entire lives on the Essodel Plantation, dying without knowing a single day of freedom. If not for Ben being owned by Master Gyzad, Harriet's father would've likely suffered the same fate as many who had come before him.

I recognize the man's voice now.

Nothing about her trip south had gone according to plan. But if she had doubts that God worked in mysterious ways, her faith would've been reinforced when the two men turned, revealing their faces to Harriet while making a mad dash to her side of the creek.

Even in human form, the men were fast. But more than the blood of an enslaved Sankofa bird shifter female flowed in their veins.

They darted up the hill and straight toward Harriet. The shorter, stockier of the two glanced at her, eyes widened with recognition. Golden-brown eyes that matched the Dragonkin who'd raped his mother, Efron ran past Harriet before skidding to a halt. Efron's twin, Abbott, did the same, slamming into his brother's back.

On any other day, Harriet would've found the action comical. But Mudspike had pounded after the brothers, forgoing his biggest advantage.

Flight.

"Harriet, I—"

"No questions, Efron. Run." She didn't wait to see if they followed her order because Barbury had taken off when Mudspike had.

Bird and gryphon slammed into each other. Beaks snapped, and feathers whipped.

"What in the hell are you doing here, Barbury? It doesn't matter because I get to finally kill you." Mudspike struck Barbury's side with his tail like a master's punishing lash.

Barbury took the assault in the same way many slaves did the sting of the whip, with unflinching resolve. But more than that, with unrestrained counterattacks. Greenish-blue wings and beaks were in constant, attacking motion. Stabbing and hitting with a force Harriet had never known Birdfolk were capable of.

But the two bodies were so entwined in their death battle that Harriet was too afraid to use the gun. With it being her first time, she was just as likely to hit Barbury as she would Mudspike.

"I'm going to kill you."

Deciding to enter the fray any way she could, even if that meant wading into the water to get closer to Mudspike, Harriet breathed deeply and then surged forward. But two feathered bodies darted past her. Not greenish blue but a pale blue inherited from their ice dragon father.

Minister Breembat.

Efron and Abbott jumped into the water, their wings extended as if capable of flight. Soundlessly, they landed on opposite sides of Mudspike.

The gryphon's robust lion's body was riddled with bloody holes from Barbury's mighty beak. Birdfolk's beaks and talons might not be so strong as to cut through a Dragonkin's tough scales, but they were powerful enough to mine without metal tools. So, a gryphon's fleshy body would be no match for a Birdfolk no longer afraid of the repercussions that normally came with physical resistance to enslavement.

The twins attacked with a viciousness that matched Barbury's.

Harriet returned the pistol to her overcoat pocket, no longer needing it. She watched the three Birdfolk rip the gryphon to shreds, turning the shallow creek crimson. She didn't enjoy the sight, no more than she relished the sound of Mudspike's pained screeches or even the disturbing silence that followed.

Bloody taloned feet exited the contaminated creek. Bits and pieces of Mudspike hung from the men's blood-covered beaks. They had ruined the tranquil landscape, but one dead gryphon had proven the cost for others' freedom.

"We can't leave him there," Harriet told the men. Not only because Mudspike's dead body would bring unwanted law enforcement to the area, but Harriet also wanted to avoid tainting the creek any more than necessary.

Then, three naked males were before her, two grinning at her as if she were a long-lost relative. In a way, Harriet supposed she was.

Still as lean and lanky as she remembered, Harriet did not complain when first Abbott hugged her, and then his fraternal twin, Efron, did. Growing up in Mistress Essodel's aviary, the brothers had been like uncles to her. Their mother, Aveline, died in 1849, having never known a day of freedom.

Harriet didn't know why the brothers had waited two years after their mother's death to run away since it was assumed the only reason they hadn't tried before was because they didn't want to abandon the ailing Aveline.

Abbott twirled her the way he had when she was a girl learning to dance. "You a sight for sore eyes, Minty."

"She sure is." Efron tapped the top of her head. "Was that a pistol I saw you holdin' earlier?"

Harriet swatted Efron's big hand away from her head. "Clean up the mess. We need to get goin' and pray no one heard the fuss you all made."

Barbury lifted his hand to his mouth, making an eating motion, then pointed to Mudspike.

Harriet walked away, recognizing the sense in Barbury's plan while also disgusted she would feast on fire-cooked gryphon meat and like it. Hunting their next meal would no longer be necessary, and her passenger count had increased to eleven.

Chapter 31

It Ain't Fair

1854

Essodel Plantation

Robert's head pounded in time with his heart, an excruciating *thump, thump, thump.*

What am I gonna do? This ain't what we planned. I can't leave her like this. Not right now. But I'll still need to go. Harriet has come all this way.

Robert turned at the sound of his wife's groans. Mary's back was against a wall with the rest of her on the pallet where they'd conceived their three children. Sweat beaded her forehead, neck, and chest. Bare feet flat on the pallet and knees bent, Mary gritted her teeth when another contraction hit.

He'd seen his wife give birth to three-year-old John and one-year-old Moses, but the sight of Mary in childbirth hadn't gotten easier. His baby would be born on Christmas Eve, which, to some Birdfolk, was a blessing. What Robert felt, watching the midwife, Peg, help Mary bring his third child into the world, could not be defined as the kind of blessing he'd prayed for.

Robert held his sons' tiny hands and moved them out of Peg and Mary's way. The boys' gazes were fixated on their mother, as was Robert's. But his mind wandered.

Me and my brothers tried runnin' away. We thought since Harriet did it, we could too. Three times. Three failures. Dragonkin and their slave catchers are more suspicious of us now. Slaves been fleein'. Some get caught, like me, Ben Jr., and Henry. But others get away. Make it north. Even so, slippin' out of Dralox County ain't easy. I ain't proud of failin' my younger brothers or leavin' my Mary and children behind. But Minister Breembat ain't left me with no good options. If I don't flee tonight, I'm gonna be sold come Monday mornin'. One night is all the time I got left. Either way, my life with my family is over.

"Robert," Peg called to him over her shoulder.

At sixty, the older woman should've been freed years ago, but Mistress Essodel and, by extension, Minister Breembat treated the manumission law as they did common decency—optional unless it benefitted them. No Miadar political or law enforcement official would dare challenge Mistress Essodel, so her slaves labored until she deemed them no longer worth the financial upkeep. Unfortunately, with Peg being a skilled midwife, Mistress Essodel had little incentive to free the woman.

"Leave the children there and come here."

Robert rushed to Mary's side and immediately fell to his knees beside her. "What do you need me to do?"

"Hold her hand and talk to her."

Providing physical and emotional support for Mary was a small ask, especially considering what Robert had planned. He grasped the hand closest to him and held it through each of the following contractions.

"You are doin' good, sweetheart."

"I-it hurts."

"I know. I know." Robert pulled an old handkerchief from his pants pocket and wiped away Mary's sweat with a hand that trembled from the gnawing guilt raging in his stomach. "When it gets really bad, look at our boys and know you can do anything. They are here, healthy and happy. You did that."

Tears flowed from Mary, more happy than painful, he hoped. But when she smiled at him, her eyes twinkled with a love he'd earned and a trust he would betray.

Robert's guilt intensified blood-churning cramps that could've rivaled Mary's contractions. Despite the possibility of missing Harriet and being sold away from Mary, Robert took comfort in being there for his wife. If Mary hadn't gone into labor early, Robert would not have been there to greet his daughter.

The newest member of the Wren family had good, strong lungs if her ear-piercing shrieks could be trusted.

Robert escorted the midwife to her cabin, where her husband and family waited. Once he fled, leaving Mary and the kids alone, he prayed Peg would make a special effort to watch over them. Robert couldn't make that request of her, no more than he could of any member of Mary's family without endangering Harriet's plan and risking his in-laws' safety. Instead, he hugged the older woman and offered his heartfelt gratitude. "Thank you, Peg. You've been a blessin' to my family."

Peg patted his cheek as he'd seen her do to her grown children. "Congratulations on the birth of your daughter. She as pretty as her momma. Now, get before Mary starts worryin'."

Never one to disobey a Birdfolk elder, Robert rushed back to his cabin. The sun had set during Mary's labor, and it had been hours since then. Robert entered his cabin.

I'm late meetin' Harriet and the others. Her message was clear. Be on time. Are they waitin' for me? What if they get caught because of me?

Robert scooped up first John and then little Moses from where they slept beside Mary and placed them on the pallet they shared on the opposite side of the room. He watched his sons sleep for long minutes, reassured by their chests' steady rise and fall but already missing them.

"What's gotten into you?"

"Nothin'." Robert pulled his gaze away from his sons and settled them on a wife whose brown eyes drooped with earned fatigue. "You should rest." Unable to help himself, Robert spooned his wife and marveled at how greedily his daughter fed from her mother. "What are we gonna name her?"

Robert hadn't thought much about girls' names because they had two boys. But there were ones he favored over others. He was partial to the name Mary but thought his wife might want to name their daughter after her sister Susan.

Robert kissed Mary's lips when she craned her head back to look at him.

"What about Harriet? Ritty for short."

The guilt that hadn't left him ratcheted up that much more because while he understood Mary meant to name their child after his mother, the

Harriet who came to mind was the sister who'd risked her freedom to help her brothers obtain theirs.

He kissed her again. "Momma will love it. Thank you."

"Now that our baby has a name, tell me what's wrong."

"I was thinkin' about hirin' myself out tonight and tomorrow. There's good money to be made on Christmas because nobody wants to work."

No one had ever accused Mary of being an unintelligent woman, so when she arched an eyebrow and glowered at him, all but calling Robert a liar, he retreated from the deception.

He sat up, despising the decision he'd been forced to make. "I know you don't believe Minister Breembat plans on sellin' me and my brothers, but he is. Harriet sent me a message. She ain't been here but a day, and she's already seen an ad about a public auction come tomorrow." Robert needlessly pointed to himself. "Me, Ben Jr., and Henry."

Robert helped Mary to a seated position so she could burp little Ritty. His daughter was as pretty as Peg had said. Silky pink feathers mixed with curly dark brown hair. He'd only seen pink that bright on Harriet. Once Mistress Essodel got a look at his baby girl, bringing his family north would be more difficult. But those were worries for another day.

"Harriet is here?"

Mary had been one of the last people to speak with Harriet before she'd fled the Tozor Plantation. Robert hadn't yet gotten around to proposing, but after seeing John all but crumble after Harriet ran away, waiting to marry the woman he loved seemed like a waste of precious time.

There he was, though, five short years later and in the same unimaginable predicament Harriet had found herself. He understood her painful choice better than he would have liked. However, unlike John, Mary wasn't physically able to flee with him. Neither when she'd been pregnant nor soon after giving birth.

I'm out of time. She might hate me for leavin'. I can't blame her if she does. But if I'm sold, there ain't nothin' I can do for Mary and our children. If I'm free, I can build a new home for us and help Harriet bring her north once Ritty is old enough to make the trip. Mary can hate me all she wants then, but she'll be free.

"I got news she arrived earlier today." Robert gently touched one of Ritty's baby-soft feathers, cautious not to wake her as she slept in her mother's arms. He situated the blanket that had pooled Mary's waist until it covered the baby from feet to shoulders and most of Mary's bare chest. "I don't know how it all works, but Harriet knows a lot of people. There's a free Birdfolk farmer she knows from Pelduth Neck. Jacob, I think. He can read and write. They exchange coded letters."

"You arranged everything through that freeborn man?"

"Yes."

"And you were gonna leave without tellin' me?"

Robert's decision to protect Mary sounded cowardly when said in her hurt voice. But her safety from Minister Breembat's wrath hinged on her ignorance. The same was true for Rit and Ben. There was little Robert could do to protect his wife except to keep her in the dark about his plans.

I guess I am a coward because facin' the wife I must leave is as hard as I feared. It's a brutal pain that claws my heart. How can I enjoy my free life knowin' my family are still slaves? I can't think like that. Harriet will know what to do. She'll find a way to free Mary and our children.

"Today is Christmas Eve, Robert. Our child was born the day before Christmas. She won't know you. John and Moses won't remember you." Mary closed her eyes, and a broken sob followed. "It ain't fair. I hate it. I hate you."

Robert accepted the hurtful lie because a child's birth should herald a day of joy, not the heartache of forced separation.

"Just go."

Despite initially planning to slip away without saying a proper goodbye, Robert wouldn't permit Mary's anger and pain to shove him out the cabin door without Robert setting a few things straight.

He first kissed the top of his daughter's head. She didn't stir, so he slipped a finger under the covers to caress her chubby arms and marvel at the feel of her tiny fingers and toes. "I love you, my sweet girl. Know your poppa loves you very much."

"Robert, please don't g—"

He kissed his wife, silencing her with the feel of his lips against hers. Robert wasn't a romantic. He didn't know the first thing about romance. But he did know that he loved this woman with every bone in his body, every feather on his head, and every tear he would shed when he left her.

No, Robert Wren wasn't romantic, but he tried his damnedest to pour all his love for his wife into what would become their final kiss. "I love you, Mary. Harriet will help me bring you all north. I promise."

Mary didn't respond, and Robert was grateful for that because leaving his family was more painful than any whipping he'd received.

Like Ritty, John and Moses slept through Robert's teary goodbye. He soothed himself with the promise that they would reunite soon. By slow degrees, his sister was rebuilding her Wren family in the North. Surely, she would do her best to save Robert's family, too.

Robert left his cabin with a final look at Mary, Ritty, John, and Moses. Minister Breembat had granted him permission to have Christmas dinner with Rit and Ben in their cabin on the Tozor Plantation. But Robert's actual plans involved meeting Harriet and his brothers.

Once out of the aviary, Robert ran toward the secret location in the woods where Harriet had said she would be. It took him more than an hour to reach the site. Robert saw signs of footprints, which could've belonged to anyone. But what he did not see was Harriet and the others.

She left. Dammit, Harriet, I can't believe you left without me.

Chapter 32
I Never Wait for No One

Pelduth Neck
Tozor Plantation

Harriet stopped at the edge of the woods. The road to Dr. Tozor's aviary was ahead. She lifted her face to the black sky, smelling rain in the air but feeling guilty in her heart for leaving without Robert.

He's my brother, but I never wait for no one. Too risky. That's one of the strictest rules I keep for myself. Followin' that rule has saved me and my passengers. Robert ain't no exception. But somethin' mighty must've happened to keep him from joinin' us. I hope he's fine. Lord, please watch over my big brother.

She was flanked by brothers she hadn't seen in over five years. The thirty-year-old Ben Jr. crouched to her right while the twenty-four-year-old Henry was to her left. Like Harriet, they observed the quiet road before them.

She'd never felt so close to home yet also so far away. But seven people relied on her, and two more awaited her pickup from Jondrin, the Dragonkin Quaker her brother Robert had met many years ago. The thought of her missing older brother troubled Harriet more than she wanted to admit, so she plowed on as if unconcerned she'd already lost a passenger.

She turned to the group, her voice a whisper. "Right up there is a corncrib. It'll put us close to Poppa's cabin. He is expectin' us but not our momma." Harriet nodded to John and Peter. They were slaves from Cosaru who'd joined her party. They were young, about Henry's age, and unknown to the aviary residents, making them perfect for the task. "When we are safe in the corncrib, you two will get Ben. It's late. He'll be up, but my momma, Rit, goes to bed early and sleeps hard. But she still got keen ears, so be careful."

The men didn't reply because none was required. Collaboration and trust were needed to travel north successfully.

Instead of creeping about, as she had when traversing the woods, cautious of slave catchers, Harriet strolled from the woods to the road with the confidence of a woman returning to the plantation she'd fled less than six years earlier. If she'd learned nothing else from her previous three missions, the first with eleven passengers in late 1851, the second with nine during the fall of 1852, and the third a single passenger in June 1854, a mere six months earlier, was that a confident leader, even if feigned, encouraged others to find their own confidence.

So, Harriet walked up the road with her head held high and back straight. Like her overcoat and satchel, her towel-covered pistol had become an essential accessory on each mission. Harriet might not have been a sharpshooter, but Majors had taken his role as instructor seriously. Luckily, Harriet didn't have reason to draw her weapon as she had when confronted by Mudspike.

"That's it," Harriet whispered.

The corncrib appeared much the same as when she had last seen the building. Perhaps more sun warped than she remembered, but it was still sturdy and would make a perfect hiding place. Corncribs were granaries used to dry and store corn. Slaves would harvest and place the corn in the crib with the husk on. Like the wooden structure, there were rooted bins elevated on wooden posts. The elevation prevented rodents from getting to the corn.

When her dancing days were over, and hard, physical labor was all that Minister Breembat thought she was suitable for, Harriet had learned to harvest corn as well as any Birdfolk man. But Minister Breembat rarely had the slaves use the corncrib she'd guided her passengers into because of its smaller size.

The walls slanted outward, with slats in the walls that allowed air to circulate through the corn. This air would initially dry the corn and then help it stay dry. However, the newer corncribs had a more extended design with ample open space in the middle for accessing corn and promoting even greater airflow. The open space could also accommodate a wagon. But Harriet only required enough space for her party to sleep without being on top of each other.

"Now?" Peter asked Harriet.

Peter and John had stayed by the closed door after the group had entered. The corncrib was dark, and the storm clouds that rolled in covered the moon's light. But Birdfolk, even in human form, could see reasonably well in the dark.

Harriet took stock of her other passengers. Ben Jr. fell in love with an enslaved woman during her time away. He'd introduced Jane as his fiancé. The twenty-two-year-old wore an oversized men's suit. Harriet did not inquire about the details, but she had heard of masters who would take their slaves' clothing at night to prevent them from running away. She also didn't mention the younger woman's bruised cheek and swollen lip. None among them had been spared their masters' physical cruelty.

Then there were George and William. They were also strangers. She'd met them earlier that day when she'd seen a public auction notice. They had stared at the same posting, although the men could no more read than Harriet. But when George and William had moved aside, permitting a flow of Dragonkin to read the notice, Harriet had waited, too. Like George and William, Harriet assumed if she exercised patience, she would overhear someone either read the names aloud or discuss the slaves who would be sold come Monday. Her patience had paid off, and by the time it had, Harriet had acquired two more passengers and knew she had to send a message to her brothers because all their names were on the public auction notice.

"Now is good. Poppa's been waitin'."

Harriet watched Peter and John through the slats in the wall that faced Ben and Rit's cabin. Again, her brothers flanked her, warming Harriet with their nearness.

Ben Jr. settled a hand around her waist and pulled her close. "You ain't seen Momma and Poppa in over five years. Are you okay?"

"I'm fine."

Henry engulfed her hand with his, and she cherished having him so near again. "You're a bad liar. They gettin' up there in age. But they are as good as can be. They miss you somethin' fierce. Moses and Kessiah, too."

Arm still wrapped around Harriet, Ben Jr. reached around her with his free hand and smacked the top of Henry's head. "You makin' her feel bad about doin' the right thing."

"That ain't what I meant. I'm just sayin' what we all know and feel. Harriet and Moses bein' gone ain't been easy on them. And we know our leavin' will hit Momma the hardest."

Harriet did know, which made being this close and not speaking with her mother the most challenging part of her plan. But Harriet refused to think about the guilt she did indeed feel for taking away two more of her parents' children. After tomorrow night, Rit and Ben would only have Robert and Rachel, and Harriet refused to leave her last remaining brother and sister behind. She would happily swallow the bitter pill of guilt when she brought the last of her siblings north because she damn well had no intention of allowing Robert or Rachel to languish the rest of their days in servitude. Her parents would decide to leave Dralox County if she were fortunate.

But those were too many moving future parts for Harriet to contemplate. She focused on one mission at a time but always with an eye to future escape plans. Although Henry hadn't mentioned his freeborn wife and two young sons, she knew it hadn't been easy for him to leave them behind, just as Ben Jr. had left the children of the freeborn woman he'd had before committing himself to Jane.

All I want to do is reunite with my family. Free them from bondage. Each time I do, another family is left in pieces. But my brothers would've been sold away if I hadn't come. Forever lost like our sisters. But I've never gone on a mission without the good Lord's consent. This is where I'm supposed to be. It hurts, yes, it does, but the Lord has shown me the way. And it led me back here to my brothers.

"Hush," she told Ben Jr. and Henry. "Poppa is comin', and I don't want him hearin' us arguin' over nothin' that's gonna change our fate."

The door to the corncrib opened, and Harriet turned. The happy butterflies that filled her stomach when her father would return home on Sundays after being away with Master Gyzad in Pelduth Neck returned with childlike flutters.

Her sixty-two-year-old father stood to the right of Peter and John. Unsurprisingly, he'd tied a handkerchief around his head, covering his eyes. If Harriet wasn't so happy to see her father, she would've laughed at Ben's future self telling Minister Breembat that he hadn't "seen" his children before they'd run off.

Ben Jr. shoved her. "Go. He been waitin' for five years."

She had always been the first of her siblings to run and jump into her father's arms when he returned home and the last to say goodbye when he had to leave again. But Harriet wasn't the child Minty anymore, begging to be spun around and tickled until laughter turned into coughs.

Still . . .

Harriet rushed to Ben, controlling her enthusiasm to not knock her blindfolded father over.

"I'd know that hug anywhere. I've missed you, my girl."

If Harriet relished her reunion with Ben Jr. and Henry, welcoming their hugs and kisses like a rain-deprived town, she all but melted into little girl tears at her father's embrace.

Harriet wept and wept, no longer concerned with her display of calm confidence in front of her passengers. To some, perhaps, five years might not be a long time, but for a woman who'd spent too much of her childhood without her parents, five years felt like an eternity and a day.

Henry had been right. Birdfolk weren't long-lived like Dragonkin. Harriet's silent fear of one or both of her parents dying while she was away had kept her up at night more often than she cared to admit.

Ben stroked her head feathers and hair the way she liked. "Havin' you home is the best Christmas gift. We can stay like this, but I bet you're hungry. The boys you sent for me have a sack of food I gathered for you all. Come, my brave girl, let's get you fed."

Harriet forced herself to release Ben, but that didn't mean she couldn't stay near him.

With Ben Jr.'s and Henry's help, Ben sat on the floor. They all sat in a line against the wall beside the door. If someone unexpectedly entered, they wouldn't automatically see them. But no one did, so Harriet wedged herself between Ben and Henry. Her brother hadn't liked it, going so far as to grumble, "Poppa's girl."

The following day, someone barged into the corncrib. Ben Jr., Henry, and George were immediately on the man. They pinned him to the ground, an arm wrenched behind his back.

Harriet retrieved her pistol and stood with it pointed at the man's head.

Everyone turned to look at her, but she focused on the man on the ground instead of the shocked gazes. Greenish-blue feathers peeked out from under the arms that held the man down, and while five years had taken its toll on a man Ben's age, it hadn't on Harriet's memory.

"You're late."

Ben Jr., dark brown eyes still on Harriet, frowned. "What do you mean late?"

Henry and George scrambled off the man, but Ben Jr. still held his arm in a bone-breaking grip if he applied more pressure. Thankfully, he didn't because Harriet had no interest in tending to a man with a broken arm.

"Get off me."

"Robert?"

"Who else? Get off me, already."

Ben Jr. obliged, although his slow smirk revealed he'd known it was Robert far sooner than he'd let on.

As if she hadn't pulled a weapon on her brother, Harriet slipped the gun into her overcoat pocket. She vowed never to mention having almost shot her oldest brother.

"That ain't no way to greet me." Robert slapped Henry's hand away when the younger man attempted to help him off the ground. He easily jumped to his feet, and Harriet thought thirty-eight looked good on Robert. His shoulders were broader than she remembered, and his arms thicker. He stepped to Harriet, glowering down at her. "You left me."

Harriet moved closer to him and matched Robert's glower with her own. "You were late. I never wait for no one."

"Not even your brother?"

Harriet pointed to Ben Jr. and Henry, who stared from Harriet to Robert with too much amusement. "They were on time. What's your excuse?"

Besides Ben, Robert was the most reliable man she knew. So, whatever had kept her brother must've been important.

Robert hugged her, and Harriet held him with the same fierceness as she had Ben. "I'm sorry. It wasn't easy leavin' Mary and the children behind. You're an aunt again."

A round of "Congratulations" followed Robert's announcement. However, instead of sharing details about his wife and newborn, Robert removed himself from the group. He sat alone in a corner, nursing his grief and guilt.

I know how he's feelin'. We've all left people we love behind. Freedom for self doesn't mean freedom for all. Somethins gotta give in this awful country. We can't go on like this. Some free while others ain't.

For the rest of the day, few talked except for Ben Jr. and Jane, who found their own corner of the corncrib. Ben visited them several times, guaranteeing they were well-fed.

Harriet rested most of the day but returned to the wall slats facing her parents' cabin. Twice, Rit had come onto the porch, looked out at the road expectantly, and then returned to the cabin.

Like Ben, Harriet hadn't seen Rit in almost six years. Unlike Ben, Rit couldn't be trusted not to wail to the point of alerting the aviary to her presence if she saw Harriet. As much as Rit wanted them to be free in the North, Harriet also understood her mother's desire to have her children near. Such conflicting emotions weren't limited to Rit, however. Harriet had seen it in others, just as she had felt it within herself.

Robert joined her, and she leaned against her brother's side, grateful he'd made it while also sad for his loss. But her brothers failed to understand that Harriet left no one behind. She had seen the desire to ask her to return for their wives and children in their eyes but also the hesitancy to make a request that would endanger her safety and freedom.

As soon as I can find fundin' for my next mission, I'll return for our sister and her children, and my brothers' wives and children. Henry and Robert won't be without their families for long.

"Momma is lookin' for us. We got permission to visit for Christmas. We promised to have dinner together, knowin' it was a lie."

As if summoned by the regret Harriet detected in Robert's voice, Rit returned to the porch. As she'd done the previous times, she cupped her hands over her eyes and stared down the road Harriet's brothers would've come from on their way to their parents' cabin.

Harriet couldn't hear Rit, but she felt her sigh of disappointment in the heart that reached for her mother's hand, offering comfort for the wound her children had inflicted in service to a greater cause.

"Poppa will explain after we've gone. The truth won't hurt less, but she'll be glad you spared us from the auction block."

"It hurts to be this close and not go to her."

"Leavin' is hard. Nothin' else in heaven or on earth would've made me leave Mary and my boys. I got a little girl now, too. She's another Harriet in the family. It's a special name. But nobody wears it better than you. You're a charm from above. Thank you for comin' back for us."

Harriet turned into her brother's embrace, giving comfort and accepting Robert's.

By nightfall, Harriet and her passengers slipped from the corncrib, well-rested and well-fed, thanks to Ben. Though they'd been holed up in a granary, Harriet had spent Christmas with her brothers, a future sister-in-law, and a blindfolded father who joked that he looked forward to telling Minister Breembat to go kick rocks because he hadn't seen "hide nor hair of my boys."

With the handkerchief securely in place, Ben waited for Harriet and her passengers in front of his cabin. Rit hadn't ventured onto the porch again since the last time Harriet and Robert had seen her, giving up on having Christmas dinner with her sons.

"She's sittin by the fire," Ben told Harriet when she tucked his big hand into hers. "Rit's in her own world, so she won't see if you take a quick look."

Ben had been right.

Harriet peered through a side window, she in front and her taller brothers behind her. Rit sat in a rocking chair, a pipe in her mouth, staring into the crackling fire, her head on her hand.

HARRIET'S ESCAPE:

"Momma's troubled," Henry whispered. "I can't imagine never seein' her again."

Neither could Harriet, but the rain had stopped, and the full moon glowed above. Harriet interpreted both as good omens they would have a smooth journey north.

"Let's go."

Ben Jr. and Robert held one of Ben's arms, permitting the older man to share the first few miles of their escape with his children. But when they reached the fork in the road, Harriet could no longer indulge in the drawn-out farewell.

"Poppa, we got to leave you here. Keep your handkerchief on until you can't hear our feet. Then wait a little longer before takin' it off."

"Be safe. I love you. I'll love you kids till the end of my days."

Her father hadn't cried a single time he'd visited them in the corncrib. But the tears she couldn't see choked the voice that bade four of his children goodbye.

"This ain't right," Ben Jr. said, following Harriet's lead away from their father.

"No, it ain't. But that there was a father's blessin'. I aim to live up to it. Now, stop your bellyachin' and walk faster."

On December 29, four days and one hundred miles after Harriet's train car had set out for the north, Harriet delivered her passengers safely to the Anti-Slavery Society Office in Pholgre. But none stayed in that city for long. While there, however, Harriet's brothers and Jane adopted new names, all renouncing the surname assigned to them by their slave master.

Her brothers chose the surname Sceeth, with Robert Wren becoming John Sceeth; Benjamin Wren Jr., James Sceeth; and Henry Wren, William Henry Sceeth. Jane changed her name to Catherine and adopted the last name Sceeth in anticipation of her marriage.

When Harriet had found her way to Pholgre's Anti-Slavery Society Office, she'd been asked the same question as every freedom seeker she delivered to the office: "What would you like your free name to be?" William Skeshru, a Birdfolk abolitionist whose parents had escaped from Miadar's Eastern Shore, carried the surname his father had chosen after migrating to New Jasu. This state bordered eastern Pyzai and had adopted a gradual abolition of slavery law in 1804. Skeshru had been as much a godsend to Harriet as to every runaway who made it through his office doors. Like Harriet and her ten 1854 passengers, most answered Skeshru's interview questions without suspicion or complaint.

Personal information, such as age, height, feather colors, family background, slave master name, and location, was shared with a similar bleeding-heart retelling Harriet had experienced when relaying her tale to William Skeshru. However, without fail, every passenger she'd delivered to Skeshru had taken his question about a new identity as an opportunity to shed their slave name and adopt one of their choosing.

But not Harriet. She had chosen her mother's name years ago, as she had John Cassin. No freedom name was better than the one she'd already claimed for herself. While she was no longer John's wife, the person defined the name, not the circumstances of their birth. So it was Harriet Wren Cassin who'd successfully fled bondage in 1849.

It was Harriet Wren Cassin, not a newly named woman, looking forward but never backward, who had led thirty-eight enslaved men, women, and children to freedom between 1850 and 1854.

And she wasn't done yet. So, within months of settling her brothers and Catherine in St. Cegri, a city in the northern country of Cothru and the home to hundreds of Birdfolk fugitives who fled Unganthu after the adoption of the Fugitive Slave Act, Harriet set off again for Dralox County.

With all of her brothers and Kessiah's family safe in St. Cegri, Harriet could turn her gaze south again.

She wouldn't rest until she also freed Rachel and her children.

Chapter 33
I Ain't Givin' Up

1855
Berzogtown

"What do you mean you ain't comin'?" Harriet had never been one to pace, but each time she met Rachel at the site of many Birdfolk weddings, including her own, her sister's unacceptable response set her off, walking in a circle as endless as their disagreement.

"I can't leave without my babies."

"I know, but—"

"There ain't no buts, Harriet. I won't leave without Ben and Angerine."

Harriet ceased the needless pacing. Once she secured her passengers, there would be plenty of walking ahead of her. There was no need to get started early. So, she grasped Rachel's hand and tugged her to the soft, green grass. Night had enfolded the woods hours ago, a silent accessory to the clandestine meeting between sisters.

Harriet had arrived in Dralox County four days earlier. She'd stayed with different friends each night, using the day hours to gather real-time information about Rachel's, Henry's, and Robert's families. She'd gone there prepared to return with three women and their children. What Harriet hadn't planned on was a stubborn sister and missing relatives.

Rachel had been twenty-four when Harriet escaped, Angerine a playful three-year-old, and Ben a chubby six-month-old. With the children being six and nine, Harriet hoped the children were still in Rachel's custody. Even if they weren't, even if they were forced to labor in a temporary master's home, as she had when she was their age, Harriet prayed the children were permitted to visit their mother on Sundays.

Unfortunately, God hadn't seen fit to answer her prayer.

"I can't leave them, Harriet. I can't. They don't have a poppa to speak of. It's just me."

During her time in the North, Harriet had met many fugitive slave women who'd left all or some of their children behind when they sought their freedom. William Skeshru's own mother had tried to flee with her four children. When she was caught and returned to her master, the next time she struck out, she took her young daughters and left her two sons behind. William Skeshru hadn't been one of those two boys left behind. He was the youngest of fourteen children born after his fugitive mother reunited with a husband who had the good fortune to have a master that allowed him to purchase his freedom.

But every successful escape came with an emotional price. And just as there were enslaved Birdfolk parents who sought freedom without their children, there were others who denied themselves the chance of freedom if it couldn't also include their offspring.

As much as Harriet had prayed for children when married to John, she recognized that having them would've made her choice to flee that much more difficult. Would John have been more inclined to risk running away with Harriet if they'd had children? Would she have taken her children with her, denying them a father's love and John access to his flesh and blood?

None of the thoughts that crisscrossed through Harriet's mind yielded easy answers. But whatever push-pull existed within Rachel—freedom without her children versus enslavement with them—she had made her decision.

Still, Harriet wasn't ready to give up on her sister and her children.

Harriet held Rachel's hand, unsure what to say but knowing only action solved problems. "Tell me where they are, and I'll steal them away."

She never liked it when someone shook their head in response to a statement she made or an action she engaged in. What followed was usually nothing she wanted to hear.

"Minister Breembat might not know it's you, but he ain't dumb, Harriet. He looks around and sees it's our kin that's gone missin'. Not only us, I know. Others have run off, too. Followin' the example you've set, even though they don't know it's you givin' people ideas and hope for a better life up north."

Harriet's goal hadn't been to inspire others. All she ever wanted was to see her family free. If Congress and the president did not see fit to end slavery, then Harriet felt duty bound to free who she could for as long as the good Lord saw her through. But freedom without the only sister she could see and touch, even if she had to travel miles in secret to do it, was like drinking tea without sweetener—refreshing but far from tasty.

"You sayin' Minister Breembat deliberately separated you from your children?"

"A test or punishment, I don't know. I've tried to visit them, when possible, but I get turned away."

Rit had experienced the same after Minister Breembat had taken Harriet to the Calis farm. She recalled how lonely she'd been, and while her heart went out to Angerine and Ben, she knew wherever they were being kept was made better because they had each other. This was a small comfort to Rachel, but knowledge of Minister Breembat's ploy did not alter Harriet's intentions.

"Tell me where they are."

"For you to fall into his trap?" Rachel lifted one of Harriet's hands to her face and then turned toward the palm.

Cupping her sister's cheek, Harriet scooted closer so she could hug her with her free hand. "I'll get them. I promise."

"You'll get caught, and it'll be my fault."

"I won't. I haven't." Harriet ran her hand up Rachel's trembling back into her feathered head, massaging her scalp and offering tactile comfort. "I'm charmed," she said, feeling the truth of that simple sentence with everything that made her who she was. "I'm charmed," Harriet repeated, needing Rachel to accept the inevitability of Harriet's success.

Rachel's fears for Harriet's safety were apparently greater than her faith in Harriet's abilities.

Rachel shook her head again, and Harriet wanted to howl her frustration at the moon.

"Trust me."

"It ain't about trust, Harriet. But I won't trade away a sister. It's just us now. We are all the daughters Momma and Poppa have left. And I'm all Angerine and Ben have. I'll find a way to get them returned to me."

Harriet was confident Rachel would try, but each rescue mission required funding. It often took Harriet months to save for another trip south. Donations to the Anti-Slavery Society helped, but money didn't always come when Harriet needed it the most.

Harriet pulled Rachel's head forward, bringing their foreheads together. "I don't know the next time I'll be back here. It might be months."

"That's fine. It'll give me time."

None of this was fine, but Rachel wouldn't leave without her children, and Harriet hadn't come there to abandon her niece and nephew. Still, Rachel was there with Harriet on a Sunday night with hours to spare before anyone would expect her in the field or kitchen on Monday. She could have her sister in William Skeshru's office in four days, sharing her story and choosing an alias. But Angerine and Ben wouldn't be there, and Harriet shuddered at the thought of her sister hating her.

"I don't like leavin' you again."

"I know. But I'll be here when you return." Rachel pulled back. Her eyes were wet, and her lips twisted into a forced smile. "You ain't come all this way for only me and mine."

Harriet hadn't, of course, because she'd promised Henry and Robert she'd reunite them with their loved ones. But she wasn't ashamed to admit that Rachel, Angerine, and Ben were her priorities. It felt wrong to have saved her brothers and others while her sister still languished under the threat of the whip.

"I didn't, but you're my sister, Rachel. We belong together." Harriet sensed the invisible thread connecting her to Rachel beginning to untwine.

HARRIET'S ESCAPE:

The sensation jolted through Harriet, stealing her breath and causing an episode.

She blacked out.

"Harriet?" *Slap.* Harriet?" *Slap.* "Harriet?"

Her eyes popped open in time for her to avoid the third slap. She caught her sister's hand. "That ain't how it works, Rach."

"You haven't called me that in years." Rachel touched Harriet's cheek and forehead with the back of her hand. "No fever."

"It doesn't work like that, either. It's not that kind of sickness. We've been away from each other too long if you've forgotten that."

"I didn't forget. I just wanna make sure you're fine before I send you on your way to get our sisters-in-law."

"I ain't ready to leave yet." Harriet reclined on the grass, her satchel within arm's reach. "What about you?"

"I got a few hours before I gotta be back."

So did Harriet. A dockworker friend had offered his home as her safe house for the night, and she'd gladly accepted.

"Stargazin'?" Rachel settled beside Harriet.

Harriet closed the small space between them and held Rachel's hand. "Sister talk."

"That's better than stargazin' any day. Tell me about your life in the North. How are Moses and Kessiah? And James and little Harriet? Why do we have so many Harriets in the family?"

Harriet couldn't help but laugh at her thirty-year-old sister's flurry of words.

I've missed Rachel somethin' fierce. I know it's been hard on her raisin' Angerine and Ben alone, but I can tell she's a good momma. She's always been a good sister, too. I won't let this be her fate. She deserves better. We all do. So, I'll keep comin' back here until I can bring Rachel and her children home. I refuse to lose another sister.

1855
Dominion of Cothru
St. Cegri

To many, Harriet's early 1855 mission had been successful. With patience and help from free Birdfolk and Dragonkin abolitionists, Harriet secured the safe passage of Henry's twenty-three-year-old wife, Harriet Ann, their four-year-old son, William Henry, and the couple's six-month-old son, John Issac. Harriet Ann's freeborn status made contacting her easier than if she had been an enslaved woman.

Harriet did not have to worry about angering a master or eluding authorities bent on capturing a runaway family. But none of those facts translated into a smooth journey when taken with young children and when unscrupulous slave catchers would sooner take their payment on a woman's body before turning her over for a monetary reward.

Subconscious of mirroring her last image of Rit, Harriet sat in a rocking chair on her porch, head in her hand, and pondered what she could've done differently during her last mission to have achieved a better result.

Spring had set in nicely, adding a floral scent to the air. The boarding house she rented was full, occupied by Henry's family, Robert, and a host of runaways, mainly from the Eastern Shore like Harriet. Kessiah and John had moved to the next town over, and Moses was like a rolling stone, never staying anywhere long.

"How long you gonna sit on those steps sayin' nothin'?" Harriet had enough of Robert. "If you're mad with me, you might as well get it off your chest."

Robert, seated on the first step of her porch, a blade of grass between his dark, full lips, twisted to face Harriet. "I told you, I ain't mad."

"Oh, you mad. You might as well spit it out because you've been stompin' around the house like a big ole elephant."

"That's what I've been doin'?" Robert moved to claim the vacant rocking chair beside her. "I made a promise to Mary."

"You did, and I made one to you. Good intentions are all we got. I tried my best. The good Lord knows I did."

Robert yanked the blade of grass from his mouth and frowned at it as if its bland flavor had turned bitter. "I ain't blamin' you."

Harriet didn't think that was entirely true because she blamed herself while admitting that forces beyond her control prevented her from fulfilling her promises to Robert and herself to take Rachel and her children north.

"I'm sorry I couldn't find where Mary and the children had been taken. I'll try again."

"You say that like it's your responsibility. It ain't. I'm the one who left. She is down there by herself with three young ones. Minister Breembat is a mean, petty dragon. I'm sure he's taken my family and Rachel's children to spite them because he can't do nothin' to us way up here."

Harriet agreed, leaving her with few good options but to return to Dralox County on a wing and a prayer that Rachel would reunite with her children by the time she arrived and Robert's family would return to Dr. Tozor's plantation.

"I ain't givin' up." Harriet pushed forward in her chair. Her grip on the arms was as resolute as her words. "I want Rachel, Mary, and the kids here with us." A rush of longing washed over Harriet, and her determination to have more nights like the one she and Rachel shared in the woods spurred her on. "I'll be attendin' the National Birdfolk Convention in October."

"The fancy gatherin' of Birdfolk abolitionists you mentioned last week. I thought you weren't goin'."

"I changed my mind. Me not likin' that kind of gatherin' don't mean I shouldn't go. Meetin' and talkin' to the right people is how I raise money for my trips south. People want to help, so I let them. Some want to show me off, and I allow that, too. I don't know if that's an even exchange, but it's more than a poor runaway like me could do by herself."

Robert eyed Harriet as he did when worry had him seeing her as a child needing her big brother's protection. "All of this back-and-forth ain't good for your health. You nodded off twice before we reached Pholgre and four more times before we crossed into Cothru."

Harriet slid back, resumed rocking, and closed her eyes so she wouldn't see her brother's expression when she lied. "I'm fine. Just a little tired."

She didn't hear or sense him move, but Harriet did yelp when Robert lifted her from the chair. One arm held her under her knees while the other supported her back. "I ain't a baby. Put me down."

"You sure actin' like one." Robert shifted her higher against his chest. "You a tiny thing, Harriet, and a stubborn woman to boot."

Harriet thought Robert would force the door open with his foot, take her inside, and glare at her until she agreed to a long nap. Instead, he claimed her rocking chair with Harriet on his lap. His big, masculine body surrounded hers, and she felt both protected and loved.

"You forever doin' for others. Let me do this one thing for you. Sleep, Harriet. Every battle worth wagin' will be here when you wake."

Sad but true.

Harriet's head dropped to Robert's shoulder. Harriet gave herself entirely into someone else's care for the first time in nearly six years. It wouldn't last, but Harriet would borrow her brother's strength for the time it did and humbly indulge in the brief respite.

Come winter, she would head out again for Dralox County. Come hell or high water, she would free Rachel and reunite Robert with his family.

Chapter 34

I Love You, Rachel

1855
Berzogtown

Despite being late December and the sun hidden behind gray clouds, Harriet wore a sunbonnet pulled low to conceal her face.

Rachel tugged one of the bonnet's strings. "I can't believe you walkin' through town as free as you please. Actin' like you don't have a care in the world."

Harriet deepened her hunch, held tightly to the waist-high branch she'd found to accompany her disguise, and shuffled along the snow-sprinkled ground.

Rachel's sweet laughter was almost enough to lighten the seriousness of their repetitive conversation. "You look ridiculous in that disguise." Rachel hooked her arm through Harriet's, treating her as if she were indeed an elderly Birdfolk woman in need of assistance. "But only to me because I know you. If I didn't, I'd be fooled."

Harriet permitted Rachel to guide her through the town, committed to her ruse of a manumitted grandmother enjoying a Sunday stroll with her enslaved granddaughter. Considering Dragonkin treated enslaved Birdfolk as if they were invisible, except when they needed their bodies for any manner of villainy, Birdfolk elders could move through town like still air—present but unfelt.

"Minister Breembat has moved Angerine and Ben. I don't know where."

Harriet was glad the hat she wore hid her frown and snarl. "He's playin' a cruel game with our family."

"No luck locatin' Mary and the kids?"

Harriet's back tightened in muscles she hadn't known existed, and she already dreaded how much worse the pain would become as the day drew on. "No luck. But I'll keep lookin'."

"What does that mean?" Rachel shifted them out of the path of a family of Dragonkin children running after their parents and hollering a list of presents they wanted for Christmas.

Harriet shook her head, disgusted by the social, political, and economic divide between poor Birdfolk and wealthy Dragonkin. Even her Anti-Slavery Society Dragonkin donors, while heads and tails above their southern slave-owning counterparts, did not truly comprehend the depth of their privilege and Birdfolk's disadvantage.

"Don't you worry about what it means."

"All you just said was that you gonna do somethin' stupid."

"Don't call me stupid."

"I didn't. I said you probably plannin' somethin' stupid. And dangerous. And . . ." Rachel stopped in front of the Berzogtown general store.

Despite the original general store having burned to the ground a day after Mudspike had thrown a weight that had hit Harriet in the head, leaving permanent, untreatable damage, she avoided the rebuilt building when she could. If she looked around the town and let her mind take flight, conjuring memory after memory of her time on the ground upon which she stood, inside the buildings she was denied entry unless on an errand for a master, or at the docks hauling goods onto and off ships that would never sail her away to freedom, Harriet would easily submit that the place she sometimes still thought of as home held more experiences worth forgetting than ones worth recalling.

The palms of Rachel's hands settled on Harriet's shoulders, gentle but firm enough for Harriet to understand her sister's silent message for her to be quiet and listen.

Harriet would, but Rachel would be mistaken if she thought any sentiment that involved Harriet giving up on the mission would hold sway.

"Minister Breembat and other Dragonkin masters have been on a tear. They've been searchin' our homes, both free and enslaved. They claim they lookin' for guns and weapons. That we plottin' an insurrection to justify their harassment of people who ain't done nothin' wrong."

Perhaps realizing that such a conversation was best not had in front of a busy general store two days before Christmas, even if spoken in whispers, Rachel resumed their stroll. But not their conversation.

However, hours later in Rachel's cabin, Harriet reclined on a pallet she'd last seen occupied by Angerine and Ben. She'd discarded her sunbonnet and overcoat when she entered her sister's quiet home and propped her walking stick next to her satchel by the door.

It was unusual for a slave to occupy a cabin by themselves. The fact that Minister Breembat had permitted Rachel to do so, saving the space for children he'd taken from her, was either a confirmation that the separation was indeed temporary, or it was a cold-blooded insurance policy he'd taken out on Rachel's heart.

It wasn't difficult to imagine Rachel staring at the empty pallet, hers across the room but near enough to watch over children who no longer slept within a mother's loving reach.

"Bold and crazy are opposite sides of the same coin, Harriet."

Rachel handed Harriet a bowl of pepper rabbit, hominy, and okra soup. On their way through the woods to Mistress Essodel's aviary, Harriet had found another use for her walking stick. Since Rachel was a better cook than Harriet, she'd cleaned and prepared the rabbit, and her sister had done the rest.

She waited for Rachel to claim the pallet across from where she sat before digging in. "Smells good. Thank you for cookin'."

"When I'm hired out, I get so tired of cookin'. When I ain't slavin' in a master's kitchen, they got me dancin'. Entertainin' their friends and family."

Rachel's fate would have been hers if not for Harriet's head injury. Instead, Harriet had been tossed into the field, working on plantations, treated no better than oxen or a mule.

When Harriet swallowed her first taste, she was reminded that the key to good soup was the right mix and amount of seasoning. Rachel might not like being forced to cook for others, but when she did for her family, she infused the meal with lip-smacking flavors that had Harriet eating a second helping.

She also hadn't forgotten her sister called her bold and crazy. "When it's only me, hidin' in plain sight is easier than you'd think. Nobody pays an old Birdfolk woman any mind. When they do, I just talk like I'm lost and confused. That gets me pity or scorn. Though, smellin' of vomit or urine gets the job done better."

Rachel's laughter rippled through the small cabin, and Harriet wished she could harness Rachel's rare moments of joy into a canteen, from which she could drink whenever she found herself missing her sister.

"Smellin' like that, I'd stay away from you, too."

"No, you'd offer to walk me home. You've always been kind, Rach. It's amazin' we aren't filled to the brim with nothin' but hatred. We could be, and we'd be right for feelin' that way. But no flowers can grow from tainted soil."

Rachel gathered their empty bowls and cleaned them with a rag hanging on the back of a chair. When finished, she pushed her pallet over until it was next to Harriet's. Rachel then removed her shoes and dress and reclined on her bed.

As she'd done throughout the day, Harriet followed her sister's lead. In no time, she wore only socks, panties, and a slip that had seen better days but still covered all the parts it should have.

Wood sizzled and crackled in the fireplace, adding much-needed warmth to the cabin. But Harriet was grateful when Rachel covered them with a quilt like the one she'd sent to Mrs. Ziet for Kessiah and her children. Like cooking, quilt making was another chore enslaved females were forced to perform for masters, only to return home in the evening and duplicate their efforts for their families.

"You thinkin' you just gonna walk onto a plantation, askin' about two children, and then leave with them, if found?"

When put so bluntly, Harriet's plan did sound bold and crazy.

"It's what I did today. Mistress Essodel's mountain ain't but a mile down the road. But she ain't thinkin' about me. Ain't nobody huntin' for a little runaway slave girl because Dragonkin can't imagine anybody doin' what I do because masters are selfish through and through." Harriet shifted onto her side to better see Rachel and hold her hand. "Minister Breembat don't think somebody's been comin' back here and takin' our kin away because he'd never risk himself for anybody. But he knows Momma and Poppa are free, and you're the only one of us still here. Unless he posts a gryphon slave catcher outside your cabin door, he knows he can't stop you from runnin'."

Rachel removed a pretty sapphire blue feather from her head and handed it to Harriet. "You're right. He can't stop me from runnin', but his gamble paid off because I won't leave Dralox County without my children. I know I can't talk you out of whatever you got planned, but if you find Angerine and Ben, show them that feather. They won't recognize you as family, but they'll know their momma's feather. Give it to them, and they'll follow you anywhere."

Harriet tightened her hand around the weighty but lightweight symbol of trust her sister had granted.

She means for me to take Angerine and Ben north without her. To not risk her children's chance at freedom by returning for her.

"Are you sure?"

"They're the air I breathe, Harriet. I've suffocated without them. I want them to be free, even if I can't be with them. Raise them as yours."

"Don't talk like that. I'll get you all to the North. Robert's family, too."

"Bold and crazy," Rachel said, but her voice held a sad whisper of wistfulness.

Harriet squeezed Rachel's hand, wanting to offer reassurance to counter her sister's silent doubt. But overconfidence could be as detrimental as having none. So, Harriet settled on voicing what had always been true. "I love you, Rachel."

No promise could be greater than the unconditional love between siblings.

Harriet repeated the declaration when she left Rachel's cabin Christmas night. She wore her overcoat and sunbonnet, carried her walking stick, and swung her satchel across her shoulder. Bold and crazy she might be, but Harriet wasn't so much of either to risk fate by creeping into Dr. Tozor's aviary again to see her parents.

Despite the confidence she'd displayed for Rachel's sake, none of Harriet's contacts had news of her niece and nephew, much less of Robert's wife and children. But they did have news of a harpy she wanted to speak with.

But family came first, so Harriet headed farther south. She mainly traveled at night, sleeping in abandoned barns or cabins when available. When decent shelter couldn't be found, Harriet would settle for a bed of leaves beside trees older than her parents. Hiding in swamps was her last resort, and she took that option more often than she liked.

She traveled as far south as Fishing Bay, where white-tailed deer grazed on wetland plants, and muskrats were plentiful. Harriet had spent years on the Calis farm setting muskrat traps in swamps like those around Fishing Bay. Luckily for Harriet, there were small free Birdfolk communities this far south of Dralox County. Unfortunately, no one had seen anyone who resembled the descriptions of her kin. So, Harriet continued to the eastern side of Fishing Bay, going as far east as where land met the Neaza River.

The Neaza River separated eastern Dralox County from western Winshogg County. If she kept moving east through that region, she would leave Miadar and be in Drethos. This eastern route was familiar to Harriet. If she'd located Mary and the kids or Ben and Angerine, she would've happily taken them into Drethos and bribed a boatman to ferry her passengers up Drethos Bay to Pholdre and freedom.

When she reached Neaza River, God had spoken to her, confirming what she'd learned from the free Birdfolk of Fishing Bay. Minister Breembat hadn't traveled this far south with Angerine, Ben, or Mary and her children. Still, Harriet found her way across the river and into Winshogg County. She hadn't walked that far to leave any stone unturned. While there, she met a runaway named Henry. Her mission hadn't included anyone other than her kin, but she told him what he needed to do and where he should go to make it safely to Pholgre and William Skeshru's Anti-Slavery Society office. Years later, Harriet would provide similar guidance to others, indirectly assisting in the successful escape of over forty freedom seekers.

However, her time in Winshogg County unearthed nothing but frustration, so Harriet turned her focus northwest. She knew western Dralox County like the back of her hand. With so many friends, family, and abolitionists' safe houses to choose from, Harriet had a roof over her head and a warm meal most nights. She visited the free Birdfolk farmer Jacob in Tobacco Stick, a hamlet of rolling hills at the southern end of Maraph Bay. The hamlet was named after cutting, bundling, and hanging split tobacco sticks, a task performed by free and enslaved Birdfolk.

No one had seen Rachel's children or Robert's family.

Harriet proceeded to Cosaru, where Minister Breembat had intended to sell Kessiah and her children. Unable to help herself, she walked past the courthouse, once again donning the disguise of an elderly woman. She visited every safe house and station she knew in the region, garnering a promise from the stationmasters to pass along any news they learned about her missing family members.

By the time Harriet had reached East New Maeroe, a harpy trading post fifteen miles northeast of Cosaru and in the heart of Miadar's Eastern Shore, it had been three months since she'd left Rachel's cabin. She had never dared to stay so long in Dralox County. Each day had brought a greater chance of discovery. But the longer she searched without a clue to anyone's whereabouts, the more determined she became to locate her family members.

However, stubborn determination didn't equate to success. So, with a heavy heart, Harriet temporarily shifted her focus to another matter. Her ability to continue evading capture wasn't guaranteed, so she required an insurance policy if the worst happened. Her dreams had never lied. But they had her tracking down a female she hadn't wanted to see again, prepared to ask questions she once thought better left unspoken.

Harriet knocked on the door. No candles were in the window, welcoming a frightened runaway to trust a stranger. There were no large trees to hide her presence on the porch or wings, clawed fingers, or taloned feet that would signal she was one of them. Harriet would appear to any observer to be precisely what she was—a Birdfolk in a town of harpies.

The door opened, and Harriet smiled. "Hello, Dorane. We need to talk about Master Gyzad's death."

Chapter 35
Close Call

1856
Dralox County
Boriaphville

Whenever possible, Breembat avoided physical confrontations. This warm May day had proven no different. However, he would rather engage in a sweaty aerial battle than return to Essodel empty-handed. He tightened his hands around the reins and pulled, commanding his horse to stop. Considering he was only a member of the posse and not the leader,

Breembat concluded he could avoid a fight but also earn the other Dragonkins' respect along with his mother's gratitude because he was party to reasserting the rights and power of Dragonkin slave owners.

Dragonkin Quakers had etched a portion of land for themselves a few miles north of Pelduth Neck. Most were common farmers, growing vegetables, fruit, and wheat, while others raised chickens and cattle. Their farmhouses were as plain and unassuming as their clothing. If they hadn't been such a pain in Breembat's backside, he would pity them for their basic lifestyle and lack of a reputable hoard.

Breembat hung back, content to allow Horcoz to take the lead. The three-hundred-year-old Dragonkin owned a tobacco plantation in Tobacco Stick. Like the other ten Dragonkin who'd decided to converge on the Quaker settlement, Horcoz had lost valuable pieces of his hoard. They'd come on horseback and in wagons from all over Dralox County. Breembat wasn't so proud to have joined them but recognized the importance of having his family represented in gathering the wealthy and powerful slaveholding Dragonkin families in the county.

None had a more impressive hoard than his mother. Still, most of the other Dragonkins' hoard could be defined mainly by the number of slaves they owned, the acres of land they'd claimed, and the money they made from their slaves' labor.

I was a fool. I've spent years investing everything I own into the purchase and sale of slaves. Slaves were the gold standard. Better than actual gold. But they defy us at every turn. And now they've taken to running away and staying away. It's been like a stampede out of Dralox County. With each successful escape, our precious Sankofa hoard decreases. Gyzad foresaw this, but I didn't want to listen. Still, until the law changes, I won't allow anyone to take what's mine. Not abolitionists, Quakers, and damn sure not ground-scrapers.

Horcoz wore a pistol strapped to his waist, and a rifle scabbard hung from the side of his saddle within easy reach. Breembat hadn't come prepared to use a firearm, and he doubted if violence ensued, it would be settled on the ground and with firearms.

As if they'd been expected, Quakers were out in full force. They were perched on roofs and trees, stationed on porches and fields, but the largest number, about twenty, had gathered in the town center. Unlike Horcoz's posse, the Quakers were unarmed, which wasn't the same as them also being defenseless.

"I'm Akolkun, the clerk of this town." The Dragonkin wore simple black pants, a shirt that had probably started off as white but was closer to dusty brown, a pair of black knee-length boots, and a hat that protected his skin from the sun. But his shirt, rolled to his elbows, revealed skin almost as brown as many Birdfolk's. "How can we help you?" At nearly eight feet, Akolkun was two feet taller than the eighteen-hand horse Horcoz sat astride.

"We came looking for runaways." Horcoz pointed a long, accusatory finger toward the town at large. "We know you got some hiding here, somewhere."

Akolkun glanced over his shoulder, and Breembat's hackle rose, expecting the Dragonkin to signal his fellow townspeople to attack.

Why didn't I think about them outnumbering us? Just because they claim pacifism doesn't mean they would take lightly to strangers forcing their way into their homes.

Akolkun nodded. It wasn't much of a signal, although Breembat didn't think more would be needed to relay an attack message. But no one other than the clerk moved.

He stepped aside and ushered with a steady hand to the town. "We have nothing to hide. Slavery is wrong. We will continue to spread God's words.

To fight to end the vile system of bondage. Birdfolk should be free, and slave owners should be ashamed for going against the will of God."

One of the possemen from Berzogtown turned to Breembat as if he expected him to enter into a religious debate with the Quaker. Minister or not, he couldn't care less about someone else's religious beliefs, certainly not to the point of engaging in a meaningless debate. The clerk would be no more moved to alter his ideologies about slavery than Breembat, so he let the wave of his hand serve as response enough to the posseman's unspoken expectation.

Dr. Tozor motioned with his head for Breembat to join the group.

I should make a good show of it. He acts as if he doesn't owe me money. Because of him, I've lost most of Ben and Rit's children. I don't know how they managed it, but Mother isn't happy with Tozor or me. Neither of us would be here if she didn't need me to run her affairs. But I've still held on to Rachel and her little ground-scrapers. I can't trust she won't run. Or Robert's wife. Tozor was good for something when he sent Robert's family to his daughter's plantation in Tregne County. Let's see Mary get her and her young ones across the Casse River.

Breembat brought his horse level with Dr. Tozor's. He leaned in close, preferring to keep his words between them. "Keep rotating Rachel's ground-scrapers between your family in Tregne and Cesthie counties. Without their mother, they're as docile as lambs, and without them, Rachel is, too."

There was something delicious about the scent of Rachel's defeated sadness. Why anyone, even Dragonkin Quakers, would think Birdfolk capable of handling freedom, had never seen a Birdfolk mother's self-determination reduced to ash when her children were used as pawns against her.

"Make sure you tell your mother how cooperative I've been. If Essodel needs anything else, she can count on me."

Breembat grinned, having no intention of relaying Dr. Tozor's message to Essodel, thereby providing her with more details about his running of her property than he wanted her to know.

"Of course. Mother will be pleased to know she has a good friend in the Tozor family."

"Come this way," Akolkun said. "We have nothing to hide but expect you to respect our homes. We have children, and no matter what you might think of us, children are always innocent. But you will leave your weapons outside."

Breembat had never known Horcoz to go anywhere without his pistol, but the clerk had planted his feet, taking a literal stand with the declaration of his single condition for them searching the townsfolks' homes.

It wasn't much of an ask, considering they weren't law, and one of the possemen would've been as gracious as the Quakers if they were in their predicament.

Breembat assumed Horcoz grasped what would happen if he refused the clerk's compromise. The other Dragonkin may have been silent, but they watched them with a deadly caution Horcoz and the others would do well to heed.

"Fine, but anyone harboring runaways will be taken into custody."

"We are law-abiding citizens. Welcome to Boriaphville." The clerk turned away from them and proceeded to walk down the road. "Follow me. We'll begin with my home."

The moment Akolkun did not protest the unauthorized search of his people's homes, Breembat knew they wouldn't find any runaways. But their failure to discover a single ground-scraper among the Dragonkin sympathizers wasn't the same as a verdict of innocence. Breembat knew that better than most because he lived his life shielding the truth of his actions from others. He revealed what he wanted people to see with one hand while concealing his secrets with the other, a simplistic but effective illusion of transparency.

So, he wasn't surprised when the posse unearthed nothing but dust under beds and cobwebs in root cellars.

When they returned to the road that would take them out of town, Breembat turned to take a final look. He didn't know how he had missed it before, but every farmhouse he saw had a lantern in the front window.

He shrugged. "Stupid Quakers."

Harriet lay on her back like a corpse in a pine box—frozen in place and silent. She shared the crawl space under the floorboards with her four passengers: Ben, James, Henry, and William.

The floorboards creaked above her with the weight of heavy Dragonkin in boots. But the floorboards were tightly secured. Even if she could see through the sliver of space between the wooden planks, a rug had been tossed over the floorboards, and a large rectangular dining room table placed atop the rug, making the room appear as it would whether or not runaways were concealed underneath.

She'd left her satchel in a dining room corner in her haste. There wasn't anything noteworthy about the bag, certainly nothing that should garner anyone's attention as being unusual to the point of suspicion. Still, Harriet would rather have the bag on her person, if for no other reason than the sense of security it brought her having her pistol near.

"Satisfied?" she heard Jondrin say to whoever had entered his home. "We have nothing to hide. No runaways are in our town."

"Maybe not now. That doesn't mean it's been that way in the past."

"We respect laws that protect all. Laws that conform to the goodwill of God."

"That sounds like double-talk to me. You follow the laws you agree with and break the ones you don't. That about right?"

"Laws should protect us all, especially the least of these. But what law gives you and your friends the right to ride into a peaceful town with your weapons and accusations?"

"What law gives you the right to try to take our property from us?"

"Freedom of speech, my friend. It's guaranteed to us all."

"I ain't your friend."

"I suppose not. You also aren't a wanted guest, yet I've invited you freely into my home. You've checked every nook and cranny. Now that you've found nothing to justify being here, I invite you to leave."

Harriet grinned at Jondrin's polite dismissal.

The other man mumbled something Harriet couldn't hear, but she needn't have because whatever he said was less important than the sound of his retreating feet.

She patted the thigh of the man beside her, offering James what assurance she could in the tight space. Hopefully, he would pass the small gesture along until it reached Ben to the far right of her.

Harriet closed her eyes, envisioning her route from Miadar to Pyzai. Once more, Rachel's children were separated from their mother, frustrating them both and forcing Harriet to leave her sister behind again. The last time she'd been in Miadar, she hadn't visited Cesthie County to search for her niece and nephew. She decided to plot a route that would lead her passengers to Pheghro Neck in Cesthie County. While there, she would meet with several stationmasters who might have news of Rachel's children and Robert's wife. With passengers in tow, she wouldn't be able to linger in Cesthie County, which was fine with Harriet, who'd already decided to return to Miadar once she delivered the four men to William Skeshru's office in Pholgre.

"It's safe," Jondrin said. "Be patient. I'll get you out of there in a couple of minutes."

If nothing else, Harriet was a patient woman, so waiting a few minutes more for Jondrin to free them was the easiest thing she'd done since she was a girl.

She heard Jondrin slide the table out of the way, and a shaft of light seeped through the floorboards when he rolled the rug back. He removed the floorboards one by one, letting in the fresh air and a lantern's revealing light.

Harriet accepted the hand Jondrin extended to her, and he virtually lifted her from the crawl space.

Ben, James, Henry, and William helped each other from the space. Like Harriet, they looked around, halfway expecting the man who'd searched Jondrin's home to jump from the shadows.

Harriet covered her heart with her hand, satisfied it no longer fluttered in warning.

"That was a close call," Ben said.

James bent to help Jondrin reset the floorboards and the rug, and finally, with the help of Ben, the three men lifted the heavy wooden dining room table and placed it atop the rug as it had been when Harriet arrived to pick up the freedom seekers from the Dragonkin abolitionists last night.

"Who was that?" Harriet sat in the chair Henry offered her.

Henry claimed the chair next to her while Ben and William sat across from Harriet with Jondrin to her left at the head of the table.

Harriet hadn't used Jondrin's home as a safe house when she ferried her brothers to safety. When Robert had met the Dragonkin a decade earlier in a workhouse, Jondrin hadn't taken an active role in helping Robert protect Linah from being sold south.

Harriet didn't know what had occurred in the intervening years that had led Jondrin to expand his definition of actions a Quaker should not engage in. She doubted such an updated perspective also included violence, perhaps not even self-defense.

"A group of Dralox County's finest slaveholders paid us a visit. That's a compliment to our anti-slavery efforts." Jondrin tapped the table in front of Harriet. "Them coming here is also a compliment to your conductor efforts. More and more Birdfolk are following your example. Runaways leave, and they aren't being dragged back in chains. They know what that means."

"Freedom," William said. "Success."

"A new home in the north," James added, his light brown eyes alight with a familiar gleam of excited hope she'd seen on every passenger she'd delivered out of bondage.

"When should we set out?" Ben asked Harriet.

Harriet intended to leave that night. But with the unexpected scrutiny of the Quakers, Harriet would rather put off setting out until she received a sign from the good Lord that it was safe for her to begin her journey north.

"In two or three nights."

Jondrin tapped the table in front of Harriet again. "I agree. I'm sure they're spying on us, waiting for any sign that we lied."

"Time is on our side," Harriet said. However, she would've rather started the return trip to the north than spend more time in Miadar with disgruntled slave owners who decided to take the law into their own hands. Not that she thought local law enforcement would punish the slave owners for any actions they would take against the Quakers and any runaway they caught.

By the third night, Harriet offered her deepest gratitude to Jondrin and Akolkun and bid them farewell. Satchel across a shoulder and her four male passengers primed and ready, she struck out for Pheghro Neck. Unfortunately, she left with no new information about Angerine's and Ben's whereabouts.

Harriet soothed herself by thinking about striking out again after fulfilling her current mission. Until then, she would stay focused and positive.

Ben, who successfully jockeyed to walk beside Harriet, nudged her with his elbow. "How much longer before we reach Weldro?"

Harriet had taken them from Pheghro Neck in Cesthie County, where they walked the roads and countryside through three Cesthie County towns: Drerez, Grulzegg, and Sakthaid. When they reached the border town of Sakthaid, Harriet crossed them into Drethos.

They cheered when the men realized they had made it out of Miadar. Harriet had only smiled before encouraging them to "Keep going."

"That little town behind us is Baniz. No safe houses, so we didn't stop." Harriet wouldn't tell them that the two stationmasters in Baniz had been caught and imprisoned a month earlier. Whether from betrayal or bad luck, Harriet did not know. She also felt a growing sense of unease the longer they walked the solitary road. "I'll feel better when we reach Weldro."

"How far is that?" Ben asked, elbowing her again as if they were best friends on a pleasant excursion.

While Harriet appreciated Ben's lighthearted attitude, the flutters in her stomach grew with each step she took.

"Weldro is about thirty miles up the road. It's the last city in Drethos before we cross into Pyzai."

Henry, who'd spent most of the journey in quiet contemplation but managed to maneuver himself to walk on her other side, flanking her with

Ben, spoke into the unseasonably chilly May air. "We've made good time, right?"

They had because Harriet plotted a linear route for them to take. But her stomach kept going flutter, flutter. She stopped.

"What's wrong?" Ben asked.

She closed her eyes and listened to a voice she knew as well as her own. *"Harriet, you need to stop here. Leave the road and take a left turn."*

"This way." Harriet rushed from the dark road into knee-high grass. *"Turn here."* She did but dropped to her knees when she heard the telltale *clippety-clop* of hooves.

Her passengers followed her to the grass, plastering their bellies to the ground.

But Harriet lifted her head level with the grass. She wanted to see the threat her fluttering stomach and God had warned was coming her way. A group of five Dragonkin men on horseback lumbered up the road. Their heads swiveled in all directions, searching the darkness with predatory intent.

Satisfied no one but them lurked, they proceeded up the road, riding at a staid pace.

Once the Dragonkin were out of sight, Harriet did not immediately move. She waited and listened, wondering if another group would follow the first or whether the five Dragonkin would double back, having only pretended not to see Harriet and the others hiding in the grass.

She tapped each man on the back, letting them know she was ready to move out. Harriet remained crouched, moving in a leftward direction as God had told her. Within minutes, she reached a stream.

"I don't see a boat," William whispered.

Neither did Harriet, but she stood to get a better look. The stream was down a small hill, but she saw nothing that would make crossing the tidewater easy. "No bridge either." She turned to the men. Their expressions ranged from defeated to fearful. She understood but wouldn't allow them to halt her train. "We crossin'."

James bit his lip and shook his head, two responses that wouldn't change Harriet's decision. "We don't know how deep that water goes. I can't swim. Can y'all?"

"I can't," Henry quickly answered.

Ben's and William's responses mirrored Henry's, which wasn't surprising, considering the vast number of things runaways were not allowed to learn or engage in.

"And you, Ms. Harriet? Can you swim?"

Ignoring James's question, Harriet guaranteed her satchel was secure across her shoulder and then took off down the hill. "I ain't arguin' with you. And I ain't goin' back to that road. I'm crossin' that stream with or without you."

Harriet had complete faith in God. Her God would not have protected her from the slave catchers only to lead her to a stream she couldn't cross safely. So, Harriet inhaled deeply and walked into the frigid water on faith.

Unlike her brothers and even Linah, Harriet wasn't blessed with an impressive height. So, she should've been afraid when the water height steadily increased the deeper into the stream she walked. She should've been even more frightened when the cold water reached her shoulders. But she wasn't because the moment she stepped into the stream, the stomach flutters that warned her of pending danger stopped.

Weighed down by her overcoat and satchel but made lighter by her absolute faith, Harriet crossed the small tidewater stream.

Ironically, James was the first of the four men to cross the stream after Harriet.

They were soaked to the bone but otherwise safe and sound.

HARRIET'S ESCAPE:

The men waded in with newfound confidence when she reached a second stream. Again, James led the men, but Harriet took up the rear.

While the road had been a straight path to Weldro, thirty miles and no more, going left added miles to an already lengthy journey. But the alternative route was safer, so it was a better choice.

Cold and exhausted, the house Harriet saw in the distance felt like a mirage. But a lantern in the window and a ribbon tied around a tree that led to the cabin marked the home as a safe place to stop for weary freedom-seeking travelers.

The free Birdfolk family was a godsend, and Harriet slept well after drying herself and eating a filling meal. The next evening, she struck out again. Her body ached but not from physical exertion.

Ben walked beside her again, but perhaps sensing she wasn't in the mood, he refrained from elbowing her. "You said you ran out of money. But you and Mrs. Ketebbie disappeared in the back room. What did you give her for hidin' and feedin' us?"

Even if this Ben had been her brother Ben Jr., Harriet would not have revealed her form of payment to him for Mrs. Ketebbie's kindness. Some things were best left between women. But traveling without undergarments after wading through two cold streams likely explained the sickness she felt working its way through her body.

Still, Harriet pushed on, arriving at William Skeshru's office a day and a half later. She sank into one of his chairs, barely able to speak above a hoarse whisper.

Harriet was used to being laid up in bed for months at a time. But she'd never had pneumonia, and the illness had so thoroughly knocked her off her feet that any plans she had of returning to Dralox County were put on hold for five long months.

Chapter 36

It's My Life to Risk

1856

Dominion of Cothru
St. Cegri

Harriet would forever be grateful for Robert. He'd taken care of her during her months-long battle with a respiratory illness that had taken her off her feet. She hadn't been able to work, much less travel to the Eastern Shore.

"Thank you." Harriet accepted her brother's arm as he helped her walk from her downstairs bedroom and down a dimly lit hallway to her living room. She settled into a chair before the warm fireplace with Robert's assistance.

"You don't have to do this." As he did each time he put Harriet to bed, Robert tucked her quilt around her. He swathed her in a way he hadn't been around to do for his daughter, Harriet.

In three months, Robert's daughter will be two years old. I've failed him and Rachel. I can't find their families to bring them north. My mind and spirit are willin' to continue for as long as it takes, but I'm a slave to my sick body. Sometimes, I just can't make it do right.

"I'm feelin' better."

"Barely. Your voice is weak, and you've lost weight. And here you thinkin' about goin' south again." Robert knelt beside Harriet's chair. "You push yourself to exhaustion and sickness. You've done more than anyone has a right to ask of you."

"Rachel, Mary, and the children ain't here with us. Momma and Poppa ain't here. How do you feel about that?"

"You know how I feel. But my selfishness has me riskin' my sister's life."

"It's my life to risk, Robert. Every time I return to Dralox County, it's for me, too. I want us all out of there and as free as possible. Now, Poppa has taken to helpin' runaways since he and Momma moved to Pheghro Neck. With all the uproar down there over slaves fleein', it's only a matter of time before the law comes for our poppa."

Robert's hand settled on Harriet's knee. She wished he hadn't covered her hands with the quilt because she would've liked to offer her brother the same physical comfort he'd granted her every day of her illness.

He ain't wrong. I'm still weak, and words don't sound like they should comin' out my mouth. But I've come to terms with havin' a weak constitution.

I won't pretend it ain't slowed me down, but on my good, strong days, I've done more than I thought possible after bein' struck by that weight. I know what the good Lord has put me here to do, and it ain't to be stuck in a bed, on a farm, or in a big city livin' life as a sickly shut-in. I'm meant to help who I can, when I can, and how I can. That's my callin'.

"You know I only take on missions God consents to. If he disapproves, I don't go. Let the man in, Robert, and we'll listen to his story together."

"I will, but it ain't right that these fugitives always come here. We all have a sad story, Harriet—a spouse, parent, or child we want to be rescued. Here you can barely talk and walk, and they still come." Robert pushed to his feet, his perpetual frown since leaving Mary and their children an outward manifestation of his broken heart. "I don't like it, but I can't protect you from yourself if you won't let me."

As with many of their disagreements, Harriet let her silence serve as an answer enough, just as she accepted Robert's bouts of melancholia. They were both too set in their ways, Harriet thirty-five and Robert forty, to change who they fundamentally were, including the scars enslavement had left on their bodies and their minds.

Harriet glanced around the living room. Although she didn't have much money, she managed to secure basic furniture for the home's common areas, including four chairs for the living room.

She laughed, realizing she sat in the solitary chair in the room. "You're awful," she told her brother.

"If he can't sit and get comfortable, he won't stay long. It's this, or he stays outside. Cothru is colder than any Miadar winter we've experienced, and you ain't well enough to go out. So go on and talk, but you'll do it in here, in front of that blazin' fire, and for as long as I can stomach listenin' to a stranger pull on your heartstrings."

HARRIET'S ESCAPE:

I can't find fault with his words. Cothru hasn't been kind to Birdfolk unused to this frigid weather. It gets into your bones and lungs and won't let go. Too many of our young ones haven't survived one of Cothru's wicked winters. This place sure ain't heaven, but it also ain't the hell we lived in the south. Robert knows that as much as anybody who's come here askin' for my help. I throw myself on my benefactors' altar, seekin' their help when I can't do it alone. I couldn't afford most of my missions south if not for them. There's no shame in askin' others to do for you what you can't do for yourself. Why can't Robert see that I ain't so different from the people who want me to save pieces of their hearts?

"Thank you, Robert. I promise to rest afterward."

Neither pleased by her conciliatory words nor put off by them, Robert's frown remained, but he nodded and left to retrieve her guest.

It didn't take long for her brother to return with a Birdfolk male barely taller than Harriet. But his small stature did not diminish the size of his request.

"Keep your visit brief, Paul. As you can see, my sister is unwell." Robert posted himself behind Harriet's chair like a disgruntled overseer. Still, his displeasure at having people in their home like Paul had never inflamed Robert's temper.

Robert is a good man. Because of Mary and the children, I think he's forgotten. Takin' care of me won't make him feel better about his decision to leave his family behind. Robert left, but Rachel refused to. They both right, and they both wrong. When a slave, there ain't any easy answers. It all makes us bleed in places we can't see, but we feel the pain like a hot poker taken to our skin.

As Robert had done earlier, Paul knelt before Harriet. He was so close she could run her hands through his gold and black head feathers. While most Sankofa bird shifters had a combination of human hair and feathers on their heads, some possessed intricate circular designs on their bare scalp where human hair would typically grow. A miniature version of their bird's head grew from the top of their human head.

He has two sets of eyes, and they both are lookin' at me as if I'm an angel from on high.

"I've been wantin' to meet the great Moses for a long time."

Harriet still hadn't gotten used to the moniker. The implications and expectations fit like one of John's oversized shirts she used to wear. It did not help that she had a brother with the same name who could not have been further from the prophet Moses than a pig was from a spider.

"I hate to come to you like this when you ain't feelin' on top. But it's been seven years, and I don't know what else to do to help my Tilly."

Unlike William Skeshru, who recorded the names of every fugitive he helped, Harriet didn't have the means to do the same. So, she relied on her memory to chronicle each person she helped to free from bondage. Each name was worth remembering because their lives had value beyond that of being someone's property.

"Is Tilly your wife?" Harriet asked, having heard Paul say the woman's name sweetly.

"Fiancée, if she'll still have me after all this time. I was gonna be sold south, so I ran, leavin' Bodan and Tilly. I told her I would be back, but one year went by and then the next, with me failin' her three times."

Harriet listened as Paul described his escape to Cothru and failed attempts to rescue the woman he loved. Harriet had heard similar stories, and she and her brothers were identical. But each shared tale of a precious loved one left behind was like a stew with distinct ingredients: sadness, guilt, shame, and desperation.

The flavor didn't suit anyone's palate, including Harriet's.

"I set aside money for the trip. I hope it'll be enough."

From past experience, most had come to her with nothing but lint in their pockets. Others, like Paul, underestimated the cost. But Harriet gratefully accepted all contributions, so she wasn't surprised when Robert's hand snaked around her chair.

"What you askin', payin' Harriet's steamboat fare is the least you can do. But she's still sick, so you've got time to add to this. I'll hold on to it until she's ready to go. If she changes her mind, come see me to get it back."

Harriet wouldn't change her mind, but she wasn't yet well enough to plan and carry out another trip south. "Tell me everything I need to know."

1856
The State of Pyzai
Pholgre City

Harriet wore her best traveling clothes and carried a new, used carpetbag. Because she disliked idleness, she would practice braiding and plaiting her hair whenever she was bedridden. While she hadn't mastered the art as well as Rit, Harriet's skill had improved enough to convince anyone she was a respectable freeborn Birdfolk woman.

She pulled her shawl tighter around her shoulders and tried not to breathe too much cool October air. Being on the Calgro Bay wasn't ideal for Harriet, who had only recovered from her long bout of pneumonia a week ago. If Robert had his way, she wouldn't be on the steamboat, going from Pholgre to Bodan to retrieve Tilly.

But she'd made a promise to Paul, and just because John had broken his vow to her did not mean Harriet scorned the sacred institution of marriage. It would do her heart good if she could reunite the couple.

So, she'd traveled from Cothru to Pholgre and purchased passage aboard the Ericsson Line. The Bodan and Pholgre Steamboat Company owned the steamboat, and the narrow propeller ships operated between the two cities through the Calgro and Drethos Canal.

I would be warmer inside than on deck. But I want to get a good look at the certificate the steamboat captain gave me.

People milled about the deck, enjoying the sunny autumn day after yesterday's heavy rainfall. Harriet had ridden on enough trains and boats that her stomach no longer betrayed her, but she still preferred land and her own two feet. Still, nothing compared to the speed of modern travel, so Harriet wouldn't look a gift horse in the mouth.

She opened her carpetbag and pulled out the certificate. According to the steamboat captain, a brother of the Dragonkin who had helped Kessiah's family escape the Cosaru courthouse, the document contained a fictitious name. It claimed she was a freeborn resident of Pholgre.

I wish what's written on this paper were true, but I can't even read it. I gotta trust the faith I placed in the captain.

However, being illiterate did not prevent Harriet from staring at the fake certificate as the steamboat sailed smoothly down Calgro Bay. She ran her fingers over letters she couldn't name and words she had no hope of deciphering.

If I stayed seated for more than five minutes, maybe I could find somebody to teach me my letters. Frederick learned his after stealin' himself away. It sure would make plannin' these missions easier if I could read. Maybe I've gone too long without learnin' how.

"Excuse me," a woman said, "is this seat taken?"

More passengers had made their way onto the deck, filling in vacant seats and enjoying the scenery. But there were four vacant seats near where

Harriet sat, so she would've preferred if the woman had chosen any place other than directly beside her.

Worse, Harriet recognized the Dragonkin woman's voice.

Lord, you stay testin' me on my missions. I was lost in thought and didn't see her until she was right up on me.

Harriet shoved her certificate into her carpetbag and, almost as quickly, grabbed the newspaper from the seat in front of her. She snapped it open and held it up to her face.

"The seat isn't taken Mis . . ." Harriet clamped her mouth shut, so close to calling the woman "Mistress Sorekoh."

"The seat is free, miss."

If Harriet dared to concentrate, she could recall each beating she'd received from the Dragonkin beside her.

Of all the people I could've encountered, it had to be one of my former masters. She didn't recognize me. Maybe time hasn't been as kind to her memory as it has been to mine. Or the nicer clothes and neat hair make me look different. My skin color isn't as dark as she probably remembers. I ain't been toilin' in the sun, but I can't be too careful. I doubt the years have smoothed out her prickly edges.

Stilling her trembling hands, Harriet held the newspaper in front of her, shielding her face from Mistress Sorekoh. She didn't know whether she held the newspaper right side up, but she was committed to the ploy and wouldn't be swayed from her path.

Within minutes, the remaining seats around her were taken by others. Whether they sought fresh air from the stuffy cabin below or wanted to take advantage of the beautiful day, Harriet neither knew nor cared. As long as Mistress Sorekoh remained beside her, Harriet would continue to play the role of an educated Birdfolk who would rather read about the events of the day than make small talk with a Dragonkin who, under different circumstances, would sell her to the highest bidder.

There Harriet sat, newspaper concealing her face and arms fatigued for how long she'd been forced to hold the paper in the air. But when she felt the first rain droplet, she thanked the good Lord for sparing her.

Mistress Sorekoh was the first to retreat to the cabin below, followed by the others and Harriet. That had been a close call. Unfortunately, it would not be the last one of the mission.

The State of Miadar
Bodan City

Luckily for all involved, Tilly was owned by the same Dragonkin couple and resided in the same Bodan City home as when Paul had last seen her seven years earlier. Otherwise, tracking a single Birdfolk female in a city that boasted the largest number of Birdfolk outside of the Deep South would've made Harriet's mission even more challenging.

Paul's direction to the single-family home where Tilly served a Dragonkin couple and their four children was easy to find. Paul was also a skilled artist, so his drawings of the neighborhood and Tilly proved invaluable.

It hadn't taken Harriet more than a couple of hours of watching the house to spot the woman she'd come there to rescue.

"Tilly likes to begin her day off with an early mornin' stroll," Paul had told her. "She's always been quiet and obedient, keepin' her real thoughts to herself. Because of this, her masters trust her to go where she wants on her day off. When I was there, it meant her spendin' time with me. Unless somethin' changed, Tilly is a creature of habit. You'll find her leavin' the house early Sunday mornin'."

From the opposite side of the street, Harriet followed Tilly. The sun had barely peeked its head in the sky when Tilly was out of the house. She didn't walk with the quickness of a slave running an errand, no more than she ambled along as if she had nowhere to be and nothing to do. Like so many house slaves Harriet had known, Tilly walked with a strained confidence that came with the frightening isolation of living in close quarters with their owners.

She'd heard slaves bicker over whether field hands or house slaves had it the worst, with field hands concluding that working in the master's house was better than tilling the field. As an enslaved woman who'd had the displeasure of experiencing both, Harriet found such arguments both pointless and divisive.

Like Paul, a small version of the head of her Sankofa bird grew from the front of her head. An orange beak led to gray feathers that surrounded two red bird eyes. The gray bled into orange-red feathers that extended from the base of the bird's head and down the center of her head. Unlike Paul, whose intricate circular patterns replaced his human hair, Tilly had a full head of curly brown hair that grew upward toward the center line of lovely orange-red feathers.

Tilly rounded a corner, and Harriet crossed to her side of the street. If Harriet had been a slave catcher, Tilly's lack of awareness would've had the woman caught and sent back to her masters. Considering Harriet was there to steal Tilly away, she tucked her newfound information about the woman away for the journey to come.

Ten quick strides had Harriet beside Tilly. "Paul sent me. No, don't look at me. Keep walkin'. I'm here to get you away from here. Nod once if that's what you want."

While Paul may have paid for Harriet's passage to Bodan, employing her to "bring Tilly to Cothru," the decision wasn't his to make but the woman he hadn't seen in seven years.

The woman didn't nod, which Harriet was prepared to take as nonverbal consent. Instead, Tilly burst into tears, which Harriet interpreted as a heartfelt acceptance.

"I'm gonna steal you away, Tilly, so follow me."

Harriet had intentionally waited until it was Tilly's day off to approach her just as she'd planned on taking her away on the same day if she agreed.

Harriet led the way, talking as she led them toward Bodan's dock. "There's a steamboat leavin' today that we'll be on. I can't risk takin' you straight north. I can't pay for a bond, and I don't have freedom papers for you to show if we're stopped."

"What we gonna do? I'm Tilly, but I suppose Paul would've told you that."

"He did. I'm Harriet."

"Thank you, Ms. Harriet. I'd almost given up hope."

On Paul or on gainin' her freedom? Tilly waited seven years, and my John couldn't give me two. I was a fool, but even now, I can't regret lovin' him.

"A southbound route," Tilly squeaked when Harriet paid their fares. "B-but, Ms. Harriet, that's the wrong direction, ain't it?"

"Walk like you belong, Tilly. Chin high and shoulders straight. Good. Now follow behind that Dragonkin onto the steamboat. I'm right behind you."

Thankfully, Tilly was as compliant as Paul had said, despite the wellspring of feelings Harriet sensed boiling in the woman.

Harriet placed the palm of her hand in the center of Tilly's back, encouraging her to follow the other passengers while gently comforting her.

This must be overwhelmin' for her. It was for me the first time, and I didn't give her much time to process. I couldn't, not if I wanted to make this boat and get her away from Bodan as soon as possible. The next scheduled steamboat wouldn't have had him as the captain.

From underneath her lashes, Harriet saw the tall, lean figure of the steamboat's captain as she guided Tilly onto the vessel. The Dragonkin stood to the left of the entryway, smiling and greeting people as they piled onto his boat. His acknowledgment of Harriet was no different than what he offered every other passenger—polite professionalism.

"Come on." Harriet grasped Tilly's hand. As she expected, it was as cold as ice and shook with faint tremors.

Tilly bent to whisper in Harriet's ear. "Are you sure about this? We're surrounded by Dragonkin."

Harriet lightly squeezed Tilly's hand while scanning the open cabin for an ideal location to spend the trip to the city of Sedriz in Drethos. Harriet preferred to have a wall to her back so she wouldn't have to worry about someone sneaking up on her from behind. When she had passengers with her, Harriet had learned it was best to have them seated separately yet close enough they could use hand signals to communicate.

But when she had passengers as skittish as Tilly, Harriet understood the greater danger was leaving their side, leaving them with the false impression of being alone. So, Harriet found them two seats in the last row on the right side of the cabin. With Bodan being the most populous city on the route, a steady stream of passengers filled the space.

However, unlike Harriet, most seemed uninterested in claiming a seat so far from the exit.

She leaned against the window wall, still feeling the motion from the last steamboat and the tiring echoes from her illness. Harriet closed her eyes. "We're gonna go south to go north. Nobody cares about two Birdfolk women travelin' south because can't nobody see the sense in goin' the opposite way if freedom is your goal."

"South to go north? It does sound crazy."

"I don't need you to trust me, Tilly. I just need you to do as I say. For now, I need you to keep an eye out while I take a quick nap."

Harriet seldom knew when an episode would overtake her, but she recognized patterns. Fatigue and strong emotions were the most significant predictors of an episode. Considering Harriet hadn't slept more than a few hours since leaving Cothru, an episode was sure to rear its ugly head, so Harriet thought to cut it off at the pass.

"Don't let me sleep too long. I got a captain to talk to."

"Yes, Ms. Harriet."

Harriet peeked at Tilly with a partially opened eye. The woman couldn't have been much older than her. But she reminded Harriet of the woman whose hanging she'd been forced to watch. Not that Harriet had known the poor executed woman, but she had imagined all the oppressive acts that had taken place in her harpy masters' household that had driven the woman to murder. Like Tilly, that woman had probably also been quiet and compliant on the outside while controlling a raging tempest within her.

But storms couldn't be contained. Eventually, everything in their explosive path would feel its impact.

Harriet settled into her nap, relieved Tilly's path had led her to Harriet instead of murder and a hangman's noose.

An hour later, Harriet and Tilly were on the deck speaking with the captain. They weren't secreted away in his personal cabin or hiding in a dark corner of the boat. Instead, they strolled the length of the deck, weaving between other passengers and speaking in tones low enough not to draw attention.

It was hard to believe there was a set of Dragonkin parents who had raised not one but three sons who grew up to sympathize with the enslaved people of Ungathu. Stranger still was that Harriet had the good fortune of benefiting from their anti-slavery stance.

Hands clasped behind his back, Captain Takshon grumbled a curse. "You want me to do what?"

"Tilly needs a travel pass. Somethin', anything that says she is free to travel."

"Your reputation precedes you. What makes you think I can create something like that?"

For every one step the ten-foot-tall captain took, Harriet was forced to take three. "Are you sayin' you can't do somethin' your younger brother can?"

Captain Takshon's loud laughter garnered looks from passersby but nothing more than inquisitively raised eyebrows.

Beside her, she felt Tilly tense, but the woman kept pace and silent.

"A war is brewing, and now that I've met you, when the time comes, the side of the righteous will need brave Birdfolk like you. How often do you play on my kind's ego?"

Harriet thought it best not to answer Captain Takshon's question. Instead, she requested a second and a third time during their less-than-leisurely stroll. It had taken another nap and three more conversations before the captain consented.

"Remember your promise," Captain Takshon told Harriet when she'd passed him on her way off the steamboat.

"What promise?" Tilly asked. Her exhausted eyes were a shade of red, prompting Harriet to enter the nearest Sedriz hotel.

While Harriet had established Underground Railroad routes that took her through Drethos, she had never hidden in plain sight. Carpetbag in hand and shoes worn almost down to the sole, Harriet walked to the registration desk, conjured every ounce of her needed bravery, looked the harpy front desk worker in the eye, and lied without a stutter or flinch.

"My name is Charlotte Golie. I'd like to have dinner for two sent to my room." Harriet stared at the harpy with the confidence she'd seen Dragonkin display her entire life. Most people lived their lives with the absolute belief they had a God-given right to possess anything they desired. Harriet couldn't imagine holding such a belief system, but she could not deny its effectiveness.

"Charlotte Golie, you said?"

"Yes." Harriet waved for Tilly to stand beside her. "This is Lucy. We require two dinners brought to our room."

"Charlotte, Lucy, and dinner. Yes, ma'am. I'll, ummm, I'll take care of the lodging first, then have someone bring you tonight's dinner."

Treating people like servants, even if for a worthy cause, made Harriet sick to her stomach. "Thank you. I appreciate your kindness."

Harriet also appreciated Robert for following up with Paul and his financial contribution to Tilly's rescue. Otherwise, her plan could not have included an overnight hotel stay.

Harriet flopped onto the bed. The room wasn't as lovely as Norveis's guest room, nor was the food as delicious as the harpy's cooking. But the hotel was clean, warm, and infinitely better than sleeping outdoors and eating off the land.

She rolled over and sat up on the edge of the bed, reminded that there was one bed and two of them. Harriet hadn't shared a bed with anyone since being with John, not even the ever-flirting Majors. Harriet removed her shoes and dress. Each movement felt like wading through waist-deep water, her limbs heavy and weak.

The bed on the opposite side dipped when Tilly joined her. "You've done this for others. I can tell. You didn't blink or break a sweat. Not when gettin' us on the steamboat or askin' a Dragonkin to make me a pass I don't have any business havin'. Not even when you bulled that harpy into givin' us this room."

"You think I bullied her?" That hadn't exactly been Harriet's intention. She'd been bullied all her enslaved life by one master after another. It wasn't a good feeling, and it didn't sit well with her that she'd done the same to another, even if to a far lesser extent.

Tilly laughed, and Harriet turned to see that the woman was already undressed and beneath the quilt. "That's all you got from what I said. Barely bullyin'. But Birdfolk gotta be bigger than themselves to get any respect. Work twice as hard to get half as much as everybody else."

"Less than half."

"It's sad, ain't it?"

It was deplorable, but Harriet knew no other way to survive this harsh world than with hard work and grit. She reclined on the bed, not bothering to crawl under the quilt as Tilly had.

"Harriet, why did you do this for a stranger?"

She shifted onto her side, seeing Tilly beside her but also seeing Rachel. "Because Paul asked."

"Only that? Are the two of you friends?"

"I barely know him. But that's not the kind of knowin' that's important. He loves you, feels guilty for leaving you behind, and wants you to have your freedom."

"Paul said all of that?"

After seven years apart, she says his name with so much love. They chose well. I wish them many happy years together. For that to happen, I gotta finish this mission.

"That and more. Tilly, I know the feel of bein' too tired to sleep because your mind is whirlin'. I can tell you want to talk, but—"

"Sleep, Harriet. I'm capable of keepin' my own company. I'll watch over you until you fall asleep."

She's as sweet as Rachel. Rachel. Rachel.

Harriet drifted off to sleep with thoughts of her still-enslaved sister making for a fitful rest.

Perhaps if she'd had a good night's sleep, Harriet would've spotted the slave dealer before he had waylaid their exit from the hotel.

The Dragonkin grabbed Tilly's arm, spinning her to face him. "You aren't going anywhere but with me. You're both under arrest."

Tilly tugged and tugged, waging a battle she couldn't win. But Harriet took stock of her surroundings. It was early morning, so most guests were still in their rooms. But the harpy front desk worker from yesterday looked on silently, likely unsure whether she should intervene.

Harriet disliked crowds, except when she needed to blend into one. Crowds brought more attention to people like her, and groups often fueled terrible behavior. But the slave dealer was alone, and Harriet was calm, even if Tilly's tugging was working her into a near fit of hysterics.

"Sir," Harriet said, employing the same confident tone she'd used with the harpy front desk worker but tempered because she spoke to a Dragonkin with the power to detain and arrest her, "we have travel papers."

From an intimidating height of thirteen feet, the Dragonkin with eyes the color of winter moss glared at her. "Don't make me grab ahold of you, too. You're both coming with me."

Harriet pulled the forged certificates from her satchel. Instead of handing them over to the Dragonkin, she unfolded the documents and held them up for his inspection.

Tilly still attempted to free herself from the man's hold. Her eyes grew wider and wilder, filling with tears with each ineffectual tug.

"Charlotte and Lucy, huh?" The Dragonkin snarled the names he'd read off the certificates, and Harriet met his angry glare with a contemptuous smile. He shoved Tilly away. "The next time you take lodging at a respectable hotel, you better show your certificate."

Harriet didn't believe in coincidences. She peered over her shoulder toward the front desk. Unsurprisingly, the harpy from yesterday had disappeared.

Harriet laced her fingers with Tilly's. "Thank you for the advice, sir. We'll be on our way."

A block from the hotel, Harriet stopped and breathed for what felt like the first time since being confronted by the Dragonkin slave dealer.

Tilly threw herself at Harriet, nearly tumbling them to the ground. "I thought we'd been found out. I didn't know what to say or do. I ain't been nowhere but Bodan and I don't wanna see that place and my masters ever again."

Harriet returned Tilly's embrace. She didn't care that they stood on a street corner and that people passed them with inquiring looks, no more than she minded Tilly's warm display of gratitude. But Harriet also did not want to linger in case the slave dealer decided to ignore their certificates and come after them. It wasn't unheard of for slave dealers to disregard Birdfolk's freedom papers—selling them into slavery and reaping the money from the illegal sale.

"Let's go," Harriet told Tilly, "we got a train to catch."

Thankfully, the train ride to Chosnos and the fifty-mile carriage ride to Weldro proved uneventful. It had taken Harriet a month to reach this point in her mission. She was happy to accept another hug from Tilly when she turned the woman over to a local free Birdfolk conductor who would see her the rest of the way to Cothru and Paul.

Tired but not yet done, Tubman happily accepted the twenty-five dollars from the other conductor, pleased one of her benefactors had provided enough money for Harriet to return to Dralox County to rescue Rachel, Ben, and Angerine.

While there was no rest for the weary, there was also no luck in Harriet's trip to Berzogtown. Yet, by the following year, God had spoken again to Harriet, leaving her with two foreboding truths.

Her father would be arrested for aiding runaways if she did not act.

Getting her parents out of Cesthie County would be her deadliest mission.

Chapter 37

You've Become Somethin' Else

1857
Cesthie County
Pheghro Neck

The sun had set hours ago, bringing a deep chill that made Miadar in May feel more like waning winter. But Harriet would take an unseasonably cold spring over almost any day in St. Cegri.

She used the reins to encourage the oxen's movement to the left and onto a dark, empty road that would take her to a cabin she'd never seen before. But the area wasn't unfamiliar to Harriet. She'd come to this part of Pheghro Neck when she'd spent three months searching for Rachel's children. She hadn't found Angerine and Ben, but Harriet had extended her Underground Network to include Pheghro Neck's free Birdfolk community.

Her parents had chosen well when they decided to move away from Pelduth Neck and to this community, but Miadar wasn't as it had been when Harriet fled nearly eight years ago, and neither was the country.

The state of slavery was changing, not only through Birdfolk's resistance and the growth of abolitionism but also the aggressive response by supporters of the slave system to the challenges to their way of life.

It's like water in a pot on an open fire. With time and more heat, the water will boil over. If I don't get Momma and Poppa out of the fire before that happens, they'll get burned. I won't let that happen. I should've come sooner, but I'm here now. Thank you, Lord, for gettin' me here before it's too late.

Harriet stopped the ox-drawn cart in front of the last cabin in a row of seven homes. Small vegetable gardens separated one house from the next. On her way up the road, Harriet had spotted a much larger garden, which was likely a communal plot for the residents of the seven cabins. Such collaborative practices guaranteed no one went hungry.

She shook her head at seeing a lit lantern in her parents' front window. *I don't have to look far to know where I got my stubbornness. They know I'm comin', but they still welcomin' runaways. I just hope ain't nobody else in there with them. My stomach has been flutterin' somethin' strong ever since I crossed into Cesthie County. The good Lord is warnin' me, but I can't turn back. If I do, I know I'll lose my parents. I know that as sure as I know somethin' is out there. But all I can do is push on with my plan and pray the good Lord will see me through again.*

HARRIET'S ESCAPE:

Satchel in her hand, Harriet hopped from the cart. But she didn't immediately move to her parents' cabin. Seeing Rit and Ben again had been all she had thought about since leaving St. Cegri. The idea of reuniting with them filled her heart with joy nearly as much as the swell of gratitude for their decades-long strength and resilience.

My actions have hurt them. My leavin'. My takin' away their sons. Now they gotta abandon Miadar, the only home they've known. At their age, it can't be easy to uproot themselves and go somewhere new and unknown. But that's why I'm here. I can't guarantee they'll be happy in St. Cegri, but I know they won't survive if they stay here. I gotta warm myself with that comfort.

Harriet stepped on the porch and raised her fist to knock on the door, but it swung open. A woman she hadn't seen in nearly eight years stood before her. At seventy, Harriet "Rit" Wren was a sight for sore eyes. Her hair, which had been a lovely mix of silver and brown the last time Harriet had seen her mother, was all silver. The silver grew like the most magnificent vines between Rit's luxurious pink and peach head feathers.

Dark circles punctuated dark brown eyes and skin blessed by the sun shone with a smoothed but weathered glow. Rit's shoulders were less round than Harriet remembered, the veins in her hands more pronounced, and her facial features sharper.

"I'm sorry" was all Harriet could think to say. The longer she observed Rit, the more she could document the passage of time on her mother's body. "I'm sorry." This wasn't how Harriet had envisioned greeting her mother after so long without seeing her. "I'm so sorry, Momma."

Harriet had assumed there would be sadness at their forced separation. Yet, she thought that emotion would be tempered by the greater feeling of happiness. However, what she did not anticipate was the soul-splitting sense of guilt.

The emotion welled up in her like so many times she'd been forced to take to her sickbed, overcome with debilitating illness wrapped in a constant thrum of exhaustion.

Harriet wept, falling into her mother's arms like the child Minty she'd once been. Back then, when Minty had been returned to Rit, knocking on death's door, her mother had planted herself before that door and told God he'd have to wait because she belonged first to Rit and second to him.

She didn't know how she managed to get inside the cabin, crying like a baby and hanging over her mother. "I'm sorry," she repeated because it hurt to see the years she missed etched in every age line on her mother's face.

"First Rit, and now you. A man can take but so many tears from the women in his family." Ben wrapped his long arms around Harriet and Rit, pulling them to him in a tight embrace. "Look at what you've done."

Forehead buried against Rit's shoulder, Harriet needn't have seen her father to know he also cried.

Being squeezed between weeping parents while she sobbed was not the reunion Harriet expected. But it was the reunion God had granted her, and for that she was grateful.

"My sweet Minty," Rit said, kissing Harriet's cheeks, "I've missed you so much."

"I've missed you, too. I'm sor—"

"Don't you dare apologize again." Rit stepped back, forcing them to disentangle from each other. Red, wet eyes met Harriet's, and her heart lurched because she could see how deeply Rit had missed her. "If you didn't go, I wouldn't be seein' you now. If you didn't go, growin' beyond Dralox County but never forgettin' where you came from and to whom you truly belong, all my boys would've been sold off. Ben and I would've been left with nothin' but a hole where our hearts used to be."

Rit grasped Harriet's hand and squeezed.

"Momma, I—"

"There's plenty of hurt to go around. None is your fault. Not the way you mean, anyway. But when Ben started openin' our home to runaways, I saw the fire in them to be free. They came to Ben and trusted him because they'd heard about you. I didn't know the woman they called Moses. All I know is Minty and Harriet. But you've become somethin' else. Somethin' more. And now you're here to take us away, too."

Rit had spoken the last sentence with a similar amount of homesickness Harriet had felt before she'd fled the Tozor Plantation, leaving her family and friends behind, unsure if she would see any of them again.

"I don't force anyone to come with me. And I won't begin with my parents." Harriet smiled from Rit to Ben, who, like her mother, had changed in ways she imagined wouldn't have seemed so stark if she'd been there as the gradual aging had taken place. But she had seen Ben two and a half years earlier, so she had time to adjust. "If the scuttlebutt is true, and I haven't any reason not to believe it, the law is suspicious of Poppa and will come for him soon enough."

Harriet watched Ben retrieve his old, well-cared-for broadaxe from beside a feather bed tick. She could easily envision Ben sleeping on the outside of the bed tick, his prized broadaxe within quick reach. If the law came for him, though, there would be little Ben could do to protect himself or Rit, no matter the sharpness of the axe's blade.

"I got a bag already packed. I'm takin' this, too."

Harriet wouldn't argue over Ben's emotional attachment to his broadaxe, but she did frown when Rit released her hands and began to roll up the bed tick.

"Momma, that ain't gonna fit on the cart."

"Oh, you got us a cart. What kind of cart?" Rit asked from where she knelt on the floor, the bed tick halfway rolled.

Harriet blinked at Rit, realizing that her mother thought Harriet had planned for them to walk and that a tick bed would be reasonable to bring with her.

"I could only manage an ox-drawn cart. It's big enough for you two and a couple of bags." Harriet knelt beside Rit and placed her hand on the bed tick. "I'm sorry, but you gotta choose somethin' smaller to take. This won't fit."

"Then I'll walk, and you put this in the cart."

"I won't have my seventy-year-old momma walkin'. And that feathered bed still won't fit, no matter what you say."

Instead of responding, Rit looked over Harriet's head. "Ben, talk some sense into your daughter."

Ben's laughter rippled through the cabin like a warm breeze. "I'd say the kind of sense we Wrens have is fine except when dealin' with each other. Rit, let Harriet do what she came here to do. And, Harriet, understand this move ain't easy on me and your momma. Your heart and feet get tied to a place after so long. This is still our home. The good and the bad. We have friends and family here, but we can't take them with us. So our little belongins are all we have. Your momma knows she can't take that bed tick; she just bein' stubborn because havin' you here makes what we've talked about since gettin' your message real."

Harriet leaned back on her heels, realizing that while material possessions could never replace people, they were tangible reminders that provided emotional comfort. "All I could afford was an old ox and a small cart. I'll sell both when we cross into Drethos to pay for our train fares. Most of my passengers only have what's on their backs. Some don't even have shoes. It ain't fair we gotta leave what little we got behind. Little treasures we've hoarded from our sweat and tears." Harriet patted a hand Rit still had clenched in the feather bed tick. "If I could make this better for you, I would."

"I'm bein' difficult, I know."

"No. You're a woman who has spent her entire life havin' things taken from her and been denied even more. I won't force this on you. But if you decide to come with me, I can't have you lookin' back. That's what I do. I need you to look forward, Momma."

"Forward." Rit released the bed tick. "Except for you kids, I've never looked forward. I'm old. And tired. What if I don't have it in me to be truly free? To start over in a place I know nothin' about?"

Harriet could've replied with one of her patented responses when she had a runaway who sought freedom but feared the unknown. None of her passengers had been as old as her parents, having spent most of their lives enslaved.

Momma and Poppa got married, had children, and raised them as best they could without expectin' to get more out of life. So, they made do, survivin' when others didn't.

But there was more to life than the daily grind to simply exist. Whatever that more was, Harriet desired her parents to have the chance to discover it for themselves.

Yet, when Ben knelt beside Rit and took her hand, stroking the back with loving gentleness, Harriet understood her mother's hesitance.

"I'll keep comin' back for Rachel. I won't leave her here alone."

Harriet pushed to her feet and walked outside. She sat on the porch, disappointed in how long it had taken her to realize the depth of her mother's hesitancy.

Once Momma and Poppa are gone, Rachel will be by herself. But if I can find Angerine and Ben, I can take them all north. Still, I've failed at every turn. *No matter how many times I've returned, Angerine and Ben ain't never with Rachel. How old are they now? Ten and eight. That's plenty old to be laborin' in someone's house.*

Harriet lowered her forehead to her bent knees, feeling a foreboding flutter in her stomach. The disturbing sensation felt like the mild cramping she got during the last day of her monthly cycle. Unlike the first two days, when her cramps were the worst, the flutters in her stomach wouldn't cease until the danger passed.

The closer the danger, the stronger the flutter. I've never ignored God's warnings this long. I should take heed and deal with this, but not here.

Harriet stood and glanced around. Despite the neighbors having freedom, they still worked six days a week, selling their labor for pennies on a dollar. It was a grueling way to make a living in the south and the north. But Harriet had chosen the middle of the workweek purposefully, as she had the lateness of her arrival.

By Wednesday, most would be feeling the edge of having worked two full days, but they would also be looking forward to Sunday if they could only get past the hump of the midweek fatigue.

Harriet returned to the cabin. Her parents sat on the unfurled feather bed tick, each stuffing odds and ends in the cloth sack on their laps.

She shrugged out of her overcoat and boots. Just as quickly, she shook her head at her parents' furrowed brows and open mouths. If she got an opportunity, she would answer their questions later. If not . . . well, Harriet refused to entertain negative thoughts.

"Poppa, I need you to wait five minutes after I leave, then get yourself and Momma out of here on that ox cart. I don't care what's in your bags as long as you've packed the tin box with your freedom papers." She grabbed her satchel and handed it to Ben, who had wasted no time getting to his feet and then helping Rit to hers. "There's a map in there. Follow the route I've drawn. It ain't the best sketch, but it'll do."

Harriet pulled her dress over her head, leaving her in a slip and undergarments. "Momma, hold on to my clothes for me."

"What? Why? What's goin' on?"

She didn't want to frighten her parents, but that was hard to avoid with Harriet's sudden behavior change. "Change of plans. I'm gonna head out first and then catch up. Follow the map. Take whatever you have in those sacks, but nothin' more. Don't push that old ox too hard, but get him movin' as fast as he can. He's stronger than he looks but not as strong as I wished he were."

Her words held a double meaning her parents hadn't missed because the second she'd said them, her mother retrieved Harriet's clothing and boots, and her father grabbed his broadaxe. There was no more discussion about the feather bed tick, no more unspoken guilt of a parent leaving an adult offspring behind, and no more anxiety about stepping into the light of an unknown future.

The flutters in her stomach intensified, squelching any thought she might have had of drawing out what she hoped would not be a final goodbye.

"If you follow that map, I'll be able to find you."

Harriet dashed from the cabin without another word.

If anybody can do this, my parents can. They have more years left in them, and I won't let anybody take them from them.

Instead of running east toward Drethos, the route she'd mapped for her parents, Harriet headed northwest.

I can't outrun what I feel in my gut. But I don't need to. I'll be a distraction enough to give Momma and Poppa time.

Harriet bolted toward the Casse River, a natural barrier separating Tregne and Cesthie counties.

Bare feet pounded against the ground. Harriet darted into the woods and yanked off her slip. She didn't bother with her undergarments. Harriet had already calculated both items as the cost of another mission.

Yet no mission ever had her stomach fluttering like a war was being waged in her belly.

Harriet envisioned her Sankofa form, as Rit had taught her many years ago. She saw her avian body vibrant with colors not found in nature. The transformation overtook her, a life-affirming shift from human to bird, from restrictive to free.

Her clawed feet dug into the grass and propelled her forward with such unbridled strength Harriet cut through the cold May air like a bullet from a pistol. She ran and ran, having forgotten the wondrous sensation of running wild and free as a bird. Harriet had long ago set aside the dream of flight.

Her wings could never be used to fly her to the sun and back, no more than they could transport her away from her life as a slave and to a land that promised freedom.

Harriet rounded a tree, the flutter stronger with each swift step. She ran toward the river, hoping no one would be down there so late at night or so early in the morning.

Harriet ran and ran. In her mind, she saw Linah and Soph. They laughed and cheered her on. Their invisible presence was keenly felt, and Harriet was buoyed by memories of her loving sisters. Their unknown fate had fueled each of her missions, beginning with her own. Their absence hardened her resolve to bring her siblings north and away from their enslaved existence as a piece of a Dragonkin's hoard.

Harriet ran and ran.

And ran.

The river came into view. Quiet and still and ... an elderly naked woman sat by the river's edge. Her waist-length, steel-gray hair sparked like fireflies caught in a cruel child's jar.

Harriet shifted and joined the woman. She looked out at the river. The water was a dark mass of liquid that could be her grave if the woman beside her chose. But this wasn't the meeting she'd expected when God warned her of the danger that lurked thousands of feet in the air.

Harriet handed the woman one of her feathers. "You once said that of my feathers, pink was your favorite."

"I did, indeed. Hello, Minty."

"Hello, Mistress Essodel."

Chapter 38

I Accept God's Will

"You are staring."

"Oh, I'm sorry." Harriet hadn't realized she'd twisted her body so far to the right that she sat facing Mistress Essodel's side. "But, ummm, I've never seen your human form."

Mistress Essodel's human body wasn't as large as Harriet assumed a dragon of her massive size would be. In fact, she could not have been more than seven feet tall, making her human form shorter than any Dragonkin adult Harriet had met. Her skin was as pale as any Dragonkin who'd avoided the sun like it was poison. Her steel-gray hair, backlit like fireflies, was straight and otherwise underwhelming. While Harriet could easily see the rippled effect of muscles underneath Mistress Essodel's white skin, taken together, the dragon looked like a human woman not much older than Rit.

Considering Mistress Essodel was likely thousands of years old, appearing seventy-plus in her human form reinforced the scaled difference between Dragonkin and Birdfolk.

Harriet gulped but didn't turn away from the once-in-a-lifetime sight.

"You are still staring."

"Yes, ma'am, I know. It's hard not to."

Mistress Essodel turned her golden eyes to Harriet. "Are you not afraid? Do I not frighten you, no matter my form?"

"Yes, ma'am, you do. I'm terrified." Harriet lifted her knees to her chest and wrapped her arms around them. She still gazed at Mistress Essodel with awed curiosity. Her mind was a flutter of questions while the flutters in her stomach had ceased to warn of danger. Why bother when Harriet had freely sat beside the deadliest creature she knew?

"What do you see when you look at me? Be honest. I will not kill you for speaking the truth." She parted thin, pink lips, revealing sharp eyeteeth Harriet had no defense against. "But if you lie, if you fail to answer one of my questions without absolute honesty, I will find Ben and Rit, wherever you think you have hidden them, and make you watch me slice them into unrecognizable pieces. Their screams of terror will haunt you for the rest of your days. Do you understand me, little Minty?"

God had gone silent, but he hadn't abandoned her to the vile Dragonkin because Harriet had known who had hunted her. While she hadn't expected to come face-to-face with Mistress Essodel in human form, she had decided to make her final stand at Casse River. If a creek was a good enough final resting place for Barbury's mother, a river should offer Harriet the same atmospheric serenity in her last breaths of life. Yet, she held one truth close to her she'd hoped would save her life. As it was, her life wasn't in danger, but Ben's and Rit's.

"I understand." Although she did not know why, Harriet understood Mistress Essodel's intention was not to pose one question but to have a conversation with Harriet that would include multiple ones. "Yes, ma'am, I'll answer truthfully. I ain't one given much to lyin', anyway."

"Except to protect your loved ones."

"Yes, ma'am. Common sense and self-preservation can make a lie necessary. You askin' me to act against nature, but God didn't put me here to watch you slaughter my parents."

"If I kill Rit and Ben, their blood will be on your head."

Harriet opened her mouth to speak but then paused when Mistress Essodel's gaze hardened to golden slits of warning.

She hadn't been about to lie, but no Birdfolk slave had spoken unfathomable truths to their Dragkonkin master without a quick and severe punishment. However, unlike Minister Breembat, Harriet had never known Mistress Essodel to lie and deceive. She was an awful brute who took pleasure in harming others, but she never pretended to be anything other than who she presented herself as. Simply put, Mistress Essodel did not lie because no one's opinion of her mattered more than how she viewed herself.

"All of God's creations are responsible for their decisions and actions. I'll take that threat as I would any other."

"Which is?"

Harriet shrugged, having no better response than: "I accept God's will."

"Such a naïve, shortsighted creature you are, Minty Wren." Mistress Essodel twirled the end of Harriet's gifted pink feather between two fingers. "This is truly lovely. Now answer my first question."

HARRIET'S ESCAPE:

Harriet didn't bother giving Mistress Essodel another thorough once-over because the answer to her question had settled in her mind when it was posed: "When I look at you, I see an elderly Dragonkin female. Shorter than average but likely shrinking from old age. This makes me wonder about your age and how old a Dragonkin must be if it's reflected in their human form. It's scary if I think too long about it."

"Is that all you see?"

Harriet shook her head, committed to speaking every bit of her truth. "No, ma'am. I see a lonely old Dragonkin so afraid of the appearance of fragility that she's locked herself away in a mountain, guaranteein' even more loneliness. There's a high cost to pride. I think you know that. You accepted it long ago. You've enslaved yourself as much as you have your hoard of Birdfolk."

Harriet turned away from Mistress Essodel, giving the dragon shifter her profile and looking out at the peaceful body of water. The Casse River ended in the small town of Drektogg in the center of Cesthie County. Steamboats traveled up and down the Casse River as far northwest as Bodan City. But Drektogg was known as much for its farm produce as for its sale of Birdfolk and the occasional harpy.

Yet, Harriet had traveled through the township, staying at Underground Railroad stations in Drektogg before moving on to Gunskac, Sozgiks, Wunghera Grove, and then to Hirshioville before crossing the Drethos border at the town of Chosnos. Each well-traveled route was seared in Harriet's mind—every settlement, town, and city. She could see them all, her southern routes to Pholgre and northern routes to the Dominion of Cothru.

If I died today, I wouldn't go to heaven a peaceful soul, because there's much more needs doin'. I ain't hardly done yet, that's for sure.

"Family is everything to me, Mistress Essodel, but you know that about Birdfolk. It's how Dragonkin have controlled us for so long. Fear of losin' our loved ones. Fear of havin' us taken from them. It's cruel, and I don't need to look at you to know you've never cared. You've demanded the truth from me, but for what purpose?"

"You are my property; I do not need a purpose to command anything I want from you."

"My sad truth is that, even after eight years of bein' free of you, I still think of myself as bein' owned." Harriet blinked away tears that threatened, then gave in to the feeling of shame and let them fall. "It's hard to get that thought out of here." She tapped the side of her head with her knuckles. "Mental enslavement. I learned those words from people smarter than me. Like you, I know the truth when I hear it. Slavery is a sickness. Mine." She turned to see Mistress Essodel watching her with eyes so golden she could've birthed the sun. "And yours."

"You speak nonsense."

"Not the same as a lie."

"You are such a disappointment." Mistress Essodel gathered her steel-gray hair at her nape, twisted it into a messy bun, and used Harriet's pink feather to hold it in place. "I remember when you climbed up my great hoard when you were a child. Frightened but not to the point of inaction. I should have known you would be the servant to defy me the most. To steal from me while ignoring my priceless gold and exquisite jewels collection. You are no richer for your high moral ground."

"I'm not. Yet, here we sit. Naked. But with you needin' somethin' from me. Information is its own kind of wealth." Harriet knew the signs of a grieving mother because she'd seen the same pain on Rit's face that she observed on Mistress Essodel's. "You know I lived with Poppa at the minin' camp when Master Gyzad died." Harriet shifted to face the elderly

Dragonkin again. "You already know the truth. But you want me to say it. To admit to knowin' more than I ever shared with anyone. I didn't want to tell you. I still don't."

"But you will trade your only valuable item if I promise to spare you, Rit, and Ben."

"Rachel, Ben, and Angerine, too."

Mistress Essodel's lips parted again, and her nose scrunched as if a foul scent had forced its way up her nostrils. Yet, her golden eyes had gone soft in a way Harriet wouldn't have thought the female capable. "You have grown to be quite bold."

"I'm merely desperate to save my family."

"Can you not see, little Minty, that what we have said is one and the same? Do you pity me for my deliberate ignorance?"

"No, ma'am."

"Do you despise me?"

"Yes, ma'am."

"As well you should. I would have broken your neck with these feeble-looking human hands if you claimed otherwise. Was Breembat responsible for Gyzad's death?"

"Yes, ma'am."

Mistress Essodel's eyes lowered, but she displayed no other outward reaction to the news of her son's betrayal.

Harriet offered no details, although she was prepared to provide them while keeping her promise to Dorane. The harpy had used her knowledge of poisons to end the life of her master and gain her freedom.

"Minister Breembat came to me," Dorane told Harriet when she visited her at the harpy trading post of East New Maeroe. "He offered me a deal I couldn't refuse. Maybe I just didn't want to refuse it. But I was Master Gyzad's cook, giving me access to almost everything he drank and ate.

Minty, have you ever wondered why masters trust slaves with their food? Their children?"

Harriet hadn't responded because her thoughts hadn't mattered, only Dorane's conscious acts of malice and vengeance.

"Minister Breembat paid Mudspike to keep an eye on Master Gyzad. He was supposed to report back to him anything he could use against his brother. Nothing panned out, so he came to me. My method was slow but effective. Without your help, gathering all the ingredients would've taken me longer. Minister Breembat is such a liar, but he kept his word. He found my contract and handed it over, as he said he would. And I tore that piece of paper up right then and there. I was free. Finally free to live my life. Now, here you are. Are you planning on telling Mistress Essodel what I've done?"

Harriet flopped onto her back. The sky on this night was unremarkable. The moon didn't shine with a majesty that encouraged adoration, and the stars didn't glow with a brilliance that tempted one to gaze upon them for sleepy hours. Yet, the uninspired May sky had witnessed a transcendental conversation between a runaway Birdfolk slave and her Dragonkin master.

"I promise to keep your secret."

"I shouldn't have used you. You were just a kid. Easily tricked but not stupid."

Dorane's assessment of Harriet back then had been accurate. Just as the harpy had manipulated Harriet, Minister Breembat had done the same to Dorane and Mudspike. But enslavement blurred the line between right and wrong, good and evil.

Harriet closed her eyes, not ready to die but prepared to suffer the consequences for her role in Master Gyzad's death. Mistress Essodel hadn't promised to spare her life, but Harriet had freely given the only thing the Dragonkin thought she had of value.

Every parent deserves to know what happened to their child. Ben and Rit don't have that because of Minister Breembat. Neither does Rachel. But apples don't fall far from the tree. Mistress Essodel should remember that before she goes punishin' others for her sins. But, ummm, why hasn't she killed me yet?

Harriet's eyes slid open, and she sat up. The night sky was still uninspired, and the river was still beautifully tranquil, but the elderly dragon no longer sat beside her. She jerked her head to the right and left, then tilted it upward.

"How did she do that?" Harriet jumped to her feet, suddenly assaulted by the chilly night air against her soft human skin, as she hadn't been when seated beside Mistress Essodel. Harriet hadn't noticed the unnatural heat that had radiated from the dragon until she had gone. "She's terrifying in any form."

Harriet shifted into a Sankofa bird and took off, confident she would catch up to Rit and Ben in two hours.

They're expectin' me, but Minister Breembat ain't expectin' what's comin' his way. For whatever a man sows, this he will also reap.

"I said fly."

Breembat stumbled over his clawed feet but righted himself before his mother boomed her command again. He bolted into the dusky sky. He didn't know the last time he'd shifted so quickly or took off without a destination.

He'd certainly never been chased before, not even when he and Gyzad played as young dragons.

"Mother . . . I . . . I don't understand."

"Fly faster."

Breembat did. His bluish-white ice dragon wings flapped harder than ever before. He chanced a look behind him, and there Essodel flew.

Unlike him, whose wings flapped like a dog paddling against an ocean wave, Essodel's wings glided relaxedly. It had been decades since he'd last seen his mother in the sky. Even when she'd left her mountain lair after Gyzad's death, Breembat hadn't seen the monstrosity that was his mother dominate the sky the way she did on this early morning.

Seeing her in her lair for so many years, lazy and self-indulgent, I'd forgotten what a terrible sight she was to behold.

"Mother, wait. Let's go home so we can talk. Tell me what's got you so upset."

"I said fly."

A heated air current slammed into Breembat. It smacked him off-balance and sliced a chunk of icy scales from his thigh. He didn't bleed because the assault was meant to warn, not to damage him to the point of rendering him incapable of following her order to run.

She knows I can't outfly her. What in the hell does she want from me? What is she trying to prove? Oh, no. Did she somehow find out about Dorane and Gyzad? Only Dorane and I know what happened, and that stupid harpy has no reason to confess either of our sins. But I can't think of any other reason for Mother to be out of her lair and to treat me like prey.

Breembat flew and flew.

"Faster."

And flew.

"Faster."

And flew.

Breembat had no idea where he was or how long he'd flown. But the sun and clouds felt like they had merged in his lungs.

"Mother, I c-can't b-breathe."

Breembat felt Essodel's heated presence in every air ripple and wind shudder. With each mile he flew, her heat intensified. Each inhalation was like having his icy nose dragged through a forest fire.

"Do you want my titles, Breembat?"

"N-no."

"Liar. My hoard, Breembat?"

"No, no, everything belongs to you."

"It all does belong to me, but you still lie. A coward. A brother's betrayer."

She knows, then. That's what this is all about. I could beg for mercy. Pledge my undying devotion.

Breembat circled to face his mother. He didn't think there was a dragon that lived who was older or as massive as Essodel. Spikes longer than most Birdfolk were tall ran the length of her back to her whipping tail. Her wingspan could shield a small town from a roaring blizzard, and her claws could cut through the longest chain of mountains in less time than it would take most Dragonkin to shift.

You're right, Mother. I want every one of your titles. And every piece in your hoard. Both are wasted on you. What good are they to a recluse? Before you tell me how much better Gyzad was than I am, he felt the same. He lied to you. He stole from you. But he was never brave enough to face you. To tell you what he really thought of you.

When he realized Essodel knew he was responsible for Gyzad's death, Breembat had given up on seeing another sunrise. He did not wish to die, and no doubt many people he'd wronged wished him dead long ago.

But he wouldn't go silently into his death. Yet, he had the misfortune of having Essodel, Eater of Bravehearts, Champion of the Deathlord, The Dark Dygen, Eternal Fire as his scale donor.

I'm so stupid. All these years, I thought her gold, jewels, and Birdfolk comprised her beloved hoard. But not just that collection of property. But also, Gyzad and me. We might hold more value to her because we're scale of her scale, fire of her fire, but in the end, property to be controlled and discarded at will.

Essodel's wings curved toward Breembat, darkening the sky around him. His instincts screamed for him to flee, but the caged reality had him submitting.

"You would have made a tolerable son, worthy of my scales, if you had half the boldness of a thirty-five-year-old nothing of a Birdfolk child who despises me to her core. But when she faced me, as you did, she saw me. The monster." The wings drew closer, locking Breembat where he hovered in the sky. "The mother. She saw me. All of me. And she was so very afraid." The wings tightened around Breembat. "For the first time in my long-lived life, I wanted to be seen in all my menacing glory. Every rugged, impenetrable scale and each age-spotted hand. The dual blade of unrivaled supremacy."

"Mother, I, please. Please." Breembat hadn't meant to beg, but he'd lied to himself. He wasn't ready to die. "I'm sorry. Please. Please."

"Such a disappointment. I only regret that you have no title for me to claim." Essodel clamped her wings around Breembat, holding him in an unbreakable vise.

"Mother. Please. P-please. D-don't."

Essodel opened her giant maw, emitting an inferno of heat that melted on contact. If she'd stopped there, Breembat would've survived. His face would have been horribly disfigured, but he would've adjusted and moved on with his life.

But Essodel wasn't yet done with Breembat, and he cursed whoever had revealed his secret to a similar fate.

Volcanic fire sprayed from Essodel like erupting lava. Fiery burst after fiery burst covered his body. Breembat's icy scales succumbed to the intense heat and weight of the lava like an umbrella unable to withstand the blustering might of hailstones.

Layer after layer after layer of volcanic fire.

Scales dissolved.

Bones disintegrated.

Organs exploded.

Breembat.

Born in 1625.

Died in 1857.

Fate known.

Chapter 39

My People Are Free

1860
Dominion of Cothru
St. Cegri

Unlike a true lady of leisure, Harriet reclined on the same kind of feather bed tick she wouldn't permit Rit to bring with her on their long journey from Pheghro Neck to St. Cegri. But Harriet had done her best to make it up to her mother by giving Rit her own bed tick until she managed to make Rit a new and better version of the feather bed tick she'd had to leave behind.

Harriet was fully dressed, except for boots that, if it were possible for inanimate objects to speak, would have many stories to tell. But none of Harriet's few possessions could regale an interested party about the last decade of her life better than her old satchel. The scarred-over bag held secrets she hadn't revealed to anyone, not to her family and certainly not to the wealthy and powerful northern Dragonkin to whom she'd shared tales of enslaved life and her many missions to free family and friends. She hadn't enjoyed the telling as much as the listeners seemed riveted by her ability to charm yet guilt them.

The funding of her missions came at an unvoiced cost. But a sympathetic, privileged audience who both viewed slaveholders as inferior to them and Birdfolk in need of their guiding hand was better than no audience at all.

She turned onto her side, taking care not to crush her most precious possession. Harriet ran a single finger over the feather.

After six years, it's as soft as when she gave it to me. Sapphire blue. So pretty. I never had a chance to use it the way she hoped I would. I had hoped, too. But the good Lord didn't answer that prayer either. I know it ain't right to expect him to answer all my prayers when there are so many others who wishin' he'd answer theirs. I can't imagine my wants are more important than someone else's. We all got somethin' we need or want relief from. But that doesn't make my failures hurt any less. I keep waitin' for the wound to my heart to heal. But it's been months, and it ain't better.

With care, Harriet held all she had left of a lost sister against a heart that hadn't stopped bleeding since that fateful night. She closed her eyes and couldn't halt the flood of memories. Her mind traveled back to Berzogtown in 1859.

Harriet approached the familiar cabin. Each time she came for Rachel, praying that the current time she would find Angerine and Ben with their mother and that the three of them would finally be ready for Harriet to take them to join the rest of the family, her heart pounded, and her head ached. Each visit ended in disappointment, with Rachel refusing to leave without her children and Harriet promising to return.

It's been two years since I could finally get down here. I couldn't just return so soon after bein' caught by Mistress Essodel. She would've been expectin' me. Dragonkin are more patient than most.

Harriet glanced around, comforted little had changed since she'd last been there. She assumed Mistress Essodel would've hired an overseer after Minister Breembat's disappearance. Uncoincidentally, Minister Breembat went missing a day after Harriet's conversation with the human Mistress Essodel. News had reached her in short order, and while no local authority would dare accuse the ancient Dragonkin of murdering her son, not a single action was taken to find the so-called missing Minister Breembat.

Life, as always, continued.

Rachel didn't respond to my messages. I planned to meet her in the woods like always, but she didn't come. I don't like comin' back here. Bein' this close to Mistress Essodel and her new overseer. But I ain't traveled all this way to go back without seein' my sister. I'd rather not return empty-handed, but Rachel is as stubborn as any Wren. I'll settle for a night of sister talk if she won't come. I've missed her. But I better get in there before I'm spotted. It might be late Saturday night, but that doesn't mean nobody is out to see me hangin' around this cabin.

Satchel swung across her shoulder, Harriet strolled up the few steps to the porch and softly knocked on the door. Considering the small size of the slave cabin, a harder knock wasn't necessary.

"Who's there?"

Harriet frowned. *That ain't my sister's voice. Did the new overseer move another enslaved woman into this cabin with Rachel? Makes sense. Never heard of a slave havin' their own cabin.*

Harriet drew closer to the door and kept her voice low. "Rachel, it's me." More words wouldn't be required if her sister were there with the other woman. Harriet looked around again. At nearly two in the morning, she couldn't imagine where else her sister could be if not in her cabin. She hadn't received word of Rachel being hired out to another plantation or, worse, sold off like her other sisters. But she also hadn't told anyone in Dralox County of her plans to rescue her sister, not even Norveis, who would've likely warned Harriet to stay away.

While she appreciated the harpy's concern and friendship, two years was too long to have gone without attempting another rescue. Rachel was the last one of them still enslaved, and that horrible fact haunted Harriet's dreams in a way John's betrayal never had.

"You lookin' for Rachel?"

Harriet didn't like the way the woman had posed the question. *Why did she sound surprised? What's goin' on?*

The wooden door swung open, and before Harriet could process the stranger, the woman yanked her inside the cabin and shut the door.

As she expected, Rachel wasn't there. Rachel had never taken to using a sheet to etch out privacy for herself, the way Rit and Ben had done. So, there wasn't a concealed nook where Rachel could've been. Even if there were, she would've immediately let her in once she heard Harriet's voice.

But that wasn't all. Harriet expanded her nostrils, taking in the cabins' scents. The old cabins carried a woodsy scent intermingled with various body odors—from pungent to fishy to sour to bitter. Occasionally, a sweet smell lingered, as did the mouth-watering aroma of cooked meats and vegetables. Yet, she could not detect Rachel's familiar scent.

"You're Harriet, right?"

"I don't know you. Where's Rachel?" Harriet's gaze shifted from the forty-something stranger with a head full of sapphire feathers the same rich shade of blue as Rachel's, to the same two pallets she remembered from the last time she'd been there. Everything about the cabin seemed to fit, but nothing felt right. She gulped, suddenly needing a drink of something stronger than water. "Where's my sister?"

The woman wrung hands that bore the same healed lacerations that began at her right cheek, traveled down the right side of her neck, and under a wrinkled dress the woman likely used for both sleeping and laboring. "Well, uh, well, the thing is . . . Rachel was sick for a while. Coughin' fits. Breathin' problems. Sweats. Fever."

Those symptoms did not sound much different from what Harriet experienced when she'd had pneumonia. Robert had cared for her, guaranteeing Harriet rested, ate well, and drank plenty of clean water.

The satchel fell from her shoulder, and she stumbled over to the pallet on the far left side of the cabin. Rachel's pallet. "Was? Is she better? Workin' somewhere else?"

Harriet closed her eyes, knowing the answer but unwilling to see the truth in the woman's pitying gaze.

"I'm sorry for your loss. I was put in here with her. Told to help her. But . . . but, I didn't know nothin' about how to help what ailed Rachel. I'm sorry."

Harriet slid down the wall onto a pallet that no longer belonged to her sister.

"I'm sorry. I'm really sorry."

Harriet wished the woman would be quiet. She did not want to hear how sorry she was for her loss. She shouldn't even be in the cabin with sapphire feathers that were too similar to Rachel's.

"I'm sorry, Harriet."

"Shut up," she said against the knees she'd pulled to her chest.

"What?"

"I said shut up. Just stop talkin'. Please, be quiet. I can't... I can't..."

Harriet didn't have to wonder the last time she'd cried so deeply, her heartache a profound pain that clamped down on her heart like a vulture claiming the body of a freshly dead carrion. Yet, Harriet still lived, but if it wasn't for her hiccupped cries, she would've sworn she'd ceased to breathe.

Harriet cried and cried.

For Rachel.

For Angerine and Ben.

For Ben and Rit.

For herself.

She cried and cried and cried.

Harriet was tired of having reasons to weep. Enslavement was brutally exhausting. Fatigue had latched on to her bones at birth, and the burdensome weight intensified with each passing year.

Harriet was sick and tired of being sick and tired.

I'm all that's left of Momma's and Poppa's girls. Mariah, Linah, Soph, and now Rachel. All gone. I'd forgotten Mariah. But I listened to the story Momma and Poppa told William. Their tears were fresh, and their grief as deep as if Mariah had been sold the day before. How can I go home and tell them Rachel is gone forever, too? I failed my sister. I don't know where Angerine and Ben are. I can't even do that one last thing for Rachel.

"Come here." The woman curled before Harriet, wrapped her arms around her, and pulled her close. "We ain't sisters, but we are still Sankofa family. I know loss, too, and it hurt like the devil. Rachel wasn't alone when she died. I was here, and two more of her friends. We gave her the love we knew her family would have if they were here. But know she wasn't alone in the end."

"B-but I wasn't here. I should've been."

"You can't be everywhere. That's God's job, and he must've wanted Rachel home because she went without a fuss or a tear. Her death was peaceful. That's the best any of us can ask."

Harriet agreed, but that truth did nothing to remove the sting of Rachel's passing or Harriet's guilt for not saving her younger sister.

Rachel Wren.

Born in 1825.

Died in 1859.

Fate known.

Knock. Knock. "Harriet, you have guests." Rit's soft, worried voice drew Harriet away from the past and back to the present.

Harriet opened her moist eyes and sat up. She still held Rachel's sapphire feather and was loathe to put it away, much less leave her sanctuary to learn who had come seeking "Moses's" help. She hadn't returned to Dralox County since Rachel's death.

"Come in, Momma."

The door creaked open, revealing Rit's still-pretty face. She smiled at Harriet, but the sweet gesture failed to reach eyes that had seen more than their share of horror. "I know it's cold out but put on your shoes and coat and meet me outside."

Harriet had no idea who had come calling. But she assumed her mother didn't think kindly of them if she hadn't offered the courtesy of a warm house afforded a visitor.

"Momma, you hate how cold it gets here. There's no need for you to go outside." Harriet was working on securing a home for her parents in northern Unganthu. Wherever she chose wouldn't be as warm as living in Miadar, but it wouldn't be as biting as winters in St. Cegri. "Robert normally lets them in the living room. I'll still turn them down, but a warm rejection will go down easier than a cold one."

"It ain't your fault." Rit stepped inside the bedroom, already dressed for the outdoors. She wore the warmest coat Harriet could afford and a matching set of gloves and hat Harriet had knitted. "You blamin' yourself ain't right. I know you hurtin'. We all are. But Rachel wouldn't want this."

"Momma, I . . . I don't know what to do anymore. Rachel, Ben, and Angerine are beyond me. Robert's family, too. I can't find them. With Minister Breembat dead, what hope do I have that they'll be returned to the Essodel Plantation?"

"You puttin' hope in the wrong things." Rit nodded to the feather Harriet held. "That ain't all you got left of your sister. But you are all the daughter me and Ben have, and we won't lose you to yourself. Now put somethin' warm on and meet me outside."

"But—"

"Harriet," Rit snapped as if she was a disobedient girl of ten instead of an independent woman of thirty-eight.

"Yes, ma'am. Comin'."

"Good. I'll see you outside."

Harriet knew better than to mumble her disagreement. Even if she did, Harriet knew which battles she could wage with her mother and win. Getting into an argument over meeting guests outside, the cold ensuring a swift denial of their request, was a waste of time. Quiet compliance would soon have her back in her bedroom and blessed solitude. Her guests wouldn't be any happier than when they arrived, but Rit would have one less reason to bother Harriet.

I know it ain't my fault. But I can't shake the feelin' of failin' my sister and parents. I've heard Momma and Poppa cryin' late at night. That type of sorrow sticks to your insides. I don't have nothin' more to offer. I didn't achieve what I set out to. My family ain't whole. We fractured. Some of us here, there, and only God knows where else.

Harriet pulled on her boots and then her overcoat. The coat was as old as her satchel, but both had served her well. She supposed it was time to lay them to rest, retiring them and her mission to seize freedom by any means necessary. If nothing else, Rachel's death reminded Harriet that no matter how hard she tried, the gulf between her desires and what it took to achieve them was sometimes too great to overcome.

Harriet exited her bedroom and walked down the hall to the front door. Before she reached it, she could feel the chill of mid-October and hear the husky voices of Ben and Robert. She wasn't surprised that Robert had taken it upon himself to size up the visitors before Harriet's arrival. However, like Rit, Ben disliked St. Cegri's cooler climate.

Why have they decided to gather outside over somethin' that could've been handled in front of a warm fireplace? I haven't taken a mission in months. Robert should've sent them on their way. What makes today different from any other?

Harriet pushed open the screen door and walked onto the porch. She stopped and stared. Her mouth fell open, but Harriet quickly closed it when the forty-degree cold threatened to choke her.

True to her word, Rit was already outside, and as she knew they would be, so were Ben and Robert. The three of them stood in front of the porch facing Harriet. They smiled at her, and each smile reached beautiful brown eyes that glistened with tears.

They are not tears of grief. I can tell they are still sad, but there's a larger emotion they want me to understand.

Ben stepped forward. "Do you see us, Harriet?"

Trying her best not to cry, Harriet couldn't do more than nod. But when Ben handed her one of his beautiful feathers, a tear escaped, and the dam broke. Rit drew a peach feather from her coat pocket and gave it to Harriet, followed by Robert.

They joined her on the porch, granting Harriet an unobstructed view of her guests. She'd expected two or three visitors, likely Miadar runaways, seeking her help in rescuing a loved one. But nothing she could have imagined compared to the sight before her.

The last time she'd seen so many Birdfolk gathered in their avian form was when she'd accepted John Cassin as her husband. All that was left of her five-year marriage was the last name she'd proudly taken on her flight to freedom.

Her parents flanked Harriet, a hand on each of her shoulders.

"I watched my Rit give birth to each of our children. Every Birdfolk child's birth is remarkable because, against all odds, they survived. But our Minty was smaller than the children that came before and the ones that came after. Rit saw her born in March 1822." Ben squeezed her shoulder and then let his hand fall away.

"But this special October day," Rit began, her voice more strident than she'd heard it in years, "is Harriet's birthday. The day she mustered the courage to set out with no family beside her. But she had a dream of freedom when she left Dralox County."

Harriet lowered her head, unable to watch those gathered for a day she'd never considered celebrating.

"Birthdays," Robert said, "celebrate another year of life. We are all here because of two decisions my sister made. The first was to flee, to seek freedom. The second was to return for all of us. Time and again. We asked you here to help us celebrate Harriet's birthday, to show her what a woman seizing freedom looks like."

Kessiah, John, and James approached. Each used their beak to hand Harriet one of their feathers.

Kessiah nudged Harriet until she lifted her chin. "Thank you. Momma would be so proud of the woman you've grown into."

With her eyes flooded with tears and her throat tight, Harriet did not know how to respond, so she nodded and accepted the praise for the love that birthed the emotion.

Moses followed Kessiah's family, gifting her with not one but three of his feathers. "I couldn't find the two friends you helped when we got to Bodan but consider these feathers from each of us. I've never been prouder to share my name with anyone."

Harriet could've melted into a puddle of hushed gratitude. As many times as she'd stood before past and potential donors, relaying her story to packed rooms of people with little space between them but stale air, Harriet should have been used to being the center of attention. But not like this. Not when presented with irrefutable evidence that her actions these past eight years could not be summed up or minimized by a single death.

Not a failure.

But life in all its pain and glory.

Barbury and his family offered Harriet their feathers and heartfelt thanks, as did her brother Ben Jr. and his wife Jane, who joined the Wren family on the porch.

One by one, most of the freedom seekers she'd rescued presented Harriet with a feather. Her arms overflowed with pink, peach, red, blue, green, and purple feathers. And still more were piled on.

Harriet's brother Henry along with his wife and children joined the Wrens gathered on the porch, and the feathers quickly became a hoard that held the sweet aroma of emancipation.

Harriet thought she would double over when she realized that the three women who had befriended her dying sister were there, too. Lavinia gifted Harriet with a sapphire feather that matched Rachel's, while Emily and Lizzie handed her a luscious mix of pink and purple feathers. Harriet had taken the women with her when she left Berzogtown. It was the least she could do for what they had done for Rachel.

"You're a good sister," Lavinia had told Harriet when she turned over the women to William Skeshru's care at the Pholgre Anti-Slavery Office. "Rachel loved you a lot. She knew you would come back for her. She never stopped believin' in you."

Harriet's arms were too full of feathers to hug the women, but she accepted their feathery embrace.

From over Lavinia's shoulder, Harriet glimpsed a grinning Tilly. When she reached Harriet, Tilly tucked her feathered offering in her hair, leading others who followed to do the same.

A group of nine approached, and Harriet recalled helping them flee in the fall of 1852. She no longer recalled their names but remembered their faces as she did the four men she led to freedom in May of 1856. That mission had been borne of another failed attempt to rescue Rachel.

Then there were others she hadn't met, but who introduced themselves to her by the month and year she had indirectly assisted their escape.

Jane, May 1854.

Samuel, August 1854.

Joseph, December 1855.

Francis, Cyrus, Joshua, Charles, and Ephraim, September 1856.

The "Drethos Eight," March 1857.

The "Cosaru Twenty-eight," October 1857.

When Harriet thought she had no more tears left to shed or places on her body to hold the gifted feathers, three wagons full of sixteen people arrived, thanking her for giving them the necessary information to flee enslavement in October 1857.

Somewhere, perhaps in her overwhelmed delirium, Harriet missed a freedom seeker she'd either directly or indirectly helped escape slavery and seize their freedom.

Harriet dropped to her knees, her body racked with tears, and she was overcome. Ben had asked Harriet if she had seen them. Until that moment, she had not—not entirely. Not in the way her father had meant. But she forced her eyes open, and through a waterfall of tears, Harriet saw them.

They chatted and mingled like old friends. Some were still in bird form, while others had shifted and dressed. Even William and Frederick had made the trip to St. Cegri, which explained how her parents and Robert managed to find so many she'd helped.

Through it all, the field of bodies and the tears that refused to stop, Harriet glimpsed four shimmers of radiant light.

Linah.

Mariah.

Soph.

Rachel.

Her sisters.

Yet, beyond them was a vision that took Harriet's breath away.

Dragonkin fought Dragonkin—in the air and on the ground. A brutal, bloody war raged, pitting neighbor against neighbor and family members against each other. In the center of the Civil War for supremacy to define the future of the United States of Ungathu stood the Sankofa Birdfolk of the great continent of Sika.

Free and fugitive.

Old and young.

Resistance had never been more vital. More violent.

But when the dragon fire cleared, and munitions quieted, a single word reverberated from the southern plantations to the northern cities.

Emancipation.

She clutched her feathers of renewed hope to a heart that pounded with the beat of a thousand angelic wings.

And Harriet said unto those gathered: "You'll see it. You'll see it soon. My people are free! My people are free!"

Epilogue

1864

Berzogtown

Essodel Plantation

War raged outside Essodel's mountain home, shaking her lair to its rocky foundation. Ancient golden nuggets, priceless gold coins, and exquisite jewels shifted and fell, creating a messy pool of the finest hoard known to the ancient and modern worlds.

Essodel growled, and the volcanic heat that formed the internal layers of her body intensified.

How dare they invade my home with their puny wings and insignificant cannons. They cannot win. They will not win.

Yet, for three years, battles of the Civil War raged in southern slave states like Miadar.

I will not allow my plantation to fall. I will burn to ash every traitorous Dragonkin and devour each ground-scraper who thinks themselves brave enough to challenge me.

Essodel used her mighty tail to shift mounds of her hoard out of her way. The fighting had displaced her meticulous arrangement. But she found what she sought with a few swipes of her tail.

Cautiously, she cradled the item and brought it to eye level. Essodel had seen only one other in her long life. To be in its presence was considered dangerous, but two or more together guaranteed death—or so the old Dragonkin bedtime stories told.

Even so, Essodel had never believed such tall tales, so she had gladly accepted the role of warden to the resident of the . . . *After all these years, your lamp is still the most unique and majestic piece of my hoard. You have made for the quietest and most accommodating roommate.* Ever so gently, Essodel shook the lamp. She might enjoy the game of torture, but she never forgot that trapped within the golden lamp was a threat beyond reckoning.

But pure, raw power did not equate to dominance. Under the right circumstances, any group of people could be subjugated.

Essodel shook the lamp again. She could hear the coarse sizzle of trapped magic.

If she'd been in her human form, Essodel would've laughed. Instead, she shook the lamp again.

Like Birdfolk, you will always be a servant to Dragonkin.

Essodel blew dragon fire onto the lamp. Despite its small size, the exterior was stronger than any Dragonkin scale she'd encountered. So, while she could not destroy the structure, the prisoner, born of the Dragonkin God's smokeless flame, or so she'd been told as a child, could undoubtedly feel the uncomfortable heat.

You are not special. None of you ever were. Essodel continued her heated assault, a concentrated beam of dragon fire. She blew and blew and blew.

Wait. Why am I doing this? I never have before. I know better. He was delivered into my safekeeping in 1822. Rendre, the Fierce, explained the rules of keeping him weak and manageable. 1822 was the same year Rit gave birth to that girl who would grow into a beacon of hope for too many Birdfolk in Dralox County. I should have eaten her that day. She could not have stopped me. But the traitorous part of my heart looked at her and wished I had been blessed with a progeny of her caliber. So, I retreated before she could see the shameful effect she had on me. Little Minty Wren. Are you out there somewhere, lending your brains and bravery to this fruitless cause for Birdfolk freedom? No doubt you are, but you will find nothing save dragon fire as a scorching reply. Your kind will not win this civil war.

Essodel dropped the lamp. Despite the concentrated heat she'd exposed it to, it was still a perfect, luscious gold.

"Keep his lamp in a cool, dark place. Don't speak to him. Do not allow the lamp to come into contact with dragon fire. But above all, do not disturb his sleep."

As much as Essodel pretended that old age had not affected her mind, it wasn't true. She might still be a physical force of nature, but she was not immune to the same cognitive decline as any other long-lived being, even if by slower degrees.

What else could explain Essodel's profound lack of judgment and careless behavior?

My aging mind aside, I know the rules. So why then did I—

The golden lamp cracked. A single line. But that was enough.

"Above all, do not disturb his sleep."

"Do not disturb his sleep."

"Do. Not. Disturb. His. Sleep."

The warning memory bounced off the walls of Essodel's lair, forcing another recollection.

His name is Vesey. He planned the largest jinn slave rebellion against our kind. For all that is holy, Essodel, do not disturb Vesey's sleep.

The jinn lamp exploded.

—freedom—

For fans of American History blended with the spirit of a woman's relentless courage, dive into the Feline Nation duology—an enchanting saga where fantasy meets bravery.

If you're captivated by tales of dragon shapeshifters and undying love, immerse yourself in "Dragon Lore and Love: Isis and Osiris."

Appendix

#HistoricVoices

This Appendix is designed to offer additional context and spark discussion, supporting deeper exploration of the novel's themes and historical background.

- **Playlist:** Immerse yourself in a curated collection of songs selected to complement the mood, themes, and historical backdrop of the novel.

- **Illustrations:** Dive into a collection of bonus images that bring the fantastical elements of Harriet's journey to vivid life.

- **Public Domain Images of Harriet Tubman:** Access a selection of historical images of Harriet Tubman to visualize the real-life inspiration behind the novel's protagonist.

- **Maps from the Historical Period:** Explore detailed maps that provide geographical context to Harriet's adventures.

- **Readers Guide:** Engage with a set of reflective questions designed to foster meaningful conversations among book club members.

- **Form to Request Educator's Toolkit:** Access a comprehensive toolkit tailored for educators, aimed at facilitating discussions and learning in academic settings.

- **Bibliography:** Delve into a list of references and resources for readers interested in further exploration of the novel's historical elements.

Playlist
#SoulMusic

Harriet's Escape Playlist Link

- Stand Up – Cynthia Erivo

- I Was Here – Beyonce

- Girl on Fire, featuring Nicki Minaj – Alicia Keys and Nicki Minaj

- Freedom, featuring Kendrick Lamar – Beyonce and Kendrick Lamar

- Rise Up – Andra Day

- I Didn't Know My Own Strength – Whitney Houston

- Count on Me – Whitney Houston and CeCe Winans

- We Won't Move – Arlissa

- Strong Black Woman – Chrisette Michele

- The Prince of Egypt (When You Believe) – Mariah Carey and Whitney Houston

- Wade in the Water – Sweet Honey and the Rock

- I Got This – Jennifer Hudson

- Change – Heather Headley

- Troubled World – Faith Evans, Kelly Price, and Jessica Reedy

Sika

Birdfolk

EASTERN SIKA

Birdfolk

WESTERN SIKA

Birdfolk

NORTHERN SIKA

Birdfolk

SOUTHERN SIKA

THREE HUNDRED DOLLARS REWARD.

OCT. 3, 1849   **THE MIADAR GAZETTE**   **RUNAWAYS SOUGHT**

On Monday, September 17th, three Birdfolk ran away from the undersigned.

HENRY: Estimated to be 19 years of age, notable for a wen under one ear on his neck. In human form, his skin is a dark chestnut. As a bird, he displays bluish-green feathers. He is roughly 5 feet 8 or 9 inches tall.

BEN: Approximately 25 years old, known for his prompt responses when spoken to. His human form shows dark chestnut skin, while his bird form features bluish-green feathers. He stands about six feet tall.

MINTY: Presumed to be around 27 years old, with dark chestnut skin in hhuman form. In her bird form, she exhibits a e combination of green, purple, pink, and blue feathers. Her height is about 5 feet.

A reward of $100 per individual is offered for capture outside the Province and $50 each within. The captured musy7t be securely held and taken to the jails in Bodan, Evno, or Cassarth, Miadar Province.

MINISTER BREEMBAT
DRALOX COUNTY, MIADAR

Harriet
TUBMAN

THE MASON-DIXON LINE

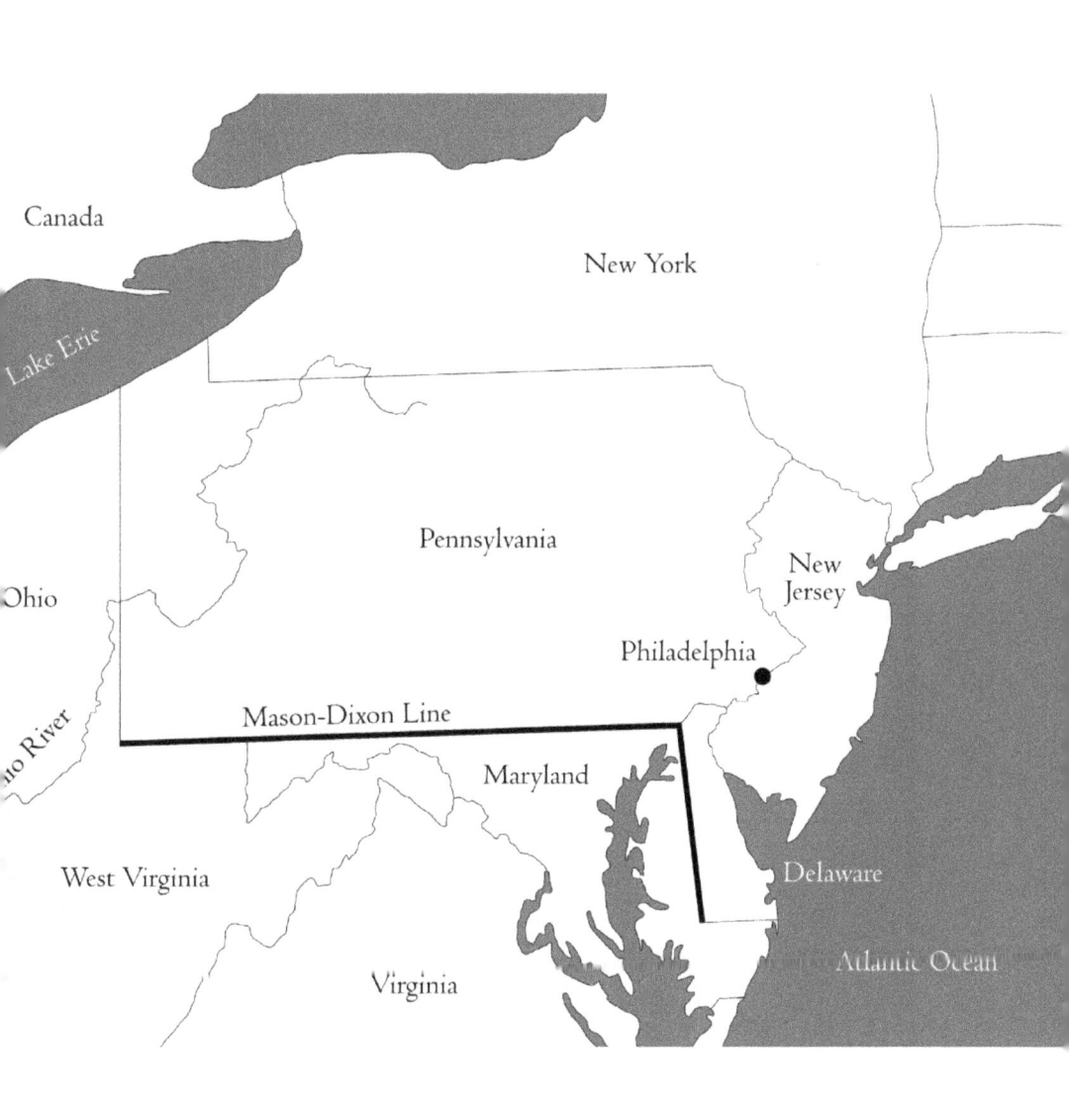

Canada
New York
Lake Erie
Ohio
Pennsylvania
New Jersey
Philadelphia
Ohio River
Mason-Dixon Line
Maryland
West Virginia
Delaware
Virginia
Atlantic Ocean

UNDERGROUND RAILROAD ROUTES

Readers Guide

#READBLACK

Discussion Questions

1. Discuss the portrayal of Harriet as a flightless Sankofa bird shifter. How did this fantastical element add depth to her character, and in what ways did it resonate with her real-life persona as a courageous freedom fighter?

2. In what ways did the depiction of slave owners as mighty dragon shifters contribute to the fantastical atmosphere of the book? How did this choice influence your perception of the power dynamics within the story?

3. How does the novel's portrayal of enslavement and resistance parallel real historical accounts of slavery, particularly in the context of Harriet Tubman's life and legacy? Discuss the effectiveness of using a fantastical setting to explore historical themes.

4. Consider the supporting characters in the story. How did their interactions with Harriet contribute to the richness of the narrative, and what role did they play in shaping her journey?

5. Reflect on moments in the book where characters grapple with the weight of their past and the desire for a better future. Have you ever faced similar conflicts between your own history and your aspirations for the future?

6. Consider the themes of courage and resistance in the face of oppression. How do these themes inspire you in your own life, and have you encountered instances where fictional stories like this one have empowered you to stand up against injustice?

7. Discuss any moments in the book where characters find strength and solace in community and solidarity. How do these themes of camaraderie and mutual support resonate with your own experiences of building connections with others?

8. Explore the theme of agency and the power of individual action to bring about change. Have you ever felt a sense of agency in your own life, even in the face of seemingly insurmountable obstacles?

9. Discuss the importance of centering marginalized voices and perspectives in conversations about social justice. How can we amplify the voices of those most impacted by injustice and ensure that their experiences are heard and valued?

10. Consider how reading *Harriet's Escape* has impacted your perspective on history, identity, and the ongoing struggle for justice. In what ways has the book influenced your thinking or inspired you to take action in your own life or community?

Bibliography

#CulturalTales

- *Harriet tubman images: Picryl - Public Domain Media Search Engine Public Domain Search.* PICRYL. (n.d.).

- Larson, K. (2004). *Bound for the promised land: Portrait of an American hero.* Ballantine Books.

- Taylor, N. M. (2023). *Brooding over bloody revenge: Enslaved women's lethal resistance.* Cambridge University Press.

- *Top 25 quotes by Harriet Tubman: A-z quotes.* AZ Quotes. (n.d.).

- *Where Harriet Tubman's journey began - on Maryland's Eastern Shore.* Harriet Tubman Byway. (2023, December 22).

- YouTube. (2012a, January 5). *All god's chillun got shoes - the Charioteers.* YouTube.

- YouTube. (2012b, April 15). *Karen Clark-Sheard"Balm in Gilead!".* YouTube.

- YouTube. (2019, October 26). *Stand up! Lyric Video Cynthia*

Ervio & Joshua Campbell. YouTube.

- YouTube. (2022, February 15). *Rocka my soul in the bosom of Abraham*. YouTube.

About N. D.

#OwnYourVoice

N.D. Jones, Ed.D., has achieved USA Today bestselling status for her captivating Black Fantasy and Paranormal Romance novels. Residing in the heart of Maryland with her loving family, N.D. is a trailblazer in the literary world of Blacks in fantasy.

Driven by a passionate desire to introduce more positive, sexy, and multi-dimensional African American characters as soul mates, friends, and lovers, N.D. embarked on a remarkable journey of her own. Determined to address this challenge, she took it upon herself to redefine the narrative.

Also by N. D.

NOVELS WITH SOUL

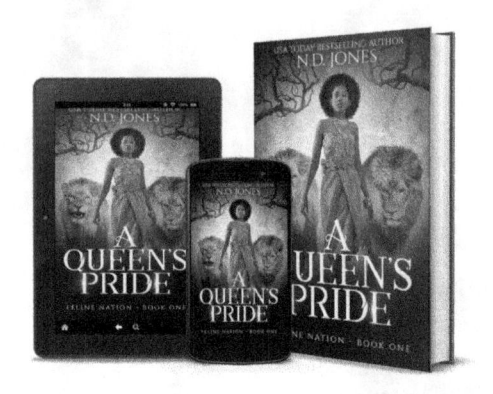

Winged Warriors Trilogy (Paranormal Romance)
Fire, Fury, Faith (Book 1)
Heat, Hunt, Hope (Book 2)
Lies, Lust, Love (Book 3)
Death and Destiny Trilogy (Paranormal Romance)
Of Fear and Faith (Book 1)
Of Beasts and Bonds (Book 2)
Of Deception and Divinity (Book 3)
Death and Destiny: The Complete Series

Forever Yours Series (Fantasy Romance)
Bound Souls (Book 1)
Fated Path (Book 2)
Dragon Shifter Romance (Paranormal Romance)
Stones of Dracontias: The Bloodstone Dragon
Dragon Lore and Love: Isis and Osiris
The Styles of Love Trilogy (Contemporary Romance)
The Perks of Higher Ed (Book 1)
The Wish of Xmas Present (Book 2)
The Gift of Second Chances (Book 3)
Rhythm and Blue Skies: Malcolm and Sky's Complete Story
The Styles of Love Trilogy: The Complete Series
Feline Nation Duology (Fantasy)
A Queen's Pride (Book 1)
Mafdet's Claws (Book 2)
Fairy Tale Fatale (Dystopian Fantasy)
Crimson Hunter: Red Riding Hood Reimagined
Bearly Gold: Goldilocks and the Three Bears Reimagined

Printed in the USA
CPSIA information can be obtained
at www.ICGtesting.com
LVHW040748180624
783403LV00007B/48